IRIDIAN
CHROMATIC MAGES

D.N. HOXA

Also by D.N. Hoxa

The Fall of the Seven Isles Series (Completed)

Mama Si's Paradise

The Evernight Court

The Eighth Isle

The Holy Bloodlines Series (Completed)

The Elysean Trials

The Elysean Academy of Darkness and Secrets

The Elysean Illusion

The Elysean Dream

The Reign of Dragons Series (Completed)

King of Air

Guardian of Earth

Warden of Water

Queen of Fire

The Hidden Realm Series (Completed)

Savage Ax

Damsel in Distress

Deadly Match

Pixie Pink Series (Completed)

Werewolves Like Pink Too

Pixies Might Like Claws

Silly Sealed Fates

The New York Shade Series (Completed)

Magic Thief

Stolen Magic

Immoral Magic

Alpha Magic

The New Orleans Shade Series (Completed)

Pain Seeker

Death Spell

Twisted Fate

Battle of Light

The Dark Shade Series (Completed)

Shadow Born

Broken Magic

Dark Shade

Smoke & Ashes Series (Completed)

Firestorm

Ghost City

Witchy Business

Wings of Fire

The Marked Series (Completed)

Blood and Fire

Deadly Secrets

Death Marked

Winter Wayne Series (Completed)

Bone Witch

Bone Coven

Bone Magic

Bone Spell

Bone Prison

Bone Fairy

Scarlet Jones Series (Completed)

Storm Witch

Storm Power

Storm Legacy

Storm Secrets

Storm Vengeance

Storm Dragon

Victoria Brigham Series (Completed)

Wolf Witch

Wolf Uncovered

Wolf Unleashed

Wolf's Rise

Starlight Series (Completed)

Assassin

Villain

Sinner

Savior

CHAPTER 1

Rosabel La Rouge

My hands were so numb I hardly felt them attached to my body. Voices called out my name, but I was drowning in this never-ending darkness, and no matter how hard I tried to break free, I couldn't. I couldn't find the light.

I wondered, *is this what it's like to die?*

Then I thought, *no matter; Taland is okay.*

My memory was perfectly functional. I remembered exactly what had happened, how I'd come to dive into this darkness, and as absurd as my mind insisted those events were, it also knew that they were *real*. That all of it had happened.

I, Rora La Rouge, had gone into the Devil's very lair and had offered him my bracelet in exchange for Taland's life, thinking it would be easy to walk back out of there. And maybe it would have been if not for the fact that the Mergenbach siblings of Selem had barged in uninvited.

That's when everything had gone to shit.

Even now, in this state that I was, a part of me couldn't help but wish they hadn't. A part of me couldn't help but wish the exchange had happened, that I'd put the bracelet into Hakim's hand, and that Seth and I had taken Taland away from that house, that neighborhood, the damn country.

Even knowing what was at stake, I wished it with all my heart.

I guess it's a good thing wishes don't really mean anything.

That voice called my name again—or maybe it said something else; I couldn't be sure. My mind still raced with memories and possibilities, with *what-ifs,* like always.

Sometimes I wondered if I was my own worst enemy.

Sometimes I believed it.

But eventually, I began to recognize the voice.

It wasn't *people* like I first thought—just one person. Just one woman who'd made me sweat ever since I was a little girl, who'd showed me how little the word *family* could mean, and how much of your life depended on the actual individuals you considered that. Just that one woman who'd made me feel like I was never enough, like there was something wrong with me, like I wasn't worthy of love and affection and patience and understanding, and I'd gone out into the world to search for it without even understanding what I was doing.

It was *that* woman's voice that called me, and that's the reason I both wanted to stay in the dark forever, and why my mind, guided by fear and panic that were completely out of my control, shocked itself awake. Wherever Madeline Rogan was, that's where I needed to be the most alert, figure out how to get the hell away from her, as far and as fast as I could.

2

It was instinct, so deeply ingrained in me by years and years of neglect that I reacted even when unconscious. Or maybe it was just the spell she was chanting?

A spell—not my name. She wasn't calling for me to wake up. The harsh Iridian words that left her lips in a rush sent a red-hot shock throughout my system, yet I was still confident that it was just the thought of her being near me that had pulled me out of unconsciousness first.

Either way, my eyes opened.

A white ceiling over me. My chest rose and fell so fast. My hands were indeed completely numb, and I couldn't blink or move at all for a good minute while my thoughts raced.

That ceiling—I knew it. That smell in the air, the faint scent of the sweet perfume lingering—I knew it. The warmth, the *weight* of her presence near me—I knew it. And even if I didn't want to believe it, I knew exactly where I was, too.

In the mansion, in Madeline's office—and she really was there with me.

"Look at me."

It was an order, one my eyes obeyed without my need to even think through what I was doing.

Madeline leaned down, closer to me. Her face came into view and our eyes locked.

I stopped breathing.

She, to me, was the boogeyman come to swallow me whole.

"Can you see me?"

I couldn't speak.

"Can you sit up?"

My lips refused to move.

Cold hands wrapped around my wrists. She pulled me to sit up the next second.

The room—her office, indeed—tilted in front of my eyes. My stomach raged, my insides threatened to come right out of me if the world didn't stop spinning so fast soon.

"Breathe," said Madeline, and if I could ever trust my own thoughts when she was around, I'd say she sounded *concerned* for a minute there. Concerned—about me.

Which was how I knew that I was hearing things.

But I breathed because I needed to make sense of the fact that I was here, at the mansion, and not in Silver Spring, in the Devil's lair. I needed to make sense of the fact that Taland wasn't with me, or that I wasn't at the IDD Headquarters, or even locked in a cell, maybe in the Tomb.

The room steadied and my stomach no longer twisted so violently a few seconds in. Madeline, wearing one of her crisp red suits that was spelled to never hold a wrinkle—at least I was pretty sure of that—sat next to me, on the same couch on the right side of her office. Her hair wasn't as perfectly combed as usual, her eyes were wide, her red lips parted, and for a moment there I thought maybe her hands were shaking, but it couldn't be. This was Madeline Rogan, former director of the IDD. Her hands didn't shake over anything.

"Can you understand what I'm saying?" she asked me, and I instinctively moved, bobbed my head up and down to say that I did.

She wasn't relieved. "Do you know where you are?"

Again, that same movement, but it was getting easier on my neck.

My mouth opened to speak, but I realized my throat was too dry and there was pain everywhere on my body.

4

Everywhere, but especially on my left thigh, where Hakim had stabbed me with that knife.

Chaos, chaos, I need to get Taland out of here, chaos—

"Rosabel."

Madeline's voice rang in my ears. I blinked and even the pain took a step back to let me focus on her, this absurd fear I had of her initially stronger than everything else.

But...it was just Madeline.

And I was an adult now, was I not? I could remind myself of that as many times as I needed when I wasn't operating on pure instinct—*just Madeline*.

"Where is he?" I said, even if my voice came out a mess, and my neck hurt, and my chest hurt, and *everything fucking hurt*.

"You mean, the Tivoux boy?" Madeline's arched brow revealed the wrinkles on her forehead.

"Yes, Grandmother. Taland—where is Taland?" Because we'd been in Silver Spring, in the Devil's lair, and I'd brought him out of that ruined house. Radock had been there—I'd left Taland in his hands.

*You can let go now. I got him—*that had happened...*right?*

A deep sigh escaped Madeline's lips, and she closed her eyes as if she were suddenly exhausted.

"What have you gotten yourself into, Rosabel?" she whispered.

A part of me wanted to start laughing and ask her, *what the hell do you care?*

But another, bigger part of me knew that this was not important. *She* was not important.

So, I tried to move, tried to stand, tried to get the hell out of there. Except the sharp pain that came from every limb as well as my ribs stopped me. Pulled me back. Held me down as the shock froze me in place for a moment.

Fuck.

"I'm going to do a spell on you, heal you, and then we're going to talk, you and I," Madeline said.

"No, I—" *have to go,* I wanted to say, but she didn't let me. The words were at the tip of her tongue. When she started chanting, red flames sprung on her hand, and extended to me instantly. It must have been a fourth-degree one because the effect was immediate.

My eyes closed involuntarily. A long breath left my lips and the warmth that spread through me from the magic was like falling on fucking clouds while the sun shone all over me. Warmed me to my bones. Relaxed my muscles and took my pain away. Some of it, maybe even half.

I'd have been tempted to think that stranger things had never happened than Madeline actually doing a healing spell on me personally, but they had. Much stranger things —like the Bluefire siblings with halos over their heads, and rooms that were in two places at once, and Alejandro Ammiz and David Hill...

Yes, stranger things had definitely happened, and when Madeline was done chanting, I opened my eyes again to find her on her way to pour herself a glass.

With her whiskey in hand and her sharp eyes unblinking, she ordered, "Speak."

Except I didn't want to speak, did I? I wanted to run the hell away from this room, and never mind that the wound and the blood loss had taken a lot of energy out of me, and that my body needed sleep and food. Never mind that I had no idea what had happened after I'd passed out or how I came to be—*again*—in this fucking mansion—never mind! I made to stand up even though my vision had become blurry around the edges.

Unfortunately, I didn't even make it to my feet before I heard her whisper again and felt her magic.

It was cold this time, and the flames basically slammed me down on the couch again. They faded soon but the magic they carried wrapped around my hips like a thick piece of rope and held me down. Even if I'd had my full energy, I wouldn't have been able to do anything against it. And my magic—

"Stay, Rosabel," said Madeline, coming toward me slowly as she sipped her whiskey. "You're not going anywhere until you tell me exactly what happened—in detail."

I looked down at my hands, my fingers empty. "Where's my ring?" I asked. "Where's my..." *bracelet?*

I wore the same clothes I'd had on when I went to Silver Spring, to that house. Ruined and bloody and dusty and torn, my jeans and shirt, though my boots weren't on my feet anymore. Nobody had changed my clothes and I'd left my ring in my pocket before the fight, but my bracelet had been around my wrist. It had been around my fucking wrist but now I could see that it wasn't because my jacket wasn't on me, either, and my sleeves were completely torn.

My stomach fell and fell, and my magic raged together with me—*where the hell is my bracelet?!*

"You had nothing on you. Your ring wasn't on your person," Madeline said as she sat on the coffee table in front of the couch and crossed her legs. "You can't do magic, Rosabel. And you're wasting my time—*speak*. Tell me what happened. Tell me everything."

I shook my head. "I..."

To look into those amber eyes had always fucking terrified me, but now it did for a whole other reason. Now, I was terrified because she *really* wouldn't let me go and there was absolutely nothing I could do about it without my ring. Without my bracelet. *Where-where-where the hell was it?* Had it fallen off me while I was dragging Taland out of that house? Had I lost it somewhere and didn't see it? Had somebody taken it from me?

Had *she*?

My eyes scrolled down Madeline's body and to her wrists—nothing but a golden bracelet she always wore on the left hand. Then I looked at the table, at the office, what I could see on the other side from her desk's monstrous size there in the middle.

My bracelet wasn't there.

CHAPTER 2

Rosabel La Rouge

"You were in Alejandro Ammiz's neighborhood, in his Regah chamber," Madeline said, her glass almost empty.

"I was." I'd gone to get Taland, and I'd offered them my bracelet in exchange. I'd gone into the Regah chamber without any idea what the hell it even was.

"Why?"

I met Madeline's eyes.

Goddess, she seemed...confused. Not just pissed, but confused, *more* confused by the second, like she was trying to *read* the answer on my face, and when she couldn't, she only grew more curious.

"If I tell you, will you let me go?" Because I could pick my battles just fine, and this wasn't one I could win no matter how hard I tried. I had no magic, and this was Madeline Rogan, one of the most powerful Iridians in the world. She wasn't going to get tired, not if she kept me under her spells all day and all night.

9

Not to mention she had at least two dozen powerful guards working for her all about her estate at any given time.

Making a deal with her was my best bet, even if my life wasn't guaranteed. I mean, this was my grandmother. She openly threatened to kill me even in front of a room full of people. She could—and she *would* if she wanted. Without hesitation.

Silence for a long beat.

"Hmm," Madeline finally said, and then whispered another spell, this one to levitate and bring her the bottle of whiskey from the liquor cabinet a bit farther away. The bottle landed in her waiting hand and she didn't once look away from me as she filled her glass again. Slowly.

The sound of that liquid pouring into the glass would forever remain in my memories.

"I can tell you this much, Rosabel—I will *not* let you go if you *don't* tell me. How's that sound?"

It sounded like one of my nightmares, to be honest. I'd literally had dreams about her hunting me down and killing me.

"Grandmother, I need to know what happened to Taland." And so what if it only pissed her off more? If she was going to kill me right now, I might as well die after I found out about Taland.

"How would *I* know what happened to that boy, Rosabel? How?"

I shook my head. "How did you get me here?" *That's* how she'd know, because if she got to me, if she brought me to her mansion, she surely knew how I came to be found, didn't she? "Did the IDD find me in Silver Spring? Or did you?"

The corners of her lips turned up just slightly—what a bitter smile. "Same difference, isn't it?"

I wanted to say *no,* but the fact that the Council had literally let me live because I was her granddaughter...

"Everything, Rosabel," said Madeline, moving her glass in circles in front of her—a nervous tick. "You've been keeping a lot of secrets from me, and I want to know everything now."

Laughter burst out of me—how could I help it? "Oh, but I think *you've* kept far more secrets from *me,* Grandmother," I said, and I was panicking a little bit, but so what? I might die in the next hour but that wasn't anything new. Since the night I received that text from the prison guard, I'd walked hand in hand with death, and today was, apparently, no different. "Imagine my surprise when I find myself in *a Regah* chamber and I have no fucking clue what it even is." No expression on her face. "Imagine my surprise when I find myself in something called *the Blackrealm,* and guess what?" I waited a heartbeat. "Nope! Never even heard the name."

"Is that tone of voice supposed to tell me something?" she wondered.

"Yes—it's supposed to tell you exactly how *frustrating* it is to be in my skin!"

She paused. "Forgive me, Rosabel, if I've given you the impression that I care." My mouth opened but no word came out. "Speak."

The *bitch.* "You first."

"Oh?"

"Yes, Madame Rogan. You first—*speak* and tell me exactly why I had no idea what the hell any of those things were, and more importantly, what more is there that I have no clue about?"

"Standard procedure, I'm afraid. IDD agents are on probation their whole careers, so to speak—a rule I created and implemented to great success. The first five years of their service, agents are given very little information about more complicated matters of magic, and after year six, new things are added to their continuous training programs. It's how we weed out the weak, those who aren't reliable, who aren't loyal. It's how we make sure that, if we choose to share sensitive information with someone, it will be when they prove themselves worthy, and not a day before."

I shook my head, wondering if she was telling me the truth or if she was simply making all of this up. But then I remembered how Taland had told me about Iridians nowadays keeping the younger generations blinded, far away from what really went on in the world. Completely ignorant to the dangers we all faced.

"That's...*insane*," I whispered because he had been right —they were taking power away from us by not telling us what we could be up against. They were keeping us weak. *Making* us weak.

"I'm sure you think so," Madeline said. "And now, tell me about the Regah chamber and the Blackrealm. I'm only as patient as this glass allows me." She waved her glass at my face.

I tried to move on instinct, to fucking slap it out of her hand because *I* had no more patience left in me, either. And since the Iris Roe, I couldn't care less about what people thought of me or what they could do to me—the world had been out to get me for a while now.

And, yes, this was Madeline Rogan, but I was as good as dead already, and even though the fear of her, the sheer panic of having her eyes on me was there, so was my anger, rivaling it. So was my anger making me want to fucking burst into flames right now, if only I could.

If only her magic wasn't as strong as it pressed against my skin, keeping me immobile. If only I'd had my own, my bracelet, my power.

As it was, she had already defeated me, and again, I came to the same conclusion—I was at her mercy.

"I'll tell you, and then you'll let me go."

Slowly, she leaned a bit closer. "You're in no position to negotiate, Rosabel. Either you tell me what happened, or you will die."

Her words rang so true that every inch of my skin rose in goose bumps.

There went what little resolve I'd gathered, out the window for a moment.

"Why?" I whispered before I'd even realized I was going to. "Why, Grandmother? Why...why don't you care? Why didn't you ever care?! Why don't you..." *love me?!*

Pathetic, Rora. So fucking pathetic.

I closed my eyes to get rid of the stupid tears that had pooled in them. I reminded myself who I was speaking to, and that I'd already decided to rely on my anger rather than my fear right now, and then I got my shit together.

The look on Madeline's face remained the same. She wasn't the least bit concerned about my questions or my tears—the two that slipped from my eyes without my fucking say-so, and I couldn't even raise my hands to wipe them off.

"I'm in love with Taland," I started, and again, she didn't react. "He promised the Devil something from the IDD Vault in exchange for his freedom from the Tomb. He came in and stole it. I was there, too. We got caught and I helped him escape—I'm sure you know this. But he lost what he stole from the Vault in the fight with the guards, and then the Devil imprisoned him." Never mind that the asshole had gone and turned himself in without telling me. He'd gone and turned himself in to the Devil, knowing he wouldn't make it out of there alive, and I knew why he'd done it.

Because of *me*. Because he figured that, if the Devil's people came looking for him, they might find him while he was with me, and they might hurt me, too. That's why he did it. I didn't have to even ask him to know it—that was his reason.

And I was going to fucking smack him in the head if I ever saw him again.

"So, I went to the Devil's lair to get him out." I swallowed hard, gave my words a moment to sink in as I watched her. No expression. Not a single hint of what she was thinking.

"I offered him a bracelet in exchange. A bracelet *I* stole from the Vault a few days prior."

Not a flinch. Goddess, she was *good*.

"I came in here that night you went to that charity event, Grandmother. I went through your library"—I nodded my head at the shelves against the wall behind her —"and I found the one called The Delaetus Army. It had pictures in it. Illustrations. I saw the army and I saw their bracelets, the same as one I saw in the Vault earlier that day."

Now she finally gave me a hint when her left eye twitched, and when she began to play with her ruby ring, to spin it around her finger like she did when she was *extra* pissed off. Or maybe just frustrated. Possibly both.

"You came into my office," she said, her voice low, and it

wasn't a question or anything. Like she was simply trying to understand the meaning of those words better.

"I did," I answered anyway. "And the next day, I went back to the Vault and I stole that bracelet." I shook my head, my own magic raging still, but she had such a good grip on my body that no matter how hard I was trying to just move my hands, I couldn't. "Remember that time you knocked me out and took me to the Council's chambers, and on the way back you said that my magic was not the *different* they were looking for?"

She stopped a heartbeat, froze completely. Didn't spin her ring around her finger or the whiskey in her glass.

I smiled just to spite her. "You were wrong. It is. It's exactly the *different* they were looking for."

Magic *leaked* out of her. I felt it in the air, coating my tongue, going down my throat. Hers had a special flavor, spicy and overly sweet at the same time. It made me so nauseous, but I bit my tongue and kept going.

"I am, after all, a Laetus, even if I drained the Rainbow. And with that bracelet, I could do colorful magic. The *different* kind of magic you were so sure I didn't need to know about."

This I said to make her feel stupid, but I don't know why I bothered. Of course, she wouldn't—this was Madeline. Instead, she just looked down at her drink for a moment, then threw it all back before filling it once more.

"Continue," she said.

So, I did.

"I went to exchange the bracelet, which is a Laetus anchor, we believe," I said and gave her another pause to see if she'd say something. Twice now I'd used the term *Laetus,* not *Mud,* and she hadn't corrected me. "The Devil agreed. He was going to take the bracelet and let us go, consider Taland's debt paid."

An arched brow. "And your magic, it was—"

"Powerful," I finished for her. "Colorful."

"And you were going to give that away for...*a man*?"

Hold up, wait a minute...she was not reacting the way I thought she would.

Now I was the confused one because I'd thought for sure she'd have a big problem with me stealing and discovering the Laetus and doing colorful magic, but she was more concerned that I'd wanted to give it away?

"A man I love, yes."

Her laughter was awful, always had been. So... *untrained*. Unpleasant. Very *unlike* Madeline.

"Love—oh dear," she said. "You were going to give away all that power for *love*." Again, she laughed.

But her spell must have been getting weaker, because when my instincts took over and I tried to get up, to move, I could, only a little bit.

Here's hoping she doesn't notice, I thought, but then again, what the hell could I do if she didn't? Even if I wasn't being forced to sit on that couch, I had no weapon on me, no anchor.

But if I did...would I actually use it against her?

The question scared me because the answer was so readily available to me.

"I guess I could laugh at you, too," I said, while she pulled herself together again. "I mean, *David Hill*." She stopped moving. "He was in your house. You taught him everything he knows—wasn't that what you said?"

"What do you know about David Hill?"

"I know who he is now," I said, and finally, I'd caught her by surprise. Finally, she was showing me emotion, frustration, *rage*. "We met, only briefly. Only until Alejandro Ammiz told us all about how they were friends, and how he, since forever, has been gathering everything he needs to bring back the Delaetus Army."

Her glass of whiskey ended up on the wall behind me.

A scream slipped out of me because it was so sudden. The sound of broken glass got to me, even though she moved so fast I hardly saw her throwing it. So fucking fast her arm turned to a blur.

"Don't lie to me, Rosabel," said Madeline, her now empty hand raised to her right as she whispered another spell to bring herself a new glass. A clean glass where she could pour her whiskey. Her eyes were slightly bloodshot now—that's the only thing that had changed about her. And her magic—it vibrated in the air around her, too.

"I'm not lying," I said, and I hated that my voice shook. I hated that even now, even after everything I'd had to go through the past year alone, my body still behaved like I was afraid of her.

Not anymore, I thought, and I forced myself to raise my chin. She could throw her glass at my fucking face next, and I didn't care. I would not cower back in front of her.

"I am not lying, Grandmother. He admitted it himself. He's been collecting everything in the Vault—the veler, the Script of Perria, the bracelet..." My eyes closed and I tried to recall what else the Devil had mentioned. "He has *soul vessels,* too, though I don't know what those are."

"Why?" she whispered, and her own voice seemed to surprise her, like she hadn't meant to ask that question at all.

"I don't know, but I would imagine for the same reason Titus created that spell when he did." To rule over the world. To be *god.*

It was almost funny. The first time I heard about it, I was shocked at the idea alone—*who even had such ambitions?!*

Men did. Iridians did.

Putting the glass down on the table, Madeline stood up. If it wasn't for her spell holding me—now weaker still—I'd have probably moved away just in case. As it was, I just watched her as she slowly made her way around the coffee table and to the shelf, ran her fingertips over the spines as she searched for what she wanted.

A moment later, she found it. Took it out of the shelf. Turned to me and sipped her whiskey.

"Did you know that this was your mother's favorite book?" she whispered, and it was like she'd slapped the shit out of me. Like she'd thrown that glass at my face.

She looked down at her book. "Yes—Titus always intrigued her. How much do you know about him, though? Do you know the *whole* story?"

She asked me that. She really asked me that.

But I couldn't speak. Something about her mentioning my mother. Something about *thinking* about my mother when it felt like I hadn't in such a long time. The best I could do was shake my head.

"Very well. I shall tell you."

CHAPTER 3

Rosabel La Rouge

"His time was long ago, long before the French and British colonies first set foot in what is now Canada. Titus was born and raised in what is now called Nova Scotia—an exceptional mage, more powerful than anything the people of his time had seen. A Whitefire and Laetus hybrid, more powerful than both combined." Madeline pressed her lips into a tight smile as she slowly paced in front of me with the book still in her hands. "It's a shame that the world hasn't seen talent such as his often. Or *ever,* after him, if you ask me."

My ears could be fucking with me. "*Talent?* He created a curse to control people." Just in case she'd somehow forgotten that part.

Her eyes brightened. "Precisely. The amount of power and dedication and attention to detail a curse of that magnitude requires...can you imagine?"

The question sounded rhetorical, but I answered

anyway. "I don't have to imagine anything—it already happened." And she knew this way better than I did, apparently.

Madeline flinched—actually flinched. "Yes, it did." She finally sat down on the coffee table again, the book on her lap. And I realized I'd never seen her so...*not-perfectly-composed* around me before. It was almost like she was *human,* like the rest of us, which couldn't possibly be. This was Madeline Rogan, and Madeline Rogan was a monster who probably had no beating heart and no soul and her insides were made of plastic.

She continued.

"Titus was, in fact, trying to find a *cure* for curses, if you will. An anti-curse—*the* anti-curse that would serve to deflect and mute every curse ever cast by magic, but he created something far superior instead."

Is it just me or is Madeline a fan of Titus? I mean, the way she was talking about him almost made me blush.

"And he wrestled with the idea for years and years. Wrestled with the morality of it, and *that* is the real reason why he went out in the world, traveled far and wide, in search—not for Laetus, but for *reasons*."

I'll be damned... "Reasons for...what, exactly? Why *not* to become so purely evil as to possess other people to make them do whatever he wanted?" I couldn't help myself, though it might have been smarter to just let her get on with the story.

"Reasons why the people deserve their freedom," Madeline said. "He searched for the good in people, sure that he'd find it, and the answer might surprise you—he *didn't*. The idea of a *good man* is only an illusion. People are bad to their core, manipulative, lying, cheating bastards, all of them. To trust *anyone* at all would be foolish..." Her voice trailed off and she looked down at the book on her lap. "He concluded."

So painfully obvious that *she* believed that, too. And I wondered, was that the reason why Madeline was the way she was? Did she really believe that all people are *bad?*

I would imagine so. *She* was a liar and a manipulator, and she knew *she* shouldn't be trusted, I guessed. After all, it all begins with our own selves, doesn't it? We see the world through our own eyes.

"Even if that was true, two wrongs still don't make a right."

"Regardless of what he considered *wrong* or *right,* he decided to move forward with his plan, to gather an army and take over the world to ensure that the people prospered under his care."

A bitter laughed burst out of me. "His *care,* yes. Where he possessed some of the most powerful mages in the world and with them threatened the same people he *cared* about, sure. I see it," I mocked, but Madeline might as well have been deaf to my voice just now.

"However, his methods were deemed *inhumane* by the people, and so they opposed him. Fought him. Died in countless battles before they came together and defeated Titus. That's the end of the story."

This was definitely the *longest* Madeline had ever spoken to me. I had never before in my life heard this many words coming out of her mouth within the same hour—or even the same year!

"Except the part where they practically banned the Laetus and called them *Mud* and cast them out of society and took away their right to have magic." I shook my head because an ache had already started to develop behind my eyes. "The story never really ended."

Madeline was silent for a moment as she went through the pages of the book.

"That is the nature of fear, Rosabel," she finally said. "That is what people who are afraid of what they cannot control or comprehend or *best* do."

That I actually agreed with, and suddenly I had this urge to ask her more, curious to see how she thought, what she believed in, but I stopped myself. Not just because of who she was but because time was ticking and Taland wasn't with me and I needed to find him and find my bracelet asap. Before things went even more to shit. Before this became...irreparable.

"What's a Regah chamber?" I asked instead.

Madeline didn't look up from the pages of the book at all, but more shockingly, she actually answered my question.

"It's a concrete space linked directly to one's soul, so to speak. To one's magic. Think of it as a bridge that links your physical location to the one that you have connected your magic to," she said.

"Two different places in one," I whispered, as the image of the Regah chamber came to my mind again, that veil of magic that separated us in Silver Spring from the Devil's cell at the Tomb penitentiary.

"Precisely. Forbidden magic for obvious reasons," Madeline continued with a deep sigh like she was nostalgic all of a sudden. "But it enables you to be present in two places at once—*only* two. The one where your physical body is, and the one you've tied your magic to. Even then, you are separated by the screen of magic that projects you to the place you are connected to, and projects the place you are connected to, to you. Basically, the entire thing is only *projection* but not only of images. Of all senses and of magical energy, too."

I nodded. "Oh, yes. I saw that. The Devil literally attacked us from his cell at the Tomb." Shivers erupted down my back at the memory of how his magic had suspended me on air. How it had taken complete control of my body, how I'd been barely able to finish that spell... "He took us to the Blackrealm, too. I don't suppose you'll mind telling me what *that* is, too, would you?"

"It's nothing but a Blackfire trick," Madeline said, and this time she did raise her head from the book to look at me. "They've created this vast space that they can connect to for short periods of time, goddess knows when. It has nothing but the color black, hence the name, I would imagine, but there's a reason why accessing it is forbidden. There's a reason why the strongest of Blackfires steer clear of it."

"Which is?" I asked when it didn't look like she planned to continue.

"You can lose yourself to the black, Rosabel. And if you do, there is no going back. One will forever be stuck in the black if one doesn't know how to navigate through it—and believe you me, nobody really does, no matter what they think." She lowered her eyes to the book again. "They used it as a punishment measure back when the IDD was first created. They would banish mages into the Blackrealm never to be seen or heard of again—which, if you ask me, is the cruelest fate of all. No in or out, virtually no senses, no time. I imagine one would want to lose their mind in such a situation—and what happens when you can't even do *that*?"

"That's...awful." Just to think about being in a timeless

space surrounded by black, never seeing or hearing or feeling anything—*fuck*.

"That's *ignorance*," said Madeline. "It was done by people who thought they had control over the Blackrealm but quickly found how wrong they were."

"But—"

"Is *this* what you were talking about, Rosabel?"

Madeline didn't let me speak when she suddenly turned the book toward me to show me illustrations of the Delaetus Army, the soldiers standing in perfect formation with their helmets on—and their bracelets.

I swallowed hard, thoughts of the Blackrealm momentarily forgotten. "Yes."

"You stole this bracelet from the IDD Vault."

"Yes."

A moment of silence as she watched me intently but just now I couldn't decipher that look at all. "And it worked."

"It did."

"You made..." Her voice trailed off, and I gladly finished for her. At this point I didn't even want to hide anything anymore. So fucking tired of secrets.

"Colorful magic. Powerful magic," I said, and I could have sworn her cheeks flushed a soft pink. "Hill has been planning for this since you were still in charge of the IDD. I know you don't trust him, are probably weary of him, but he used me for that mission in school because I am your granddaughter, because if something went wrong, *you'd* be implicated as well, and the Council has a soft spot for you." I leaned forward as far as her magic allowed me, which was actually more than I expected. "He's a double agent, Grandmother. His mother was a Mergenbach, his grandfather the founder of Selem. *He* took Taland to that school to steal the veler."

"He wouldn't," Madeline whispered, but even she didn't believe herself.

"He did. Then he sent me to supposedly *stop him,* but he was never really going to allow Taland to actually steal the veler. He merely needed an excuse for the Council when he demanded they take that veler to the IDD Vault. I imagine it must have been *easy* at that point for him."

"It was quite easy, yes," she said, surprising me again.

"So, he has the veler that he needs right there, and he has all these other things, too. No idea how he collected them, but he has them. And the Devil helped him. He actually broke Taland out of prison to try to steal something from Hill, so that when Hill rose in power, he said, he'd rise with him. They'd planned everything in detail." And nobody had even figured it out.

I wouldn't have ever figured it out either, had I not stolen that bracelet when I did.

"I always knew Ammiz was a dangerous man. Him, I could even be persuaded to throw into the Blackrealm," said Madeline, shaking her head.

"He's in the Tomb. There's only so much he can do. I think Hill is far more dangerous."

"Oh, but Ammiz is *weak.* Weak men are the most dangerous out there," she insisted.

"Regardless—Hill is the guy who actually plans to find and bring back the Delaetus Army, as absurd as it sounds."

She slammed the book closed so abruptly I jumped, and this time I could. Either she was willingly letting me move more freely, or her spell had faded and she didn't seem interested in reinforcing it.

I had no complaints.

"I guess I should have seen it," Madeline whispered. "There were signs."

And as much as I would have loved to rub that in her face, I stopped myself. "You can still put an end to it. Where is Hill?"

Madeline looked me in the eye without even blinking for a good long moment. I thought for sure she'd tell me that he was captured, that he was in jail or something, but no. She didn't answer me at all.

"Where is the bracelet, Rosabel?"

Fuck. "I don't know."

"But you had it. You used it."

"Yes. I destroyed the screen of the Regah chamber with it and that's how the Devil lost control of...*our side* of the room."

"You destroyed the screen of the Regah," Madeline repeated.

"I did." Except...that's not *all* I'd done, was it? The memories kept coming back to me, and I remembered dragging myself and Taland out of that basement, up the stairs and out the door, the yard...the *ruined* basement and stairs and yard. All of it had been ruined, the people knocked out, the ground with holes in it. *Holes.*

"It takes a lot of power to break a Regah. That's the connection of magic between a person and a place. It takes... *a lot* of power." Slowly, Madeline put the book down on the table and crossed her legs again. "You did it by yourself?"

I analyzed her for a moment. She didn't seem suspicious and she didn't judge me or despise me or anything like that—no, she simply seemed curious.

"Yes."

"You used all the colors of magic." Again—a statement.

"I did, Grandmother. All the colors of magic and more. But right now, I don't know where the bracelet is, if it fell off me when I passed out in Silver Spring, or if it was taken. Either way, I need to leave." I pushed against her magic, and though it let me move, it still didn't let me stand up, like this invisible blanket wrapped around my legs that was as strong as fucking concrete. Impossible to break through by myself.

"Who else was there in the Regah?" she asked instead.

"Grandmother, let go of me. Please, just let go. I need to leave." I needed to go to Silver Spring or The Diamond Club to look for Taland. I needed to leave right now.

"Who else?" She leaned forward, her eyes dead and dull once more. "Answer me, Rosabel." And the hold of her magic tightened around me.

Fucking hell... "Taland and Seth Tivoux. Aurelia and Zach Mergenbach. Three of the Devil's men—Hakim, Bes, and another I don't know the name of. Hill came at the end."

"How long did it last?"

"I. *Don't. Know,*" I said through gritted teeth. "Let me go."

"I can't do that, Rosabel," she said. "What kind of a spell did you use to break the screen?"

"What do you mean, *you can't*? We made a deal, didn't we? You said—"

"I said I wouldn't let you go if you didn't tell me. I never promised that I would if you did," the bitch said, and by now I was fuming at the ears. "Tell me what kind of a spell you used."

"No," I spit. "I am not telling you a single thing anymore."

For a moment, she just looked at me passively. "I don't think you understand the gravity of the situation, Rosabel."

"No—it's *you* who doesn't! I was there, Grandmother. I understand just fine." My voice rose—I couldn't help it and I didn't care. She was *really* not going to let go of me, and now I was starting to panic again.

"The Council is on their way."

I stopped.

The entire fucking world could have stopped spinning just now.

"What?" I breathed, sure that I'd heard her wrong because no fucking way...

"The Council is on their way here."

My lips opened but no sound left me.

"They insisted I take you to them, but I told them that you weren't capable of staying awake yet, that I would take you to see them later. They must be in a hurry because they decided to come to us instead," Madeline said, and I couldn't even believe my ears.

"Grandmother," I whispered again, and it sounded like both a pleading and a warning.

"Hill is missing, Rosabel. Alejandro Ammiz, too. When the IDD went into that house, they didn't find anyone you mentioned except *you* in the front yard, alone. I had to come personally to bring you back here instead of leaving you in a jail cell."

"The Mergenbachs," I whispered. "And-and-and Seth, they..." But Radock had been there, hadn't he? And I bet whoever worked for Selem had taken Seth and the Mergen-bachs out before the IDD arrived. Of course, they did—and left *me* there. I wasn't one of them, was I? I was an outsider.

Tears in my eyes, angry ones now that I didn't care enough to hold back.

"They weren't there, only the ruins that *you* left behind, apparently," Madeline said. "I wonder how much more power you could have used with that bracelet." This last sentence she said under her breath, like she was thinking out loud more than talking to me.

"Taland," I said and squeezed my eyes shut to get rid of those tears faster. "I need to see Taland."

"How silly of you, Rosabel. To go and fall in love with your target?" She sighed. "Regardless of how things turned out—you shouldn't have. I always knew you weren't capable of doing a spy's work. You're way too honest. You *feel* too much, and you are not very good at keeping yourself under control."

"I did! Hill saw me himself—it was my ability to control myself that got me that fucking job in the first place!" She was there, too, and she knew this.

But Madeline raised a perfectly manicured finger and shook it in front of my face. "Your ability to control your *expressions* got you that *fucking* job, Rosabel." That was the first time I'd ever heard her cussing. "Controlling your emotions is a completely different thing. You could never force yourself to let go of something or to believe something you know is a lie. You could never manipulate yourself, not even when it suited you. Never—I've been watching you since you were a little girl."

Fucking hell, this woman.

"I know you mean it as an insult, Grandmother, but that's a compliment to me." I didn't want to manipulate myself, close my eyes when it was convenient. Pretend I wasn't aware of things to make it easier on myself. I *chose* not to do that, despite what she thought.

"Not an insult, for goddess's sake. Just an observation. You are so very sensitive, Rosabel—so very, very sensitive.

You take everything personally when you shouldn't, because nothing ever is."

"Is that why, then?" I asked despite my better judgment. "Is that why you always choose Poppy, why you wanted Poppy to go on that mission for Hill?" Because Poppy could most definitely rearrange the narrative in her mind to suit her, to make things easier for herself. She'd admitted it to me herself, even though I'd never really noticed it. She had. "Is that why you could never stand me, didn't love me, Grandmother? Because I can't manipulate myself? Because I am not *like you*?!"

Those fucking tears again—goddess, I hated them so much. I hated that I was crying, and I hated *her,* and I hated *me,* and I hated the entire fucking world that was standing between me and Taland.

"Quite the contrary. It's because you're exactly like who I used to be that I don't trust you."

She could have slapped me, and I'd have been less surprised.

I am nothing *like you,* I wanted to say because she must have lost her fucking mind if she thought I was going to just let her say that and get away with it, but Madeline suddenly stood up. Redfire magic danced on her fingertips as she raised one hand toward the doors on the other side of the room and the other at me.

Her magic let go of me all at once.

"They're here."

CHAPTER 4

Taland Tivoux
A few hours earlier

Whatever place this was, wherever they'd taken me to, Rosabel was not here, and that was pretty much all I needed to know.

I pushed the doors open at the same time and with all my strength, as if I hoped the sound of them slamming against the walls was going to do something—*anything*—to alleviate the anger and pain weighing my chest down. Not physical pain because I'd been healed, it seemed, but the pain of not knowing where she was. What had happened to her. *Why* she wasn't with me, when it had been her who took me out.

I remembered it just fine, even though I'd had a foot in the grave—I remembered. She'd carried me, dragged me all the way out of that shit show by herself when she could barely stand on her own.

My stubborn little criminal.

And now she wasn't here. I'd woken up in a small dark room all alone, *without* her.

At the end of the narrow corridor outside that room were the others, and they all stopped speaking when I barged in. The doors did slam against the walls on either side, and it was definitely satisfying to hear the cracks as the handles dented them in, but the satisfaction didn't last.

Aurelia and Kaid were sitting on a couch farthest to the left of the room, while Seth sat alone on the floor near a table with weapons on top of it, resting his elbows on his raised knees as he played with his feather. And on the other side, near a dark grey desk stood Zachary, Radock and Violet—one of the elder members of Selem, a Bluefire that could kill you twenty different ways with nothing but two pocket knives in her hands.

Or she *used to* when she wasn't sixty years old, I guessed.

No Rosabel.

I stepped into the room as they watched me, some flinching, some concerned—Seth just looked bored as he rolled his eyes at my naked torso. I hadn't taken the time to change or shower—I couldn't have cared less.

"Bro—" Radock started at the same time as I said, "Where is she?"

They all knew who I was talking about. They could all see that she wasn't here, but her bracelet was. It was right there in the middle of the grey desk's shiny top. The bracelet, but not her.

"I imagine you're feeling well, Taland," said Aurelia as she stood up from the couch and fixed her leather jacket.

"'Course he does, the bastard. After all those spells the

dead would feel great, too. Meanwhile, I can't get any of you to do more on *me*," Seth said. His voice was low but the entire room heard it because of the silence.

The entire room ignored him, too.

Radock turned toward me with his hands in his pockets. "Glad to see you're okay, Taland."

I moved closer to him, to that desk. "Where is she?" I asked again, and he had to see that I was holding myself back from screaming my fucking guts out. I hoped he answered me before I did something stupid. My magic was at the ready, and that bracelet was right there. I didn't even need a feather—or the pain that came with it. I'd already used that bracelet with Rosabel so I knew how easily I could best all of them here if it came to it.

"She's home."

I turned to Violet Asher while she crossed her arms in front of her chest. Since I was a kid, she'd always looked strange to me with her wavy hair that fell down to her hips and wrapped around her shoulders like a silver blanket—and she still looked almost exactly the same somehow.

"She went home. Madeline Rogan took her," she added.

Every drop of blood in my veins turned to stone. *Madeline Rogan.* "The IDD—"

"*Not* the IDD—she's in the mansion in Baltimore. She's with her grandmother."

I took another step closer, and I felt the cool tiles underneath my bare feet as if they were trying to call to my mind, to my attention, to remind me that I was in a room full of killers who could take my head if they wanted.

Here's the thing, though: I could take theirs easier. I *would* take theirs because whatever kept them alive and clinging to this world was much weaker than *my* purpose.

"Why isn't she here with me, Radock?" I asked my brother because *he* had been there at the Devil's lair. I'd seen him before my body gave up on me. He'd been there.

Radock took a moment to look me over. "Because I was concerned with getting my brothers out of the ruins, Taland. Because I didn't need Madeline Rogan on me while I was tending to you."

"What you're saying is, you're a coward."

The words slipped out of me—in normal circumstances I'd have kept that thought to myself. However, there was nothing *normal* about any of this and it hadn't been for a while now, so I'd lost the will to bother.

Radock clenched his jaws so hard the whole room could hear it.

Then Aurelia was coming toward us. "That's no way to talk to your brother, boy."

And I had plenty to say to her, too, but Radock didn't let me. Maybe because he knew and he didn't want me to make a bigger mess out of this little meeting they had going on here?

He was right.

"There was no time to hide her properly when they came. I wasn't about to risk *everything* for her the way you continuously do."

A bitter smile stretched my lips as I moved back a couple feet and rested my hip on the edge of his desk. Then I slowly reached for the bracelet he'd left there—*her* bracelet.

"You didn't have time to hide her, but you had time to take *this* off her wrist?" He was a fucking liar is what he was —and he knew I knew.

"Yes. It was fairly easy, too. She was unconscious," my brother said, and I hadn't wanted to slam my fists on his face so much since he was torturing Rosabel in the basement back home.

"We couldn't have kept her hidden, Taland," said Aurelia, stepping in front of me. "Look at me."

I did. I was taller than her, so she had to look up at me, those wide blue eyes as intense as always. Like they held secrets. Like they knew *my* secrets.

"There was nothing we could have done. The Council would have come after us with their everything the moment they found out what happened. She's safer with Madeline Rogan."

I leaned closer just a bit. "Move out of my way, Aurelia."

She was shocked and she was pissed and probably feeling plenty of other things, but before she could voice any of it, I was in front of Radock.

"She told you. I know she told you the truth. She saved me. She saved *us* from the Devil, too. Yet you decided she wasn't worth the effort when you know she can use *this*." I raised the bracelet between us.

"She also told me that *you* can, too," my asshole of a brother said.

"And it didn't occur to you that I would use it against *you* if you don't help me get to her and bring her here safely right now?" I didn't even care where *here* was, but wherever I was, that's where she had to be.

Otherwise, I was going to fuck something up.

"If you're thinking about starting a fight, you can't win against all of us, Taland. Not in the state you're in," said Kaid, shaking his head with a sigh. "Drop the attitude. We did the best we could. We got *you* out—and Seth, too."

"If only his own life and mine were as valuable to him..." Seth said from where he sat on the floor—and he was absolutely right.

"But you left her there," I reminded them. "And now... what? What happens when the Council gets to her? What do you think they'll do?" I went closer to Radock. "Do you think Madeline Rogan is going to save her, brother? *Spare* her? Do you?"

Radock held my eyes but said nothing, and I knew he was tense. He hated to be spoken to this way, but I currently had zero fucks left to give. They were all back in Silver Spring where he left them behind—together with Rosabel.

The guilt ate at me, gnawed at my insides like a living beast. I had been too weak to make sure she was okay. Too weak to stay conscious.

"Of course, you don't," I said after a second of loaded silence. "You know they won't. They'll kill her—and you don't care. Maybe you even prefer it."

"I don't. She saved you, despite everything. But if her own grandmother will allow the Council to kill her, who am I to try to intervene?" Radock said, having composed himself as fast as always.

"*My* brother," I said, and it was hard to keep the bite out of my voice—so hard.

"Is that so? And was I your brother when you betrayed me and yours for her? When you called Madeline Rogan herself to come for her granddaughter?"

Words died on my tongue. I had no idea he'd found out —not that it mattered. I would have told him myself when the time was right.

The problem was that the time seemed to never be right. For those shorts hours when Rosabel and I were together in that safe house, everything had made such perfect sense, had aligned as it should. But then I had a fucking debt to pay, and so here we were again in this old dance.

"I need a car." Because I was realizing it was useless to stand here and talk to him. His opinion wouldn't change no matter what I said.

"You're not going anywhere," said Radock, and I would have laughed any other day.

"What you need to do is sit down and call to your mind and forget about Rosabel for a second—she can take care of herself, okay? I met her. She will be just fine." Aurelia again, and she pushed both me and Radock to the sides—we'd come much closer to one another than I'd realized. "What *we* all need to do is figure out how to find David Hill before everything goes to shit because if he wins, Taland—you know what happens?" Again, she looked up at me with that conviction. "Then *we all* die. Not just Rosabel, but *all* of us." She gave her words a moment to sink in.

Fuck, she was right.

How I hated that she was right.

"So now that you got your head out of your ass, help us figure out how to track Hill, and once we stop him, the Council will have no reason to want to get rid of anyone, will they?"

"You'll have your girl back and everybody lives happily ever after," Kaid said.

"Nobody's going to be *happy* anytime soon, I assure you," Violet muttered.

"Just help us," Aurelia insisted. "Help us find the Devil, at least—they are surely together. You spoke to him. You worked with him when he helped you escape the Tomb—you must know something about him."

"David Hill," Radock said. "He's the most important thing now. We need to find him."

Violet came closer. "And the best part?" She smiled as if to show me that two of her upper teeth were missing. "The best part is that we'll still need to contact the Council if we do."

"We *don't,*" Zach insisted, but his eyes were closed and he had sweat on his forehead—his *clean* forehead. Just now I was realizing that everyone in this room was clean and dressed in fresh clothes, healed and rested, probably fed. Meanwhile my stomach was growling with hunger, and as much as I hated to feel the weakness of my muscles, I still did. Healing spells were miracles, indeed, but they still needed the body's own energy.

"We don't need anybody's help," Kaid agreed, but Radock didn't.

"We do," he said. "Unfortunately, Violet is right—we do need the help of the Council. Alone, we cannot defeat Hill."

"Or maybe we can." Zachary came closer, too, and even Seth was finally interested enough to get up and come closer. They were all around me now. "Maybe we can with the help of *that* thing." He pointed at the bracelet in my hand. "You can use it. The Drainage in the Roe turned you Mud—that's what Rosabel told Radock. You can use it."

Suddenly, all the pieces clicked in place in my noisy brain. I might have been tired and hungry and still not fully recovered from the torture that Yuri and the Devil's people put me through for those few days, but I still had the upper hand here.

I could still win. I was *going* to.

"That is true—I could," I said, raising the bracelet again, inspecting the details, the mud-like surface, the thickness of it, how cold it was to the touch.

Then how it fit my wrist, just slightly tighter than I'd have preferred.

I released a bit of my magic just for show, just to allow small flames in all colors to dance on the tips of my fingers so they could see. So that each and every person in this room could see that I was not fucking around.

They did.

The way they watched those tiny flames could have been funny.

"Here's the thing, though. Not only will I use this to help you against Hill, but I can do something far better—recite the Script of Perria the Devil sent me to steal. I can recite it to you as many times as you'd like."

The greedy look in their eyes intensified.

"Remember what you taught me, brother?" I asked Radock. "When dealing with important documents, we never know when we'll see them again, so it's important to memorize anything we can, as fast as we can memorize it." This he'd told me before I went to the Iridian School of Chromatic Magics—at the request of *David fucking Hill*.

"You memorized it," Radock said, both afraid and impressed, though he'd never admit it. It wasn't his habit to allow anybody to see how he really felt about anything.

"I did. And I'm assuming they already told you everything that happened in the Regah chamber so I'm not going to repeat any of it to you—but if you want to find David Hill, you will have to go where *he* is going." To Perria, the place where they buried the Delaetus Army seven centuries ago.

The fucker wanted to actually bring those soldiers back and conquer the world, which was mind-blowing on its own.

But there would be time to think about that.

"So, why didn't you give it to the Devil then? You said you didn't know what it was," Seth asked, and all the others seemed suddenly curious, too. "I mean, you could have spared yourself all the torture."

"Does it matter?" I said because I didn't have the patience to explain to them that I *had,* in fact, tried to give the Devil the contents of that script engraved on the marble plaque. I'd turned myself in to do just that, but turns out, the Devil wasn't interested in the contents at all, only the plaque.

I'd been confused then, but now it made sense—he couldn't sell David Hill something he already had in the IDD Vault.

"He's right," Aurelia finally said. "Taland didn't steal the script so that means Hill has it. Hill can *use* it, if he hasn't already." Her eyes squeezed shut. "Goddess, he could be in Perria right now, reviving the dead!"

Everyone in the room shivered visibly.

"You *will* tell us what the Script of Perria contained, right?"

"I will," I said. "We leave for Madeline Rogan's mansion right now, we find Rosabel, and then you can have the Script of Perria—and you can keep the bracelet, too."

"The bracelet is useless to us—we're not Mud," Violet said.

"You can't be serious," Zach and Radock said at the same time.

If only they had a clue what it was like inside my chest. If only they had a clue of the lengths I'd go to for my girl.

But since they didn't... "Two options." I raised two fingers in front of me. "I can take this bracelet and my memory of the script with me right now and leave on my own. *Or* you can come with me, and once Rosabel is with us, I will write the whole thing down for you myself."

I gave my words a moment to sink into their brains.

"So, what's it going to be, friends?"

In my mind, I was already preparing for them to stay behind. I was already picturing the details of my solo trip to that mansion from wherever the fuck they'd brought me. I'd need clothes and food and water—lots of water. I'd need feathers, too, though I planned to use the bracelet until I got to her. But once I found her, I'd still need to be able to do magic until we got to safety.

"Well, I mean, to be fair, there's a good chance that the Council is already on her. It's been almost twelve hours since she ruined the Regah chamber and we made it out."

Twelve hours.

"She'd be unconscious, I would think, but yes. The Council could very well be onto her already," said Aurelia.

"And how do you propose we fight off the Council, assuming we don't even need them for Hill? How do you assume we *win* and take your precious Rosabel out?" Violet again, and her voice had turned even more bitter.

"We don't fight them," I said, struggling to keep my calm now. *Twelve hours.* That was a long time.

Could it really be that they'd already gotten to her?

"They'll want Hill as much as we do. Where is he now?"

"Disappeared," said Radock. "Nobody knows—not the IDD and not the Council."

I nodded. "Then I'll give them the script as well."

"You said you'd give that *to us*," Zachary insisted.

"What difference does it make? We're all going to him, aren't we? Didn't you just say that we'll need the Council to defeat him?" It made perfect sense to me already because I was in a rush to figure out how to get to Rosabel and how to get them all to join me.

It took the rest of them a minute, but they all came to the same conclusion.

"So, we go back to Baltimore, and then..." Kaid started.

"Then we go to the Council, if they haven't killed her already," Radock said, his eyes never leaving mine.

A cold chill rushed down my spine at the idea. Rosabel, *killed?*

Never.

"Then we tell the Council we know how to find Hill if they agree to fight with us," said Aurelia.

"I can see that happening. They have a lot of people. A lot of soldiers and agents. People trained to fight. Yes, yes..." Violet's voice trailed off as she stared at her feet.

"And then—" Zach started, but I'd run all out of patience already.

"Then we all go and find Hill and stop him," I finished for him. "Now, I'm going to turn around and I'm going to leave. Come with me or don't—it's entirely up to you."

A moment, that's all they had. A single moment of thick, heavy silence that I could feel in the air going down my throat.

Then I turned, just as I said, and walked for the doors with the bracelet around my wrist.

The rest of them, *all* of them except Violet, came after me.

To say that I wasn't relieved would be a lie. The Council was still the Council, the most powerful mages in the world even without their soldiers and guards and agents. Against them I'd have died on my own. They would try to kill me without hesitation, right away, and even if they didn't, there was a good chance that they wouldn't take me seriously if I went alone. Having Radock and Kaid and the Mergenbachs there would change that.

As much as I wanted to just *fly* over to that mansion and

get Rosabel and disappear, I couldn't, so I had to play by these rules for now.

Lucky for me I had something they all wanted, and right now I was going to use that as best as I could. Hill and the Devil and the Delaetus Army could wait—for now. Everything could wait.

I'm coming for you, sweetness.

CHAPTER 5

Rosabel La Rouge

Every thought in my head disappeared just as fast as Madeline's magic that was holding me down on that couch. The doors to her office opened. Now I couldn't get up for an entirely different reason—my legs would never hold me. Not when the face of Helen Paine was in front of my eyes, and not when I realized that the rest of the Council was coming in through those doors, too.

Had my heart stopped beating? Because suddenly I couldn't feel it or hear it—I could only hear those footsteps slamming against the shiny wooden floor of Madeline's office.

Then the doors closed.

Madeline was on her feet by the coffee table where she'd just been sitting, hands folded, not a wrinkle in sight on her red suit. The Council members stopped in front of her, and they looked so *big* from down here because I still couldn't bring myself to stand. They looked so different, too, because they were wearing ordinary clothes, pants and dresses and jackets, not the black robes they'd had on when I met them the first time—but the suspicion, the rage in their eyes was the same.

The *hatred* they all felt for me was perfectly visible across their faces when they looked at me—except the Mud councilman. I didn't know his name, but when he looked at me, analyzed every inch of me, he looked more concerned than suspicious. More *sorry* than angry.

But I knew that that wasn't going to make a difference.

"She just woke up."

Madeline's voice rang in my ears and it felt like the entire room held their breath for a moment until her words made sense.

"I suppose it was too much of a bother to put her in a car unconscious," said the Redfire woman, her eyes just as fiery as I remembered, her dark skin shimmering like she had golden blood in her veins and it was just slightly peeking through—or maybe it was the warm overhead lights of the office.

"It wasn't—but I wanted to bring her to you awake," Madeline said, not in the least bit concerned, even though she could see the way the Redfire woman looked at her.

"Time is of the essence here, Madeline," said Helen Paine. "No matter. We're here now."

With the fabric of her long white dress in her hand, she moved around Madeline and the table. She was now barely three feet away from me, looking down at me and assessing me with her eyes the same way I was assessing her.

The memory of her sword with the handle made of bones was in the center of my mind. How long until she drew it this time?

And was I really going to just sit here and take it?

No, I thought. *Fuck that, I won't.*

Except...what exactly could I do against the most powerful Iridians in the world when there were six of them and one of me—*without* weapons or magic?

Sweat on my brow.

"Have you found him?" Madeline said, as the rest of the Council members came around her and spread about the room, all their eyes on me. Some—the Blackfire and Bluefire—were already helping themselves to a glass from the cabinet.

"No," said the Greenfire woman, her copper hair shining golden, too, under the lights as she slowly crossed her arms in front of her chest and raised her chin so she could look down at me better. "We haven't found David yet, Madeline."

My stomach turned.

"And the IDD?" she asked.

"The IDD is fine." The Redfire threw Madeline a look. "The managing body is perfectly capable of taking care of business for a few days without a director."

Madeline didn't look happy about that. Of course she cared about the IDD. As far as she was concerned, that was her *baby.*

"She spoke to me, told me what happened," my grandmother said in the end, her cold amber eyes falling on me.

Now every Council member was looking at her, as the Blackfire and Bluefire offered everyone drinks.

"And?" asked the Mud as he threw back the contents of his glass at once, then wiped his mouth with the back of his hand.

"Please, sit down," said Madeline, raising a hand as she whispered. Red flames danced on her fingers as her magic came to life. Two chairs that were near her desk and the armchairs on the other side of the room slowly slid toward us, and all the Council members took their seats, leaving a good distance between each other as if they were disgusted —no, as if they *didn't trust* one another enough to sit closer together.

Only I remained seated on the couch, even though Madeline's magic no longer held me back.

"I'll tell you everything she told me," she said, and she began without wasting time, while the others used their magic to bring themselves liquor bottles and filled their glasses and drank.

I closed my eyes, focused on breathing, on the way the air went down my throat. I focused on my limbs, my muscles, clenching and unclenching them to make sure they were working properly. I focused on my fingers, too, and my magic.

It was there. It was *livid* as it slithered under my skin, searching for a way out, for an anchor, a gateway through which it could protect me. I had none on me, though. No bracelet and no ring.

I was completely naked in front of these people.

Madeline told them everything I had told her in detail, and she didn't stutter. Her voice didn't waver.

And even though I was constantly trying to think of a plan of escape as I looked in the faces of the Council members, I came up empty-handed.

The windows were on the other side, the drapes drawn, so I had no clue if it was even daylight outside. I had no clue how much time had passed since Radock took Taland away from Silver Spring or when I came to this mansion. Goddess, I wished I could see Poppy right now. She'd tell me what time it was and what had happened. She'd help me—I was sure she would.

But Poppy couldn't even come through the doors now that the Council was here. And I was glad for it—the ugly voice in my head knew that I wasn't going to get as lucky as I did with them that first time. The ugly voice in my head insisted that I was going to die soon. This time it sounded like it really *meant* it.

And in the mansion. In Madeline's fucking office, the place I despised the most. Here was where I'd die, after everything I went through. Taland in prison and the torture of the Tivoux brothers and the Iris Roe and the Devil's Regah chamber. I survived all of that just so I could die at the hands of the very people who were supposed to protect me. The *good* guys—what a fucking joke.

No way out. For real this time. There was no way out. Even though no magic was holding me back now, the moment I tried to stand they would turn on me. The moment I tried to move they would attack me.

No way out.

"And you believe her, Madeline?"

My attention fell on the Greenfire woman, who spoke after that moment of deafening silence when Madeline finished telling them the story as I'd told it to her.

"I do," Madeline said, but at this point I wasn't even surprised. "I do believe her, not only because the story makes sense, but because hearing it now, I can connect the times I found David's behaviors strange but didn't even realize it. I know that man." Madeline drank her whiskey slowly where she sat on the recliner—the white one. The same as the one she'd had to throw away last time because *I'd* made it dirty when I'd sat on it.

"We all know that man," said the Redfire. "We all know what he's capable of. The question remains, would he dare?"

I almost laughed. If she thought David Hill was afraid of anything, she was fucking delusional.

"He would," Madeline said. "He's smart enough. Powerful enough. Arrogant enough to convince himself that he will win."

"Why—you don't think he will?" asked the Blackfire—Ferid was his name if I remembered correctly.

"You do?" the Bluefire guy asked him in turn.

"I don't have an opinion about it yet, nor do I know enough to make an assumption, at least not an accurate one. What I do know is that if it were me wearing his shoes, I would have done anything in my power—and I mean *anything*—to keep this a secret until I knew that I was absolutely one hundred percent ready," Ferid said.

"He's right, George," said the Redfire, shaking her head at the Bluefire. "He's right—I wouldn't have let word get out if I wasn't ready, either."

"Except he didn't simply *decide* to let the word get out, did he?" This from the Greenfire, and she looked right at me.

Shivers rushed down my back.

"You broke the screen of the Regah chamber, did you not, girl?" she asked me.

My nails dug into my palms. I was most probably bleeding, but I didn't even feel it. All I felt was their eyes on me. The weight of their attention. The cruelness of my fate. The knowledge that my life ended right here, today, by these very people.

"Rosabel, answer the question," Madeline said.

"I..." My voice was so dry. I didn't want to talk. I didn't want to *help* these people, but the truth was that I wouldn't be helping *them*. The truth was that, as much as I hated it, they were the only ones who could put a stop to Hill's absurd plans of bringing back the Delaetus Army.

And wasn't that just fucking comical?

Because I *had* to help them. Taland lived in this world. Taland would no doubt try to stop Hill—and you know what, I'd rather *these* people did. Taylor lived in this world, too, and so did Poppy and Cassie, every other person who had done absolutely *nothing* to deserve the fate that Hill would bring upon the world if he really took over.

Tears slid down my cheeks so fast I hardly noticed them. For that moment that all of these things crossed my mind, I felt like I wasn't me at all.

How cruel was life. How very cruel.

My hands shook when I raised them to wipe the tears. "I broke that screen, yes. Hill tried to stop me. The Devil held us all motionless in the air from his side of the Regah chamber, and Hill *swam* in the air to get to me. Both he and the Devil knew that they wouldn't make it, so the Devil let us go at the last second. Hill reached me when I already finished the spell. Grabbed me by the head, tried to pull it off my shoulders." My hands were on my neck now, too, like I thought maybe Hill was still here trying to pull my head off for real. "My magic released before he could hurt me."

Silence in the room, another eternal moment.

"He didn't want his secret out and he hoped to keep the Devil silent before he told us, but he couldn't. He sent his guards to the Devil's cell in the Tomb to try to stop him, but they didn't get to him in time. He told us everything in front of him, too, and Hill confirmed it. Hill hoped to kill us all before we left the Regah chamber—but again, he couldn't get to me in time. We made it out."

"Because of you," said the Redfire. "Because you broke the screen."

"With the bracelet that you claim is an anchor." The Greenfire woman raised a red brow as she looked down at me even though she was sitting on the couch across from me. "A Mud anchor."

"It seems to have behaved the way an anchor does," said Madeline before I could answer.

"Colors," said the Mud councilman. "You really made magic with *colors*."

"I did." And he'd had no idea it could be done—it was plain to see. These women and men who held themselves above all others hadn't bothered to try to figure out if something like an anchor for the Mud even existed. I doubted they'd cared much to learn anything at all about the people they had labeled with that name, with that *fate*.

I realized this was exactly what Taland had been talking about when he spoke about our elders leaving *us* in the dark, blinding us to the real world.

And I wondered, had *they* been left in the dark, too, by their parents?

"So, it really exists," the man said.

"Of course, it exists," said the Greenfire. "And you're going to use it, Nicholas. As soon as we find it."

"All of it exists—it isn't just tales," said the Redfire. "David has really been stealing from us from right under our noses. All our noses." The way she looked at each and every one of her colleagues made me flinch, and her eyes stopped on Madeline. "You vouched for him, Madeline."

"And you agreed with me," said my grandmother without batting a lash. "All of you tested him, and you agreed."

Most of them looked down at their laps for a moment, but not the Redfire. "All of us trusted *your* judgment, too. Throughout your whole career."

"It has served you, that trust, hasn't it?" Again, Madeline couldn't have cared less about the accusations.

"Flora, we don't have the time to dwell on the past now. The future isn't looking very bright for us at the moment," the Greenfire said. "That is what we shall focus on."

"And who put *you* in charge, Natasha?" snapped the Bluefire—George.

"Oh, don't start with me," the old woman said.

"You are all ridiculous—a circus, a circus!" the Blackfire said, throwing back his whiskey before he reached for one of the bottles on the table to refill it.

For a moment, most of the Council members spoke at the same time. It was so surreal to sit there and watch them, like they were *ordinary* people, not the ones who held the fate of the world in their hands.

Meanwhile Madeline played with her glass and looked at me, her face perfectly passive, and for a moment there, just a split second, I could have sworn she looked *bored* while the members went at it, accusing one another, bickering about useless things.

"Enough," the Mud councilman finally said. "That's enough. We don't have time for this. Put yourselves under control."

I thought for sure they'd burst out again and ask him who put *him* in charge, but nobody did. The rest of them closed their eyes and took in deep breaths and drank more alcohol, but none said anything for a good moment.

"Enough time has already been wasted," the Redfire continued. "I'm afraid we'll have no choice but to believe Rosabel's tale and to take action before it's too late."

"He wants to raise a dead army? Fine," the Greenfire muttered. "Our ancestors have stopped a mad man once. We'll stop another again."

"Of course, we will," said George. "As soon as we find him, we kill him. I've always wanted to see the light die in his eyes, to be frank."

Through all of this, Helen had remained silent, sitting near Madeline in the second armchair, sipping her drink slowly, thinking.

"So...*arrogant*, indeed," said Ferid with a frown on his face as he no doubt thought back to whenever he had met Hill.

"Thinks he's entitled to everything," George muttered next, shaking his head at his almost empty glass.

"Behaves like he has the world in his pocket," Natasha the Greenfire whispered to herself.

"We will do this away from the public eye," Helen finally said, and when she spoke, the rest of them fell silent. "We will find him, and we will take care of him *in private*. Is that understood?"

They all nodded at the same time.

"There's a lot wrong with this system that we've inherited, and it's time we did something about it. It's time we made changes to ensure that the power doesn't slip from us again the way it has been doing for a decade now, apparently." Her eyes locked on Madeline's. "We will restore the order once more, Maddie, and you will help us."

"I will," Madeline said without a moment's hesitation.

Words were in my mind, coming up my throat, ready to slip out my lips in a rush. I wanted to tell them exactly how *wrong* everything was right now, inside the IDD and outside, too, in the Tomb, a penitentiary that was controlled by a criminal, an inmate, and the fact that Selem even existed; about how awful the Iris Roe was and how absolutely absurd draining people was, or labeling them *Mud,* treating them as the scum of society for no reason at all. I wanted to talk to them about every single thing in detail and *demand* that they fixed it, fixed everything, made it better. That was their fucking job!

Except now was not the time, was it?

And let's be honest—they would *never* listen to me, would never even let me finish speaking.

I tried anyway. "There's a lot going on at the IDD that isn't right. And out there, too, in the world. The Mud are treated like—"

"The bracelet," Flora cut me off. "Where is the anchor?"

I swallowed hard and my magic raged. "I don't know."

Helen turned to Madeline. "Where is the anchor?"

"She's telling the truth. It wasn't on her when they found her. It was taken."

"By whom?" the Greenfire asked me.

By Radock Tivoux, I thought. "I don't know," I said.

"You stole it from the Vault," said the Mud councilman —Nicholas. "Did it speak to you—is that why? Did it connect with you right away?"

I shook my head. "No. I just saw the picture of it in that book." I looked at the copy of *The Delaetus Army* still on the table where Madeline left it. "I got curious. I took it. I didn't find out what it could do until"—the memory of those colors in the woods coming out of Taylor Maddison's hand was at the center of my mind— "later."

"We tested you," said Helen in wonder. "I saw your Redfire with my own eyes. We all did."

"I was under the impression that the Mud *can't* do magic of one color at all," said Flora. "That's what I've known my whole life." And she sounded pretty fucking frustrated about it.

"That's what we all thought," said the Greenfire with a bitter smile. "I knew about the bracelets. I've seen drawings of them—I knew they wore them, but never did I even entertain the idea of finding one or trying to make it work. *Never.*"

"David Hill did," George said, then clenched his teeth. "He thought about it and he actually found it."

"It's *lucky,* I guess, that your granddaughter stole it," Helen said to my grandmother.

"Lucky, indeed," Madeline said.

Goddess, how I hated that world—*lucky.* I despised it.

"Not only the bracelet," I said, like something suddenly came over me. And I knew—I *knew* exactly what awaited me, yet I couldn't help myself, refused to keep my lips sealed. Refused to *not* help them, at least with what I could. "He found everything else—the Devil told us. The veler that you allowed to be locked up in the Vault when I stopped Taland from stealing it at the school, something called *soul vessels,* the bracelet, the Script of Perria. And he said he still needed *more* soul vessels and..." My eyes closed and I was violently thrust back into the memory of that Regah chamber, and the Devil was laughing and Hill was pissed off. The words came back to me despite the fear and the panic. "*His bones.*" I raised my head and looked at the Council members. "The Devil said that Hill still needed *his bones.*"

Silence, that heavy silence.

"The bones of Titus," Flora finally whispered.

"Yes," Helen said with a nod. "I imagine he would need the bones to bring back the army."

"Goddess," the Greenfire said after a moment. "He *really* is going to do it!"

I found myself in a state of disbelief, too, even though I had already known that Hill wasn't fucking around since the moment the Devil told us his plans.

"We have to find him—now," Ferid said, and his hand shook a little as he brought the glass to his lips.

"It's gone, it's all gone," said George, and all our eyes turned to him. He was sitting on my grandmother's desk chair with a big phone in his hand as he typed furiously. "Everything—gone, gone, gone."

We were all sweating by then, even Madeline.

"What's gone? What's gone?" asked Helen, but she knew. We all did.

"The veler. The vessels. The-the-the Script of Perria—it's gone," said George, looking up at her with bloodshot eyes. "He took everything, burned the physical reports, erased the digital footprint. Everything."

Suddenly Flora jumped to her feet. "This is *madness!* How are we to find him now—*madness!*" Her voice was so loud my ears whistled.

My eyes closed, and those angry tears returned and I cursed myself in my head over and over for not returning for the Script that night when Taland found out it had fallen off him.

If we only had it now. If we only had *something* to make sure Hill failed...

"Enough," said Helen, drinking the last of her wine. "That's enough. We focus on one thing at a time."

"But we must find him! Now, before it's too late—we must," Madeline said, and for once she wasn't as perfectly composed as ever.

"And we will. We'll find him. We'll search every inch of the world," Helen said. "But first we must do what needs doing to ensure that we win when we do capture him."

The sky fell right over my head. Every set of eyes in the office turned to me again.

It's over, the ugly voice said.

"We'll find that bracelet," Helen continued, putting her empty glass on the table slowly. "And you will use it, Nicholas. With the magic of the Rainbow in you, you will."

I swallowed hard, raised my chin. "So, you're just going to kill me." Goddess, I hated that my voice shook.

"Not necessarily. We'll take the magic of the Rainbow back. You...*might* survive," said Ferid.

"We can't harness a new Rainbow in such a short amount of time," Nicholas said, shaking his head as the wheels turned in his head—he was the only one trying to find an alternative.

"No, we can't," Helen said and stood up, slowly undid the buttons of her silver jacket and took it off. "We'll take back the Rainbow, Rosabel. *Now*. With it, we'll defeat Hill."

My stomach twisted. My magic raged, went wild inside me, nearly split me wide open when I stopped it from bursting out of me. *Never again.* I would never open myself up like that again.

"Then what?" I choked the words out. "Then what happens? Will you really make the changes you know you ought to make, or will things simply...go back to the way they were?"

Not a single word. They all looked away from me, too, except for Helen and Madeline.

My grandmother who was going to not only stand by and watch them kill me but would help them if needed.

Not a single fucking word.

"Very well then." Two big tears released themselves from my eyes and I saw their faces clearly again. "Get on with it."

I was ready, as ready as one could really be to die, I guessed.

I was ready when all of them slowly stood up and left their glasses on the table.

My eyes closed. I didn't pray. I didn't think—I just imagined Taland's face. After all, that was the only thing that had ever brought me any peace, and right now peace was all I could hope for.

Magic in the air, thick and heavy, buzzing in my ears. I felt them coming closer, heard it when they pushed the table farther back to give themselves more space.

Then one of them began to chant—could have been Helen or Flora. Not that it mattered, anyway.

My magic began to react, too, instantly, but this time not in rage. This time not with the intent to burst out of me to protect me.

No, this time, it was being *pulled,* like the words of that spell they were chanting so furiously was a magnet for it.

My magic was being torn off me. My own energy, my life force was being cut off with every new word that woman chanted. There was no way I'd survive this, and they knew it. They would take the Rainbow out of me, they said, but the Rainbow no longer existed inside me; it had become me. It had merged with my own magic and energy. That's what they were going to take out—*me.*

"Nicholas, are you ready?" someone asked, and I imagined the Mud councilman nodded.

Then someone knocked on the door.

CHAPTER 6

Rosabel La Rouge

It was so sudden, that sound. So...*ordinary* in a sea of strange magic buzzing and harsh Iridian words being thrown at me like fucking daggers.

Everything came to a halt. My eyes opened, and I saw how all of them had gathered around me, except for Ferid, Natasha, and Madeline, who'd remained a few feet behind.

Now everyone was looking at the door, especially when it opened.

It actually opened without Madeline telling whoever it was on the other side to enter, and every person in the room held their breath until we saw the face of the guard. That same guard who'd taken me to the Iris Roe, who'd smuggled me in. That same guard who was now pale as a sheet when his eyes found Madeleine.

"It's an emergency," he said, and he strode over to her like he couldn't even see the members of the Council—and me sitting there on the couch, waiting to die.

Goddess, is this real?

The magic that had been pressing against my chest disappeared. It no longer buzzed in my ears, either, and everyone was still looking at the guard as he whispered in Madeline's ear.

I thought for a moment I could make a run for it. I thought for a moment I could jump to my feet and run and protect myself when they came after me, but that's only until I remembered that I didn't have the bracelet on me—or my father's ring.

"What is the meaning of this, Madeline?" Natasha the Greenfire demanded when the guard stepped back and waited, his unblinking eyes on my grandmother.

My grandmother who had been looking at the floor for a moment before turning to Helen—it had been *her* who'd been chanting that spell to pull at my magic. Which made sense since she was the only Whitefire in our midst.

"Selem is here," Madeline said, and every inch of my body raised in goose bumps.

Silence—such a long and heavy silence that could make a person believe she'd gone deaf.

Then...

"They wouldn't," said George in a whisper, and his voice trailed off as a strange smile spread his lips.

And I thought, *no, please no, please no, please no...*

"They're here and they claim they know how to find David," Madeline continued, and now my stomach was doing all kinds of horrible dances.

"By the Goddess," said Nicholas and fell on the armchair with a deep sigh, almost like he was relieved. Not because of what Madeline said, but because he wouldn't have to go through with what they'd wanted to do just now

—*drain* me and give him my magic. My life source. *All* of me.

"And..." Madeline said, and her eyes locked on mine just for a split second when she said, "They have the bracelet."

Fuck, Taland, run! my mind shouted, while another part of me was thankful, so thankful I wanted to burst out in tears with relief.

He'd come back for me. He'd brought the bracelet—that fucking bracelet. He'd come back for me, and I honestly thought it was only him. I honestly thought he'd made it to me himself.

"Very well," Helen said, stepping away from me, and all the others did the same. "Invite them in, I suppose. Let's have a chat."

Everyone was already taking their seats and filling their glasses. Madeline turned her head to the side just slightly and nodded, and the guard understood. He walked out the door, closing it behind him, leaving us alone once more.

Meanwhile, I had made a mess of my palms and my eyes were closed and air went down my throat with ease. I was breathing. I was alive. *For now.*

Never before had I felt more helpless than I did in those moments, not even in that alley in Night City, when the other players had been chasing me, coming to kill me. That's why I already decided that I was *never* going to allow myself to be in that position again even before the door opened—this time without a knock.

The first to come in was Aurelia Mergenbach, and my heart took a long pause at the sight of her face. Behind her was none other than Radock Tivoux, and my eyes refused to blink for fear he'd disappear. Zachary followed, and behind him was Seth.

Behind Seth came Taland, and the room around me disappeared.

Taland was in Madeline's mansion, in Madeline's office.

Taland was here.

Our eyes locked. The people spoke, but I couldn't understand a word they said, and I didn't care to. Taland was here, and he was standing on his own even though he looked like shit. He had a clean black shirt and a new jacket on, but his jeans were a mess and there was dirt around his neck, too, like he hadn't had time to even shower.

He wore boots—and an expression on his face that said he was *this* close to setting the fucking world on fire.

"That's far enough."

The sound of Madeline's voice fell in the center of my mind like a big piece of rock. I was suddenly aware that Taland and I were not the only people in this room. I was suddenly aware that I had made it to my feet, too.

I'd stood up without even realizing it, and now everyone was standing, and the office had never looked so *small.*

The doors closed. The tension in the air was so thick I could feel it pressing against my skin, and Taland was there still. He hadn't disappeared. I hadn't imagined him—he was there and he was looking at me and he seemed calmer by the minute.

Calmer because he didn't know what these people had been about to do to me, and I preferred it that way. Because now he was here and now the Council had access to him. Now he was here and the Council could kill him just as they'd been about to kill me, so I needed him to remain calm. To not piss them off.

Goddess, please, don't piss them off, my fear begged.

"Isn't this a surprise," said Helen, as she stood in the

middle of the room with the rest of the Council and my grandmother at her side. They'd created a wall in front of me, separating me from the newcomers, but I could still see them just fine.

Radock Tivoux stepped forward with his chin raised and a gleaming in his dark eyes, not an ounce of fear or hesitation anywhere on his body. "Maybe to you. I suppose it came as a shock to you to find out that you've been lied to and spied on for years."

"Who *are* you?" said Ferid, shaking his head, pretending to be disgusted while he looked everyone over, but then Aurelia stepped forward, too.

"I think you know who we are, Mr. Nagi," she said to him. "Just as we know who *you* are."

"One little thing you *didn't* know, though, was that David Hill was one of ours." This from Zachary, who slowly crossed his arms in front of his chest, and I saw it because he was standing next to Taland.

Taland who hadn't once looked away from me yet.

"True," said Natasha. "Very true—we had no idea that he was screwing us over." She flinched. "And *you* had no idea that he was screwing *you* over as well."

"Enough," Helen said. "We all know who we're talking to here, and we've all been blindsided by a man we trusted —the same man."

"Agreed," Radock said with a nod, his eyes boring into Helen with such intensity I could have sworn she looked a bit nervous. "David Hill brought us together, as strange as that may sound. He's not our guy and he's not your guy— he's nobody's guy, apparently, and right now the only thing that matters is that he's stopped." He stepped closer. "I assume Rosabel has already told you everything that happened in Silver Spring."

"And my guard told me that you know how to find David," Madeline said, her voice ice-cold, so fucking terrifying—or maybe just to me.

"More importantly—we were told you have the bracelet," said Nicholas.

Aurelia looked behind her—at Taland.

Taland stepped forward, pulling the left sleeve of his jacket up to reveal the bracelet around his wrist.

My eyes closed for a moment, chasing out the tears that had gathered in them. *Goddess, thank you.* He had the bracelet. He could survive if the Council turned on him. He could survive.

"I don't just have it," Taland said, and his voice raised every inch of my skin in goose bumps. He sounded calm, as certain of his every word as always. "I can use it, too."

"Show us," said Helen.

We all looked at Taland's hand, and we all expected him to start chanting, when...

"No." Once more, everyone in the room held their breath. "I've also memorized the Script of Perria that Alejandro Ammiz sent me to steal from your Vault. I imagine Hill has already taken it and has left behind no records, so you will need that as well, to find him."

He said all of it with such ease, you'd think he was talking about something as ordinary as the fucking weather.

Are you out of your fucking mind?! I wanted to shout at him, and I hoped he looked at me now so I could show him with my eyes how fucking absurd he was being, but he didn't. His eyes remained on Helen—who was already livid.

"How *dare* you? What do—" she started, but Taland didn't even let her finish.

"Rosabel," he said, and he raised his hand toward me.

Fuck, the way I wanted to run, to jump, to fucking *fly* until my hand was in his.

But Madeline stepped forward, closer to Taland, and told him, "Rosabel is not going anywhere."

Taland didn't even look at her at all, like she didn't exist. "I have the Script of Perria in my mind, and the only way any of you is going to have it is *if* Rosabel is by my side right now and she tells me to give it to you."

Damn it, Taland!

A smile spread on my face—silly, I know. I couldn't help it because *this guy*. This fucking guy came here just as I was about to die and saved me, once again, and looked the fucking Council in their eyes and told them that. Said those words.

This fucking guy.

"My granddaughter will—" Madeline started again, but this time, I didn't let her finish.

Because *fuck you, Madeline*. Fuck her and the Council and Hill and everyone.

"Let me through."

Helen and Nicholas who were standing in front of me turned to look at me and I didn't hesitate. I moved between them, pushed them to the side, and for a second there I thought I would make it. I thought I'd walk all the way to Taland and take his hand in mine and then we could get the hell out of here.

Except both Helen and Nicholas put their hands on my shoulders the moment I stepped between them and stopped me.

Wands were drawn. Magic released in the air from the mages in the room in an instant—all that power.

Taland aimed his palm at Helen now—that same hand he'd extended for me.

Fuck.

I closed my eyes, took in a deep breath.

"Rosabel isn't going anywhere without the bracelet and without the Script," Helen said, and her fingers dug into my shoulder, and I could have sworn that magic leaked out of her, whether intentionally or not.

"I would normally agree with you," Radock said, half a bitter smile on his face as he slowly, casually put a hand in the pocket of his black pants. "But see, that girl saved my brother twice." He raised two fingers. "And now I am in her debt, which doesn't sit all that well with me, to be honest." I could hardly believe my ears. "So, I'm going to have to insist on this, too. Let the girl come to us and then we can sit and talk."

"*Talk?*" George said, and he meant to *mock* him, but then Aurelia said, "Yes, *talk,* Mr. Levington. We all need to talk about Hill. We all need to *work together* to stop him before he actually brings back the dead army and dooms us all."

Silence in the room. I didn't look away from Taland, and Taland didn't look away from me.

Then he winked at me, and I smiled again. It was automatic—when he was calm, my nervous system decided there was nothing to worry about. I trusted his sense of judgment more than my own, I think. Or I just *believed* that we were both here now and we both knew there was no such thing as impossible because of everything we'd gone through. We both knew we had no limits when it came to one another. There was nothing we couldn't do.

And that put me at ease.

Fascinating how my entire mindset changed simply because he was here. I'd been surrendered to death just minutes ago, but now I had a thirst for life deeper than ever before.

"He's going to do it," Zachary said when nobody else spoke.

"He has everything he needs," said Kaid. "We have word that the Devil has already found the bones of Titus. And the Devil is working with Hill."

My stomach fell. Could it be that Kaid was telling the truth?

"The girl," said Radock. "Let her go and we can talk."

"*Or* you can keep your little brother under control and give us the Script as a leader ought to do," Flora said, her condescending tone sending ice-cold chills down my spine.

Radock laughed—actually laughed. "You think he told *me* anything?" He shook his head again and again. "How do you think he got us to come here in the first place? My brother is very thorough when he wants to be, and he's always wanted to be thorough when it comes to this girl."

Behind him, Zachary smiled mischievously. "Yep. Afraid we can't help with that, but we're sure hoping you'll help us. *All* of us."

The hands on my shoulders seemed to grow heavier by the second. I shook my head at Taland just a bit to tell him that he was fucking *nuts* to be doing this, and that I loved him for it.

The corner of his lips curled up just slightly in a smile. My heart all but leapt out of my ribcage to go to him.

"And if we don't?" asked Ferid, who had his feathers in his hands—two of them, big and shiny and ready to be used.

They were preparing, all of them. Even Madeline had spread her fingers as she watched Taland, *hated* him with all her being the way she usually did me.

"If you don't, we'll fight," said Aurelia with a shrug of her petite shoulders. "You'll lose—and I'm not saying that to try to scare you or anything. I've just seen what this thing can do." And she pointed her finger at Taland's wrist. "A single spell and the Regah screen was in pieces—not only that but a good portion of the entire neighborhood shifted, and everyone within a mile radius fell unconscious. A single spell did that—from her." She nodded at me, and grinned. "Him?" She then pointed her thumb at Taland by her side. "He's even more powerful, far as I know. And he really doesn't give a shit about anything, so..." Again, she shrugged. "Your call, I guess."

"You really expect us to believe that this boy will go to war *with us* knowing his family will die if we don't hand Rosabel over?" This from Natasha, who shook her head like she couldn't even believe her own ears.

"Well, considering he called Madeline Rogan and gave her the location of *our* own headquarters just to get her out..." Radock said, and the look on Madeline's face.

I would *never* forget the shock, the terror that darkened her eyes. "It was *you*," she whispered, then pressed her lips like the words slipped out of her involuntarily.

"It was," said Radock. "I was furious, too, when I found out—but what can you do, I guess. Young love." And he grinned that awful grin that made you think of anything but positive emotions. That made you think of certain *painful* death instead.

"Helen?" Nicholas said from my left, but I refused to look away from Taland still. I refused to do anything but stand there and wait until they made up their minds because I knew one thing by now. I *believed* one thing with my whole heart—no matter what happened next, I was getting out of here with Taland. One way or the other.

"We *really* should get this over with sooner," said Kaid. "Hill is on his way to the dead army right now. Do you really need us to remind you what happens if he actually succeeds?"

"He can't succeed without that bracelet," said Madeline.

"Who's to say this was the only one he had?" said Radock.

This time, you could *see* the way they were all defeated by the thought of loss. Defeated by the certainty that David Hill might be out there right now, summoning the dead, coming to kill us all, to rule the world.

"*Tick-tock,*" Zach whispered, and he was still smiling, like the gravity of this situation was completely lost on him.

"The power of the Rainbow," Nicholas started, and slowly he removed his hand from my shoulder as he looked at Helen first, then his colleagues. "I am almost certain it won't work on me. It cannot be separated from her anymore. It has merged with Rosabel's energy already. It *won't* work."

I could kiss the guy for saying that right now, but...

"Is that what you were trying to do," said Taland, his voice low, barely a whisper, and I knew what he looked like when he was angry, even if the expression on his face didn't change at all. I knew the shade of brown his eyes took on—and right now, he was raging on the inside.

The next moment, tiny flames in all colors sprung on his skin, on his hand that he'd aimed at Helen, demanding the focus of each and every person in here with me.

I shook my head once—*no.* He was not going to attack now when we were close. *No, Taland, don't you dare,* I thought, and I like to think he understood.

"A fight isn't going to serve anyone," Radock said. "We

will win against you, but as much as it pains me to say this, we need you to win against Hill, just like you need us."

His words fell over me, warm and comforting—because I had been thinking the same thing—but heavy as well. Because he was absolutely right. As much as these people had worked against one another for years, now was not the time to fight. Now was the time to stand together—at least until the common threat no longer existed.

"Who would have thought?" said Natasha, shaking her head, and she took her seat on the couch again, reached for her glass on the table. "The likes of David Hill to force a truce between us—who would have thought?"

"Natasha," Helen said, but the old woman waved her off.

"Sit down, all of you. Let the girl go. Let's talk."

I didn't think, didn't blink, didn't even breathe as I waited and waited...

Helen dropped her hand from my shoulder, too, and I moved. My legs carried me to Taland, and I fell in his open arm with my whole being. He wrapped it around my waist and held me to his chest tightly, his other hand still raised. Still not entirely convinced that the Council was going to stand down. That they'd actually *agreed* to let me go and talk.

"It's okay," I whispered, holding onto his neck tightly, eyes squeezed shut, the sound of his heartbeat and mine in my ears. "It's okay, Taland. I'm okay."

His other arm wrapped around me as well, and he took us a couple of steps back while the others moved forward. All of them, closer to the Council.

"All right, then. If you would be so kind as to pour us a drink, too, we can begin to plan," Zachary Mergenbach said, but I still hadn't opened my eyes or let go of Taland, and he still hadn't let go of me.

For a moment there, he lowered his head and pressed his lip to my shoulder, and I heard the deep sigh that left him—the relief. I could only imagine what it must have been like in his head—but it was over now. I was smiling because it was over.

"You're *mad*, Mister Tivoux," I said, and if we were anywhere else, I'd have laughed my heart out.

"I am, indeed," he said without hesitation.

I wouldn't have had him any other way.

CHAPTER 7

Rosabel La Rouge

Madeline Rogan sat about five feet to my side with her eyes on my lap where I held Taland's hand between mine tightly. We were sitting together, *all* of us. Selem and the Council, Madeline and me, in her mansion.

Impossible seemed like a small word just now, but here we were.

"You are certain that this is the Script of Perria," said Flora the Redfire as she looked down at the piece of paper in the middle of the coffee table that they'd put back in place again. Madeline had called up for more empty glasses from the liquor cabinet with her magic, which had been another shock.

Then Taland had asked me, in front of all of them, if I wanted them to have the script, and I said *yes*. Not because I cared about any of them, but because we all had to work together, unfortunately. Just like Radock said.

Nicholas had given Taland a pad and a pen for him to

write down exactly what he'd memorized from that script the Devil had sent him to steal.

"I am," Taland said.

"Why didn't you give this to the Devil?" I whispered under my breath, though there was a good chance that others would hear, too. I didn't really care.

"I tried. That's why I turned myself in. He wasn't interested," Taland told me without batting an eye, completely at ease now that I was sitting next to him.

"It *is* a search spell, all right," said Radock as he, too, analyzed the letters on that piece of paper.

"A very specific one," said Zach as he drank his wine slowly, savoring every sip. "Very old, too. We haven't created or used eighteen-line spells for finding things since..."

"Five or six centuries ago," George the Bluefire finished.

"Because we've learned how to simplify the use of magic," said Helen. "But just because this spell is *old* doesn't mean that it's what we're looking for."

Her cold, almost white eyes fell on Taland. She, out of everyone else, was the most suspicious of him.

"I had the script in my hands. I read it twenty times. Memorized it. Then I lost it," Taland told her. "*This* was what the Devil sent me to steal."

"And the fact that it's not there anymore, this script, is proof enough. *That* means that this is what we're looking for," Aurelia told her. She, Taland, and I were the only ones not drinking alcohol right now.

"Exactly. Why would he take it with him if he didn't need it or if he didn't care if you could find it?" asked Kaid.

Meanwhile Seth stood by the wall and played with his feather and drank his white wine like it was water. Any time I looked up at him, he grinned and winked, and I was tempted to smile back. I would have if we hadn't been in this situation because I was really glad to see that he was okay, that he'd made it out of the ruins in one piece.

"*You* do it, then," said Natasha the Greenfire. "Do this spell and give us a location. Wasn't that the deal?"

"The deal was to work together to stop him," said Aurelia. "And if we do the spell, we'll do it together."

"Are you assuming we *trust* that the boy hasn't hidden a curse in there somewhere?" asked Flora.

"Why would he bother to hide a curse in there when he wants Hill found as much as you do?" Kaid.

"Together. We chant the spell together," said Radock. "*That* will be your guarantee. Unless my brother wants to kill us all, I trust this is exactly what he says it is."

"And *you* trust him after he betrayed you—what am I supposed to make of that?" said Helen.

"Make of it whatever you like," Radock said, and he didn't sound happy in the least. "But we either do this together or not at all."

Suddenly, everyone started to speak at the same time. Everyone had something to say:

Hill is your *guy—he operated under your nose this whole time!*

And you assume we're stupid to trust in anything you say! Have you no idea who we are?

If this goes south, which it will, who will take responsibility?

If we chant this spell and we find nothing, what happens then? Are you really ready to die here, now?

On and on they went.

"Look at me, sweetness."

Taland's voice snaked its way into my mind and took hold of all my thoughts, all the fear and the panic. I looked up at his wide eyes that were alive.

"You pulled me out."

"I didn't even have to walk over bones to do it. Just a couple of unconscious guys," I muttered, reaching out a hand to touch his cheek. "Are you okay?"

"Perfect. You?"

"I could use some food, to be honest."

He put his hand over mine and turned his head just slightly to kiss my palm. "Soon, baby. Soon." Then he took my hand down, and while he held my eyes, he put the bracelet around my wrist so fast, I doubted anybody had seen it—they were still bickering, all at the same time. I didn't see him moving either, only felt the cold of the metal against my skin.

"You should keep it," I said, though to have that thing around my wrist made me feel like I could *fly* again. With it, I was safe—perfectly safe. With it, I didn't fear for my life or Taland's for a second. Not after a single spell with it ruined that screen, and the entire neighborhood, apparently.

"It's yours," Taland said. "It belongs to you."

"But you can use it, too."

"I prefer it when you do," Taland said and slowly touched the tip of my nose the way he always did—*small I-love-yous* to carry around, Seth said. That's what that touch meant to Taland and his brothers because of their mother who'd always done the same to them.

"We'll make it out of here," I said, and I sounded so sure.

"Sweetness, we made it out of the Iris Roe and the Blackrealm. Mansions don't really scare me."

Laughter burst out of me for a second, and to my horror, it did so in the same second that *everybody* stopped speaking, so they all heard it. The sound echoed in Madeline's office, and now every one of them was looking at us.

I suddenly felt like I was sitting on hot coals as I straightened in my chair.

Taland didn't let go of my hand, though.

"Something funny?" Helen asked in that tone of voice that meant to humiliate us. And she thought she could—of course she did. She'd just been about to kill me not an hour ago, and I'd just sat there and waited, had been perfectly defenseless against her, and my own grandmother would have allowed her to go through with it without a word of complaint. Of course, she thought she could humiliate me —except I was not the same girl as I was when I was sitting in that couch before, confused and scared and helpless.

I had the bracelet around my wrist now, and my magic had already connected to it without my even having to think about it at all. But most importantly Taland was here. And I didn't blame them for not knowing the kind of impact his presence had on me. Even I didn't understand it myself how my entire view of the world changed when he was near, but that was okay. I'd show her exactly what she was dealing with now.

"*You* are," I said, and her brows shot up, but if she planned to say something, I didn't give her the chance. "You're funny—all of you. The whole world turns to *you* in times of crises because *you're* supposed to be calm and rational and work toward a solution. Well, we are in a crisis, even if the world doesn't know it yet, and what are *you* doing?"

I wasn't looking at her only, but at the Mergenbachs, too, and finally at Radock who had that small smile on his face like he was thinking inappropriate things—like how to skin me alive.

"You're sitting here arguing about who to trust. Trust has nothing to do with this—we have a common enemy.

After we're done with it, by all means, go back to being enemies or whatever you are, but right now, let's find Hill and let's stop him. *Calmly.*"

I expected them to start laughing at me, at least half of them.

Nobody did.

"Very well, then," said Aurelia, and she pulled the piece of paper toward her. "I'll start and you can tag along, whoever feels like it." She looked up at Helen. "Save the bickering for later, like Rosabel said. Shall we?"

She didn't wait. She didn't let anybody make a single sound before she began to chant the long spell exactly as Taland had written it.

Which made every single person in the room hold their breath.

I looked at Taland. He winked at me. We were okay.

He didn't let go of my hand when we stood up and went closer to Aurelia so we could read the spell, too. I might have been weak, but my magic was still there, and after we did the spell, we could eat and rest and do whatever. For now, we began together, joining Aurelia as she read through the second sentence slowly, to make sure we didn't miss a single letter.

Magic in the air.

The others came closer, too, one by one. Zach and Flora and George and Helen, Radock and Kaid and Natasha, too. Meanwhile Nicholas and my grandmother remained in their seats, and Ferid kept looking at us, unsure whether to panic or stop us or join us.

He chose to do nothing.

The spell lasted a while indeed, and when the magic of each and every one of us began to come out of our skins, I was afraid.

Afraid that it would work and afraid that it wouldn't. Afraid of what either of those options meant.

Colorful magic burst out of my hand as I raised it in the air together with all of them. My flames were brighter than the rest, and I was sweating by the time we started on the last paragraph.

Slowly. Steadily. We chanted every single word, and our magic, in so many beautiful colors, stretched and stretched until we couldn't see through it, until it became a thick box of colors hovering in the air.

Then the last word of the spell left our lips at the same time, and the colors of our magic faded.

A golden dot remained in the middle of the room, so bright it could have been a miniature sun, but none of us looked away from it. None of us *could*—I felt that light as if it was inside my veins. I felt it and it held my attention and it took the air out of my lungs and it forced me to follow it.

To someone watching, it remained in the same place, burning there a couple of feet over the coffee table.

To me, and to the others who brought the spell to life, it moved at the speed of light.

Images popped in my head. It was like watching a movie, except the movie held me prisoner, frozen in place, my muscles locked, my lungs empty, my eyes unable to blink. The only thing that was moving inside me, that *could* move and was being forced to, was my magic.

It was tearing itself out of me and rushing down my arm, and the pain was even more intense than when I used my ring after draining the Rainbow. I gritted my teeth to keep the scream inside, but it was no use—the whole room heard it.

And *I* heard the screams of most of the people who'd been chanting with me.

A curse, said a voice in my head. It was really a curse. I couldn't move, and I couldn't do anything to stop the magic that was being *dragged* out of me with such force.

But...

Taland wrote this spell. Taland memorized it from that script. Taland would have *never* let me chant if he even suspected that this wasn't what we thought it was.

No, that wasn't it. The tiny sun that was pulling my magic out of me—*all* our magic out of each and every one of us—was not a curse, but it was powerful. And the heat of the colorful flames that sprouted on the palm of my hand without my say-so almost burned my skin.

Another scream ripped out of me because I was holding that light in my palm now, and it was just as hot as it had looked from a distance. The others screamed, too, until I couldn't tell my voice apart from theirs.

Pain. So much fucking pain.

Then I touched it.

Just when I thought I was *never* going to feel cold again, I did. Just when I thought I was never going to get my body to obey *my* commands again, I did. Just when I thought that I was dying once more, I breathed. My lungs worked and I was alive.

The ball of light in my hand was gone, and inside my fist was something hard, something cold, something that I had never seen before.

A parchment scroll with dark wooden handles on the sides.

I blinked, half of me focused on the air going down my throat to convince myself that it was real, that I wasn't dying. Nobody was screaming anymore, and...they all had those same scrolls in their hands, too. Everybody was holding onto their chests and breathing deeply, heavily, and Taland's hand was on my cheek as he looked at me. He'd been in that same pain, too. He was breathing like he'd been racing, and his eyes were bloodshot, his hair all over the place.

"I'm okay, I'm okay," I said, and we could all see that we were okay, but it took us a little while to get our heartbeat to slow down and our breathing under control.

Meanwhile the others who hadn't chanted with us were standing on the other side of the room, watching us with wide eyes, curious, concerned.

"What the hell happened?"

"What kind of a spell was that?"

"I swear it felt like it ripped my arm off..."

"But it *worked*."

We all stopped.

We looked at Radock who had already opened his scroll and was smiling at the brownish parchment he held in front of his face, though it was empty.

"It worked," said Helen from my other side, and she, too, was rushing to open her scroll, so we did the same. Maybe Perria's location would be in these. We had nine—one of them was bound to contain that map.

And *mine* did.

"It worked!" I repeated in awe as I watched the shimmering silver on the brownish parchment slowly reveal to me a shape—what could have been a valley between two mountains.

"Holy shit, it actually worked," said Zachary. "Are you guys seeing this?! We have it! We—"

I looked at his scroll as he held it up for us with a big

smile on his face, and I saw that it was empty just a second before Radock said...

"Empty." Zachary stopped. "Yours is empty—mine isn't." And Radock showed us his.

His scroll that was also empty, which I'd seen the moment I came to my senses.

"*Yours* is empty, not mine," Zachary insisted, and then we were all turning our scrolls so everyone could see, only to realize...

"We can't see them," said Flora from behind me, raising every inch of my skin in goose bumps. "I can only see mine, and you can only see yours—nobody else's."

"Fuck," Kaid said, leaning to look at Taland's scroll, and I did, too. Empty.

All of theirs were empty except mine—to my eyes.

"It's a puzzle," Radock said. "It's a puzzle spell—of course. An extra layer of protection."

"Does that mean I should have done it by myself?" asked Aurelia.

"It wouldn't have opened to you," said Helen. "This was created by the original Council. It requires at least five people to work." She was looking at her parchment and shaking her head.

"We should be able to read it, though. When the parchments are together..." Natasha said, bringing her parchment closer to Helen's. "Anything?"

"No. Yours remains empty to me," the woman said.

Everybody sighed at the same time. We all folded the scrolls and took a moment to gather ourselves—that spell had been intense. The magic that had come out of me, had been *forced* out of me by that burning sun...

It was gone now. I looked up and I expected to find it there still, hovering in the air, but it was gone. It had disappeared as soon as those scrolls had materialized in our hands.

"Let's sit," Taland said, and took my hand in his again, took me back to the chairs we'd been sitting in a moment ago. Everybody sat, and everybody was still shaken, except for Radock and Helen, who seemed to be lost in their own minds as they stared at the tabletop. I could see the wheels turning in their heads as the others spoke, gave ideas.

How about only the Council tries it?

How about we do the spell over?

What if we said it wrong?

What if the boy remembered it wrong?

What if we mixed the spell—how are we going to get the whole picture?

We draw *it,* said someone—Kaid, I think, and he was already by Madeline's desk, getting pads and pens, while she looked at him like she wanted to drink his blood for dinner.

Some thought it would be useless to draw out parts of the map, and some said it would work, but we all got a piece of paper and a pen to draw ours. It made sense at first to create the shape I was seeing in my parchment in detail on that blank piece of paper. It made sense, except...

I could also see what Taland was drawing beside me, and I couldn't get any of the lines to make sense to me.

"I think it's a river—do you see?" he asked when he was halfway done, but I saw no river. All I saw was a straight line.

And the others were looking at one another's, too, but... a voice in my head was whispering. A voice that was almost coming from my bracelet.

I could have sworn it was coming from my bracelet, and

the harder I tried to see what Natasha was showing me from the other side of the couch, the louder it got.

Dark. It was too dark to see the drawings in detail, wasn't it? The drapes were drawn, and the lights overhead were very bright, but it still seemed too dark to me. That's the word that voice whispered, *dark.*

My eyes closed.

"Sweetness, you okay?" asked Taland, but I was suddenly feeling...*fatigued.* Weak. I was feeling so damn weak, and I just wanted to sleep. I wanted to eat and sleep until I couldn't keep my eyes closed anymore.

Dark.

"I'm fine," I thought I said while the others continued to argue about who got what shape right and who sucked at drawing more.

"We'll figure it out," Taland said, bringing my hand to his lips and kissing my knuckles.

"I know," I said, though I could have been lying. But when my eyes opened, I felt *hers* on me like sun rays.

Madeline stood at the corner of her desk with her hands crossed in front of her chest, watching me. She looked... unusual, a look I hadn't seen on her before. Calm but furious. Unbothered but curious. Her eyes could melt the skin off my flesh, my flesh off my bones. And if I could somehow look inside her mind right now, I'd find out exactly how much she despised me, even if she sometimes looked like she didn't. Even if she hid it well.

The others talked. Taland pulled at my hand, but I couldn't turn, couldn't look away.

Madeline reminded me of *bad* things, always had. She was synonymous with every ounce of pain I'd ever felt, and right now the pain of that spell was the most vivid in my mind. I couldn't tell you why I was so caught up in the way she was looking at me, why I felt the heat of her hatred on me so perfectly, why my bracelet kept tugging at my arm and why that voice wouldn't stop whispering, *dark, dark dark.*

It was dark outside, no doubt, even though the drapes wouldn't let me see the sky.

It was dark outside, and *that's* why we couldn't see.

"The sun," I said, and the word could have popped into my mind from that old voice, not mine, but my lips said it all the same.

Only when the others stopped talking did I realize how loud it had been in the room until now.

Madeline raised a brow at me.

"The sun?" Flora said, and I nodded.

"The sun. That light that gave us these looked like a little sun, don't you think?"

A moment of silence.

Laughter—Natasha. "The oldest trick in the book," she said. "The girl is right."

"We'll need sunlight to see the full picture," said Radock, and Seth was already by the windows, pulling the drapes to the sides to reveal the dark sky with a million stars twinkling in the distance.

"We can't see the map for another...six hours then, give or take," said George, looking at his watch.

Six hours.

"Sweetness."

I broke eye contact with Madeline to look at Taland. The heat of all that she felt for me disappeared into thin air instantly.

"Do you want to get out of here?"

I thought, *more than anything in the world.* I said, "I think we should stay."

Taland nodded. "Then we'll stay."

Madeline continued to look at me. The others continued to talk about ideas—not bickering at the moment, but talking. Exploring possibilities. Wondering how Hill would have gotten his own script to work, and if we would even find him wherever these scrolls said the Delaetus Army was.

But we would, I was sure of it. Hill was not a fool—on the contrary. He might be the smartest man any of us had ever met. He'd have figured out how to find the Army with or without that script.

As I rested my head on Taland's shoulder for a moment, I just prayed to the goddess that he hadn't brought them back to life already.

CHAPTER 8

Rosabel La Rouge

The Council insisted that nobody was going anywhere with those scrolls until the sun came up and we found out if we could actually see the whole thing. To Madeline's horror, they asked her to accommodate the Mergenbachs and Taland's brothers, as well as all of them.

When I say *asked,* I mean that they didn't give her the option to decline. They simply told her that she had the space and the money for it, and for the next six hours, she would be our host.

The look on her face would have made me laugh in any other situation. As it was, I just took Taland by the hand and guided him to my room while guards took the others to wherever Madeline had decided to let them stay until sunrise.

That's how I ended up in my bedroom with Taland. That's how I walked inside, turned the lights on, and closed the door, resting my back against it for a moment just to catch my breath.

"Fancy," he said as he slowly walked to the middle of the room and looked around. "I want to fuck you in every corner of this room."

Laughter burst out of me at the same time as tears spilled out of my eyes. The whole moment was so surreal that I could hardly get myself together.

Walking on my own was out of the question. I stayed there by the door, hanging on to the handles, and I watched him and I laughed and I cried until he came closer. Until he took my hands in his and pulled me to the middle of the room with him, then held me against his chest while he laughed, too.

It took me a while to stop crying and making those awful sounds.

"You're in my room," I finally said, cheek against his chest, my arms around him and his around me.

"Mhmm," he muttered and kissed the top of my head before he rested his chin against it again.

Like that we spun around slowly, just to keep moving.

"You have a nice room, sweetness," Taland said after a little while, and I nodded.

"I also have a nice bathroom. I think we need a shower." We were both covered in dried blood and dirt from the last time we barely escaped with our lives.

Taland chuckled. "Don't be shy, baby. Just say you want to fuck me in the shower first."

The butterflies in my stomach went nuts and my knees actually shook a little. "I don't..." I closed my eyes and bit my lip for a second. "I want to fuck you in the shower, yes."

Taland grabbed my face in his hands and raised it until we were eye to eye. Goddess, he looked like a completely different person from the guy he had been when he first came to Madeline's office. He always looked like another Taland when other people were around, and I adored that he saved this side of himself only for me.

"Good girl," he said, and my toes curled and my cheeks flushed like I'd never heard those words before. Like I was just discovering that I adored them, too.

"Come with me," I said, and with his hand in mine, I walked us to the bathroom and turned the lights on.

Taland stopped me in front of the large mirror over the sink and began to take my clothes off without a word. Goddess, we were a mess, both of us. I wanted to feel bad or afraid as I looked through the mirror at him slowly pushing down my jeans but I couldn't.

And the moment the wound on my thigh was visible to me was the moment I noticed the pain that was coming from it. Hakim had done a number on it, and I'd been so focused on everything happening, on the pain that I'd felt all over me that I hadn't noticed how tender my thigh still was. Madeline had healed me but that wound had been deep, so it was still there, my skin red, the scar angry.

Closing my eyes, I put my hand over it, and I began to chant a more advanced healing spell on myself. At this point we were already moving slowly. We were already weak, both of us, so even if it cost me energy, it was worth it, that spell. Colors came out of me, the bracelet around my wrist heating up for a moment. Then the magic slipped in the wound and the way it mended it within seconds was fucking miraculous. I was breathing a bit heavier, and Taland chuckled as he came in front of me and pushed my hand back, then kissed my thigh that was just slightly red.

The wound was gone and so was the pain. And I still

looked at the bracelet, in awe of it just like I had been the first time I witnessed what it could do.

The spell did take a lot of energy out of me together with the pain. Goddess, I was too tired. I just wanted to shower and fuck Taland and sleep, and when I woke up, I'd eat. I'd get my strength back then, I was sure of it.

That's exactly what I did.

We walked into the shower together. The cabin was more than big enough to fit us, and at first, we let the water wash away most of the dirt from our bodies. We held onto each other and we kissed slowly, and I swear his kisses were life. The more I felt him, the more alive I came, the more I wanted, the faster my heart beat.

We scrubbed the dirt and dried blood off one another thoroughly, and the more we did so, the faster we moved because he was hard and I was wet between my legs, too, and we needed each other more than we needed sleep.

"Sit down," I told him when we were as clean as we were going to get, and I pushed him back toward the white marble bench that lined the wall at the end of the cabin. I'd always loved that bench—it made shaving so easy, and now I loved it even more. It wasn't big by any means, very narrow, but the seat wasn't slippery so we made it work. Taland sat on it with a wondrous smile on his face and watched me as I straddled him while the shower over us continued to spill warm water.

His arms were wrapped around my waist tightly. Our lips were pressed together as I held his cock up and slowly lowered on it, taking him in inch by little inch. It slipped inside so easily because it was wet, too, and when I sat on him all the way, I felt right at home.

Goddess, the way he stretched me. Even now, I still needed a moment to adjust to the size of him, and he needed a moment, too. To kiss my entire face slowly, dig his fingers in my ass to hold me in place, to analyze every bit of me that he could see in this position.

"How do you become more divine every new time?" he whispered as he ran his other hand down my chest and touched my breasts with his fingertips, my nipples, trailing the drops of water on my skin.

I didn't know the answer to his question, and I was pretty sure that it was just him who saw me that way, so I said nothing, only moved.

I fucked him slowly, our skins slippery from the water, and my knees hurt from the hard surface of the bench but I didn't care. Taland guided me up and down with his hands on my hips. Sometimes he raised his own and pulled me forward and back until I felt him in my very core. The sound of the water falling from the shower muted half of our moans and whispers, and it was a moment as perfect as any other when we were together like this, connected in soul and body and mind.

Chest to chest, mouth to mouth, we came together a little while later, holding onto each other, calling each other's names with the last of our strength.

The water had gone cold by then but neither of us complained while we cleaned ourselves up, wrapped ourselves in towels, and made it back to the bedroom, walking like we were drunk or high—or both. By the time we crashed on the bed, we were completely spent. I didn't even have the time to tell him that I loved him, that I'd dreamed of having him in this bed possibly more than a million times before.

I fell asleep right away.

～

A knock on the door.

My eyes opened and I was a bit confused because my mind insisted that the warm body next to mine and the heavy arm draped around my waist was Taland's, but then my eyes were telling me that I was in *my bedroom* in Madeline's mansion, and that couldn't possibly be. Taland sleeping with me under the same roof as Madeline?

No way in hell...

"That's the third time they're knocking, sweetness. Want me to get that?"

I sat up, breathing like I'd been racing for hours, and I looked behind me—at *Taland* in my bed, his gorgeous head on my pillow.

"I don't mind," he continued, grinning because he could see just how confused I was, just how *shocked* at the sight of him, but the memories were already coming back. The memories of last night, of him coming to my rescue, *again,* this time in Madeline's mansion. Of him putting the bracelet around my wrist and scrubbing the dirt from my back and guiding my movements on his cock by my hips— *holy fuck.*

"No, no, I-I-I got it."

I made to jump off the bed when he grabbed me by the arm and spun me around. Then my face was between his hands and his lips on mine.

He kissed me softly, just a small peck, and whispered, "Breathe, baby."

So, I breathed.

And good thing I did because when I breathed I realized that I was completely naked—we both were—so I had the good sense to put a robe on before I went for the door, smiling. Impossible to help it—Taland was here, in my bed, and so of course I would be smiling even though little made sense and the sky outside my windows was still dark.

Then I pulled the door open to find Fiona with a big tray in her hands that must have been very heavy.

"Oh, Rora," she whispered, like she was both surprised and happy to see me.

"Hey, Fi," I said, pulling the robe closer together as I looked over the empty plates and the silver domes that surely hid food.

Oh, goddess, there was food on that tray and I was fucking *starving*.

"So sorry to bother you—I've been trying to bring you food all night. Poppy insisted. I hope I didn't wake you."

Poppy. The mentioning of her name sent shivers down my spine. Poppy was here.

"You're not bothering me at all—thank you. Do you need help with that?" Though now that I was thinking about carrying that tray, I realized just how weak my limbs felt.

"Not if you let me through," Fiona said with a little grin, like she already knew my secret.

Like she already knew that I wasn't alone in my room.

My cheeks flushed bright scarlet. "Of course, yeah," I said, and stepped aside, pulling the door open for her.

She came in with the food. Taland was sitting up in my bed, his body covered in my red silk sheet.

I was mortified.

"Hello, sir," Fiona said to him with a nod and went to put the tray on my bedside table.

"Hello," Taland said, a little mischievous grin on his face.

"Taland, uhm...this-this is Fiona. Fiona, this is Taland,"

I barely managed, and I had no idea why it was so hard to look either of them in the face just now.

"It's a pleasure, Mister Taland," Fiona said.

"Just Taland is fine."

"Do you need anything else from me, Rora? Any medical help maybe?" Fiona stepped by the door again and looked me over quickly with her hands folded in front of her, like always.

Her smile was genuine and her eyes warm, but even so, I felt like my skin was on fucking fire.

"Nope, nope, I'm fine. Thank you for the food, Fi. I'm fine," I assured her.

She threw a quick look at Taland, and I could have sworn her cheeks turned a bit pink. Fuck, it was so hot in here...

"If you need me, you know where to find me," she said with a bow of her head, and then she turned around to leave.

"Thank you, Fi," I said, and by the time the door closed, I felt like I was standing right below a scorching sun.

Then Taland chuckled.

He wore nothing but a towel around his hips as he came to me, took my hands and pulled me toward the bed, sat me on the edge.

"You know, for someone who grew up with maids and slept in silk sheets and had a bathroom the size of most apartments, you should be more spoiled, baby," he told me, then reached for the huge tray and put it on the bed between us.

I realized it had two of everything—plates and glasses and cups and hardboiled eggs and silverware—that's why it was so heavy. It was almost twice the size of what Fiona brought in for me after I had one of my (now pretty consis-tent) near-death experiences.

"I'm plenty spoiled," I muttered, and my mouth watered when he pulled the silver domes open to reveal two large plates full of everything—pancakes, waffles, scrambled eggs, bacon, sausages, and in smaller bowls there was melted chocolate and maple syrup and mustard and that garlic sauce that Fiona made, which made me want to literally drown in it.

"I don't think I've ever seen a better looking breakfast," Taland said in wonder, pulling the white and red cover from a small basket at the edge of the tray that had four croissants in it—my favorites. "And no, sweetness, you're everything *but* spoiled." He broke a croissant in half, brought the bigger piece to my lips, and bit into his at the same time I did.

Heaven.

It was heaven. Soft and warm and so delicious I wanted to cry.

Instead, I ate more.

I ate another three croissants and two waffles and drank the whole glass of milk, too, so fast that when it was time for the coffee, I felt like I'd explode if I took a single sip.

Meanwhile Taland smiled and chuckled and laughed at me while he watched me stuff all that food in my mouth at once, while he ate like a normal person. I didn't even care—I had been starving for real, and now that I had all the food in my system, I fell down on the bed and breathed. For real this time.

Fuck, I kept forgetting how much better everything looked with food in my system, how much clearer my mind could get.

"This was good," Taland said, wiping his mouth with

his napkin when he was done. "Not as tasty as you, though." He stood up and put the tray on the bedside table again, then lay down on the bed sideways with me.

His kisses after all that food were twice as powerful, especially when his lips lingered for a few seconds everywhere on my face.

"I always forget what it means to be full," I muttered, eyes half closed as he continued to kiss me. "What time is it?"

"Your clock says it's a little past four a.m. It will be dawn soon," Taland said, and I flinched.

"The others?" I knew he didn't know—he'd been with me the whole time, but he could guess.

"Probably somewhere bickering. Waiting." He wrapped an arm around my waist and turned me to the side to face him.

"Do you really think it's going to work, the sun? Or did I just have a bullshit idea?" It was very possible, considering everything that had brought me here.

"I don't think you've ever had one of those," he muttered, kissing the tip of my nose. "I think it will work— why else would a little sun appear as we were given the scrolls?"

I closed my eyes and sighed deeply. "I don't want to be here." Goddess, how I wished we could be all alone in that safe house again.

"I don't mind where we are as long as we're together," he said.

"But you didn't care about being together when you ran from me and left me alone in that safe house." And I wasn't trying to be a bitch here, but remembering what it had felt like killed me a little bit even now. Not my fault for trying to

95

understand, for trying to make sure it wouldn't happen again.

With his eyes squeezed shut, he brought his forehead to mine. "I'm sorry, sweetness. I had hope that the Devil would make that deal with me. I had hope that he'd let me go so I could come back to you."

"How about next time you *talk* to me," I said, bringing my hands to his face to touch the stubble that had grown on his cheeks just slightly.

"I don't plan to end up in the Tomb again anytime soon, so...I don't think I'll be owing anything to anyone again," Taland said. "But I promise you this—I will *never* again assume or hope. I will never let anyone or anything get between us in any way. I promise you, sweetness. I'll kill them all first."

His every word rang true. My stomach tied in a thousand knots, and even though I didn't *want* to like it, I did. Whatever it was about Taland when he said things like this, when he threatened the world on my behalf and *meant* it, something primal inside me worshipped him more for it.

"Just don't die," was what I said, even if a part of me thought I should tell him that that was wrong. Killing people was wrong—but he knew that already, didn't he? "Whatever happens next, let's just make sure we don't die, okay? Not you and not me. Neither of us."

He nodded, grabbed my hand and kissed my palm. "We live."

"We live." Because in the end, that's all that mattered.

"Did it ever occur to you when we were in my dorm in school that we'd end up here, talking about staying alive, just three short years later?"

I laughed a little. "Not at all. I thought we'd be arguing

about holiday locations, honestly. I thought you'd hate the beach and I'd hate skiing—but that's it."

His shoulders shook as he laughed, too, then kissed the palm of my other hand. "I do hate the beach when you're not there. When you are, I love it."

My toes curled. "I'll still hate skiing even if you're there, though," I teased.

He grabbed me suddenly and spun me around and put me on his chest while he bit my jaw, and I laughed out loud when he tickled me, stuck his hands underneath my robe and gripped my ass. Of course, he was hard.

"Then we won't go skiing," said Taland. "I think I can survive on beaches only."

I kissed his lips a hundred times. "I'm sure you'll convince me a time or two."

"I'll just have to work very hard at it," he said, and his fingers were dangerously close to my pussy, so I jumped off him right away.

"Don't you dare," I warned. "We need to get ready and go downstairs. We need to be out there when the sun rises, Taland."

He sat up, a tent in the white towel wrapped around his hips.

Now my mouth watered for an entirely different reason.

"Yes, yes, I know. I'll just need to use your bathroom real quick," he said and stood up, took the towel off and threw it on the bed.

Naked. He was so perfectly naked and hard and fucking delicious I wanted to devour him.

"Taland," I breathed, my eyes on his body, and the asshole chuckled as he walked backward to the bathroom.

"You wouldn't happen to have a razor I can use, do you? My face is itchy," he said, grinning.

"Second drawer," I muttered absentmindedly, then closed my eyes to gather my thoughts. "Damn it, Taland."

"I'm sorry, baby, but my clothes are in the bathroom." He shrugged, his eyes glistening. "Join me if you want." He slipped inside the bathroom and left the door open just a bit.

And I was going to just go to my closet and put my clothes on. That's what I did—I went in there and I picked up washed clothes and I was going to put them on and walk out of the room.

I was going to.

But then I didn't.

Cursing under my breath, I put the clothes down and dropped the robe on the floor and went to the bathroom. I was so damn horny I couldn't even find it funny that Taland was shaving his face with a pink razor. I just jumped him like a fucking savage.

The razor ended up discarded for the moment, and I ended up with my hands on the edges of the sink and my ass in the air while Taland fucked me from behind like it was the first time we were doing this.

The mirror was right there. I saw him through it while he pounded into me, looking down so intently at how his cock disappeared inside me, like it was the most fascinating thing he'd ever seen.

I *absorbed* every little inch of him with my eyes as well, but when he saw me looking and our eyes locked on the mirror, it got even better.

We came seconds later, holding each other's eyes, moaning each other's names. Taland pulled me up until my back was against his chest, and he wrapped me in his arms with all his strength, all his desire, like he wanted me inside his skin, too.

The reflection in that mirror was the most beautiful thing I had ever seen. Us, together, one for real. Naked, bare, exactly as we were.

In love.

～

We didn't really get to think about what was happening, Taland and I, or what awaited us in the next day—or days, or weeks. It was for the better. We both needed a moment of peace before we faced our new reality.

So, when I got dressed and walked out of the closet, I planned to go downstairs immediately, ask Fiona for some clothes for Taland. I had no idea if someone from the staff was the same size, but we'd make it work.

Except the moment I opened my bedroom door, Poppy was there in the hallway, leaning against the wall, waiting for me.

She ran and hugged me with all her strength, and her eyes glistened with tears, and she *screamed* in my ear about how she was going to pay me back for all the scares I gave her and for not going to see her before I slept last night.

"I'm fine," I assured her for the twentieth time, and eventually, she believed me.

"Tell me everything," she said, squeezing my hands. "Is it true that Taland is here with you?" She rose on her tiptoes to see into the room, though she didn't bother to keep it down. "Fi told me that you weren't alone, but I can't believe it. She was messing with me, wasn't she? It's not—"

"It's true, I'm afraid."

Taland's voice sent shivers down my back as he walked out of the bathroom, clean and shaved and wearing my white robe that was a bit too small on him.

My cheeks almost fell to the floor.

"You must be Poppy," he said, and Poppy, who opened and closed her lips a dozen times couldn't bring herself to say anything yet.

Goddess, I thought Fiona was bad, but *this* was a thousand times worse.

"Um, yeah," I said, stepping slightly to the side to block her view of him. "Yes, yes, this is Poppy, and Poppy this is Taland, and he needs clothes, as you can see—that's why he's wearing my robe."

If I didn't die of embarrassment in those moments, I never would.

"It's a pleasure to meet you, Poppy. I've heard great things," Taland said, and by the sound of it, he was coming closer.

Goddess, how I panicked.

"Right, so, I need to go get him some clothes, and—" I was going to walk out of the room, close the door and *run* down the hallway, but...

"Stop."

Poppy put her hands on my shoulders.

"Stay. I'll bring clothes."

Without even blinking her eyes, she turned on her heels and she ran just like I'd imagined doing a moment ago. She ran like her tail was on fire.

"Poppy, wait, you don't have to..." I whispered, and it was pathetic. *I* was pathetic, too.

Meanwhile, Taland chuckled.

"You're an asshole, you know that?"

All he did was shrug. "I have no idea what you're talking about."

Luckily, when Poppy came back to bring me a pair of jeans and a green shirt that looked to be Taland's size, I managed to convince him to stay in my closet. Poppy still hadn't stopped blushing, though now she was smiling, too, eyes darting back and forth from me and into the room.

"He's in the closet; he won't come out," I assured her. "Poppy, I—"

She suddenly came close until our noses almost touched. "He's *hot!*" she whisper-yelled, then stepped back and cleared her throat. "Grandma and the others are waiting for you downstairs. The sun will be up in less than twenty."

Again, she ran, but this time she also *jumped* every few steps like she couldn't contain her joy. I watched after her with my mouth open until she turned the corner and disappeared from my sight.

Five minutes later, Taland and I were in the backyard with everyone else.

CHAPTER 9

Rosabel La Rouge

We put the scrolls on the grass in the open field at the back of Madeline's mansion. The sun would rise from the horizon in front of us, and we'd catch the first of its rays here. The sky was already gray with the coming light, and every person in the backyard was jittery with nerves.

They all looked well rested, better than the night before. They all watched me and the bracelet around my wrist like it was both a thing of wonder and the most dangerous weapon they'd ever seen. I didn't let it get to me, of course, and it helped that Taland was right there by my side—wearing *green*. It suited him, even if it wasn't his color. And the grin on his lips remained even after Madeline continued to look at him like she was disgusted by his very presence. I thought he thrived on her judgmental attitude—he kept winking at her every time she dared to meet his eyes.

I loved him a little more for it.

"Just to be clear," said Radock Tivoux, who wasn't all

that happy that he'd had to spend the night at Madeline's. He seemed more aggravated than he had been the night before. "If this works and we have a location of the Army, *we* will be going there ourselves. We will not be sending soldiers to do the work for us."

Silence for a moment.

Then Helen Paine, wearing white pants and a white shirt and her hair in a braid that made her look a decade younger, turned to him and said, "Of course. We'll all be there. Madeline will be in charge of the IDD soldiers that will assist us. But Hill will be ours to defeat." Her eyes suddenly stopped on me. "Just as soon as we receive that bracelet, we will be on our way."

Ice in my veins.

"The bracelet is not going anywhere," Taland said. "It belongs to Rosabel."

Then Flora stepped forward and said, "I believe we can all agree that that magic will be much more effective and useful in *our* hands."

And she could have been right, except... "You *can't* use it," I reminded her. None of them could.

"I'm sure Nicholas could. He is Laetus," said Helen.

"Except he hasn't received the power of that Rainbow," I said, smiling bitterly. "That's why you were going to kill me last night—or did you forget?" Because I hadn't.

The women looked at one another, then back at me.

"It could help us win, that bracelet," Helen said.

"You are but a child. To join us in this fight is suicide. *We* shall have the bracelet," said Flora, and it sounded like a damn order.

"I am not a child," I spit, stepping closer because right now I couldn't have cared less about who she was. The shit we were in was equally deep for all of us. "And you *can't* use the bracelet if I handed it over to you right now."

"She's right, Helen," Radock said, playing with the bottle of water in his hands. "Don't underestimate her—she's tougher than she looks."

I'll be damned.

"We're talking about—" Flora started, *screaming* now, but Helen stopped her when she turned to me and said, "Would you?"

I blinked. "What?"

"Would you hand over the bracelet and let us try?"

My heart fell all the way to my heels. Taland was beside me in an instant, his hand around mine. "Easy, baby. Breathe," he told me, and I was breathing. But a part of me wanted to say *yes* to Helen, because what if they were right and Nicholas could actually really use this bracelet as his anchor? What if *we* didn't have to go with them and die in a fight with David Hill—what if?

Another part of me thought me a coward for even having that thought, but I wasn't. I wasn't a coward—I was trying to be rational here. Because as much as I hated it, Flora was right. Compared to them, I *was* a child, and if any of them could use the bracelet, they would be a hundred times more powerful than I could ever be. This was the Council we were talking about—the most powerful people in the world.

"Rosabel?" Taland whispered when I raised my hand and looked at the bracelet around my wrist.

Suddenly it had gotten so heavy. "If it works..." I started, but I couldn't even speak the words out loud—*we'll stay behind.* Goddess, I didn't want to stay behind. I wanted to look Hill in the eye again and fight him until my dying breath if I had to.

"If it works, our chances of winning against him become much better," said Helen.

I looked up at her. "And if it doesn't?"

Silence in the air. The sky had become so light so suddenly, and the sun had just peeked from behind the horizon in the distance.

"If it doesn't, we'll return it to you."

I searched for a hint on her face that would tell me if she was being truthful. I found none.

"Do I have your word?"

Are you seriously doing this!? my own mind screamed at me.

"You have my word," Helen solemnly said.

I took the bracelet off.

"Rosabel, you don't have to do this," Taland told me, but he knew, too. He knew that it was for the better, that if one of them could use this bracelet, winning would be guaranteed.

"It's okay, I want to," I lied—but it wasn't *all* a lie. Just half.

Helen came over and took the bracelet from my hand without a single expression on her face.

My stomach turned. Bile in my throat while I watched her put it on and close her eyes and look up at the sky, then chant, whispering Iridian words with her hand raised.

Try once, and twice, then try again the third time, harder.

It didn't work.

"*Breathe,*" Taland said.

But I couldn't breathe easy when Flora took the bracelet next and put it around her wrist, either.

"You're wasting time, but what the hell." Radock

shrugged. "We've got a few more minutes to kill. It's not going to work."

Helen stepped closer to him—and I could have sworn that she wasn't looking at him the same way she did last night. She was...*wary* of Radock now. Almost like she feared him, which made me wonder about what had happened in this mansion while Taland and I had been locked up in my room, how many conversations had taken place within those walls.

"How do you know?" she asked him as we all watched Flora chant—in vain.

"Because we tried it," Radock said.

"All of us. Didn't work," said Aurelia from the other side where she stood next to Zachary.

"It will for Nicholas," said Helen, and that's why when Flora was done, the others didn't bother. The Redfire, angry now, put the bracelet on the Mud councilman's hand.

His eyes were wide as he looked at me and stepped forward, almost like he was saying *sorry*. I liked Nicholas; he had never hated me, not since the first time he saw me. Maybe because he understood or maybe because he was a good guy? Didn't really matter.

But the bracelet didn't give him magic, either.

He tried. With four spells he tried, called up simple ones, then more advanced, with his eyes open, then closed, whispering, then screaming until the fresh sunlight reached us.

It didn't fucking work.

And when he was done trying, he didn't hesitate. He strode over to me with a smile, like he was *glad* of the outcome, and he put the bracelet around my wrist while Taland loomed over him at his side, watching his every movement like a hawk.

"There. Where it belongs," said Nicholas, smiling down at me, his brown eyes warm. He patted my hand and stepped back, looked up at Taland. He just nodded at him then went back to his place near Ferid.

Nobody spoke for the longest time, as long as it took for the sun to finally fall on the ground and to touch those parchments laid out on the ground in wait.

It hadn't worked. The bracelet refused to work for any of them—the most powerful mages in the world. Yet I felt it when it touched me, like it was a living thing. Like it was whispering to me—just like it did the night before. It whispered.

Taland took my hand and pulled me to the side, toward where they'd set the open scrolls. Everybody was already standing around them, eyes wide and breaths held.

Everybody except Madeline, who was on the other side, a few feet away from the rest of us, watching me without an ounce of emotion in those cold amber eyes.

A strange feeling settled over me, one I'd never really felt before. *Detachment.* I almost *saw* strings being cut between us in the new light, as if my mind was trying to tell me that nothing tied me to her anymore. I was my own person now—because I had power. Because I had Taland.

And, most importantly, because I'd *never* had her.

"Look," someone said, their voice full of wonder, and it was Aurelia with both her fingers pointing at the parchments, but I couldn't see anything yet. Just my parchment, those shapes that looked like mountains—that's all.

"I don't..." Helen began, but her voice trailed off just as my breath caught in my throat.

Because slowly, so slowly, shimmer was appearing on the surface of the parchments that had been empty to my eyes until now. That same shimmery ink that painted the one I'd been given, was now creating shapes on every inch of those yellowed surfaces.

Within the minute, the ink had created all that it was going to create, and it was really difficult to make out, too, because it was almost translucent when the light hit it right, and...

"It makes no sense," Helen said, kneeling so she could see it better. "None of this makes sense."

And she was right.

"A puzzle," said Zachary. "It's a puzzle."

"Like the ones we used to do when we were kids," said Aurelia, lowering to her knees on the grass and picking up the first parchment.

"Yeah, I remember those," said Kaid, squatting down, too. "Shouldn't be too hard."

"I can't really see anything," said Natasha, and she was trying, leaning closer, squinting her eyes. "What puzzle—I can't see shit!"

Some laughed. Even I was tempted to crack a smile.

Taland said, "Wanna play?"

I shook my head. "How about I just watch you?" Not because I was lazy or didn't want to help, but because I was still processing all these feelings. It was amazing how I could postpone feeling something for a while if needed, but then when it got to me, it got to me good.

The Regah chamber. Seeing Taland chained to a wall, knowing he had been tortured. Having the Council *almost* kill me by sucking out my energy not even half a day before, and then having them all trying to get my bracelet to work because they thought they could do a better job, be more powerful with it.

Regret coursed in my veins as thick as blood—I shouldn't have let that woman have it. I shouldn't have let any of them touch my bracelet; I should have kept it myself. After all, the only reason these people hadn't killed me was because Taland stopped them and offered them something they wanted. The only reason these people allowed me to have my bracelet back was because they couldn't use it, and they were afraid of Hill. Afraid of what he could do. Afraid *they* wouldn't be enough, and so they'd agreed to work with Selem. With *me*.

And it made me wonder, when this was over, what exactly was going to happen to us? What would the Council do to us, assuming we managed to defeat Hill and make it out of that fight alive?

Too much. It was way too much to think about right now, so I didn't. I just kept my eyes on the others who were moving the scrolls around, the Mergenbachs, Kaid and Taland, Helen and Flora. Even George the Bluefire had decided to join them, too curious not to.

They weren't bickering, which was surprising. They actually worked together and they were confident that they knew what they were doing, even if it didn't look like it to the rest of us. I mean, it was shimmery, almost transparent ink on old as dirt parchment.

But when I noticed Madeline coming toward me slowly, I forgot to pay attention to what they were doing completely and focused on her. I didn't turn, didn't make eye contact, pretended I didn't even see her when she stopped at my side. Just her presence had such a good hold over me that it took me a few moments to get myself under control.

"Here," she said, raising her hand, and it was impossible not to look down. My father's ring was in the middle of her palm, just like the last time she'd found me when I was unconscious.

Shivers ran down my back.

"It was in your pocket. Take it if you want," she continued.

I did. Of course, I did—even if that ring was no longer my anchor, it was still *mine*. My father's. I inspected the golden band and the red ruby in the middle, and my heart ached. It was too big for my fingers, so I put it in my pocket again, just for good luck. Maybe it was time to finally take it to a jeweler and make it my size. I wanted it on my finger the whole time. Just as soon as this was over, I figured.

"There's a good chance you'll die if this thing actually works and we find David," she said when she realized she wasn't going to get a *thank you* any time soon.

"And what—you want me to leave you my money?" Goddess forbid that she would care about *me*, and we both knew it.

"This isn't about money," she said. "I am not a good person, Rosabel. I couldn't be one to achieve the things I wanted, and I've made my peace with it. This isn't about me, either. But if this works, you really might die soon. If you do, I'll bury you next to my daughter, and if you don't..." Her voice trailed off and I resisted the urge to rub the goose bumps from my arms. Taland must have noticed her approaching me so his eyes were on me, on her, watching us intently as he pretended to be focused on the parchments.

"If I don't, what?" I spit because how dare she speak about my mother *now*? Call her *her daughter* now?

"If you don't, you will take the position of the IDD Director when you come back. With *my* guidance."

"*No.*" I said the word so fast it was a miracle I didn't scream it. But she must have been out of her goddamn mind if she thought I was going to ever return to the IDD as anything ever again.

"Yes, you will," she said. "Under my guidance, you will continue to keep the power in our family."

This time I laughed. Out loud, and people heard me, but most were busy with the parchments so they didn't stare for long. Except for Taland.

"You really are a piece of work, you know that?"

"Yes," said Madeline, hands folded, her hair perfectly combed and her eyes burning amber with the fresh light of the morning. "I understand what having power means, even if you don't yet."

"I understand—"

"*Nothing,* Rosabel. Not yet," she cut me off. "And to paint the picture for you, had you not had *power,* you wouldn't have been in a position to do something against... well, the threat of the end of the world, now, is it not?" I clamped my mouth shut. "You would have been in your room, reading or watching a movie or doing whatever it is that you would be doing, clueless that it was even happening until it was too late. It's *power* that has brought you here."

I shook my head because I actually couldn't find it in me to argue with her about this, not now.

"Our family will continue to *be* the power in the front lines and trust me when I tell you that I tried to prepare Poppy for this role—I tried." She gave me a look. "However, she doesn't have what it takes. You do, as much as it pains me to admit it. You're made for this."

Made for this, she said, and it took me a good moment to understand that she wasn't kidding. Madeline was *not* joking—she meant everything.

"*Never,*" I said because I wasn't going to waste a single

second more with this. That she would think I wanted to *be in power* so that *she* could be in power with me was too absurd a concept to engage in right now, so that word would suffice.

Her eyes widened.

A few feet behind her, Natasha watched me like a damn snake, her eyes as green as the grass we stood on. She had heard us, I was sure—and I was glad for it. Let everybody hear because I had nothing to hide.

Luckily, before Madeline could try to say something else, Aurelia Mergenbach shouted, "It's working!"

My heart leaped. I rushed forward, Madeline and her dreams of power forgotten, to see the parchments on the ground in the way that they'd arranged them under the sunlight. And I saw with my own eyes how the ink, once almost translucent, was gaining color little by little, line by line, becoming a dark blue, the shimmer still there, like stars in the night sky.

Until it revealed the whole image to us, and it was a map, indeed.

It had no names and addresses, only shapes, but shapes that made sense now. The image had become whole, and the people were already trying to guess where the mountains and the curved roads and the towns that were depicted in that strange dark blue ink were—or were they cities? I, for one, had no clue what any of it was, and I didn't even have an idea to offer. Meanwhile, Seth had his phone in his hands, reaching up his arms as far as he could, standing on his tiptoes, taking pictures of the map.

Taland came to stand by my side again. "This could be anywhere," he said, almost like he was talking to himself more.

"We'll figure it out," I said, taking his hand in mine. "We'll take the day and figure out where this place is."

I had a mind to go grab a pad and a pen like George was doing to draw the shapes so that we could see the whole thing on a smaller format, when...

"Got it!"

This from Seth.

He was grinning ear to ear as he looked at the screen of his phone, and we all narrowed our brows at him in confusion.

"You...*got* it?" asked Aurelia, as skeptical as the rest of us.

"Yep."

She shook her head and whispered, "How?"

Seth shrugged. "I asked ChatGPT."

I burst out laughing together with a few others, while we all rushed to Seth to see what his phone was telling him. He had pulled up the maps app on his phone and was showing us someplace called *Triades* in West Virginia. According to the map, it was about four hours away by car.

"Are you sure that's the same?" asked Radock, and Seth zoomed out the map again to show him.

"Look," he said, pointing at the roads, and then at the curved lines on the parchment that had come to life with sunlight. "And this town here—Franklin. And a branch of the Potomac River right here—look! And the North Folk Mountain in the west. It's all right there."

Hard to see with so many people trying to look at that small screen at the same time, but I could just make out everything he was saying.

Holy shit, Seth was right.

"Send it to my phone," Kaid said.

"And mine," said George, and Aurelia, and soon Seth

was sending the location to everyone, while Taland and I stepped aside and continued to look at the beautiful shimmer on the parchments.

In the heart of it was the location we were looking for— or at least where we thought David Hill had gone to find a dead army of Laetus soldiers.

No way is this real, a part of me said, and I almost laughed at it, but how could I blame my own mind for being skeptical of this reality?

"Perria," said Taland, putting his arm over my shoulder. "Over there—that's Perria. It has to be."

He was pointing at the middle of the map, right where I'd been looking, too, to those big pointy structures that could only be mountains. Five of them, two bigger, three smaller, set in an almost perfect circle.

"That's where they buried the Army." And the words sounded just as strange out there in the world as they did in my head.

"Assuming this map opened to Hill, that's where we'll find him," Taland said.

"I can't believe you actually memorized all that spell." *Impressed* was a small word, and despite knowing that Madeline was behind me somewhere and could probably see me, I leaned in and kissed him on the side of his neck.

Shivers erupted down his arm that was over my shoulders, and I saw the hairs on his forearm rising.

He growled low in his throat. "I've memorized your moans and screams of pleasure even better," he whispered, so low I would have never heard if his mouth hadn't been right next to my ear.

Those butterflies that hid in my stomach and only ever came out when he was around went nuts.

Heat between my legs.

"Not the time," I told him because everyone else was preoccupied with that map location and we were over here, getting turned on.

"It's always the time, sweetness," Taland said with a chuckle and kissed my temple. "When we're done with Hill and we come back, every second of every day will be the exactly right time."

Didn't that sound like heaven. "When we're done with Hill and come back, we're going anyway, Taland," I said. "We're going far away from Maryland, to another country, maybe another continent. And we're going to just...*be*." That's all I wanted, to just *be* with him, take our time together without fear and without lies and secrets keeping distance between us.

"Done," said Taland. "We'll go wherever you want and stay as long as you want. We don't ever have to come back."

He stuck his nose in my ear and sniffed hard, making me laugh a little.

"We'll see about that. We'll see—but first, we leave here." Everything else we could figure out.

"Your attention, everyone," Radock said as he stood on the other side of the map with Helen, the sun at their back. Everyone stopped talking and speculating, though most had their phones in their hands and that map on their screens.

"It seems we have a location already, and it's only a four hours' drive. Mister Tivoux and I have agreed that our best bet is to be there today, in case David already is—which we'll know soon as we've sent teams to scout the area," Helen said.

"The plan is to arrive at our location by three p.m. at the latest, so that we'll have plenty of daylight at our disposal should a fight happen with David Hill and whoever he has working for him," Radock continued, and he was so at ease standing there with Helen, like they'd both done this a thousand times before. "Which is why we have to prepare to leave in approximately three hours."

"By then Madeline will have agents and soldiers at the site waiting for us, and I trust they'll remain there as backup should we need them," Helen continued. "More will be on standby close to our location."

"We will act right away," Radock said. "We will engage in the fight and chances are it will be bloody."

"Some might not make it," Helen added so effortlessly —again, like they'd done this a thousand times before together.

"So, if you have any doubt in yourselves, by all means, stay behind." This Radock said with a wide grin on his face.

"That is all," Helen concluded with a nod.

"Is it just me or is my brother rather...*friendly* with that woman?" Taland whispered in my ear.

I shook my head—it did seem like it. "I wouldn't trust Helen Paine even if she looked like she was in love," I whispered back.

"And I wouldn't trust Radock, either," he said.

"Let's just get inside and rest." I pulled him toward the back door as everyone else moved for the mansion, too. Madeline was there, watching them like a hawk, chin raised and shoulders back. I imagined it was a dream come true that the Council had basically put her in charge of the IDD once again. I didn't even glance at her until we were inside, and Taland whispered in my ear again.

"*Rest?* I'm afraid you have the wrong idea about what the next three hours will look like for the two of us, baby."

A miracle my cheeks didn't melt off my face completely.

"There's rest there somewhere. There has to be," I said, and he chuckled.

"Not today, there isn't. You're going to come again and again and again, on my cock and my fingers and my tongue. I've got to make the best out of these three hours because who knows how long that fight is gonna last?"

"We need to *rest*," I insisted.

"We will on our way there. Unless you want to make a couple stops..." He wiggled his eyebrows with that devilish grin, and laughter escaped me before I thought to bring my hands in front of my mouth.

He was absolutely *insane* because he meant it. That's why I laughed—we were in *this* situation and he actually meant what he said, and if I asked him, he'd really stop *while on the way to Hill* to have sex with me as many times as I wanted, everything else be damned.

Then...

"Hi."

Poppy.

Black dots in my vision for a moment, probably from the shock of hearing her voice, but Poppy was right there at the top of the stairs on the second floor, hands folded behind her back, hair neatly tied behind her head, eyes big and sparkling and her smile painfully fake as she tried to hide what she was feeling but failed.

I envied her for it, to be honest.

On instinct, I made to let go of Taland and step away from his reach, except he didn't let me. He held me right there by his side with his arm draped around my shoulders still.

"Hey, Poppy, hi," I said, almost choking on my own spit, and I couldn't even tell you why I was so mortified all of a sudden.

"Hello, Poppy. Good to see you again," Taland said, and I heard the grin in his voice just fine.

"You, too."

I couldn't see her hands, but I could just tell she was trying to rip her fingers off from nervousness. I realized we'd *never* done this before, never saw each other with guys, and that's why it was equally weird for both of us.

"Ro, I was wondering if you wanted to grab some coffee in the kitchen?" Then she looked at Taland. "I hope you don't mind."

"He doesn't," I said before Taland could say anything. "I'll be right there. Go ahead, Poppy."

She didn't even hesitate.

"No fair," Taland muttered when she disappeared behind the stairway.

"Looks like I'll be resting for a little bit after all," I teased, and with a quick peck on his lips, I made to follow Poppy.

Except he grabbed me by the arm and pulled me to his chest and squeezed my ass like he couldn't fucking tell that there were others coming up the stairs. He licked the side of my neck just a little. Just to get me perfectly breathless.

"*Taland!*" I hissed, but he was already letting go.

"Don't take too long. I'll be waiting."

My heart was still trying to beat out of my chest when I made it to the kitchen.

CHAPTER 10

Rosabel La Rouge

"...and you know what else she did? She called all my brothers, too—tell her, Tal. She called them and told them to *talk to me* and tell me to *behave*—can you imagine? Can you fucking imagine how pissed off Radock was?" Seth said from the backseat.

Yes, Seth was in the backseat, riding with us to West Virginia, and I'd had to stop Taland from violently dragging him out of the car when we found him there a couple hours ago.

Madeline had given us a car, so we were driving behind the SUVs and the trucks of the rest of Selem and the Council, and Taland had been happy that we'd be riding alone, but then Seth had already been in the back, waiting. Claiming he'd rather ride with *me* than with his brothers because they didn't let him talk and I was a great listener.

The look on Taland's face...

I still giggled every time I remembered it.

At first, I regretted not letting Taland kick Seth out of the car, but then I was thankful for him. Because it was almost one in the afternoon and we were on our way to another fight that could potentially kill us all and I had no space in my head to worry because every corner of my mind was occupied with Seth's stories about him when he was a kid, and about his friends, and about his girlfriends, too, all the *"crazy exes"* he'd had to *"go through"* he said. The perfect distraction, and I even laughed a few times.

Then, Seth continued to tell us about the fights he'd picked at school, about how he'd created a system to challenge himself, how he'd felt mighty smart to come up with it.

"It was all Kaid's fault," Taland muttered, just when I thought he was focused on the road ahead, on the SUV where his brothers and the Mergenbachs were riding, and the other cars and trucks and vans of the Council and the IDD soldiers and agents Madeline had sent here with us.

A lot more were behind us, too. To see them through the side mirror made me feel like I was going on a mission with my old team.

"It was, it was," Seth confirmed. "He taught us spells when we were *this* big." Grabbing our seats, he pulled himself between them and almost came all the way to the front, then held up his hand to show us how big he meant. "All kinds of spells—to fight and to manipulate, even kill spells, too."

I looked back at him, suspicious. "Kaid taught you kill spells?"

"Yep—when I was eleven," Seth said.

"He taught me when I was nine," said Taland.

And I shook my head. "Who taught *him* a kill spell?" Those were the most dangerous kinds of spells out there,

120

able to stop a heart in an instant. Dangerous stuff—I only ever learned a couple at the training academy with the IDD. Kill spells were not common knowledge and one needed special permission to even learn them just like one needed a permit to carry a gun around in some states.

"Radock," Seth and Taland said at the same time.

"Not only that but Radock made him responsible to teach it to us," Seth said, laughing. "So, imagine my teenage self walking around with two kill spells in my memory, and I felt like I had a loaded gun with me even when I couldn't do magic. Just the idea that I knew words that could kill someone on the spot gave me a boost of ego—never mind that I *couldn't* kill shit yet."

"Wow," I whispered because what else was there to say? On the one hand, I couldn't believe that Kaid or even Radock would tell his brothers kill spells at such a young age, and on the other, I *envied* them so much. To have brothers with whom you did mischief or who told you things you weren't supposed to know or who just made you miserable every day for the fun of it—yes, I envied that so much.

"You know what else he taught me?" Seth said. "A dream haunter spell—and, boy, did I have my fun with it for a while when I first got my feather." He laughed and laughed as I shook my head.

"A dream haunter," I said, and I asked Taland, "Really, was there a forbidden spell or curse that you guys *didn't know* growing up?"

Dream haunters were considered curses—not dangerous per-se, except for the fact that they gave you the worst possible nightmares, all tailored to your own thoughts and fears, the kind that could leave you without sleep for days. They could ruin lives, which was why they were considered forbidden, and you could actually go to jail if you were arrested for doing one.

"Unlikely," said Taland with half a smile on his handsome face—a smile that made me think about all the things he'd done to me just before we were on our way, even though we'd only gotten an hour.

"There was this kid—Jace, who lived in the Blue House with us..." Seth started, telling story after story about how he basically tormented Jace in his sleep because Jace was a big kid and he beat the shit out of him whenever he got him alone during the day.

Meanwhile, half my attention drifted back to the mansion, to Poppy and the talk we'd had about Taland. How relieving it had been to tell her the truth about everything, even the Iris Roe, and even Fiona had been there and had heard everything. I hadn't cared and I'd felt *free* for the first time in my life.

Even better when Poppy was so happy about it she literally did a dance in the kitchen before she grabbed me in a bear hug.

Before leaving, I told her about Taylor Maddison, too, and asked her to make sure she was okay at all times if something happened and I didn't make it back. Just in case.

And even though she insisted that there was nothing in the world that could kill me, Poppy agreed to check in on her regularly without Taylor knowing about it. That was good enough for me.

When I made it back to my room, I froze by the door and had to pinch my arm to convince myself that this was real—Taland was in the bed, naked, waiting for me with one of my books in his hands.

The way my heart fucking burst at these small, ordinary

things. I craved a simple life with him so badly it wasn't even funny.

Then Taland made me come with his mouth first, then his cock, then his fingers, just like he said, but to his horror, we'd only gotten one hour before Fiona came to the door to tell us that they were waiting for us downstairs.

Now here we were. We'd eaten. We'd rested as much as we could, and we were driving to what the original Council had called *Perria* back in the day—what was now a mountain site in West Virginia.

Seth kept on talking. I was starting to think he was nervous—more nervous than before, and unfortunately so was Taland. I could tell by the way his eyes darted from the windshield, to the rearview mirror, and to me lightning fast every couple of minutes. I could tell by how white his knuckles were, too, and by how *furiously* he switched gears while he drove.

To be honest, so was I.

There was a good chance that David Hill was waiting for us with an army of revived Laetus at the end of this road. Even though I laughed at Seth's jokes and interacted when it was appropriate, the closer we got to our destination, the heavier the situation became. The more *real* the whole thing seemed—we were actually doing this.

"Hey," said Taland, and reached for my hand on my lap, kissed the back of it, and held it there over the stick for a little while. "We're going to be okay."

I nodded, and even though I was starting to feel like I had rocks in my stomach, I smiled for his sake. "We will."

"Are you guys even listening to me?"

Seth stuck his head between our seats.

I laughed. "We are. You were telling us about when Aurelia pulled that prank on you and your friends," I said because I had been listening to him as well. Only with half my attention.

"Good," Seth said and sat back again before he continued to tell us his story.

I kept my hand over Taland's because it felt so much better when I was touching him. But eventually even that didn't help. Eventually, the gravity of the situation fell on me and no amount of Seth's stories or Taland's warmth calmed me down.

And the worst part was that we were already there.

∾

Breathing wasn't helping. Wishing we'd stayed behind now wasn't doing anything, either.

What the hell were you thinking?! my own mind kept screaming at me. *Both Selem and the Council have joined forces to come here today, and I thought I was ready for something this big?!*

Goddess, I was going to throw up.

"We have movement."

I blinked my eyes and focused on Ferid, who was standing next to a soldier dressed in a dark blue uniform that covered his face almost all the way, and he'd whispered something in the ear of the councilman.

"It seems he has close to fifty men with him," Ferid said, his cheeks paler than usual as he looked at Helen.

"David is here," Radock said, and she nodded.

"We're expecting a visual from the drone that he took down as soon as it was close enough," said Helen, looking at a tablet one of the soldiers had given her—could have been the same guy who was still standing behind Ferid.

"You okay?" Taland asked me, and I nodded automatically.

"Yep. You?"

He could probably tell from my tone of voice alone that that was bullshit, but he said, "Same. Look at me." I did. It was almost three in the afternoon and the sun was still high up in the sky and he looked really, *really* good in it, but he still looked better in the dark.

A silly thing to notice in this situation.

"We're together just like before," Taland whispered.

The Iris Roe. The Devil's Regah chamber. Madeline's office while the Council themselves were trying to find a reason to end me.

We were together.

Some of the panic and the fear faded. "Together," I said.

"And we're going to walk out of here just like we always do."

"Like always," I repeated, the words giving me life.

"Just another fight we gotta win."

Taland winked at me. Impossible not to smile.

"There," Helen said, taking our attention to the screen of her tablet as she held it up. "He's there. And he's not alone."

Every drop of blood in my veins froze when I saw the short video that drone had captured, that replayed over and over again because it was only four seconds long. But in it we could see perfectly fine what was going on down that road that snaked around the foundation of the first and smallest mountain, and went to the other side.

A hole in the ground, like a large bowl in the valley between the mountains, possibly a hundred feet wide, with escalators and all kinds of tools and woods and metals about, like it was a construction site. Grey rocks and dirt everywhere, and the ground was dug all around the edges of the mountain farthest to the left made of yellowish and light grey rocks, with a few trees growing on the sides as if by accident, and with a landing that extended right over that valley, wide enough to fit several people.

Right now, though, only one was standing on top of it, on his knees doing something I couldn't even see because the moment he noticed the drone in the sky, he jumped to his feet and raised his hand toward it, and white flames burst out of his skin just before the magic reached the camera.

The video started again.

This time, Radock pressed pause, and he moved the video forward and back so we could see everything that was happening clearly—Hill on that landing, kneeling in front of what could have been *eggs*, with three pieces of paper in front of him. He had been chanting before he saw the drone and stopped to attack it.

But Hill wasn't the only one on the rocky walls of the mountain or in that bowl-like valley below. Soldiers dressed in white were everywhere with machine guns in their hands as they walked around the excavators and the piles of dirt on all sides.

Halfway up the mountain where Hill was, Alejandro Ammiz sat on the rocks with one leg over the other, looking around with a cigar burning between his lips.

"Is that...a skeleton?" someone asked—could have been Aurelia.

My stomach turned as I followed her shaking finger moving closer and closer to the screen to point at the shade behind the mountain right across from where Hill was.

Indeed, that was a skeleton standing—and it wasn't the only one.

Memories from the book in Madeline's office spun in my mind as I took in the three rows of skeletons, which I was sure continued deeper behind the mountain where we couldn't see. Actual skeletons standing on bony legs, wearing armor and helmets over their skulls, swords strapped to their hips, as still as statues.

Every hair on my body stood at attention when I realized what they were.

"He's found them," George said reluctantly as he looked down at his own tablet. "The soldiers who are stationed nearby can see all—thirty skeletons so far, all wearing armor."

"The Delaetus Army is truly here," Helen said, as if she was more fascinated by *that* fact than anything else.

Surreal.

The others were already talking, and I half heard them, though most of my attention remained on Hill.

"We have soldiers surrounding them on all sides. They will take care of David's help, while we take care of him," Helen continued.

"As you can see, he already has the vessels, I imagine for all thirty of them, if there aren't more," Radock said. "We have to stop him before he uses those vessels."

"What the hell can he do with those? Are they *eggs*, is that it?" Seth asked before I could because I had no clue how the hell a soul vessel worked, either.

"They are artificial eggs, yes, as the eggshell preserves harvested souls the best way," said Flora, a murderous look in her eyes. She looked completely feral, though her hair was pulled up neatly in a bun over her head and her red leather suit fit her perfectly. It was her eyes that seemed even more fiery under sunlight. "I imagine he's been making the vessels for a long time now."

"The Devil helped," said Taland from my side. "Word in the Tomb was that he put anybody who crossed him in an egg eventually. I thought it was just an expression."

Goddess, they were sick. Not the first time I heard of it —that woman whose case Cassie was working on had taken the souls of twenty familiars for herself, but Hill and the Devil had done it to people. They'd actually sucked the energy out of *people*. And they hadn't used it on themselves like that woman had to keep herself young. No—they'd put them inside fucking *eggshells*.

"He needed more," I said, my voice small. "In the Regah chamber, the Devil said that Hill needed more soul vessels."

"Well, it seems he got them," Radock said with a flinch. "We can still stop him. It should take him a long time to complete the transfer of those vessels to the skeletons. We can get to him fast."

"Eight of us," Helen said, looking at him. "I believe eight will suffice to begin with."

"Agreed," said Radock.

"I'm going. I need to see that prick die," Aurelia said.

"Me, too," said Zachary.

"And me," said Flora.

"I have no trouble staying behind," said Natasha, and it had surprised me that she even came all the way here. At her age, it was a miracle she could walk straight. She had to be well into her eighties.

"Very well. Flora, Ferid and I from our side," Helen said to Radock, then turned to me. "You, too, Rosabel."

"I am not on your side," I said, and I knew I shouldn't have bothered because now was *not* the time, but I couldn't help myself.

She wasn't offended in the least, though.

"Regardless, you have the bracelet. We will need it in

the fight," said Radock. "And I imagine Taland won't stay behind, so"—he looked at Helen again—"the three of us, and the Mergenbachs. My brothers will be on standby."

"Not fair," Kaid said, at the same time Seth cheered, "That's what I'm talking about!"

"We will be watching," George said when Helen handed him her tablet.

"Madeline will, too. She will guide the soldiers through the cameras we have on our persons," Helen said, and I flinched. "There is no way that he can win this. The odds are in our favor."

Except...something told me that that wasn't going to matter much. It was Hill we were talking about. A man who'd fooled both sides for decades, had pitted them against each other, had planned and plotted to his heart's desire from a position of power.

"We might be walking into a trap, too," said Taland before they all spread out to go prepare. "We should take that into account."

"He knows we're here, and there's a good chance that he saw it coming, true," Radock said. "But even if he prepared a trap, he won't win. He's not only outnumbered, but neither he nor Alejandro have more power than we do right now."

I wanted to believe him. I did. "What if he has a bracelet? *Another* bracelet," I asked because I had felt exactly how much power that thing had, how much magic it could unleash at once, and in the hands of someone like Hill...

"Well, then I suppose it's lucky *you're* here," said Helen, then turned around and walked away with her head high together with Natasha and George.

There it was, that word again—*lucky*. Goddess, I hated it so much.

It didn't matter now, though. Hill was just a couple miles away from us, and we weren't leaving here without a fight. He wouldn't surrender, and we weren't going to just let him summon the dead army—that he'd even found them was horrifying enough. All those skeletons...

"Go ahead and spell your clothes, prepare. We go in in ten," Radock said when we walked back to the SUV they'd been driving. The wide road that led here was blocked by IDD soldiers and their vans, and no civilian was going to be able to drive by here anytime soon, for which I was thankful. Open fields and forests and mountains on either side of the road, so nobody else would have to pay the price of Hill's greed, at least. If everything went right, the world would never have to even know this happened.

"I think we should all go in, brother," Kaid said, and earned a slap on the shoulder from Seth.

"No, you stay out here. Keep an eye on them."

"You don't trust them?" Kaid asked.

Zachary snorted. "This is still the Council, the reason why Selem was created in the first place." He looked behind him as if to make sure that none of them were close, but they weren't. They'd gone to their own vehicles, the standard mission vans of the IDD farther up the road.

"Our war with them hasn't ended," Zach continued, his voice low now. "Right now, we're in a truce because of David Hill, because unfortunately, we don't have the resources to take him down ourselves, and he's already gone too far. But this is not permanent."

"As soon as this is over, as soon as Hill is dead, we disappear. There's too many of them and I have people moving in closer when the fight begins to take us out. Do you underhand?" Radock's eyes stopped on me. "As soon as Hill is dead, we destroy everything he had, the scripts and the spells and the vessels he prepared for the Army, and we get out. There's no telling what they can do once we win."

Shivers down my back because he was absolutely right. When David Hill was no longer in the picture, we had to make sure that any scripts or spells to bring back the Delaetus Army were destroyed, just in case someone else in the future decided it was a good idea to try to conquer the world.

Or...someone from the Council.

Because I'd seen the way Helen looked at that video of Hill working on the soul vessels. The curiosity in her eyes— the *greed*.

No, we definitely could not trust the Council with any of what Hill had here. We had to destroy everything before we left.

Assuming we even won against Hill.

"Let's focus on one thing at a time, though. Let's focus on David. He will be hard to kill," Aurelia said.

"But not impossible. Not with all of us together," Radock said, then looked at me. "Not with that bracelet. If it ruined the Regah screen with a single spell, it can kill Hill, too."

"He could be protected. He could have wards about him —" I said because the fear, the *pressure* of having to chant that final spell almost crushed me under.

But Taland was there to squeeze my hand when Zachary said, "And we'll break down all the wards he has if we have to. But we *will* kill him."

"A single kill spell," Taland whispered to me, and when I looked at him, he winked. "What's the shortest one you know?"

"Cheining," I whispered with half a heart, as the words of the spell came back to me like my mind was trying to make sure that I remembered it right.

I did—it was a curse created by Apollo Cheining some four hundred years ago, and it was the shortest spell that they taught at the training academy. It made the heart basically *explode* in someone's chest.

"Good one," Taland said. "Use it."

"I will." On anyone that got in my way, I'd use it. At this point I wasn't going to even bother thinking about remorse.

"We're here now," Radock said. "And we're all powerful enough to survive this—I know it. So, keep your eyes open and your ears sharp, and do whatever you have to do." He looked each and every one of us in the eye, and I couldn't believe that that actually worked. It calmed me down, if just a little, to know that they were all in on this, too. "Everything else, we'll figure out after."

So, we went back to the car, and I used the bracelet to call the most powerful wards I knew on both Taland's clothes and mine. They were not IDD uniforms by any means, but they would do just fine. I had a pair of leather pants and a leather jacket zipped up all the way, and Zachary gave him a thick leather vest to put on over his shirt. The magic that wrapped around us was what mattered the most.

"That's enough. Save your energy," Taland said when I considered doing a third spell, too.

"I'm fine. I feel great." Which wasn't a lie. Physically I felt great—save for my twisting stomach. My limbs were strong. My leg didn't hurt at all. I was fed and hydrated, and even though we hadn't exactly *rested*, I was full of energy. More motivated than ever because Taland was with me.

For now, I was happy that I had the chance to be here

for real. As much as I hated to agree with anything Madeline said, I was happy that I got to be here and fight, *try* to win. Not a good guy or a bad guy—no, just a girl fighting a mad man who wanted to bring back a dead army and take over the world.

That's all I wanted to be right now.

That's all I was when we followed two dozen soldiers around the mountain together and made it to the other side.

CHAPTER 11

Rosabel La Rouge

Not ready, I am not ready; not ready, I am not ready—my mind spun with the thought, and by the time we were on the other side of that mountain, the voice in my head screamed it until I *felt* those words on every inch of my body.

I was not ready to be here.

But that was nothing new, was it? I wasn't ready; of course, I wasn't. I'd been an agent for a year and a half and none of the missions I'd been on even came close to this. None of the people we'd had to fight against even came close to Hill and what he was trying to do—*of course I am not ready!*

But that didn't mean I couldn't win.

That's what I told myself. I wasn't ready for the training academy, or to take on the job of an agent when I did; I wasn't ready to be Mud; I wasn't ready to survive and win the Iris Roe, or to undo the Devil's Regah chamber. And most importantly I was never ready to lose Taland over and over—but I did. I did all of those things, and here I was now.

Just because I am not ready doesn't mean I won't win.

My thoughts slowly changed as I took in the sight in front of me, and it was incredible how much power I had when I decided to take it. It was incredible how I could control my heartbeat with a simple thought when I chose to not let the panic and the anxiety control me. I was here now and there was no going back. It was time to assess my surroundings and fight until I couldn't anymore.

Laughter.

The sound of it echoed in the bowl valley between the mountains that had looked a bit smaller on the screen. Those excavators on the other side had dug about fifty feet deep searching for those skeletons.

Meanwhile they were standing on the other side of them, and even though I couldn't see them from here yet, I knew they were there.

So was Hill atop that landing farther up than I'd realized. So were his men wearing white, spread everywhere around us.

And so was Alejandro Ammiz, sitting on the same place —and the laughter was coming from him.

"Greetings! Welcome, welcome!" he shouted, waving his hands up and down and to the sides, as if he thought we might not see him.

All of us spread out in a line, and the soldiers who'd guided us here were already getting closer to where the ground began to descend into that hole.

"We've been waiting for you!" said the Devil, his voice echoing a million times. "Tell them, David! We've been *waaaaiiiting!*"

Goose bumps down my arms. I looked at Taland and he

winked at me, an easy smile on his face, like always, though I knew him well enough to realize he was calculating distances and trying to come up with a plan of action just by the look in his eyes.

"Our goal is simple—either apprehend or kill David Hill and Alejandro Ammiz, and whoever else gets in your way. Just *don't* let them bring those skeletons to life," Helen said as she stepped forward, her hair wrapped behind her head, her dark grey leather suit zipped up to her neck.

"Safe to say he doesn't have another bracelet. That's the first good news," Radock said, putting on black leather gloves.

"The second is that those skeletons hopefully will break easy," said Zachary.

"I'm going after Hill," said Aurelia.

"So am I," I said because I already had an idea of how to run all around the edges of the valley to get to that mountain and start climbing. The rocks had a lot of sharp edges. *Should be easy enough,* I thought.

"Good luck," Helen said, and without another glance our way, she ran.

She ran and jumped straight into the bowl just as the gunshots began all around us—from both behind and ahead. Snipers.

The IDD soldiers and Hill's men were trying their luck with bullets first.

Taland pulled up my hand and kissed the back of it. "Let's kill David Hill."

I rose on my tiptoes and kissed him on the lips. "He has no chance."

I didn't actually believe in the words I said, but I ran. Together with Taland, I followed Aurelia and Zach all around the edge of the bowl. They had probably made the same calculations and figured that this was the easiest way to that mountain.

We would make it, I thought. And there were soldiers maybe fifty feet ahead, who didn't bother with guns but were waiting for us with wands and bones in their hands, but it was nothing we couldn't handle.

Except...

The explosion came out of nowhere. The ground shook and groaned, and a wave of energy slammed onto my side so hard it was impossible to push back even if I had seen it coming. It picked me up and threw me to the side like I weighed no more than a feather, and then I was falling. The view in front of me moved, and I flew and I fell and I was too shocked to scream, but I realized what had happened even before I hit the ground. They'd planted an explosive spell somewhere on the ground, and we must have activated it when we ran past it.

Now all four of us were in the air—and we crashed against the soil in the bowl almost at the same time.

Goddess, it hurt. I fell on my side and it felt like my shoulder caught fire and my neck snapped and broke, and then I continued to roll and roll until I was at the very bottom, all my insides trying to come right out of my mouth.

Get up, get up, GET UP! my mind shouted at me, and I did. My body moved on pure instinct and I was on my feet even before I knew I could stand and even before I could actually see my surroundings.

A hundred blinks later, the view cleared. I did see, and somehow, I could keep standing. Taland was beside me, taking my hand in his, the other raised as he chanted furiously—putting up another ward around us.

"The fucker planted them all over," Aurelia said from

my other side as she helped Zach to his feet, and she was right. We were looking at where Helen and Radock had been leading the group to the skeletons of the Delaetus Army, and they'd been met with an explosion, too.

And all around the edges of the dug-up valley, IDD soldiers were fighting Hill's men already.

For a moment, it all felt like a dream. Everything had happened so fast, and that fall was like a wakeup call shaking me awake to what was really going on around me, all that blood that was being spilled, all that magic hanging in the air, making it almost too thick to breathe.

"Hey, you're okay," Taland said, pulling my hand to get my attention—and I was. By some miracle the fall hadn't hurt me too much. My shoulder still throbbed, but I wasn't bleeding and I could move just fine.

"I am," I said and focused on him for a moment. He was slightly bleeding in the corner of his lips, but he seemed to be okay, too. He was putting away a gigantic raven feather in his pocket that shone with all imaginable colors under the bright sunlight. "Need a healing spell?"

"Nope. Good as new," he said, looking up at the mountains, at that landing that protruded from the side of it, atop which was Hill.

"C'mon, weaklings. Race you to the top!" Zachary called as he started running up the steep incline of the valley right where we'd fallen, and Aurelia followed.

"Ready?" Taland asked, and I nodded even if I wasn't. But we were here now, and we were going to make the best of it.

Together, we ran.

The soil was slightly wet and stuck to my boots, but it also made it a bit easier to climb all the way up the the edge again. By then I no longer really expected to make it to Hill or even the Devil who was still smoking his cigar sitting on that rock, grinning at us. Aurelia and Zach were already fighting a group of soldiers who'd been waiting for us.

I started chanting even before I made it up the edge behind Taland. He'd pushed back the two soldiers from the bigger group a bit farther away fighting the Mergenbachs, who had been throwing their Bluefire at us—standard combat spells, which meant these guys were trained in the academy, too. Hill had taken them from the IDD.

My bracelet heated up and my magic rushed down my arm—faster than ever before, it seemed to me. I could have sworn that the more strongly I felt about any given situation, the more magic I had access to, and right now I was thankful. For the fear and for the thrill that went through me when I raised my hand forward and aimed it at the soldiers.

Eleven of them. Eleven were fighting the siblings and Taland, who, when he saw me chanting and aiming my hand, shouted, "*Get down!*"

Flames full of colors burst out of me just as they moved their heads down. My magic shot forward, so bright even in the sunlight, and slammed against the soldiers like it was something solid, pushed them back and threw them to the ground much like that explosion had thrown us down the valley.

Power hummed in my veins, raw power.

"Let's go!" Aurelia shouted when the colors faded and all those soldiers we'd been fighting remained on the ground, still trying to get up.

We didn't bother with them, though. We just kept on running toward that mountain, and *more* soldiers dressed in white were waiting for us, but I wasn't afraid. There simply was no room for fear in my mind—*surviving* required all my focus.

We clashed with the second group of soldiers, and the others we'd left behind would be on us soon, too. At least most of them. The magic might have broken a few ribs, but it hadn't killed them. I'd used a third-degree, but right now I was thinking I wanted to go with fourth-degree spells only because I could. Because all those colors that were buzzing inside me could absolutely handle it.

"Go, go, go!" Zachary said as he pointed his wand at the group of eight soldiers throwing spells at us from a distance, clashing onto our wards.

"C'mon!" Aurelia called, waving for us to follow her while Zach kept the soldiers back with his bright blue flames, the halo over his head unwavering.

"Just keep running, baby. I got your back. Keep your focus forward," Taland said while we ran, and I believed him. I heard him chanting and throwing his magic behind, and I assumed the soldiers were already on us, but I kept my eyes ahead on Aurelia as she ran, closer and closer to the edge of the mountain, to another group of ten soldiers who were waiting for us with their hands raised.

How many more of them would there be? I wondered, my ears already used to the screams and shouts and the sound of bodies slamming against the ground.

Goddess, this was worse than the Iris Roe.

"Move aside!" I called at Aurelia as she ran, and she did, just as another blast of blue flames left her wand and slammed onto the group of soldiers, who were under a stronger ward than their friends. No matter. I was already chanting my second spell—a fourth degree energy blast this time, and I had my hand raised and ready.

They all tried to attack me, too, and a couple even fired their guns at me, but the bullets fell before they reached me. And my magic charged at them like a vicious animal full of colors that faded before the blast slammed onto them, picked them up and threw them against the rocks of the mountain at their back—and not only that. It made the entire mountain shake and groan, and it made the Devil laugh out loud like he'd just witnessed a damn miracle.

Meanwhile Aurelia cheered. *"Woohoo!"* then proceeded to chant another spell to hit someone behind us. I turned for a second, but all I saw were the blue flames of her spell, and the black ones of Taland.

"Don't die!" Aurelia told me, pointing her index finger at me like she was ordering me.

I could have laughed.

"Keep your eyes ahead. We'll cover you," Taland called, and I did. More than that—I was starting to feel *ready*, like maybe being here wasn't a complete disaster. Like I could actually make a difference in this fight and not hold anybody back—I already had! Those soldiers were down, and the ones who'd tried to get to their feet again had already met Aurelia's magic, and even Zach was running toward us again, having beaten the soldiers that he'd stopped to fight, too.

Hope—such a beautiful, terrifying thing. It took over me, fell around my shoulders, wrapped around me like it had arms, clung to me as I ran. More soldiers dressed in white came from the side of the mountain, but I was climbing because Taland reminded me to keep my eyes up. He and Aurelia, and even Zach took care of the rest, and I saved my energy and I looked upward—right at the face of the Devil who had stood up and thrown his cigar away. It finally felt like he was taking us seriously, at least enough to stand and wait, prepare himself.

I had no illusion that he'd be as easy to get through as those soldiers. I had no doubt that his wards would be much more problematic to break. His wouldn't be standard protocol wards that all IDD soldiers and agents used—no, his would be personal and stronger, but *my* magic? Those fourth-degree spells that I seemed to be able to push out of me with the same ease as Madeline did?

They would be hard to keep back, and he knew it.

That's why he stopped laughing and started chanting when I was still only halfway to him.

I was right—the rough surface and the sharp edges of the rocks made it fairly easy to climb, but the Devil could see me from where he stood just fine, and so when he raised his hand toward me and chanted his spell, there was nowhere I could hide or get out of his way.

My wards were about me, two that I'd made with the bracelet, so I had hope that they would hold against his magic as well as they held against bullets. But even so, I raised my arm in front of my face on instinct when his Blackfire shot out of his hand and came for me lightning fast. A scream built up in me and stuck in my throat, and the taste of his magic coated my tongue, even though I felt no pain and my wards held back the worst of it.

Still, the effect of his magic vibrated on my skin, and I knew that if he kept at it, I wasn't going to be able to withstand it forever. That's why I forced myself to keep moving, even while he chanted his second spell, this one longer, and I had a plan. I was going to let him do his spell, hit me with it this time, too, while I got closer. The smaller the distance between us, the more effective my magic would be. And hopefully, when he hit me with the second spell, I'd be ready and close enough to unleash mine on him.

So, when his magic slammed onto my wards for the second time, it was much more powerful, indeed, definitely a fourth-degree, and it was a miracle I managed to hold onto the edges of the rocks. The Devil was done playing around, and if he hit me with that same spell again, my wards was going to shatter, and I was going to feel the full strength of his magic.

That's why I was chanting even before I blinked the stars away from my vision—and he did, too. Except he chanted out loud, and he was going for another fourth-degree, but so was I, and I was going to complete my spell faster. But I kept my head down while I whispered so he didn't see it, didn't know what I was preparing, couldn't protect himself as well as he should have.

I only raised my head and my hand toward him when I was on the last words of the spell, and colorful flames were already taking shape on the palm of my hand, my magic so eager to come out of me, to *destroy,* it would have scared me any other day. As it was, I watched the colors shoot for the Devil, and I'd never forget the look in his eyes when he realized he couldn't move away in time.

No smile on his lips. His eyes widened and he still tried to step back, but my magic was faster. It hit him straight in the face, and of course his wards protected him, but the sheer force of my magic pushed him back a couple steps, then knocked him down on that rock, too.

Go, go, go, go, I kept repeating to myself, as if that was going to make me move faster.

Behind me Taland was already climbing together with Zach, while Aurelia still fought a few soldiers who were left standing. Goddess, I only looked back for a second, and when I saw the bloodbath and the trail of bodies we'd left behind, I was fucking sick to my stomach.

Then I had no choice but to focus on pulling myself up to stand on that rock where the Devil was struggling to make it to his feet.

My legs shook a little and my arms hurt, too, from the climbing. My fingers were bloody, but I still raised my hand at him, prepared to chant.

Before I could, Taland put his over my forearm. "Save your energy," he said, his eyes focused on the Devil.

"Move out of my way!" Zachary called, and we stepped to the side to let him up. The guy was smiling and he sounded cheerful, and Aurelia was coming up fast behind him, too, *laughing* like the Devil had been doing until now.

"We got this," Zach said, wand raised at the Devil who was on his feet already, pretending to dust off his pants as he watched us and smiled. But it wasn't a real smile—it was one he forced himself to keep on because he was afraid.

Oh, he was afraid, all right. And to see that fear in him boosted my hope even more.

"Go ahead, keep climbing," said Aurelia. She had a cut on her cheek that was bleeding but seemed otherwise perfectly fine, too. And focused on the Devil.

"Have fun, friends," said Taland, pulling me to the other side so we could continue to climb higher.

"Oh, that's awfully rude of you. You don't think I'm worth the effort?!" said the Devil, and when his Blackfire shot out of both his hands at the same time, the entire mountain seemed to shake in its foundation again. Even though the magic didn't reach us—both Zach and Aurelia were already countering it with their Bluefire that had spread like a shield in front of them—the ground was uneven enough that I couldn't keep my balance. I fell on all fours, and so did Taland.

Before I could get back up, I looked.

I looked out into the valley, and all the hope I'd felt swelling in my chest until now faded away.

Here I'd thought that Helen and Radock and the others had already killed every soldier that stood in their way and they'd already ruined the bones of the Delaetus Army, but I was wrong. They were still fighting, and the ground beneath their feet seemed to be loaded with fucking mines because it kept exploding and throwing them off the closer they got to the Army, and the more of those soldiers they took to the ground.

Holy shit, they were bloodier than we were, slower, covered in dirt. The skeletons were still there—and Hill was still up on that landing.

"Move!" Aurelia screamed at us, and Taland was already pulling me to my feet, basically throwing me against the rocks. The Devil's magic came at them again, and Aurelia and Zach stepped in front of me to act as a shield. For a moment, Zach looked back and his nose was bleeding, probably from the sheer pressure of the magic he held back with his own, and in his eyes, I saw that same hope that had faded from me just a moment ago.

"*Go!*" he said, but I didn't hear his voice over the screams in my own head, only read the word on his lips.

I turned to the rocks again and I started climbing with Taland right behind me.

Don't look, don't look, don't look, I was telling myself now because if I looked down and saw that the Devil was winning, I might lose my grip on these rocks. If I turned to find out why he was laughing—*again*—I was afraid I'd have no choice but to get down there myself and make sure he died.

Why the fuck was he laughing still? Could he not see that he couldn't win?

Who says he can't win? said the ugly voice in my head, and it was a bloody battle up there in my mind.

"Keep going. Keep going," Taland said, as if he could tell that I was struggling and I needed his voice to keep me grounded. In the moment. To make me hope again simply because if these men won, they'd kill us. They'd kill Taland, and that just wasn't acceptable. I'd never allow it, hope or no hope.

These men could not—*would not* win.

Even though the thought didn't clear my head all the way like I hoped, I was able to focus on moving my limbs faster, getting up there in time so that I could kill David Hill and put an end to this bullshit once and for all. No more threats—couldn't I just have that? One day and month and year without fearing for my life or the life of my loved ones. That's it, that's all I wanted, and only David Hill was standing in my way.

It took us a while to climb all the way to him, and not only because the surface of the mountain wall became smoother, with less edges to hold onto, and steeper as we went, but he was higher up than I'd realized. Blood on my fingers and my limbs were screaming in protest, my muscles aching, but I kept going.

Ignoring the sound of the battles around me, I kept on climbing until I could see the edge of that landing, and I could see Hill kneeling up there with those eggs in front of him in my mind's eye, too.

"Just a little more, baby," Taland said. He was just as breathless as me, but he refused to stop, too. I had no idea for how long we climbed, but he never once fell behind or stopped to take a breath.

Until finally, I gripped the edge of the landing and pulled myself onto it, and he followed. We were both on our stomachs, breathing heavily, and when we looked up, we finally saw Hill—standing. Chanting.

That's when we realized that we were too late.

CHAPTER 12

Rosabel La Rouge

That man made my skin crawl even when I couldn't see his face. He could make me want to close my ears just to keep his voice out of my mind.

I breathed like I'd been climbing for days while I struggled to make it to my feet and help Taland to stand, and we were close, so close.

Not close enough, though.

His voice echoed in my head. The words of the spell he was chanting didn't sound like Iridian words at all, and he still had those pieces of paper with him right there on the smooth, flat surface of the landing. Those pieces of paper that remained in place, didn't move with the breeze at all, like he'd frozen them there with his magic as well—and the eggs...

My goddess, the eggs were all cracked open, and inside them was light. Small white lights like enlarged fireflies were slowly rising from the broken eggshells as Hill held his arms up and chanted furiously.

"Taland!" I screamed because I was trying to get closer, to call for my magic, but I couldn't. Fucking hell, the magic radiating from Hill was keeping me perfectly motionless, and it was *pushing me back!*

Taland as well. I couldn't turn my head to the side at all because whatever spell Hill was doing, it was keeping me frozen while it pushed me to the wall of the mountain, all the way to the sharp edges that were trying to dig into my back.

"I can't...break...through..." Taland said, his voice strained as he tried to push the magic back but couldn't.

I *couldn't move.*

David Hill was right there, not even twenty feet away from me at the edge of that landing looking out at the valley beneath him, with his arms spread and those lights rising all around them, defying the light of the sun—and I couldn't fucking move.

Panic squeezed my throat and stopped what little air had been going down to my lungs completely. The magic pushed me back, tried to make me one with the rocks behind me. Hill continued to chant as his voice rose, and those lights...

Those fucking lights were *buzzing,* vibrating in place like they contained the energy of the entire world and they were about to burst open any second.

I wanted to call Taland's name again, but I couldn't. My magic raged inside me, and I tried to force my jaws to move, to chant, to *do something* other than just stand there, but I couldn't.

I could do nothing but watch as my bracelet heated to a point that I thought it would scorch my skin, and my magic raged but couldn't come out of me, and Hill chanted and chanted and looked up at the sky and those lights buzzed and buzzed and became brighter—until they moved.

For a second, just as Hill stopped chanting abruptly, the lights stopped vibrating, suspended in air, frozen just like I was. Then they shot toward the ground, below the landing to where we couldn't see, fast as lightning.

David Hill laughed.

The magic that had been holding us against the rocks let go and we both fell to our knees.

Screams somewhere below and I *had to-had to-had to* see. That's why I was already crawling toward the edge on all fours, until my limbs gave up and I fell on my stomach again, but I could see the valley now just fine. I could see the people screaming—Helen and Flora and Radock, too.

I could see *why*.

The lights had stopped right over the skeletons, and I still couldn't see all of them, but I saw plenty. I saw how the lights slowly descended onto their helmets, and how the others were being kept back just like Taland and I a moment ago. I saw how they tried to get through the magic, to stop whatever was about to happen, but couldn't.

It was too late, indeed.

The small lights that had come from those eggs slipped into the helmets of the skeletons. The ground underneath their leather-covered feet moved. I could have been looking at a fucking movie because no way was this real—yet it was happening. The lights must have traveled down the skulls because now they were shining in the middle of their ribcages. Right in front of my eyes, in front of *all* our eyes, pink flesh was appearing out of thin air and wrapping itself around the skeletons. Blood—all that blood was just sprouting into existence over them, and layers of skin were stretching from under their armor plates, up and down their whole bodies. Making them whole. Making them *alive*.

While the rest of us watched.

Somewhere below us, the sound of the Devil's laughter reached our ears, but there was no time to fear him. Those skeletons were no longer skeletons—they were men dressed in armor, but...

They weren't moving. They were still as the rocks to their side, and though I couldn't see their eyes, I was willing to bet anything that they were closed.

The soldiers of the Delaetus Army had gained flesh and blood and skin, but they were still not fully alive.

I confirmed that when Hill, no longer chanting or spreading his arms around, turned to me. Our eyes locked. His were bloodshot, sunken in, like he'd lost a lot of weight since we last met in the Regah chamber.

His smile sent shivers up and down my body when he raised his hand toward me and said, "I'm going to need my bracelet now."

Ice-cold chills ran down my back and it felt like a flame ignited in my core that was threatening to melt me at the same time. The image of those skeletons gaining flesh and blood and skin remained in front of my mind's eye as Hill continued to smile with his hand outstretched, as if he really thought that I would give him the bracelet, just like that.

A hand over my leg.

My heart jumped until I remembered that I wasn't alone up here with Hill. I remembered that Taland was right behind me, and he was pulling me toward himself with all his strength while he tried to make it to his feet at the same time.

At the sight of him struggling, a brand-new energy came over me, enough to help me reach for the rocks for support and stand when he did. My heart beat a mile a minute. I was breathing heavily, black dots still in my vision here and there, but I was moving. I could chant and I could fight and I could use my bracelet now—nothing stopped me. Nothing held me against the rocks.

And Taland was the same.

"Don't tell me you're going to make me come and get it," Hill said, lowering his hand again, putting both in the pockets of his white pants. He wore all white—even his boots were made of white leather, and his hair had grown longer than I'd ever seen, and the hollows of his cheeks made him look sick.

His eyes, though. His eyes were still as wide and as alert as ever. As *greedy*. As empty. They say eyes are the windows to the soul, and his would make you think that there was *nothing* in there. No soul to speak of. Just pure, raw malice.

"We won't let you get away with this," I said through gritted teeth because I couldn't help myself, and I couldn't help the fear or this voice in my head that insisted that he couldn't be beaten. He was far too powerful now—and the Delaetus Army was complete, the skeletons turned to people.

Though nobody was screaming yet, so I hoped that they were still not moving.

"And how do you plan to stop me, Rosabel? With your Council? With your pathetic soldiers?" Another laughter. "I have an army of undead."

And I have the bracelet, I thought. "Nobody's invincible," I said—only because Taland was chanting under his breath, and I was foolish enough to think I could keep Hill distracted so he didn't see it coming.

"Except *me*," he calmly said. "You've come a long way, Rosabel. When I ordered your superior to kill you, my heart wasn't in it, really, and I didn't even mind that much that you survived, and he didn't. I'll be the first to admit I ended up slightly regretting that."

The way he spoke, so calmly. I'd known all along since Taland told me about Hill being in Selem that *he* had been the one to order Michael to kill me that day in the catfairie forest, but even so, I was shocked for a moment. Even so, I couldn't help but feel *sorry* for Michael now, knowing that it was Hill who'd probably threatened him, told him that he'd kill him, if Michael didn't agree to kill me.

"You're pure evil, aren't you," I said, despite my better judgment. "Erid was my friend. You almost killed Taland— you're fucking *evil*."

His brows shot up. Here I was, completely worked up and shaking, while he acted like he had the whole day ahead of him and he took his time in looking around as if to make sure I wasn't talking to someone else.

"Is that supposed to make me feel bad, Rosabel?" he asked. "Goddess, you're worse than your grandmother." Shivers ran down my arms. "Imagine my surprise when I saw the video of you stealing my bracelet. *You* of all people." His head fell back and he laughed, but this time it was bitter. "I should have definitely tried harder when your superior failed. I should have done it myself when you came back from the Roe."

Superior, he said. And I wondered if he even knew Michael's name, but did it matter?

Because Taland had finished his fourth-degree spell, and he raised his hand the same moment his Blackfire shot for Hill.

I thought I'd kept Hill well enough distracted, that he hadn't noticed.

He had. He'd probably been perfectly aware of it the whole time, and when the Blackfire reached him, he simply raised a hand and whatever ward he had about him swallowed Taland's magic whole, made it disappear as if it had never existed in the first place.

Hill sighed then. I looked at Taland, tried to find courage in the dark of his eyes but he knew just as well as I did that we were screwed.

Even so, he smiled for me.

Even so he winked to try to calm me down.

I love you, I thought. "Through summer breezes," I said.

"Through fucking hurricanes, baby," he said.

Then we began to chant at the same time.

We knew very well who we were up against. We knew that the chances of us making it out of this fight alive were slimmer than ever before, but we still tried with our everything. Just like in the Iris Roe and in the Regah chamber, we fought with every ounce of strength we had, and the magic coming out of us spread around the entire landing, wrapped us in a cocoon.

Hill didn't spare himself, either. He pushed back the Blackfire magic and the colorful one that came out of me constantly, then hit us with his Whitefire as many times as he could. I called up a new ward on Taland and me first, just as an added layer of protection while Taland attacked Hill, but that didn't hold for long, and I didn't get the chance to call for another. Hill was relentless, and he still managed to push us back until we almost reached the side of the mountain again, even though we never stopped chanting. I threw at him every possible spell I knew, short and long, third- and fourth-degree—whatever I had the time to summon.

And I wasn't tired, couldn't even tell you if my body was weak, because my magic was still buzzing, far from spent, but I thought it wouldn't be enough. I thought we wouldn't be able to even put a dent in Hill's ward.

We did more than that, though.

When he hit us with his magic and slammed us against the rocks, and then to the ground, I had been chanting a spell on the longer side, a magic blast almost as powerful as that with which I'd ruined the Regah screen. There was simply no time to do the same, but I unleashed this one at him when I was still on the ground, and he was on his way to us.

Maybe finally I caught him by surprise because my magic slammed onto his ward and I *heard* it when it cracked open, fell to pieces all around him, invisible to the eye. The magic vanished into the thin air, and Hill hit the smooth rock on one knee.

Our eyes locked. Blood trickled from his nostrils. His jaws were locked tightly as he held it in—the pain. He had to be in pain.

A tiny bit of that hope I lost came back to me in that moment, and it never left my side again. I stood up, already chanting, and when his magic came at me, Taland's blocked it by slamming onto him.

It worked. The Blackfire almost knocked him down all the way, something it wasn't able to do at all until now. Hill's wards were gone, all of them, and this was our chance.

Taland and I exchanged a quick look, but we both knew what to do next. My bracelet, my magic through it would make the biggest difference here, and if we had a chance against Hill, as crazy as that sounded, we needed to hit him with that magic. So Taland jumped forward and he kept calling for second- and third-degree spells because they were faster, giving me enough time to chant a proper fourth-degree blast like the one I'd used in the Regah chamber.

It didn't work right away. Hill overthrew Taland's spells and hit us both with his own, and I ended up on my back another two times. I had to start the spell over for the fourth, and now I was getting pissed off. My magic was getting pissed off, too.

Except the spell was really long—longer still when we were fighting face-to-face with someone who kept throwing magic at us like he didn't even need to chant at all. And Taland was tired, too. Even though he never stopped moving, never stopped whispering, I could tell he'd gotten just a bit slower, his Blackfire just a bit weaker.

And when I was almost ready to finish that spell for the fourth time, Hill dodged Taland's spell and was able to hit us both, again, with his own magic.

I ended up on the ground on my side, ready to fucking scream my guts out at the world.

Instead, I forced myself to continue chanting because even though Hill was coming, Taland could keep him away for another moment. Just until I was done chanting. Just until I was fucking done.

Taland did jump in front of him when he aimed his Whitefire at me, with a shield that was so fresh black flames were still dancing on the transparent surface, but the Whitefire shattered it at once. And when Taland fell to his knees for a second, I did make it to my feet as I continued to whisper under my breath, and I ran for him, too.

Maybe I'd lost my fucking mind, and maybe being thrown against rocks had already gotten the last of my patience. Or maybe it was just because he was looking at Taland as he whispered. I had no clue, but I ran for Hill, knowing I still had two whole sentences of my spell to whisper with these jaws that seemed more reluctant to move by the second.

But I was already operating on instinct, and my body knew how to move even if I sometimes forgot that I could fight. That I'd been trained by the best of the IDD. That I'd worked on missions for a year and a half. By some miracle, before Hill could finish whatever spell he had coming next, I managed to spin around with my leg raised and catch him on the jaw with the heel of my boot.

Maybe it was luck. Or maybe Hill didn't see it coming. Or maybe he was tired—*finally*—from using all that magic for the goddess knew how long, but he moved to the side and lost his footing and fell on one knee again.

"*Move!*" Taland called from behind me, and I stepped aside just as his Blackfire flew past me and slammed onto Hill's chest, taking his breath away.

My bracelet heated, and colorful magic started to slowly appear on my skin. Hill launched himself toward me, and this time *I* was too slow to stop him, too surprised.

His fingers were on my bracelet, trying to pry it from my wrist.

The last word of my spell left my lips in a whisper. I put my hand on his shoulder and screamed.

Colors burst out of me so fast that the energy threw me back. I hit the ragged edges of the rocks at the mountain's side once more, then slid to the ground on my back. The blast had thrown me at least five feet in the air, and it had done the same to Taland. He was on the ground right next to me, and he was breathing just as heavily, face a mess of blood and bruises, probably similar to mine.

But we were both still alive and aware.

We raised our heads as well as we could to see Hill, moaning in pain, clothes torn and bloody and dirty as he tried to make it to his feet.

He was going to make it if we gave him enough time.

"Rose," Taland choked, but he wasn't looking at me. He was looking at my wrist, where my bracelet barely hung on my finger. Hill had *almost* taken it off me completely.

Goddess, everything hurt, but I prayed that my ribs were only bruised, not broken. I prayed that I had enough energy in me for one last spell.

Tears in my eyes as I looked at Taland. "Together?" I whispered, and the moment I raised my hand, the bracelet fell from me completely. Taland grabbed it on one side and held it between us. I touched the other.

"Together," he said, as Hill spewed curse words at us, still not steady on his feet but pissed. And weak.

And ready to fucking die.

"Cheining?" I asked in barely any voice, and Taland nodded.

We both knew the spell. We were both Mud. The bracelet would channel magic from both of us.

Goddess please, let it work...

Together, we chanted the words at the same time, much slower than we ought to, but we were getting faster. The more we breathed, the better control of our jaws we had, and eventually, I even managed to sit up and pull Taland with me. The bracelet was in both our hands, and Hill was bleeding, pissed off like a rabid fucking dog as he came for us. Except that spell I did on him must have damaged him more than he was willing to accept because he was holding his right shoulder with his hand and he was dragging his foot behind, almost like my magic had paralyzed his entire side completely.

That sliver of hope I felt before now turned brighter and grew bigger and gave more voice to the words of my spell until I was shouting them. He was only halfway to us, and Taland was already on his feet, pulling me by the arm, his other hand still on the bracelet.

Hill's bloodshot eyes were open wide. His teeth were gritted, and he was growling like a beast as he kept trying to get to us, even though he could see that it was no use. Even though he knew the spell would be long finished, and he didn't even have the strength to turn to his magic anymore.

Colorful flames shot from both Taland's and my hands. The bracelet had released both our magics, indeed.

The killing spell was on its way to Hill.

Though it moved fast, so fast, to me it felt like ages until it hit home. Until it fell on Hill's chest, slipped under his skin, and cut off his breath completely, leaving his eyes wide open.

Even my heart stood still for a good moment, waiting to see...

The asshole still didn't go down. His hand was still moving, rising toward us slowly.

Taland fell to his knees beside me, exhausted.

I lost my fucking mind for real.

I didn't look at Taland at all, afraid it would somehow stop me when I had such little energy left. I just dropped the bracelet and ran forward, wrapped my arms around David Hill and took him to the fucking ground.

"*Die, die, die,*" I said, or maybe I just thought it, but I was planning to wrap my arm around his neck and cut off his breathing completely until he died for real, except...

It was a mistake.

Goddess, I should have waited. I should have given the spell a little bit of time to work. I should have stayed put, shouldn't have gone to him at all.

Because the spell did work, and by the time I realized that his heart was indeed going to explode, it was too late.

All that magic we'd put in him *released* itself from his body when not only his heart, but every organ inside Hill exploded like he'd had dynamite under his flesh. Taland called my name but I couldn't answer, couldn't even look at him, couldn't stop the magic that made Hill's body explode from throwing me up in the air.

Too close. I was too close to the edge.

I should have waited.

Blood everywhere, on my face and mouth and eyes—and hands. Magic pushed me back violently and I tried in vain to grab the smooth surface of the rock.

I slipped.

I fell.

No voice left me. The scream got stuck in my throat and paralysis came over me as if from a spell. Taland called my name again, but I was falling so fast...

Then—*"Grab my hand!"*

The voice came out of nowhere. My instincts must have still been working because I reached out both hands toward where the sound came from, even though I had no idea who'd spoken or where I was or how the hell I was going to grab anybody's hand while I was falling.

But I did.

Two strong hands grabbed me by the arm and stopped my fall, but it felt like they tore my arm off my shoulder completely. Zach's face was looming somewhere over me, and the pain sent live flames all over my body.

Goddess, I couldn't fucking breathe. I couldn't tell him to let go, that he was tearing me apart!

But maybe I should have been thankful that he caught me, that I didn't fall all the way into the valley from that altitude because I'd have died. And there was a good chance that I *would* die, after all, because Zachary was wounded himself, and he couldn't hold onto me. I was too heavy, and he was too bloody, too weak.

"Hold on—just hold on!" said Aurelia, who was dragging herself by her arms over that rock where she and her brother had fought the Devil. They had won, apparently, but they were both just as messed up as I was.

And my leather jacket was covered in blood—*Hill's blood*—so it slipped from Zachary's hands. He couldn't stop it. It slipped fast, so fast.

They called my name, screamed it.

I fell again, but this time not for long. Maybe mere seconds before I hit the ground on that same shoulder that didn't feel like my own at all. Then I rolled and rolled and there was dirt in my nose and mouth and eyes, and Hill's blood was all over me, and I just wanted to burn. I wanted flames to eat at me, cleanse my skin from any stain of him. I wanted to scrub any sign of him off my body forever.

Instead, when I stopped spinning, I found I couldn't even open my eyes. The best I could do was lie there in whatever position I was in, and focus on breathing.

Sound came from somewhere far away—a voice, but I couldn't understand a single word it said. Darkness pulled at me harder and faster with every new breath until I heard nothing at all anymore. Until even the thoughts in my head, the terror, the panic, the *hope* faded away into nothing.

I let go.

CHAPTER 13

Rosabel La Rouge

Hill is dead-Hill is dead-Hill exploded!

My eyes popped open, and my panic reached its peak before I'd taken my first breath. I could see nothing but brown at first, and something awful was on my tongue, and my body felt like it had been through the fucking sewer—but I was awake. I could hear voices, could understand that I was conscious. I could remember, could think back to the reason why I was here, almost completely paralyzed, with blood and dirt in my mouth and eyes, forcing myself to draw in air.

David Hill was dead. He'd *exploded* while I had my arms around him still, when I'd taken him down for fear that he'd make it to his feet again and would somehow survive. He didn't, though—that bracelet made sure of it. The magic that came from both Taland and me made sure that not only his heart, but his entire body came apart.

The bracelet that wasn't on me—I felt it, even now. Felt

the absence of it around my wrist, and before I even knew what the hell was around me, I felt vulnerable without it. Weak.

Hands on my arms, pulling me to the side, then putting me on my back. A blue sky was over us and I saw masked faces, two of them. Navy colored masks—IDD soldiers, and one of them was saying something, trying to get me to respond. The best I could do right now was blink my eyes and try to clear the view. Wait for Taland to come down here and get me so we could disappear.

Because Hill was dead and there was a good chance his blood was in my mouth and nose, even eyes, and we could leave now. We could get away, run to the edge of the world, be alone. It had worked—*goddess, it worked!*—and I could cry with happiness. With relief. With gratitude.

It had worked, our plan, and now everything was over.

Thinking back now, I wished I hadn't been so utterly *happy* then. It almost felt like I jinxed the whole fucking thing—but I digress.

The soldiers pulled me up by the hands even before I was able to tell them that I could. That I wasn't dizzy. That I wasn't going to fall unconscious again. But wasn't it a miracle that I'd even survived? I'd fallen from so high up. The magic of the explosion had pushed me right off the edge and I couldn't hold on.

Then...Zach and Aurelia.

I remembered the voice—*Grab my hand!*—and Zach's face, his wounded arm. I remembered Aurelia trying to make it to me when her legs didn't even work at all. I remembered how they'd tried to save me but all that blood on my leather jacket had made sure I slipped right through Zach'a fingers—yet I'd survived. From that rock the fall wasn't long, and I'd survived.

I was alive and Hill wasn't, and that was all that mattered.

Until I was pulled up by the same soldiers who were still speaking and I still couldn't understand. I was pulled up all the way to my feet, and both of them held my weight because, turns out, my legs couldn't really carry me. Not yet, anyway.

But finally, I forced myself to focus, to push down the thoughts in my head and reach for my face to wipe the dirt from my eyes, and I focused on my ears, too.

I'd fallen in the valley, indeed, and the first thing I saw in the distance was the soldiers. The fucking soldiers of the Delaetus Army, with their flesh and their armor on, their eyes closed as they remained perfectly still. Another wave of relief crashed onto me—Hill had managed to use his soul vessels, but he hadn't awakened them. He'd needed the bracelet for that, and the bracelet was ours. Mine and Taland's, and even if it wasn't on me right now, he had it, so it was okay.

Tears in my eyes when I raised my head to look at that protruding piece of rock where we'd fought. Goddess, it looked even higher from down here. And I was laughing and crying at the same time to see Taland standing at the edge of it with his hands on his hips as he watched me.

Alive. I couldn't see his face from so far up, but I knew he was looking at me, and I knew what he was thinking: *we made it, baby. We fucking made it.*

As if he read the thoughts in my mind, he raised two fists to the sky.

Laughter burst out of me, and I imagined he was laughing, too. Fuck, I couldn't wait to kiss his face, to wrap my arms around him already. I couldn't fucking wait for someone to heal me—and him, too, because he'd fought just as much as I had—so we could get the hell away from this place together.

Except...

"Rosabel."

The voice held my heart prisoner for a good beat, and I looked down to find none other than Helen Paine with her sword in her hand, with George on one side and Natasha on the other. She looked like shit, too, her white clothes covered in blood and dirt, but the others didn't have a speck on them.

Regardless—it was the look in Helen's icy-grey eyes that made me pause.

"Where is the bracelet?"

The bracelet, the bracelet, the bracelet—I raised my head and looked at Taland again.

Taland who wasn't holding his fists to the sky anymore but was simply looking down from the edge now.

My jaws opened, but I found I was going to need a moment to be able to speak.

I never really got the chance to answer before I heard the screams.

Aurelia's screams as she and her brother were being *dragged* away from the rocks where they'd fought the Devil, and they had definitely won because he wasn't laughing. But now those soldiers wearing their navy uniforms were dragging them both away, right through the edges of the valley and back where we first came from, where *more* soldiers were coming, jumping into the valley with their guns and their wands and...

Radock and Kaid and Seth, bloody and on their knees.

I did a double take because there was no way I was seeing right. There was no way that the Tivoux brothers would be forced to their knees and held there by a dozen soldiers, with cuffs around their wrists, all bloody and dirty, when Kaid and Seth hadn't even been in the fucking fight. Just like George and Natasha, they hadn't been in the fight —so why were they bloody?!

Why were they being held to their knees?

"Very well," Helen said. She stepped back, waved her sword around as if to show the aftermath of the fucking massacre—the blood and the bodies and the body pieces, too. Most of them wearing those white uniforms. Most of them soldiers of Hill.

"Kill them all," Helen said—loud and clear so that her voice echoed and every soldier in that valley and around it heard.

And I thought, *wait, wait, hold on a minute...*

But she didn't. She just raised her sword toward that landing where Hill died. Where Taland was watching, waiting...

"And bring me that bracelet!"

She turned around to walk away.

My thoughts clashed onto one another, and Radock had his head up and he was laughing, and the soldiers who'd been holding me up until now put me down on my knees, too.

There was still a part of me that insisted this wasn't happening, or that it was simply a prank, or that Helen was messing with us or something. There was still a part of me that refused to accept that she had said those words at all.

But she had. Of course, she had said those words, had ordered her soldiers to kill us all when we were wounded from the battle, when we'd barely gotten out with our lives. Of course, she would order the soldiers to kill us because *she had* soldiers. Soldiers that my grandmother sent here for her, lots and lots of them—countless.

What could we do against all of them now?

I raised my head and I screamed at the top of my lungs, "*TALAND!*"

Tears streamed from my eyes because I was weak and I couldn't even stand on my own and my magic barely even slithered inside me because I'd exhausted it properly; and Radock laughed, and Kaid tried to stand up, and Aurelia screamed and screamed while they dragged her and her brother away—and I just wanted Taland to make it.

Goddess, was that too much to ask? *Can he just* make *it?* Because then all of this wouldn't have been for nothing. Because if he climbed that mountain and disappeared somewhere far away, then neither of us would have died in vain.

Except...Taland wasn't by the edge of the landing anymore, looking down at us.

My heart leaped, and another scream left my lips when I imagined they'd gotten him, too. The panic, the fear gave me energy, and I tried to stand, tried to jump to my feet and run all the way to him, except the guards holding me down didn't let me. They put their hands on the back of my neck, pressed the warm tip of a wand against my right cheek, and a gun barrel on my left.

Over-over-over, my mind insisted, and my goddess, I couldn't believe it. I didn't want to. I *refused.*

Then...

"Madam Paine!"

A soldier called her name before she'd made it out of the valley together with the rest of the Council. He was already by her side and he was pointing up the mountain, and she raised her head to see.

He was pointing up the mountain were Taland had been just a moment ago.

My heart paused again, this time for longer.

And just like that, the entire world changed once more right in front of my eyes.

Taland was still there on that landing, and even though I couldn't see him well enough because he'd stepped back a bit, I could still see his raised arms.

"*Stop him!*" someone called—Helen and Flora and Ferid —all of them.

Stop him, stop him, stop him!

Then a rainbow burst out from the landing, and it was coming from Taland's hands. He was wearing the bracelet and he must have been chanting, must have been trying to attack these soldiers holding us down.

I wanted to tell him not to bother—we were too far, and his magic couldn't reach us in time. *Save yourself, Taland! Run!*

Except his magic, all those bright colors that looked even brighter now that the sun was getting ready to set, weren't coming for *us*. No—they moved toward the other side of the valley, toward the edge of the mountain across from where he stood. Toward the ground on its other side, lightning fast.

Screams erupted all at once. Guns fired. All kinds of magics took over the sky, aimed at that landing, at Taland.

Then *his* magic, all the colors, *fell* over the motionless soldiers of the Delaetus Army.

The ground groaned. The sky darkened. The mountains seemed to be screaming, too, but none of it made any difference.

The soldiers opened their eyes.

My mind was empty. The screaming and the chanting, and the protest of the ground and the mountains stopped for a short second.

Everything just...*stopped*. Watched. Waited.

Then Taland stepped to the very edge of that landing again, and it was dark now, so I barely saw the shape of him against the grey sky. I barely saw his hand outstretched, the colorful flames dancing on his fingers—and I barely saw it when he moved it up.

The screams started again.

The soldiers of the Delaetus Army moved.

"*Attack!*" called someone—could have been Helen or Flora or whoever, but every single soldier who'd been holding us down, who'd been in that valley or by the edges of it, was already running.

Running to meet the seven-hundred-year-old men who had been just brought back from the dead, and who were marching in unison toward them.

I could hardly believe my eyes, and I'd have thought I'd lost my mind, had gone insane, or maybe that this was only happening in my imagination, except everybody else was seeing this, too. Everybody else was reacting the same way. I risked a glance at Radock, where he had been kneeling with his brothers, laughing like a maniac, and our eyes locked for a moment.

He saw, too. They all did.

Then there was magic. Colors of it, bright and beautiful and fucking *deadly*, this time coming from the soldiers. The soldiers who were moving together still, raising their hands at the same time, not with weapons but with magic.

IDD soldiers *fell*. Like their strings had been cut, they fell all over the ground, and there was no blood and no wounds that the eye could see, but none of them moved again. I couldn't really tell if they were breathing because the more of them fell, the better I saw the soldiers—the *dead* soldiers who were alive. The dead soldiers whose eyes were white spheres without a pupil or an iris, but who saw just fine as they broke formation and started to move in either direction as IDD soldiers kept attacking them with their magic—bullets were useless against them, it seemed. Whatever wards they wore on their skins couldn't be penetrated by them.

The magic hardly worked, too. The soldiers spread and fought those who attacked them, and more were coming, possibly over a hundred IDD men running into the valley while they shot their magic, but it wasn't enough. It *wouldn't be* enough, I realized.

And then I noticed four of them were coming toward me from all around the massacre going on right in front of my eyes. I was too shocked to speak, or to even make sense of this thing, but I somehow stood up, like my instincts insisted that I needed to protect myself from these creatures. I needed to move, to do something, run or fight—because they were coming for me.

Except they didn't.

Needless to say, I was too weak to even call up a spell, even if I'd had my father's ring on my finger. So, all I did was stand there as the soldiers—four of them wearing helmets, white marbles for eyes, and bracelets around their wrists—came for me, surrounded me on all sides, then...

Turned their backs to me.

Tears spilled down my eyes, though I'd been sure that I was too shocked to cry. The soldiers were *right there* within my reach, if I had enough control of my body to raise a hand right now. Their backs were turned to me and their hands were raised in front of them as they waited, completely motionless, for any IDD soldier who wanted to come and attack them.

Attack *me*.

My knees shook and I looked up at the sky, at Taland still standing there at the very edge of the landing, looking down at us. He saw everything and he stood there and waited, and I had no voice left in me to even whisper, let alone to call out his name again.

Goddess, this couldn't be happening, yet my eyes insisted that it was. My eyes insisted that the IDD soldiers were *retreating* and that at least fifty of them were on the ground, dead now, motionless. The rest who had tried to fight the Delaetus Army were moving back, out of the valley, around the mountain where we came from.

There, atop the edge was Helen Paine and the rest of the Council, and I could have sworn her eyes were on me. A part of me wished I had enough energy to give her my middle fingers. That fucking bitch! *Kill them all,* she'd said, and with such ease. *Kill them all,* after we'd risked our lives in this fight. After we'd almost died to stop Hill.

Look at us now.

She'd made Taland raise the dead fucking army himself.

She'd made Taland bring the Delaetus Army to life, and now four of them were around me like fucking robots, ready to kill anyone who dared to come close. Another dozen of them were practically *chasing* the IDD soldiers who were moving back up the incline of the valley as fast as they could, while the rest just stood there in the middle, in perfect formation, motionless, watching with their colorless eyes.

Too much.

Radock, Kaid, Seth—Zach was with them now, too, with Aurelia in his arms—and they were all smiling. Laughing. No soldiers had created walls around *them,* but they were surrounded by the bodies of the IDD ones who'd been keeping them down, had been about to kill them just moments ago.

Too much! my mind screamed, and I looked up again, hoping to see Taland, but the sky was almost completely black.

The solider to my right turned toward me, and his face —*my goddess, his face.* It shocked me and wiped my mind clean, and by the time he grabbed my arm, my legs had let go of me.

Whether I died right now or didn't made no difference to me in those moments. The darkness was pulling me under faster the better I felt those hands around my body— the hands of a man who'd been dead for seven hundred years.

In my mind, I screamed and thrashed and cried and ran.

In reality, I just let go again.

CHAPTER 14

Rosabel La Rouge

Birds sang—*what a nice sound to wake up to*, I thought.

The air was light going down my throat, and I could have sworn there was sunlight falling on the side of my face and on my shoulder, all the way down to my hip. I felt it, felt the heat like a soft, fuzzy blanket, and I wished I could move a little to my right just to feel it everywhere on my body as well. Except I was too lazy. Too tired. I just wanted to listen to the birds singing and sleep a little longer.

Or a lot.

I could really, really use this break, but even so, the memories started to come back to me slowly.

I remember how Taland had come through the doors in Madeline's office at the mansion, and how I'd thought for sure I was dreaming. How he'd sat there and basically saved me from the Council by bargaining what he knew.

I remembered him in my room, in my bed, naked and

delicious and smiling at me, his eyes full of light just like always when he was looking at me. When he was happy.

And I remembered him fighting beside me in that awful place, too, that looked like a construction site in a valley between mountains but wasn't. Nobody had constructed anything there—David Hill had dug up the ground to search for the skeletons of a dead army, and he'd actually found them.

I'd seen them, had fought him, had tasted the magic, his blood on my tongue, and dirt, dirt—all that dirt.

Then...

Kill them all.

Three words that rang in my ears and chased away the beautiful song of the birds. My eyes finally opened as my heart picked up the beating, and the pieces of the puzzle in my mind connected, and I finally saw the bigger picture. I finally saw where I was the last time I was awake, whose hands had been on me.

Armor, helmets, bracelets, white eyes—I sat up with a scream stuck in my throat that didn't even let me breathe properly now. I blinked my eyes possibly a thousand times to convince myself that I wasn't in that fucking *grave* between the mountains, but instead I was surrounded by trees and birds and sunlight.

And Taland.

It took me a moment to notice him standing not fifty feet away from me in a wide pathway between large, green trees, his back turned to me. It took me a moment to see where I was, understand that there was no danger near me anywhere, convince myself to allow the birdsong to calm me down a bit so I could think straight. The air was light here, indeed, and it smelled like flowers. I wasn't wearing my jacket, only my shirt and jeans, and most of the dirt and blood on my hands had been cleaned, but more remained. Under my nails, in the cracks of my skin. All of it remained to remind me of what had happened, as if to prove to me that all of it had really been real.

I sat up, reminding myself to breathe, to shake the numbness out of my hands, to not panic or fear because Taland was right there—alive and standing between those trees, looking out at something. And I was alive, too. Though my limbs were weak and numb with anxiety, I didn't think I felt any pain, at least right now.

My clothes, though. Goddess, they were a mess of dirt and blood, and the memories of how I came to be covered in so much blood were right there suddenly, at the center of my mind. It was like I was reliving the whole thing all over again, like I had my arms wrapped around Hill, like he *exploded* between them and threw me off the damn landing.

A muffled cry escaped my lips before I could catch it with my hands, but it was loud enough in the quiet of this forest we were in.

Taland heard.

Taland turned and looked at me.

A whole new kind of terror took hold of my body and mind and heart.

My eyes rolled in my skull and I passed out again.

Minutes, or maybe years later, I came to. Felt the slow breeze, and the sunlight now on more than half my body. The birds were still singing, and the air was still featherlight.

My mind still insisted that what I'd seen—minutes or years ago—was real.

Taland with his hair back and his skin pale and his eyes white.

The same shock and fear pulled me awake violently, and again, I sat up, hands to my heart to keep it inside my ribcage. It wanted to fly out right now—*right now*. It wanted to stop beating, too, with the same intensity.

Taland was sitting about ten feet away on the wooden railing of what was a porch to a house I'd never seen before, with large trees and large leaves falling all over the roof and the pillars. The top of the railing was as thick as a bench, probably on purpose, and that's where I was lying, too, though on the other side of the low stairs that led to the porch.

On the other side, so far away from him, yet I could still see with perfectly clarity that his eyes were white.

Like white spheres, white marbles stuck to his skull. No color. No iris. No pupil. Nothing but white.

"Baby, don't be afraid of me."

If he'd have slapped me in that moment, I'd have probably been less surprised.

"You...you..." I shook my head, swallowed to wet my throat. "You're a *damn fool*."

When I made to move, to stand up from that railing, I didn't actually think my legs would hold me, but they did. When I walked as fast as I could I didn't actually think that I'd ever make it all the way to Taland, who had also stood up and was looking at me like he expected me to fall unconscious again.

Tears streamed from my eyes when I wrapped my arms around his neck and fell against his chest and I held him to me with all the strength I could muster. He was alive and it was *him*—his face and his voice and his warmth. He'd made it. *We'd* made it. Somehow, in some fucked up way, we'd actually made it and we were here, wherever *here* was.

He kissed my hair and buried his face on my neck and breathed in the scent of me like I smelled better than the air. The birds sang louder, and they came closer and sounded more cheerful—or maybe it was just me. We stayed there for a good, long moment, soaking up each other's warmth, allowing our hearts and minds to calm down for a bit.

"You passed out," Taland whispered eventually, and I could have laughed.

"You have white eyes."

"I thought you were afraid." And he sounded *horrified* by the fact.

"I *am*." I let go of him to lean back a little, to see his face, half of me sure that I'd only imagined it, that his eyes would be the same as always. Dark and rich with color and secrets and sparks that could make the stars jealous.

They weren't.

"Of course, I'm afraid, Taland. You have white eyes!" As if he needed me to remind him...

He squeezed them shut and shook his head, a ghost of a smile on his lips. "I thought you were afraid *of me*."

This time I did laugh even if the sound was awful and chased the birds nearby away. "I figured that much when I didn't wake up in your arms, asshole." I rose on my tiptoes and kissed his lips, both to feel him all the way and to ease this terror that had gripped me by the throat.

"I'm sorry, sweetness. I...I didn't know how you'd react," he whispered, and his eyes were still closed as he caressed my cheeks and pushed my hair back.

"Look at me," I said, and it took him a while to open his eyes. It took him a while to *look* at me.

I couldn't even tell you how I knew that he could see me when his eyes really were purely white. I couldn't tell you how I knew that I was at the center of his focus, but I did. I *felt* it.

I shook my head, battling that terror still. "*Why* are your eyes white, Taland?" I sounded breathless because I was.

Again, he closed his eyes and tried to lower his head, maybe because he still thought I was afraid of him. "No, don't!" I said and pushed his chin back up again. "I'm not afraid of you, Taland. I couldn't care less what color your eyes are, but I need to know that you're okay." That I even had to tell him that was ridiculous, but right now neither of us were really thinking straight.

He smiled again and it looked painful. "I'm fine. I promise, I'm fine," he said.

"Then tell me why. Can you...*see*?" I thought he could, but I still needed to hear him say it.

"Better than ever, actually. I can see every color of your hair. Every speck in your eyes. Every single freckle that my normal eyes missed." His hands were on my face and he traced his thumb on my skin like he really was witnessing wonder.

"How?"

"I..." He shook his head. "I lost it, sweetness. They were going to kill you. They were holding you down and I couldn't stop them. I couldn't get there in time—and even if I could, I wouldn't have been able to do anything against them on my own. So I just...lost it. The spell was there. I picked it up and I chanted. I didn't think—whether it would work or not, I didn't think."

Again, that bitter laughter came out of me—poor birds. "You...you brought back an army of dead soldiers for me." And wasn't that just fucking *wonderful*?!

He touched his forehead to mine. "I'll bring the sky down for you, too, if you want."

All those tears that slipped out of my eyes made my view of him blurry. "Let's just leave the sky alone for now."

He kissed me with his breath held and his whole body frozen, like he, too, wished we could just stop right there forever, in that moment, in that place. But we couldn't stop time, unfortunately for us, and so eventually, we had to face the voices in our heads. We had to face our reality.

"Talk to me," I said, my lips against his still, our hands on each other. "Where are we? What happened at Perria? Where are the others?"

The images flashed in front of my eyes as I spoke—of the Council and his brothers, and Zach carrying Aurelia in his arms.

"We're in another Selem safe house, the only one they have on a mountain that I know about. We're on Mount Rhoden in Virginia, about two hours away from Perria," Taland said. "The others are all alive. I made sure the IDD and the Council were gone before I left them and took you away."

Took me away.

I stepped back, the feel of those hands around my arms suddenly in the center of my mind. "Where...where..." I couldn't even bring myself to ask, but Taland knew exactly what I was trying to say, so he answered.

"They're here," he said, and how was I still standing?

"They're *here,*" I repeated, just to make sure I'd gotten it right.

He nodded. "They're...around."

I drew in a deep breath. "I—" *want to see them,* I was going say, to go against every single instinct in my body and say those words that were absolutely not true. I *didn't want* to see any dead soldiers come back to life. I didn't. Not now and not ever.

Except I knew I had to.

Taland cut me off, though. "Shower first. You're covered in his blood and I can't keep looking at it. Then we eat."

Goddess, the relief I felt could have been funny.

"*His* blood," I said—again, just repeating it because I was too scared to even say his name.

Taland nodded and stepped back, took my hand in his. "Hill's blood." I could have sworn those eyes darkened when he said his name, or maybe it was just my imagination.

Goddess, it was so strange to look at him like that. His entire face had changed. Had become...less human. I always knew that eyes made the most difference, but I'd never seen a face like this before.

Well, except for those soldiers...

"He's dead."

"He exploded."

"Cheining," I said with a sigh—one of the most brutal kill spells out there.

"The bracelet worked for the both of us at the same time," Taland said, raising his right hand to show me that the bracelet, in fact, was right there. And he was just as dirty as me. He hadn't showered, and I would bet anything that he hadn't eaten without me, either.

"Is it the same?" I asked because those soldiers had had bracelets around their wrists, too, and they'd called up magic—*without chanting,* if I recalled correctly.

"Kind of," Taland said, but before I could ask what that meant, he added, "Let's shower and put on some clean clothes first."

Again, that relief.

"What time is it?" I asked, and the wooden doors engraved with pretty flowers and chipped paint in all colors were right there in front of us now. Taland pushed them open, and I looked back at the trees surrounding us on all sides, but luckily, they'd didn't let me see very far in case those dead soldiers were there somewhere. *Around,* like Taland said.

"Just after eight in the morning," he said. "Welcome to this safe house, sweetness."

Shivers ran down my back. Those words awakened another memory in me, so when he walked inside the house, I remained outside still and said, "Do you promise to not disappear on me for any reason in the world while we're here?"

His lips stretched into a wide smile. Those eyes made him look like a fucking alien for a moment.

"I promise, baby. I am *never* going to disappear on you again for any reason in the world."

I released a long breath, both because of how he looked, and what he said. "Good. Then it's good to be here." It really, *really* was.

The house, just like the first safe house of Selem he'd taken me to, was on the smaller side. Here, the hallways were wider, full of light, the walls dotted with small windows everywhere. The rooms were bigger, too, and it smelled clean even though the furniture was covered in white sheets. Taland didn't stop in the three rooms across from one another that we passed, but when we turned the corner, he headed for the wooden doors at the end of the corridor.

The bathroom was unlike any I'd ever seen, and I stopped by the door again to take it in. Half of it was outside, and those big branches and leaves curved over the low wall that surrounded the bathtub area. Birds and geckos on the walls, rushing away at the sound of us. On the left was the toilet, the shower on the right.

"It's safe," Taland said. "I checked every inch of this place. We're safe. The wards are working. Nobody can get to us, baby, I promise."

I stepped inside on the dark grey tiles. "It's not that. It's just...*wow*. I've never seen a half-open bathroom before."

"This whole place is very beautiful. I'll show you my favorite spot later," Taland said, and maybe it was just the exhaustion he must've been feeling, but his voice was duller than normal. It lacked the excitement he spoke with normally.

"Are you wounded?" I asked when he began to pull my shirt off.

"No. I've done healing spells."

He threw my shirt back and began to unbutton my jeans. I touched the bracelet around his wrist, and he reacted instantly. Looked up at me—again, it was so fucking weird that he had *white* eyes, and weirder yet that I could feel it when he was focused on me. "What?"

"Nothing," he said, then moved behind me to unclasp my bra.

I looked to the side. "Did you just freeze because I touched the bracelet, Taland?" Because it seemed to me like he did.

A deep sigh escaped him, and he rested his forehead to the top of my head. "I'll explain everything later."

"No, not later." I turned to face him again. "If you're going to tell me that you've turned into a power-hungry asshole and you now won't let anybody even touch that thing or take it—"

He raised his hand, took the bracelet off, *threw* it in the marble sink near the toilet.

"I *am* an asshole, but not a power-hungry one. And I don't care about anybody touching that thing as long as *you* don't."

I flinched until the bracelet settled on the marble and stopped making so much damn noise.

"Meaning?"

"Meaning it's dangerous." I opened my mouth to argue, to ask, but he didn't even let me. "Shower. *Now*."

It was a damn order, and my body had a way of obeying him without much caring about what *I* thought on the matter. So, before I knew it, I was standing under the shower while he was kneeling in front of me, taking my boots and my jeans off, and lastly, my panties.

His hands moved up my legs, and I could have sworn that he looked at every inch of my body as if for the first time, even if he had no pupils for me to be able to even tell where his focus was.

Talking now would be pointless—he'd just insist on waiting, and to be honest, when he turned the water on, I no longer felt the need to want to know everything *right now*. I just stayed under the shower and allowed myself a moment to breathe while the water washed away most of the dirt and dry blood, and I watched Taland take his own clothes off and join me. It wasn't sexual, that moment—at least not as sexual as usual, and we just hugged each other for a good long while, rocking slightly from side to side, then in slow circles.

"What's going on, Taland?" I said after a while. The words slipped from me almost accidentally because I was still trying to pretend that my tears weren't actual tears, just water from the shower pouring on us.

"Things...escalated," Taland whispered, then kissed the top of my head.

"You brought a dead army back to life."

"They tricked us. Betrayed us. Which I saw coming, but I thought they wouldn't act while we were still on the battlefield." His hold around me tightened as he remembered.

And I remembered, too. I remembered that bitch Helen Paine when she gave that order—*kill them all.*

Goddess, if I was ever face-to-face with that woman again...

"My grandmother basically told me she wanted me to become the director of the IDD when we came back." More tears. "I wonder if she knew. If she just said it to throw me off, to distract me from what was coming for me."

"Does it matter?" Taland asked.

Unfortunately it does, I thought. "It doesn't," I said.

"I'm going to rub this dirt off us now, baby. Can you just stand there under the shower for me?" said Taland, stepping back. And I pretended he thought it was just water on my cheeks, not tears, too.

"When we're done, we're going to sit down and eat, and we're going to talk, okay?"

Not like I had any choice, but I nodded anyway.

Then I stood there and cried in silence while Taland scrubbed every inch of my skin clean, then proceeded to clean himself, too, until the water turned cold. We used the old towels that kinda smelled like rain on the rack near the door, and finally, when I dared to look at myself in the mirror over the sink, I was clean.

No dirt, no blood, just me.

I didn't cry again.

~

We got dressed in clothes we found in the rooms. The brown pants and white shirt I had on were a size too big, but they worked just fine because neither of us wanted to wash or dry the same clothes we'd fought in. I'd rather wear anything else.

Taland dried our washed boots and socks, and then he took us to the kitchen, which had a large glass door on the third wall that slid open to let you out onto another narrower porch that wrapped around half the house.

From there, I could see just how far up we really were, and the mountain on the side of which this house was built was so incredibly green—and steeper than I realized. I could make out no sign of civilization—not even a road in the distance.

The food wasn't ideal—canned tuna and frozen vegetables that Taland put in an air fryer, but there was plenty of it, at least, and our full bellies had us feeling a bit closer to *normal* within the hour.

But even after we ate, we just sat there on the chairs by the dining table that Taland had dragged to the porch, and we looked out at the view, at the green trees and the clear blue sky. We breathed in the air and listened to the birdsong.

We just existed in those moments, with no attachment to the past or future. That was all we had.

Unfortunately, it was time to get back to reality once more.

"It's probably too late to say this, but you *really* shouldn't have done that," I said after a long time.

Taland chuckled—it brought out my smile.

He continued to chuckle, and so, of course. I joined him

ten seconds in. We laughed together at the utter absurdity of our situation. What a fucking nightmare...

"I don't regret it, though," Taland said eventually.

"Not even the part where your eyes turned white?" I said, to tease him, but I was also genuinely curious.

"Not even that part, no," he said, and again, he sounded so...*depressed*. I wasn't used to it. In fact, I hated it.

I reached for his hand across the table. "You did what you had to do."

"I did," he said. "I am *not* going to let anybody near you again. Nobody deserves to even be in your presence, let alone order an end to your life."

Is it wrong that I loved him for saying that?

Yes, probably. But did it make me feel like the most important person in the world? Also, *yes,* so...

I just changed the subject. "It's the Council—what the hell did we expect?"

"Oh, I expected them to turn on us, just not right away."

"The same second Hill died," I said, flinching at the memory. They hadn't waited for us to even go back to Headquarters, or the city, or even to our fucking cars.

"I'm glad for it. If we'd gone back, I couldn't have stopped them."

I looked at him. "If we'd gone back, we'd have had a chance to escape. You wouldn't have had to..." The words didn't come because I had no idea exactly what Taland had done—or rather, what *it* had done to Taland. "Can you explain it to me? How could you just...*awaken* them? What exactly does that mean? Are they...*yours* now? At your command?" *And what the hell were you thinking, getting yourself in this kind of trouble?!* was what I didn't say because I didn't want to make it harder on him.

After all, he'd done all of this to protect *me*. And needless to say, I'd have done the exact same thing in his shoes.

Taland took a moment to think as we looked out at the trees. Goddess, it was so peaceful here, I never wanted to leave this place. But then again, I suspected the key element to many places I never wanted to leave was his presence.

"Hill employed the soul vessels he'd collected," he eventually started, and I had to interrupt him already.

"I still have no idea what exactly that means." And I couldn't wait to start learning about magic—*for real*. Not what they taught us in high school or the IDD training academy—for everything magic could actually do.

"He basically gave an energy source for the soldiers to latch onto, to come back to life, something to *use* to...exist. Those little lights he sent into them contained *life energy*, and through it the soldiers could recover everything death took from them through the centuries. Flesh and blood and skin—and a functioning mind."

I flinched, both because the explanation made sense—our souls were what kept *us* alive, too—and because it didn't. Because how in the world could a soul still work on seven-hundred-year-old skeletons?

"He had everything prepared, thought through every single detail, and sweetness..." he squeezed my hand until I looked at him, and it was still a shock to see those eyes. So strange. Beautiful, but so damn strange. "He would have succeeded if you hadn't stolen that bracelet."

Heat rushed to my cheeks. "I didn't even know what the hell I was doing," I muttered because it was strange to be complimented for *theft*, too.

"My little criminal," Taland said with a grin that didn't last, but it was the exact same grin as always, and I appreciated it. It reassured me that he was okay still, just...a bit changed.

"Like I said—he had everything prepared. They even found the bones of Titus, the same guy who *made* them with his curse, together with the spell to basically call them to service. He planted the bones *onto* each soldier before he planted the soul vessels, and so the army was actually capable of moving and performing magic exactly like before. Then all he needed was the actual magic to make his call."

"The call *you* made instead."

"The spell wasn't complicated, believe it or not. Very standard necromancy, not even close to what Hill did to plant the soul vessels on them," Taland said.

"And where are those spells now?" I dared to ask.

"Burned them; all three of them," he said. "Destroyed the Script of Perria, too, though I suppose it's useless now. The Army isn't there anymore."

I closed my eyes for a moment. "So...it really happened. You really...*really* awakened the Delaetus Army."

"I did," Taland said.

"Why are your eyes as white as theirs?" This I asked in barely a whisper, and when Taland flinched, I added, "Not that I care about the color of your eyes, Taland, but I want to know what it did to you. I want to...I want to know the side effects." Because no magic came without cost. That much we'd known since forever.

"I..." Taland paused for a good long moment. "I *hear* them, sweetness."

My stomach dropped all the way to my heels. "Hear them how?"

Taland stood up. "Come on. Let me show you."

CHAPTER 15

Rosabel La Rouge

When Taland said that the soldiers of the Delaetus Army were *around,* he meant it literally, it seemed. Because we walked out the front of the house and down the wide pathway between those gorgeous trees for a minute or two, and then we saw them.

They were standing *all around* the land where that house was built, with their backs turned to it and their eyes closed, as still as the trees at their sides.

Goddess, they were in perfect formation, creating a wall of bodies all around the house, leaving barely enough space for us to fit through between them.

I didn't think I'd ever seen a stranger thing in my life.

We said nothing, Taland and I, as we went to their front and we analyzed them. Or rather *I* analyzed them while Taland watched me and focused on anything else around us every now and again, as if looking at these soldiers made him uncomfortable.

Goddess, I understood why. These men looked so *real,* yet unusual at the same time because their eyes were closed and they *weren't breathing.* How strange it was to see a being that looked alive but didn't breathe, I realized. I had never before known how much I *saw* people breathing without realizing it, or maybe I just noticed the absence of those slight chest movements much more than I ever thought I would.

Their skin looked like normal, ordinary skin, and even though at first glance they'd all looked the same, they weren't. Different heights and different builds, different skin tones and different hair on their chests and forearms and brows that I could only barely see through the copper-colored helmets.

The swords strapped to their hips were huge, and they looked really heavy. Their armor plates were made of the same metal, which looked light and smooth through patches of dirt here and there. They wore brown pants and armor plates around their hips and groin area, too, and their brown leather boots looked a million years old, with metal on the tip of their toes as well as their shins. Their arms were naked from the shoulders down, save for leather gloves and the bracelets on their left wrists.

They weren't *exactly* the same, though. The metal of it—yes. The color was exactly the same, and the image of it, like dried mud, was identical, but these bracelets were thinner and they were sealed shut—like cuffs. I couldn't see a key lock anywhere—like the metal had hardened around their wrists like that and they could never be taken off again, which made me wonder.

"Can I touch them?" I asked Taland—too curious, even if the request did sound a bit ridiculous.

"Of course," Taland said without hesitation. "You never

have to fear any of them, sweetness. Their sole purpose now is to protect you."

That made me feel all kinds of weird things, but I didn't let myself dwell on his words for long. I slowly reached out my hand and touched the bracelet of one of them, my eyes on his face.

"*Fuck,*" I breathed when a second passed and his didn't open. They remained shut—they all continued to look like they were carved out of marble or wax or something with those still chests.

But the feel of their bracelets was exactly the same as the one I'd stolen from the Vault. The only difference remained their width and the fact that theirs were closed—and *tightly* around their wrists, impossible to take off without breaking them or cutting their hands off.

"How many?" I asked Taland as I moved around the soldier one more time, this time touching his back and his arms and his armor plates as I went, his chin and cheeks—*so terribly real*—and his helmet, too. The guy didn't even flinch.

"Thirty," Taland said.

"I thought there'd be more."

"There were. A hundred and twenty in total. The others were destroyed in the War of Mages," Taland said. "These ones who remained were sort of...*deactivated* by Titus's death."

"They're all men," I said in wonder.

"They are," said Taland. "Seven hundred years ago I don't think they taught a lot of women combat. Titus needed men who were very good at hand-to-hand, as well as magic."

Again, I circled the soldier I was basically studying.

"They're not really *alive* though." They weren't breathing, yet they were still standing. *How very strange...*

"They are puppets, sweetness. That's it—they're puppets." This he said as if the words were being cut out of his very soul.

"How so?" I asked because I wanted him to choose what to tell me himself, hoping that would make this whole thing easier on him. It was obvious that he was...*struggling* with something.

He turned around, turned his back on both me and the soldiers. He seemed to be more at ease when they weren't in his line of vision at all, and I didn't mind. I went to stand beside him.

"If you don't want to talk about it," I started, even though I wanted to know so badly.

"I always want to talk to you about everything," Taland said, and my heart tripped all over itself. I wrapped my arm around his and rested my head on his shoulder, waited until he thought about what to say.

"I...hear them."

"Yes, but how?" He'd said so before and I had no idea what he meant when the soldiers were so perfectly silent.

"In here." He reached up his fingers and touched his temple. "I hear their voices. It's...I don't know how to explain it, but they're *talking* to me."

Every inch of my skin rose in goose bumps. "Taland, you're scaring me." I wrapped my arms around his tighter.

"It's nothing to be afraid of—I just hear their thoughts, that's all. I hear their voices. It's like we're...connected on a deeper level."

"You mean like *mentally?*"

"Mentally, too."

Too, he said. "But that...that's..." *What?!*

I had no word for something as twisted, as scary, as fucking *impossible* as this.

"The curse," Taland said, lowering his head. "That's the curse, sweetness. This thing—this whole thing is not what we thought it was. It's more, so much more." His eyes squeezed shut, and he clenched his jaws so hard his teeth popped. "He *tethered* these people's souls to his own. He linked them to his mind, to his magic."

"Like...bonding?"

Taland turned to me, suddenly excited, and said, "Yes, exactly. Exactly like bonding."

And suddenly I understood him better.

Even though only Greenfire mages were able to bond with familiars, I had experienced the whole thing in the Iris Roe, too. Whether it had been fake or real, I was made to bond to that vulcera, and the emptiness her disappearance had left me with was still there. I doubted it was ever going to go away. *She* was still with me every time I closed my eyes to sleep. Every time I through of *green*. Every time I didn't know what I missed, until I remembered her face.

"But you can't bond with *people*," I said, trying to make sense still. "And Titus was Whitefire, right?"

Taland nodded. "Laetus, but his primary color was White. But all Laetus could bond if they chose to, sweetness. And when he created this curse, his basis was the bonding ritual. That's the very foundation of this...connection." It sounded like he was figuring all of this out, too, as he spoke.

"Fuck, Taland," I whispered, throwing a look back at the soldiers—they hadn't moved a single inch. Not even a little bit. "I don't get it. *How* are they able to *be alive* without actually being alive? They don't breathe—do their hearts beat?"

"Magic," Taland said. "They function solely on magic. The curse is a sort of self-maintaining system. It uses magic to produce magic—it all started with the initial burst. That's all Hill needed to bring them back—a burst of Laetus magic."

"The bracelet. Just the bracelet," I said, shaking my head over and over.

"Just the bracelet," he confirmed.

"But...but he *wasn't* Mud, was he? He wasn't Laetus. It wouldn't have worked for him!"

Taland thought about it for a moment. "Unless he had already drained himself, turned Mud. Then consumed a massive amount of energy to fire himself up—like you did with the Rainbow."

"You think?" Because I had a very hard time picturing someone like David Hill rendering his own magic useless and counting on someone else to help him get it back. I had only been able to drain the Rainbow because of Taland. Whom did Hill have that he could trust so fully, I wondered?

Was it Madeline?

"I think so based on his behavior," Taland said. "Think about it—he had everything else prepared. When he told you he was going to *need his bracelet,* he seemed very certain that he could make it work. I don't know—he just did everything else exactly right, and he would have known that he *couldn't* reactivate the curse without Laetus magic. That's why he even had that bracelet in the Vault to begin with."

And it absolutely made sense. Sounded like Hill. *Exactly* like Hill.

"All these years he went behind everybody's back," I whispered, closing my eyes for a moment, trying to get the image of his face away from my thoughts. Impossible.

"And he was incredibly smart about it. Gathered everything he needed, put it in the Vault. Not only did he make everything look *legal,* hid it in plain sight, but he ensured the best security system and countless trained soldiers would be there to keep it safe." Taland shook his head. "The only part of his plan that went astray was *us,*" he whispered. "He couldn't foresee that we'd fall in love."

Goddess, how I loved those three words.

"I think I know why he *chose me* that day, and not Poppy. I think he thought I was too damaged, too closed up to allow anybody in." That's why he'd showed me those pictures of my parents, and why he'd asked me if I was sad or happy. I'd said no and he'd believed me. Or at least he didn't know how I really felt.

So, in the end, maybe my ability to play a rock *did* help me. It didn't doom me—it saved me. Saved us all from him.

"He had a plan for everything," said Taland in wonder.

"Imagine that kind of dedication to his actual fucking job," I spit. He'd have made the world a better place for real if he'd spent all that energy being the actual IDD Director, instead of plotting to take over the world.

"He's dead," he said, as if he was reminding himself, too. "He's gone—that's all that matters."

"Except now you're stuck with thirty dead guys who live off magic, not air, and you have white eyes, and I have *no clue* what we're going to do next!" I laughed—couldn't even tell you why. The pressure, the fear, the paranoia?

But the bitter sound was cut off abruptly when something moved to my side.

I turned, heart in my throat, but Taland said, "*It's okay,*" before I started screaming.

Because one of the soldiers who'd been perfectly motionless until now, standing in line with his eyes closed, was walking down the mountain. His eyes were open and as white as I remembered, as white as Taland's, and he stepped out of the formation and continued to walk ahead like we weren't there at all. He must have been six foot seven, shoulders as wide as most tree trunks in this place, yet you could barely hear his footfalls on the forest floor as he moved. Walked, just like normal people, even though he was everything but.

That my heart didn't leave my body was a miracle.

"What...what...what the hell?" I finally managed when the soldier went too far for me to see or hear, and then I turned halfway to the others, expecting them to come alive and open their eyes, too.

None did, though.

"Someone's close to the wards down the mountain," Taland said. "He's going to check to make sure they go away."

I shook my head again. "Are you serious?"

"They have our location. I wasn't trying to hide," Taland said. "They've come before—twice now. It's fine."

I stepped away from him and looked down at the trees, laughing like a fucking lunatic. "Who?! Who the hell is— *who?*"

"The Council, the IDD. Soldiers, agents," Taland said, hands in his pockets as he looked at me with his white eyes.

"*And?* What happened?!"

"Nothing. They realized they can't get through, and they walked away. They're gonna keep coming back for a little while longer, I suspect, before they leave us alone for good. They'll want to make sure that we stay here, I suppose." And he was awfully calm about it. Not in the way that Taland was usually calm, no—it was a different calm, one I didn't like at all.

With my eyes closed, I took in a deep breath and I tried to get my shit together. I really tried.

"What if they come through?" I asked in a whisper, but Taland had come closer to me so he heard.

"They won't. *Can't.*"

"But...but..." I didn't even know what to say. Fuck, I was freaking out and I didn't even know how to stop.

Luckily, Taland did.

He grabbed my face in his hands and came close until the tips of our noses touched, and even though his eyes hadn't changed, hadn't gained their colors back, in my mind I saw them for how they really were.

"Breathe with me, baby," he whispered. "Breathe with me."

So, we did.

I breathed and I forced myself to cling to him, to let him ground me like always. To calm me down.

"Who does this for you, by the way?" I ended up asking after a little while, as if that made any difference. But it was the perfect distraction because I'd always been curious to know. He always calmed me down, but who calmed him?

"You do," Taland said. "When you breathe."

"No, I mean—"

He grinned and it was a glimpse of the old Taland that stopped my heart for a second. "I know what you mean, baby. When I ask you to breathe with me, I do it for *my* benefit, too. When you're okay, I'm okay."

This guy.

I rose on my tiptoes and kissed his lips with all my being, and fuck, it felt good. It felt *great* to be wrapped up in his arms and to have him squeezing me to his chest as he deepened the kiss, to hear the soft moans that came from him, to be reminded of what mattered.

Him. Us. Forever.

And then I also remembered that there were dead and sort-of alive soldiers from the past standing in a perfect line just a few feet away from us.

I moved back, eyes on them, expecting to find them moving, watching us. They didn't.

Taland shook his head. "They are not going to move— and if they do, they will do so to *protect* you."

"I know, I know. It's just so new," I said, closing my eyes for a moment. "You're incredibly comfortable around them, though." He hadn't once glanced at them at all.

"I am. You should be, too." And I believed him. I did.

But I still turned and looked for where that solider had gone off to, to see if he'd returned. "Where is he?"

"Still down there," Taland said, wrapping his arms around me from behind, resting his chin on my shoulder.

"Do you think he maybe needs backup?" I wondered.

"If he does, they'll know." He didn't need to explain that he meant the other soldiers.

"How? We can't see him from here—and all their eyes are closed."

Taland thought about it for a moment, then said, "We can all sort of see through each other."

That gave me a good pause. "I don't...get it."

"They see through my eyes. We all see through that soldier's. If he needs something, we all know—*they* know. It's like...a network," Taland said. "I still don't understand how it works exactly, but think about it this way: we're all connected to the same computer, if you will. The same curse."

I turned my head to him, and he kissed my cheek. "So, you're all...*one?*"

"I think so," Taland said. "Though I can *give orders* to them without really needing to say anything, just think it. Just...*want* it. I tested this since I brought you here," he said. "If I think about them doing pushups, they do pushups. If I think about them jumping up and down, they do. Hours ago, I thought about them standing here in a perfect half circle around the house, keeping watch, feeling the wards of this safe house, and here they are."

"Goddess, Taland, that's incredible."

"It's...heavy," he said. "Crowded."

My stomach sank. "Your mind?"

Taland nodded. "I'm...not alone anymore. Not for a second."

"What are they saying?"

He didn't tell me for a little while, and when he did, I knew he was being as vague as possible on purpose. "Just things. Images, flashes of who they used to be. What they used to see."

"You can't make it stop?"

"I'm trying, sweetness," he said, and the soldier who'd gone to check on whatever danger was out there seemed to just *materialize* between the trees and went back to his place without ever even glancing our way. He turned around, kept his arms loose to the sides and closed his eyes —and it was like he'd never even moved in the first place.

"Are they gone?" I dared to ask.

"Yes," Taland said. "Nobody's out there right now. Wanna—"

"Go inside, yes," I cut him off. "Let's go inside."

When we turned, the two soldiers who'd been directly

behind us opened their eyes, stepped out of the line and moved back just a couple feet.

"They're just making way," Taland whispered, eyes on me. "I know they're making you uncomfortable."

"You just thought about them making way?" He nodded. "And they just *heard* that? Just like that?"

"Yep," said Taland, trying to wave me off like it wasn't a big deal, even though he knew it was.

My goddess. Thirty super soldiers who were connected to your own mind and all you had to do was *think* something to get them moving?

Yeah, it was a big deal, all right. Maybe that's why I laughed all the way back to that house again.

CHAPTER 16

Rosabel La Rouge

We went straight to bed together because I didn't want to sit and watch the trees and the sky anymore. I did want to hear the birds, so Taland pulled a window up just a bit and put the thick curtain halfway over it. Plenty of light came through to the bed. Not the most comfortable bed, but Taland was there with his warmth and his muscles and his satin-smooth skin, so you wouldn't find me complaining. I made a pillow out of his shoulder, and he had an arm wrapped around me to make sure I couldn't move if I tried. With his other hand, he touched my face and caressed my hair, my arm, played with my fingers over his chest while they traced the shape of my favorite tattoo on him. The tallarose, which was *us*.

We stayed like that for a long time, just listening to each other breathing, listening to the birds, *adjusting* to this new reality we seemed to be facing. Out of all the things that I *never* saw coming in my life, being on a mountain with

Taland while a small army of super-soldiers guarded us was at the top of my list—*for now.* The Iris Roe or the Regah chamber or anything else couldn't compare.

Yet as I listened to his heart beating so close to my ear, I began to feel more and more at ease. I began to realize what it meant that David Hill was dead, and the Devil was possibly dead, too, and the Council knew where we were, yes—but what exactly could they do about it?

"We're okay," Taland said, and he said it like he just came to the realization, the same as me.

"Apparently we are," I said in wonder. "Apparently we're *really* okay." As much as my paranoia insisted that there had to be loopholes, that we couldn't just *be here* at peace and not worry when we were both fugitives and the Council knew where we were, I couldn't deny this.

Once more, when I started laughing at the sheer absurdity of this whole thing, he did, too. So that's how we ended up laughing our hearts out in bed, possibly scaring away the birds outside the window that could hear us, but that was okay, too.

I had tears in my eyes a minute in, and the bed was shaking with our bodies, and Taland pulled me up higher so he could see my face, look into my eyes with his white ones. Just now, I wasn't startled. Just now, I *expected* them to be white. It was Taland, no matter what colors he wore. And him I *felt* more than saw.

"Apparently we are," he repeated in a soft whisper, holding my face in his hands, smiling—for real this time.

"I love you so much it hurts," I blurted because it was the truth and it was the only truth that mattered.

For a moment, Taland froze, looked up at me like he didn't even understand what those words meant.

"Even now?"

I shook my head, in awe of how utterly silly he could be sometimes. I lowered my head until the tips of our noses touched, and said, "Especially now, Taland. And especially tomorrow, and especially the day after. Through summer breezes and fucking hurricanes."

His eyes closed like he was suddenly relieved. When I kissed his lips, he let me. He just lay there with his eyes closed and let me plant little kisses all over his face for as long as he needed to convince himself that just because his eyes were white, nothing had changed between us. On the contrary—I felt him more than ever before.

Then his hands moved down my back and to my waist, and he squeezed me to him harder until a moan ripped out of me.

Now that I'd calmed down and accepted that this was our life, I could move that doubt and that paranoia out of the way and focus on him completely. On his body under mine. On his hands, the way his fingers dug into my back. Of his breathing that became faster with every new kiss I planted on his skin.

Then he raised his hips and his cock touched my leg— hard. Unsurprising because I was already wet between my legs, too.

Suddenly, Taland moved. I screamed when my back hit the mattress and he was on top of me, eagerly waiting for my mouth to open so he could stick his tongue in my throat and kiss me until nothing else but him remained in my mind.

"I heard you, baby. Loud and clear," Taland said as he sucked my lips between his teeth and bit them. "Now I'm going to show you exactly how much I love you—*especially* now."

I moaned again, and my whole body came alive at his

words, so I raised my hips to meet his. When he pushed them down and let me feel all of his hard cock, I swear I touched the fucking sky with my hands.

"What do you say, sweetness? Would you like that?"

"Yes," I breathed, rubbing against his cock as well as the position allowed. "Please, yes..."

He leaned his head back just a little and looked at me with those strange eyes that were becoming more and more beautiful to me every new time I saw them. Maybe because I was beginning to understand them, too, the way I always understood his real ones.

"Have I ever told you how much I love it when you beg for me?" he asked.

But before I could tell him that he had and that I loved that he loved it, Taland slammed his lips to mine again and kissed all the air out of my lungs. From that moment, all I knew how to do with my mouth and voice was scream and moan and sometimes whisper his name in pure bliss.

He continued to kiss me furiously as he took the clothes we'd borrowed off our bodies—mine first, then his. Meanwhile I couldn't stop touching him, playing with his hair, rubbing the short stubble on his cheek that had just begun to grow out. Goddess, he felt so good it was no wonder that the whole world hung on him for me. I couldn't get enough. The way his tongue felt in my mouth as it devoured me, the way he moaned when I sucked on it with all my strength, only made my appetite grow.

When he rose on his elbows to play with my boobs, I pushed him to the side and climbed on top of him, burning with need.

Taland grinned, and those white eyes gave him an even more devilish look that had me fucking *dripping* even before I sat up and rubbed my pussy against his hard cock. Fuck, what a feeling. To be looking at his perfect face, to be touched by him with such passion, such desire, to move my hips on the length on him until I almost came—what a fucking feeling.

"Keep moving," Taland whispered, and I didn't have the brain cells to form words, so I just obeyed and while he played with my boobs, slapped them and rubbed my nipples, twisted them between his fingers.

"Come closer," he then ordered, and I fell on my hands while he dragged himself lower until his mouth was on my nipples.

He bit hard. I screamed harder. His fingers were on my pussy, thumb on my clit, while he thrust a couple in and out of me fast.

I was close, too close, but I needed him in my mouth first, so I moved back.

"Sweetness," he warned with a growl, but I pushed him down and I moved lower on the bed on all fours, kissing his lips and chin, his chest and stomach, and finally the pink tip of his cock.

There was no patience left with me—I was *this* close to falling over the edge, so I didn't tease him, couldn't take my time with it. I just made myself comfortable between his legs and I took him in my mouth all at once until he touched the back of my throat and blocked my airway.

Fuck, yes, I thought, and Taland held my head down with his hand and thrust his hips up to stay in my mouth for a good moment, until I almost choked.

Then he let me move at my own rhythm like he knew I needed to taste him thoroughly before he fucked me. Pulling my hair away from my face, he held it up over my head and watched, his head up, his eyes on my mouth as his cock filled it. He watched me like a man possessed, and seconds in I couldn't even tell you what color his eyes were, if they looked strange or not—I was used to them. His attention was on me and that's all I cared about as I sucked on him to please us both—and to give him a show.

It worked even better than I expected because he came close to the edge within the minute, and when I took him in all the way again, felt him pulsating against my tongue as I massaged it slowly, he almost tipped over.

With a hiss, he pulled up my head by the hair until my scalp was on fire, and I cried out, both from the pain and in complaint.

"Come up here, *now*," Taland ordered before I could speak, but it was okay. The day hadn't ended yet, and we still had the night. We had *all* the nights now.

So, I obeyed again and I slowly crawled up his body, letting him guide me until his hands were on my ass and he pushed me up all the way.

"Sit on my face, baby. Sit on me, sit on me..." he kept whispering, like he'd been waiting for this for years and he couldn't wait to have me in his mouth.

I wasn't shy in the least, so close to coming as I was, and I did exactly as he said, positioned my knees on the sides of his head. I sat on him without hesitation.

Goddess, the way it felt. The way it *looked*.

He slid his tongue up my folds slowly, those white eyes on me. When he reached my clit, he sucked on it gently.

"Hands on the wall, baby. Hold on tight for me," he said, making himself comfortable, digging his fingers in my thighs.

Then he dove in again and he didn't stop until my throat was raw from screaming out his name.

I lost control ten seconds in and then I was moving up and down his face, taking everything he could give me. I felt his tongue all the way inside me, then on my clit, slow and fast, exactly as I needed it. I held onto the wall over the headboard, and I tried to hold back, I really tried. But Taland slipped a finger inside me while he pressed his tongue to my clit, and I was a goner.

My throat hurt for real. When he finally stopped licking every drop off my folds clean, my legs were slightly shaking, and I thought he would let me lie down.

I was wrong.

"Stay," he ordered, and I fucking adored his voice. It made me want to moan, the sound of it, but I was still busy trying to catch my breath.

I stayed put while he pushed himself back and sat up on the bed, then came behind me. Took my hair and slowly smoothed it over my shoulder while he kissed the other one. Ran his hands down my arms and put mine against the wall again.

"Keep them there," he whispered, licking a trail from my jaw and to my neck, touching my breasts, squeezing my waist until my lungs were empty again.

All the while he muttered praise under his breath, told me how incredible I felt in his hands, how he could never get enough of touching my skin.

I didn't understand half of it, completely delirious with pleasure, eyes half closed as I stayed there on my knees, facing the wall while he had his way with me.

He was on his knees, too, and when he was done caressing every inch of me he could reach, he put his hands on my thighs and pushed my knees a bit closer together. Then he took his cock in his hands and brought it to my entrance slowly from behind.

I pushed my hips back automatically, trying to take him in, so turned on again already it wasn't even funny. But

Taland was in control of me and with a hand around my hip, he held me in place, brought his knees to the sides of mine, and slowly played with me.

He leaned his shoulders back as he teased me with his cock at first, ran it over my skin and watched it disappearing between my legs, until he couldn't hold himself back anymore. He pressed his chest against my back and thrust himself inside me all the way. Pushed me until I was one with the wall, too. Until I was sandwiched between it and him.

Fuck, I didn't want to be anywhere else. He came so deep inside me my eyes rolled in my skull, and then he got to work. He fucked me from behind and didn't let me move a single inch as he increased his speed by the second. I held onto that wall for dear life with both hands, and Taland pushed me forward with his powerful thrusts until my cheek was against it, too. Like that, I could lean in and raise my ass up as far as he let me, and we kept going for a long time.

When Taland was close, he whispered in my ear about how much he wanted my pussy to squeeze him, and he brought a hand forward, massaged my clit like he fucking made me himself. I saw the stars again less than a minute in, and he followed right behind.

He held my hips in place and he pushed his up all the way until I felt him in my core. Even the pain of being stretched so fully by him was fucking delicious.

When he was done whispering my name, he held us there still, rested his forehead on my head while we both took a moment to catch our breaths. And when he pulled out of me, a little bit of his cum slipped down my thighs.

He grabbed me gently and put me on the bed, and he finally let me lie down.

We were covered in sweat with goofy grins on our faces, our hearts chasing the same rhythm, and the sun outside had just begun to descend behind the horizon.

We looked at each other, Taland and I, and we knew without the need for words. We knew exactly what we were both thinking, but he said it out loud, too, "The sun's setting. That means we haven't even started yet."

"We can still go another round before it's fully dark."

His face broke into a huge, mischievous grin. "How about *two* rounds?"

He moved lightning fast and fell on top of me again.

It was a long, long night, indeed.

And when the sun came up again the next morning, we were there to see it climbing, sitting out on that porch with the kitchen door wide open, covered in thick blankets, talking, or just holding hands in silence for minutes at a time.

With daylight, we finally went back to the bedroom to sleep, and Taland never once let go of me while we did. I could tell even when I was unconscious.

And even though things had gone to shit beyond anybody's imagination at that point, and the future was incredibly unclear, I wouldn't have changed a single day that led me here.

CHAPTER 17

Rosabel La Rouge

The first few days passed by in a blur. I still felt like I was on the run, like someone was right behind us, chasing us, like eventually, we were going to get caught. No way to help it —I'd been on the run for so long now that it had become the only way I knew how to exist.

Taland helped, though.

He was at peace when we were together, and he was there to smile at me and kiss me every time I woke up with a start, sweating and breathing heavily from one nightmare or the other. But he was there, and the nightmares had no chance against his touch, and they faded by the third night completely.

By the end of week one, I'd become perfectly comfortable.

We spent almost every waking second together. That first day when we fell asleep with sunrise, Taland had been to the nearest town, which was over an hour and a half away, apparently, to get supplies and groceries possibly for the next two months, if not more. He came back long before I woke up, so I didn't even notice he was gone.

"I wasn't alone," he said, and I knew he meant those soldiers. Those men that didn't look like men at all, but I didn't blame them. They'd spent the last seven hundred years being dead and buried under a mountain.

But despite everything, I was glad they were here now, that they kept him safe. Kept *us* safe. We never even heard it if someone came close to the wards of this safe house, or if they tried to get through. The soldiers took care of it. I was blissfully unaware, and Taland no longer even paid it any attention.

He joked and said they were our fairy godmothers, and I was tempted to believe him. He sometimes went out there to check on them, and sometimes I went with, but they never seemed any different—visually speaking—and that seemed to please him.

Yes, Taland was at peace—but only when we were together.

When we weren't, some...*strange* things happened.

He'd gotten electronics, too, when he went shopping while I slept. A laptop and two tablets, no phones but a couple of games, subscriptions to most streaming services, and though 5G sucked up here sometimes, it worked the better part of the day. We ate and watched shows and movies, and we had a lot of sex, too. We went on walks and on hikes, and we spent time at his favorite place as much as we could—a waterfall with crystal clear water that fell into this pool on the other side of the mountain from the safe house. It wasn't big by any means—maybe about fifty feet wide—and tiny fish lived in there, but it was perfect. The waterfall went on to pour into a bigger pool down the mountain, but we had no desire to go explore it when we had everything we needed barely a ten-minute hike away.

It was there that I noticed something off for the first time.

I was lying on the biggest rock at the edge of the pool with a towel underneath me and a pillow under my head, sunbathing. The sound of the water was perfect in keeping me distracted, not letting me think. It was loud, but loud was good. We didn't much need to talk, Taland and I, not when we came to swim.

Which was why I found it odd to hear his voice when I was almost sleeping while the afternoon sun kept me warm.

I opened my eyes, blinked the stars away, looked at where that voice was coming from, certain that the sound of the water falling was making me hear things. It wasn't.

Taland, who had been relaxing in the water, was now on the other side of the pool, sitting on a rock at the edge, talking to himself. *Yelling* to himself—or rather, at the thin air in front of him.

I stood up, heart in my throat, wondering if maybe there was somebody there that I couldn't see, that was invisible, because Taland was waving his arms around and those white eyes of his were focused ahead where only the trees began maybe six or seven feet away, and there was nothing else. Not a soldier from his army, not anybody else.

Yet he seemed so fucking frustrated, I could have sworn his fists were shaking when he raised them.

"Taland?" I whispered, so low I couldn't even hear my own voice through the sound of the waterfall.

So, I tried again, this time screaming out his name as loud as I could.

Taland heard.

He stopped, froze in place for a split second, then turned to me so fast I was tempted to think I'd imagined it. He slid from the rock and into the water—it was hip deep around the edges.

And he...*smiled* at me.

"Sweetness," he said, and I read the word on his lips rather than heard it.

I shook my head, looked back to where he had been sitting. "Who were you talking to?" I asked—screaming still because he would not hear me otherwise.

Taland was surprised. His brows shot up and he shook his head, too.

"Over there," I said, pointing my finger to where he'd been sitting a moment ago as he slowly came closer to me, walking in the water, keeping close to the edge of the pool. "Over there—who were you talking to just now?!"

Taland looked behind, right to where I was pointing, but when he turned to me again, he seemed perfectly confused.

"I wasn't talking to anybody, sweetness. There's nobody there."

The worst part? He *meant* it.

He meant those words and he believed them.

A bad feeling settled in my gut in that moment, and from then on, it only intensified.

From then on, I watched Taland more closely, and I saw a lot more.

～

Two days later at about ten p.m., we were lying on the couch in the living room, the laptop on the coffee table while we ate cherry-flavored ice cream. Taland had woken me at five a.m. that morning with kisses and touches and a hard cock begging for my attention, and we'd been up a while. We hadn't gone back to sleep at all, so we were both kind of slow the whole day, which was perfect. We decided to sleep early, too, right after we finished the movie, but then Taland needed to use the bathroom, so I pressed pause and stretched while he was away. I had a smile on my face, a full heart, and a *really* full stomach, too.

Seriously, I had probably gained a couple pounds in the last five days alone.

My smile fell, though, when Taland was gone for longer than usual, and that scene at the pool was still playing in my head every now and again. Even though I'd tried to convince myself that it was nothing, that *I* had been the one seeing things or that Taland had just been messing with me, my gut knew. That's why I got up and I went to the bathroom to check on him.

I heard his voice the moment I stepped into the hallway.

"Taland?" I called, hoping maybe he was talking to me or calling for me or something, but he wasn't.

He wasn't calling for anyone—he was *arguing* with someone in a hushed voice, in a language I had never heard before. It sounded familiar, though, but I couldn't put my finger on it, maybe because of the sheer panic that took over me completely—either because someone was here, in the bathroom with him, or because Taland had never before mentioned that he could speak foreign languages.

And it didn't stop.

"Taland?" I said louder when I couldn't take it anymore and I was already thinking about the bracelet he kept in the bedroom because he didn't want it on him all the time, how fast I could go and grab it, how fast I could attack someone if it came to it.

I tried the door—*locked*.

Which was funny because we didn't lock doors.

But before I could run for the bracelet and break that thing to pieces, the lock turned and Taland opened the door, a small smile on his face.

"Couldn't wait to see me, could you," he said, grabbing his face in my hands, coming in for a kiss like he normally did.

Except I moved away—of course, I moved away. I pushed him to the side and walked into the bathroom, sure I'd find someone, *anyone* sitting there in the toilet or the shower or on the fucking sink, but there was nobody there.

I looked up at the walls surrounding the tub area—had someone climbed up and jumped to the other side?

"Sweetness, what's wrong?"

Taland was right behind me.

I turned to him, trying to keep myself under control. "Who were you talking to, Taland?"

His smile dropped like I'd just slapped him across the face. "Nobody."

Impossible, my mind insisted. "I heard you. Right now— I heard you talking to someone, Taland. In a foreign language, and I didn't know you knew foreign languages! And why the hell did you lock the door?!"

His arms were already around me. "It's fine, baby," he told me. "I promise you nobody was here. I wasn't talking to anyone, I swear it."

Again, he *meant* it, which was the problem. Because he swore it and he believed that he was telling me the truth and I knew that either *I* was completely losing it, or...

"Hey, look at me," Taland said, and I blinked the tears

away to focus on his face. He looked concerned, but nothing out of the ordinary. "It's fine, baby. You're okay. *I'm* okay. We're fine."

He repeated that to me over and over again and took me straight to bed, held me in his arms, kissed me and caressed me until I slept—maybe because I was tired or maybe because I just wanted the night to end, to escape this absurdity. All the while he whispered to me that we were perfectly fine.

That was the first time that I didn't believe him.

Day ten.

We'd never gone so long without something happening, without being found by someone, being chased by someone—or without one of us disappearing into thin air. Nobody had come to bother us, and life was so simple, so beautiful, everything I'd ever dreamed to have with Taland. Just the two of us watching movies and eating delicious food, sleeping together, being together—and that waterfall was an added bonus I never even knew I needed.

Even though I missed Poppy and Cassie and Taylor, I had Taland. It was the perfect getaway, better than anything my imagination could ever come up with.

Or maybe I should say *almost perfect*.

Small things haunted me, not just having heard Taland talking to the air twice now, once in a foreign language that I was sure was Portuguese because I'd been doing some research online—*without* admitting it to myself—whenever I could. It was the way he sometimes stared at something in the distance, too, and his entire body locked down and he wouldn't respond to me when I called for him.

One morning, I woke up to find him staring out the

window, and I had to fucking slap him across the face for him to come to his senses, then swear to me that he had been sleeping, that he hadn't been looking at anything or anyone.

And, while I had been gaining weight, eating more each day, he didn't. In fact, I was pretty sure if we had a scale it would be telling us that he lost a lot. His cheeks were hollowed out and the bags under his eyes were bluer than usual, and I could have sworn I could touch his ribs when he was on top of me. I could make them out perfectly on his back, a lot more than usual.

Something was definitely up, but I was busy fighting with myself for those ten days to allow myself to admit it. To allow myself to look into it deeper, maybe confront Taland, figure out if he really didn't know what was happening or if he was just lying—*what for?*

I didn't have it in me to face that music yet—or even the possibility that *I* had lost my mind somewhere in the process of running for my life or trying to make sure Taland was safe. It wouldn't have surprised me, now when I thought back to it, but in those short, blissful days, I wasn't ready for any of it.

Until night twelve.

CHAPTER 18

Rosabel La Rouge

Strange how I could tell whether Taland was in bed with me, his body next to mine, most times through sleep. Like, even when I was unconscious, my body knew his and craved his heat, and my instincts knew when it wasn't there.

On night twelve, I felt it clearly, like I'd kicked my blanket off while asleep and now I was freezing. The feeling was so powerful that it actually woke me up.

The blanket wasn't the problem, though. It was there, covering half my body, but the heat I'd been missing was Taland's because he wasn't in bed with me.

He's probably in the bathroom, I thought, forcing my eyes closed again, hugging the blanket to my chest as I waited. The digital clock on the nightstand said it was a quarter past midnight, so we'd only slept two hours ago after quite possibly the best sex of my life. We'd been going at it for four hours nonstop, and that's why every muscle in my body was slightly aching in the best possible way.

I focused on those memories. On the way his hands felt on my body, his lips on mine, the way he filled me when he was inside me all the way. The way he bent me over and spun me around and had his way with me while he pleased me—that's what I focused on for a little while.

Except when I opened my eyes again, thinking a minute had passed, the clock insisted that it had been eleven, and Taland was still not back.

That bad feeling in my gut took over me in an instant.

I jumped off the bed, calling his name, and I went straight for the bathroom—empty. The kitchen and the living room, and the other bedroom we never used, they were all empty.

He was not inside the safe house at all.

I stopped in the middle of the hallway, took a deep breath, tried to stop my thoughts from racing so fast. They insisted that something was wrong, that somebody had found us, that our time here was as good as over. Worse yet —they insisted that Taland was gone, taken away from me again, and this time I was never going to find him.

Maybe that's why I screamed at the top of my lungs, "*TALAND!*"

Not caring if someone was close or if they could hear me—I just screamed out his name with my everything.

I got no response.

I wore an oversized men's shirt and some loose pajama bottoms, but I didn't bother to change. The wood of the porch was smooth against my bare feet when I went outside, biting my tongue to keep the tears back. The sky was dark, but I couldn't see if there were stars on its canvas because of the roof that extended over the porch. Even so, I cursed it—cursed the sky because I seemed to be moving in a circle, a never-ending fucking circle where I only got days of happiness before my whole world was taken from me again.

It wasn't fair, damn it. It wasn't fucking fair, but I wasn't going to quit. I was going to fight back. Just to spite the universe, I was going to go back to the real world and find Taland again, and this time it would be over for good. This time, we'd hide somewhere where even the sky couldn't see us.

Except...

Nobody had taken Taland away from the safe house. I didn't need to go back to the real world to find him at all. I heard his voice the moment I stepped down the stairs of the porch and my bare feet connected with the slightly wet soil.

It had rained. The smell of the leaves and the wetness of the ground said so. The sky was indeed clear and a million stars winked at me from above as if to encourage me. That voice I heard was Taland's—I'd know it anywhere in the world. And he was talking in a foreign language again, though this time not Portuguese. This time, I was almost a hundred percent sure it was French.

I ran.

The cold, wet dirt beneath my feet could have been trying to slow me down, but then again maybe it was just that I couldn't breathe very well, not until I ran almost to the back of the house, following the sound of his voice.

Until I saw them.

Five soldiers of the Delaetus Army were standing in a half circle around four trees that were just slightly grouped together, a bit farther away from the rest.

Kneeling in front of the third tree was Taland, spewing those French words relentlessly, a knife in his hands as he engraved something on the bark. Judging by the fact that the first two trees had lines and words engraved on every inch of them, I'd say he had been here a while.

I meant to call out his name but all that left my lips was a whisper. I was breathing too heavily and I had tears in my eyes, but it was okay now because the sky hadn't fallen yet. Taland was right there and whatever he was doing, we'd figure it out. Together, we could figure anything out and start from scratch if we had to.

This time when I ran, I knew exactly where I was going. This time when I ran, I thought for sure he would hear my footfalls and he would turn, snap out of it the way he'd done at the pool and in the bathroom—he'd for sure come to his senses right away.

Except he didn't. I made it all the way to him and called out his name, and kneeled next to him as he continued to cut the wood with that kitchen knife, but he didn't even turn his head toward me.

He just kept hissing those French words, white eyes on the tree, every muscle on his body strained, and I could see because all he had on was his pajama bottoms. He was barefoot, too, his torso naked so I could count every protruding vein around his neck, even though not much light reached us here from the moon and the safe house at our back.

I kept calling his name.

"Please," I said, those damn tears spilling down my cheeks without stop. "Taland, look at me. Snap out of it— just *look* at me!"

He didn't.

It was so strange to see him like that, so completely lost. So strange to be ignored by him that every time he stabbed that tree it felt like he was stabbing right at my heart.

"Taland! Taland, please, just—" I grabbed his arm, tried to pull him to the side.

The soldiers around us moved.

All five of them who'd been standing by the trees as still as the night took a step forward, toward *us*, and their eyes were open. Had they been open until now? I couldn't really remember—I was so used to them being perfectly motion-less any time I came across them, that I no longer even cared to look at their eyes.

"Taland, listen to me," I tried again, telling myself that I didn't have to be afraid because those soldiers weren't going to attack us. Of course not—they belonged to *him* now. "Please, baby, listen to me. Look at me, Taland, look at me!"

I grabbed his hands and tried to pry the knife out of them, but it was like trying to move fucking steel.

And Taland pushed me to the side with all his strength the next second.

It was so unexpected, like someone had pulled me back by invisible strings, had slammed me against the ground hard.

The soldiers moved again.

Everything happened so fast.

Hands on my arms, pulling me up to my feet. Two soldiers were holding me, while another two stood in front of me, moving like they'd just materialized out of thin air.

Fear gripped me by the throat because I thought they were coming for me, that they would hurt me, or try to— and Taland couldn't even tell. I couldn't defend myself because I didn't have the bracelet on me, hadn't even thought to put it on, but...

The soldiers hadn't turned on me. The ones who pulled me to my feet had already let go of me, though they remained by my sides, and the other two had their backs to me. They were all looking at Taland.

I could hardly believe my own eyes.

They were *protecting* me *from* Taland.

A scream ripped out of me, and it came from my very soul. Not only because I didn't understand what was happening, but because Taland couldn't hear me.

Fortunately for me, that scream must have pierced through whatever spell he was under because, finally, he did.

Finally, he stopped hissing at the trees in French, stopped stabbing them.

He blinked slowly, looked down at his hands, at the knife in them. He looked up at the tree again, then at the soldiers between us, and *me* standing behind them.

He saw me. This time, he *saw* me.

"Sweetness..."

My knees gave and I hit the ground. The soldiers moved away from me and took their places around those trees again. Taland stood up, brows narrowed, shaking his head. The knife fell from his hand and he came to me, kneeled in front of me, touched my face, wiped my tears that wouldn't stop coming.

"What...what happened?" he asked me.

He asked *me.*

Laughter burst out of me, the bitter kind that scratched my throat on the way out. I could hardly stop for a second to draw in air, even when Taland wrapped his arms around me and pulled me to his naked chest.

We didn't calm down for a long time.

· · ·

My legs refused to carry me no matter how cold it was outside at this hour. Taland was burning, though, his skin hot. I was still against his chest, hands hanging onto his naked shoulders, and minutes could have passed since he came to his senses—or hours.

"We're okay," said Taland eventually, but I no longer believed that. And not only because of a gut feeling, but because I'd *seen* that. All of that—I'd seen it. I'd seen *him*.

Slowly, I leaned back to look at his face, those strange white eyes that I'd gotten so used to that the memory of his *real* eyes had gone cold. Distant.

"Talk to me," he said, and he was freaking out just as badly as me. His voice was shaking, which never happened. "Talk to me, sweetness. Why are you crying? Talk to me..."

It killed me worse than watching him just now when he wasn't himself.

He *wasn't himself.*

I shook my head, but the memory stopped the tears for a moment, at least. "You...you were stabbing trees."

As absurd as it sounded out loud, I didn't expect him to laugh. He just followed my eyes, looked where I was looking—at those trees that had no bark left on them.

"You...you had a knife, and you were stabbing at the trees, and I called for you but you didn't respond. You were talking, Taland, you were talking and talking..."

"Hey, hey, look at me," he said and took my face in his hands. "What was I saying?"

He'd begun to get himself under control already, and sometimes I wondered if he did it for *my* sake. If he held himself together to calm me down.

"I don't know. You were talking in French."

His brows narrowed. "I don't speak French."

"Yes, I know that!" Except now I couldn't even laugh at

the absurdity. "I know you don't speak French, but you were speaking French! And when I tried to grab that knife from your hand you pushed me and I fell, and then the soldiers, they-they-they..." I stopped, took in a deep breath. "They pulled me away from you and got between us."

This didn't surprise him in the least. "They are ordered to keep you safe even from me if needed," he said. "Come on, let's get inside. You're freezing."

He stood up and pulled me to my feet.

I could hardly believe my ears, but he wasn't even kidding. His face said so, and when he tried to pull me toward the house, I jerked my hand away from his.

"No, Taland—*no!*" I moved back, toward those trees, pointing at them without looking. "What the hell were you doing here? You've been talking to yourself and I hear you, but you never tell me—*why,* damn it?! Why are you talking to yourself like that? How can you speak French when you don't speak French—*why*?!" Goddess, I was losing it, and the way he looked at me only made it worse. "Tell me what's going on. Just *tell me.*"

He shook his head and looked so fucking hopeless that it killed me all over again. Clear to see that he didn't want to tell me anything, but he knew. He *had* to know.

"Can we talk inside?" he tried.

"*What. The. Hell. Is. This*?!" I hissed, pointing at the trees behind me.

If he thought I was going to let him off the hook just like I did the first and second time, he was dead wrong. None of it had been in my head—none of it. Not at the waterfall, not in the bathroom, not those strange looks that came over him every now and again—it was all real, and tonight proved it. He couldn't lie to me, not again. I wouldn't stand for it.

And Taland must have seen it on my face because he sighed and lowered his head for a moment. Then he came to me slowly, like he thought I might be afraid of him again.

"It's them," he whispered, looking at the trees now, walking around me and toward them. I turned, too, followed him with my eyes, so I saw the small nod he gave to nobody in particular, a second before the five soldiers simply turned on their heels and walked away down the mountain without ever looking back.

Chills on my back as I watched them.

Meanwhile, Taland had stopped in front of the first tree he'd basically assaulted, and he touched the places where he'd cut into the bark—senseless lines, I first thought, but now that I was seeing more clearly...

"It's their names," Taland said, and every thought in my head came to a halt.

I went to his side, looking at the lines his fingers traced.

"Hugo," he whispered. "Warin. Richard. Philip, Ada, Symon..."

"The soldiers?"

"The soldiers," Taland said with a nod. "They...*talk* to me. I hear their thoughts. I know all their names."

"*Fuck.*" What the hell could I even say to that?

Taland looked at me, that sad, desperate smile on his lips. "I'm trying to find a way to shut them out, but so far they've proven stronger. Sometimes they take over completely," he said. "I'm sorry, baby. I didn't want to scare you. I thought I had it under control but when I sleep, I slip."

I fell against his side with a sigh, looking at those trees again, and I wrapped my arms around his torso. "The only thing you should be sorry about is that you didn't tell me."

"I know," Taland said. "I didn't want to worry you.

You've gone through enough already. I wanted to spare you."

"And I want to smack you on the head right now, but I know it's wrong, so I won't do it."

"I mean, I do deserve it," Taland said, and I knew he was trying to make me feel better, but it didn't work.

"Let's just get inside." I didn't want to have to keep looking at those trees or be out here a second longer now that I knew what those names were.

Taland held me to his side, arm around my shoulders, and we went straight to the bedroom. I was no longer cold, but I slipped under the covers and welcomed the heat of his magic when he lay down with me and whispered a heating spell.

It was something to do, something to occupy my mind with until he got comfortable and started speaking.

"It started right away when I awakened them," Taland said. "I told you before—I can hear them."

"Yes, but I didn't think that also included you waking up in the middle of the night to stab trees."

He pulled me closer until we were face-to-face, our noses almost touching.

"I've been trying to keep them back, but it's not working," he whispered, not a hint of amusement in his voice.

"Why not?" I whispered back.

"Because they're too strong."

"But how did Titus do it? Did he go around stabbing trees and carving out their names, too?" Taland shook his head. "Do you think Hill would have agreed to bring them back to life if he knew they could literally take control of him like that?"

"Not for a second," he admitted.

"So, *it can* be done." That's what it sounded like to me.

227

"Yes," Taland said. "It's just *me* who can't do it."

"Why not?"

"Because it requires me to...*shut them down* completely. To order them to stay silent."

"And you won't do that, because...?"

Taland closed his eyes and breathed in deeply for a moment. I reached out and touched his cheek, and his pain was my pain, so I felt my shoulders crushing together with him.

"They were tricked, sweetness," he finally said. "Each and every one of these men who signed their souls to Titus were tricked. They were lied to. They were taken advantage of." He swallowed hard, held my hand against his cheek. "I can hear their memories. Titus promised them freedom as soon as the war was over—he lied. Titus promised them that their families would be safe and taken care of—he lied to get them to give him their souls to link to, and now they can't pass through to the other side." Shivers rushed down my back. "I can hear the ones who've already been physically destroyed, too. They remain here still; they're trapped, all of them. They can't *rest* in peace or in any kind of way— they're trapped and they're relentless and they just want to cross over. They just want this to be *over*."

"Oh, my goddess, Taland..."

"And every second of every day they're speaking into my head, *begging* me to release them. *Screaming* for me to set them free so they can finally get the peace they deserve. They are so, so loud."

Closing my eyes to release the tears that had pooled in them, I dragged myself closer and hugged him tightly, hid my face under his chin.

"Most of them were fathers. They all had families, people they loved. People they left behind for this. To silence them, I have to order them to keep all that pain to themselves, like Titus did. And I'm the only one who can hear them, sweetness. Nobody else can. Nobody else *has* for seven hundred years."

My shoulders shook as I cried, even though I was holding onto his body with all my strength.

"That's *awful*," I managed to choke out while he kissed my head and rubbed my back to get me to calm down.

"It is. Which is why I won't order them to stay silent. I'm hoping to....find another way, but if I don't push back, they take over. It's a losing battle," he said, desperate, but now pissed off, too. I could tell by how rigid every muscle in his body suddenly became.

For a moment, a long moment, all we did was breathe. Hold onto each other and think and breathe and try to come to terms with this heartbreaking revelation.

Well, *me*—because he knew about this possibly since the first day. Or he figured it out soon after. And I knew he didn't want me to worry, but I fucking hated it when he kept things from me.

So, I said, "You don't trust me."

He stopped. Pushed my head up and looked at me. "I trust you more than I trust myself."

"You kept *this* from me, Taland."

"Because I didn't want to worry you, I didn't—" And he was feeling awful about it, but he could suck it up and deal with it because I felt bad, too.

"And you think worry is going to break me?" I rose on one elbow. "Newsflash, Taland—it won't, but you continuing to keep secrets from me will."

"Fuck, baby," he said, closing his eyes for a moment.

"It makes me feel weak," I admitted, even if I would have rather not said a word, but I was preaching about not keeping secrets, and I didn't want this to weigh on me and turn to resentment later. "It makes me feel like this fragile little thing when you *don't want to worry me.*"

Throwing his head back, he laughed, and it was bitter.

"You're the strongest person I've ever known, sweetness. Nothing about you is fragile," he said, and I knew he believed that, but it was nice to be reminded. Because if he thought I was weak, then I was afraid that I would believe him, and if I believed him, I would really *be* weak.

"Then stop keeping things from me. I can handle it, damn it. I can handle it." I handled putting him in prison— he should know by now that I could handle anything else.

"I know. I won't keep anything from you again," he said and hugged me to him tightly, kissed my lips. "Like the fact that the only time when they're silent is when I'm with you. Talking or...doing things to you."

"Maybe *they're* afraid of me and don't think I'm a weakling," I teased, just to try to lighten up the mood.

"Actually, at first I thought they were just as fascinated by you as I am, but now I think it's because of how fully you hold my attention. There's no way for them to get through. It's been keeping me alive."

I kissed him back, pushed him down on the bed and climbed on top of him, arms wrapped around his neck.

"Taland, you have to release them," I whispered, so low you'd think I was terrified that someone might hear. Someone might think that it was an absurd, ridiculous idea.

Closing his eyes, Taland just lay there and breathed for a moment, let me kiss his face.

Then, he said, "They make sure we're safe. They make sure *you're* safe better than I ever will be able to."

"Nobody's going to come for us anymore, Taland. It's been two weeks."

He smiled, eyes closed still. "They've been trying to get through twice a day, every day."

My breath cut off and my heart skipped a long beat. "Are you serious?"

Taland nodded. "They've been sending drones, soldiers, agents."

Goddess, the way my stomach twisted. "*And*?!"

"And nothing. They can't get through."

"The soldiers—"

"Are more than capable of stopping them, sweetness. There's absolutely nothing to worry about even if the Council comes here themselves—which they won't," he cut me off.

My eyes squeezed shut and I breathed in deeply. Fuck, my thoughts were racing with too many possibilities and imagined scenarios now. I'd forgotten was it was like to have a chaotic mind in less than two weeks, and I understood why. My head was so, so heavy on my shoulders all of the sudden...

"Which is why I've been hesitant to figure out how to release them," Taland continued, playing with my hair, his lips against my cheek. "If they're gone, the Council will get to us."

"Apparently, they will," I said, moving off him to lie on the bed again because I needed a moment.

"I've been trying to come up with different ideas, different spells on how to take *them* off the radar. Me and you, I can erase us from anything, no problem, but they stay together, and together, they emit too strong a signal. I can't seem to be able to keep it under. I can't just...*turn it off*."

"And you've been figuring all of this out without me," I said, and I tried—Goddess, I tried not to be bitter about it, but I was. At least a little bit.

"I'm sorry, baby," Taland said. "But your safety is *my* responsibility. I should have told you about the voices and the soldiers, but it's my job to protect you and I will do that job thoroughly whichever way I see fit."

Just now he didn't really sound sorry at all, actually. "I'm not a baby you need to babysit, Taland," I spit, and he smiled.

"Noted."

"And it's not *your job*—"

"We can argue about this. You won't win," he cut me off, then gave me a peck on the lips.

I sighed. "Fine." I didn't want to argue, anyway. There were apparently more pressing issues that needed to be addressed first. "We'll argue later. Right now, I need to know if there's anything else you've been keeping from me since we came here."

"Aside from having made up my mind that you look much better naked—no, I think you know everything."

"Asshole," I muttered, but when he pulled me in to kiss me, I didn't stop him.

"I'll be anything at all as long as I'm here," he said, raising my hand to his lips to kiss my fingertips.

All that anger was starting to fade away already. "What else?" I asked, even if I hated to take him back there. But I needed to know. I wanted to understand this whole thing better, how deep it went. "What else have they been telling you?"

Taland didn't hesitate. "Stories—mostly about their loved ones. Their families. It's not so much that they're *telling* me these things, more like...I'm seeing their memories."

"Like you saw mine when you carried me through the Drainage?"

"Exactly like that," Taland said, and when he was done kissing my hand, he leaned in to kiss me on the lips, too. "It's like the images in their minds are mine—for me to read like books or see them like movies. This one man, Luigi from Romania, whose parents abandoned him when he was four, left him in the middle of the street, was raised by three prostitutes in a brothel. He grew to love them like his own sisters. He took Titus's deal because he offered all three of them houses and enough money to live comfortably without having to set foot in a brothel ever again. He was nineteen."

Shivers ran down my spine. "That's fucking sick." And it made perfect sense, unfortunately. A man like Titus, a power-hungry fucking *monster* would use his money to trick and entrap someone as young as that boy.

"I can see him, you know," said Taland, and my breath caught all over again. "I can see him through their eyes. Through their memories. He was...*good*. Really good."

I rose on my elbows again. "Good, how?"

"At tricking people. At making them trust him. Believe in anything he said. He was strikingly handsome, with long hair and an easy smile—and a fortune in his pockets he didn't seem to mind spending. Every single one of the soldiers who linked themselves to him genuinely believed he was a good guy."

"Goddess, that's *incredible,* Taland. This kind of magic..." I shook my head, at a loss for words.

"Should be wiped from all books and the minds of everyone in the world," he whispered. "Sweetness, he's tied them to himself like animals. Worse than animals. He's made slaves out of their souls."

I snuggled closer again, rested my head over his shoulder. Goddess, his heart was galloping like it was being chased by a storm.

"He was a monster," I whispered, kissing his skin. "But you're not."

"I know," he said. "I would never even dream of trapping someone like that, let alone work the goddess knows how many years it took him to create that curse."

"Tell me more," I whispered. "Do you mind?" Because I wanted to know. I wanted to share his pain with him. I wanted to understand him fully, and I could only do that if I knew what he knew.

"You don't have to, baby," he said.

"I know. I want to."

"You sure?"

"Unless you don't want to talk about it, I am."

"I do. It's actually...easier than I thought," he said in wonder. "Talking about it out loud, I mean."

I nodded, kissed him on the chest again, right on his tallarose. "Then tell me everything."

The night was young, and Taland spoke slowly, told me stories about the soldiers that had been tricked and manipulated by a man seven centuries ago like they all had happened these past few years. I listened to every word he said, absorbed every little detail, and by the time the sun lit up the sky outside our window, I felt like I knew those men as personally as Taland did. I felt like I'd sat with them, had talked to them, had created connections with them, too.

And for a while, I couldn't stop crying silent tears for all of them.

CHAPTER 19

Rosabel La Rouge

Fresh sunlight warmed the side of my face, fell over my shoulders like it wanted to hold me in its embrace. Like it knew exactly what I was feeling as I looked at the soldiers in silence, side by side with Taland.

They were different now, so different. Not just monstrous beings with white eyes like I'd thought when I first saw them, but now they were alive to me. Victims of an evil, cunning man who'd offered them slavery masked as freedom.

One choice they'd made and look what it had cost them. One choice, and they were suffering because of it seven hundred years later.

I bit my tongue so hard my mouth was full of blood, but I'd cried enough. While I lay on the bed with Taland and he told me about them all night, I'd cried enough for days and weeks and years.

These soldiers didn't need my tears now—far from it.

"Why is he bloody?" I asked as I walked in front of a soldier with blood on his chin and a cut on his arm that looked deep, even though the blood over it had long dried.

Taland came closer, his eyes on the soldier I spoke of. He was shorter than the ones by his sides, his shoulders wider, his lips thin and his wounded chin pointy. They were all so different from one another, even though they looked like copies of the same man from a distance or when you first laid eyes on them. They were all individuals. You just didn't see it unless you spent time watching them, I guessed. Unless you didn't know their stories.

"He fought a few agents alone," Taland said as he stopped beside me, looking at the soldiers, too. "The wounds weren't deep. He healed himself right away. That's just old blood."

"Can they do that? Heal themselves?"

"They can when I tell them to. Basically give them permission to do magic. It all comes from me," said Taland, and I pretended I understood exactly what he meant.

"They bleed yet they don't breathe. Their beards don't grow. They don't eat," I said in wonder, and continued to walk in front of them, thinking about which of the stories Taland had told me about them belonged to which soldier.

"They run on magic," Taland said. "They're...animated corpses, sweetness."

Goddess, those words didn't sit well with me at all.

"I think this is him," I whispered, ignoring the tears that had welled in my eyes, blinking them away as I focused on the soldier in front of me now, who had only three fingers on his right hand. "This is the one whose stepmother tortured him."

That story was particularly sad, I thought. A reverse Cinderella story, where he was the son of a rich man whose mother died, and whose father married again within the month. And his stepmother was an awful woman from what Taland saw, who'd tortured the kid physically whenever his father wasn't home. She'd cut a toe and two fingers off him, as well as pulled out most of his teeth, among other things. All of it when he was only a boy, powerless to do anything to stop her. Too afraid to tell his father—or maybe he just knew nothing would change if he did.

And finally, Taland said, when he'd gotten the courage to strike back, he had gone into the house one night to kill both her and his father in bed. He'd found her sleeping in a nightgown and had noticed her growing belly.

He couldn't do it, couldn't kill her, not with a baby inside of her.

So, he'd ran away from home instead and had lived in the streets for the next few years, stealing, killing for food, nearly dying of plagues.

Then Titus had found him, had offered him a house anywhere he pleased, and a fortune to live with for the rest of his days if he served in his army.

Look at him now.

"The one whose stepmother despised him," Taland said, looking at the soldier's missing fingers.

Goddess, my heart ached as I tried to imagine it but couldn't get the details right; and then I imagined the bigger picture, the pain he must have felt; and then I tried to *stop* imagining—all within the same minute.

"Do it," I whispered, digging my fingernails into my palms, trying to keep from screaming my lungs out—at the sky, the earth, everything that had stood by and just watched such cruelty happen without interfering.

But the man responsible was already dead, his bones inside the bodies of these very soldiers, and now I wished that I could bring back David Hill again just to feel him exploding to pieces once more. I wished I could somehow bring back Titus, too, and watch the life drain from his eyes little by little.

Taland said nothing for a little while.

"Do you hear me? Do it, Taland. Set them free," I repeated as he walked over to my other side, all the way to the last soldier in line, to the very edge where the mountain continued on a steep rise of smooth rock, impossible to climb. Even so, I knew someone would try to get to us from the other side eventually, but I was prepared.

Because this was inhumane. This was unacceptable.

"I can't," Taland whispered, lowering his head, his jaws clenching.

"We're *part of it,*" I said, shaking my head at myself, at him. "The longer we keep them here, the longer we are a part of this cruelty." I went to him, grabbed his hands. "We're no better than Hill or Titus, Taland. We're—"

His finger pressed over my lips. "*Don't* ever say that again," he told me. "There's not a single part of you that could compare even remotely to what those men were capable of. What *I* am capable of. You are not us and you never will be."

Funny guy. He made me laugh. "Oh, you think you're on the same level as Hill and Titus? Why don't you try saying that to me when you actually order these soldiers to stay silent, and you don't lose your fucking mind to their cries of help. Try then, Taland, and maybe I'll believe you!"

Because I could be wrong, and we didn't compare to the likes of David Hill and Titus, but *he* wasn't evil. Taland, as much as he tried to appear so to the world, had a bigger heart than anybody I knew.

"Sweetness—"

"And maybe we're not those men, but we will be if we keep this up. We will be just as guilty if we don't release these soldiers." That, at least, was a truth even he couldn't deny.

A bitter smile curled the corners of his lips. "I *can't* do it, baby. Not only because I can't keep you safe on my own now, but because I don't know how." His hands framed my face. He touched me gently. "I don't know how to release them. Hill only had the necromancy spell with him, not the original spell that *made* them, or anything that could set them free of this curse."

My stomach turned. I held onto his wrists and rose on my tiptoes to give him a peck on the lips because it almost seemed like he was expecting me to push him away or something because I was pissed off and panicking.

"Then let's figure it out." We were no experts on revived soldiers or curses to basically possess them, but we could learn, couldn't we? "There must be somewhere we can go to search for answers, someone we could talk to."

"There isn't," Taland said. "I've been thinking about it since we got here. I've been searching their minds, their memories, trying to figure it out, but Titus was very thorough. He left no loose ends and if he ever created a counter spell for his curse, he never shared it with anyone. Not that these soldiers know, anyway."

I shook my head, turned to look at them, then back at Taland. "Then we'll *make* one," I whispered. "You have the power, don't you? If you can control all of these soldiers, you can create a spell to break this curse."

Taland paused for a moment, and I knew that he wasn't focused on me, even though his eyes were still just as white.

"You there?"

He sighed, smiled a little, and leaned in for a kiss. "Yes, of course. I'm here, just thinking."

"You're a Blackfire. Necromancy is kind of your thing," I whispered. "Well, you *were* a Blackfire, but now you have the power of a Laetus and the expertise of a Blackfire. To me that sounds like a very good start."

"It's not so simple," Taland whispered. "Titus didn't use necromancy to create the curse—he used Whitefire. He created—*forged* this inter-soul link from scratch."

"But you can destroy it," I said—not because I knew he could, but I was just hopeful. Desperate.

"Destroying it doesn't mean they will be free, though. That's the thing—merely undoing the curse doesn't guarantee that they're released from the bond with Titus. He still lives, in a way, through them. Through his bones that Hill planted in their bodies."

Taland's eyes squeezed shut, and I understood. My head was killing me, too—all of this was too complicated, and I couldn't even begin to understand what it took to make—or *unmake* something of this magnitude.

But I knew one thing, though. "We have to try." For the sake of these men who were tricked and trapped and suffering every second of every day.

"We will," Taland said. "We'll try."

"It's going to work," I said, not because I knew it for a fact, but just because I wanted to believe it. I *needed* to believe it. "It's going to work, Taland. You are very powerful —that you were even able to bring them back proves it. And even after they're gone, we will be perfectly fine because we still have the bracelet. We can both use it—together. That's how we killed Hill, remember?"

Again, he smiled, but this time it was sad. Heartbreaking. "I do. I remember everything."

"So, you know that we will be just fine, you and I. We'll disappear somewhere, live off the radar."

"On another mountain. Maybe an island somewhere," he said, with a nod.

"And we can create our own protection shields and wards from scratch. We can be invisible to the whole world." Maybe not invisible, but we could find a way to make wards last for a long time. Like the charm his mother made him—we could take that spell and alter it, enhance it. "As long as we're together, I don't mind living anywhere at all. I don't care where we are or if we have to run and hide all the time."

He wrapped an arm around my shoulders and brought me closer, hugged me to his chest tightly. "As long as we're together," he repeated in my ear because he wouldn't mind living anywhere, either.

"We can't keep them here forever." *That* was unacceptable. The rest we could work with.

"They'll be coming for us. All the time, they'll be coming," Taland said as I kissed the side of his neck, held onto his waist with all my strength. "They'll be coming for the bracelet. I doubt another exists out there, and without it, the Council can't figure out how to recreate it."

"But they won't get to us. They can try, but we won't let them get close."

A heartbeat later, Taland kissed my cheek. "They can try," he agreed. "We'll make it work. Whatever it takes."

"Whatever it takes." Pure joy came over me, as strong as the crippling fear that rivaled it. But it was okay, wasn't it? "We've done the impossible before. We're still here." And that gave me hope.

Taland laughed and my toes curled. Goddess, I loved that sound.

"We'll be just fine."

I believed him.

We didn't have access to books or any kind of online data that we could use to help us figure out how to undo the curse, set those men free. All we had was what we knew, and for the next three days, we spent every waking second going over different ways to undo spells and curses, or to null a spell or curse in its entirety.

When we weren't sleeping—or fucking—we were trying to come up with the most effective spell, even while eating.

"I think it's more a linking issue," Taland said at noon on the third day. We had a decent plan on how to null the curse, how to basically reverse it, but we still had no clue how to separate his soul from those men. "I think it should be a reverse-bonding spell—is there such a thing?"

I shook my head. "Not that I know of. I'm no Greenfire, but unless the mage or the animal dies, the bond stays in place."

Taland thought about it for a second. "Except this isn't an ordinary bond—remember, Titus died and they remained connected. Almost like his soul remains here while the soldiers' do and probably vice versa. And, sweetness, I'm pretty sure the bonding that happened in the Tree of Abundance in the Roe was real. If the Drainage was real, so was *it*, and they separated us from our bonded, didn't they? We were...*unlinked* from them when we came out of the game."

Shivers ran down my back. "Yes—unless they actually killed the animals." The words brought bile up my throat because the idea of my beautiful vulcera dying made me want to lose my mind just like in the Whitefire challenge. It had been the reason why I'd taken to attacking ice and that roc statue, with nothing but a little hope that she'd make it. It had worked, true, but who was to say that they hadn't killed the animals when the game was over?

"They absolutely have the capacity," Taland said in the end, just as sick at the idea as me. Then he dropped the pen he'd been scribbling on a pad with and ran his fingers through his hair furiously. It had grown again, just like in the Iris Roe, and I'd asked him not to cut it because I loved to play with it when we were in bed.

"Nulling the spell," I whispered, feeling a little defeated as I paced around the porch while he sat at the dining table we pretty much always left outside now. "We have to start there and hope for the best."

He nodded. "I'll try again to see into their minds, try to find any details that might help."

I flinched. "That drains you." Whenever he spent hours at a time staring at the sky and *searching* the minds of those soldiers, he was completely exhausted because he felt every feeling they'd felt, heard and saw whatever event exactly as the soldiers did when it happened to them. That would drain anyone.

"I don't mind. You can sit with me and read." He tapped the tablet on the table that we used to both read digital books and to watch movies sometimes.

So, I sat down beside him and hugged his arm to my chest and kissed him. "I love you. I won't leave your side if you need me."

That small, almost *surprised* smile that stretched his lips made my heart trip all over itself. "I love you, too, baby. More every day." And he kissed me again.

Then he stared away at the sky and the trees, and for a

while, I stared away with him, my head on his shoulder, my eyes half closed. I had faith that if there was any kind of way for him to figure this out in this way, he'd do it. Taland was something else. He was extraordinary. I believed in him just as he believed in me.

I knew it would take time. Possibly days and months and years, but I was okay with that as long as we kept trying.

What I didn't expect was for Taland to wake me up three hours later with, "I think I got it. I think I know how to set them free."

∼

The sun had already chased away the night not half an hour ago. Taland and I walked hand in hand through the trees, toward where the soldiers had created a wall of bodies that pretty much nobody could get through with weapons or magic.

Taland had wanted to sleep last night—a trip down the minds of those soldiers had drained him worse than we'd imagined because he'd been searching for details this time around. He'd willingly navigated their memories, searching, and that had taken a toll on him. He'd need energy to do what needed doing, and now he looked well rested. Though he was paler than I'd ever seen him before, and he hadn't even bothered to shave, which never happened. But he was rested, and I'd even made him eat a little.

For now, it only mattered that this worked.

Taland had the bracelet around his wrist. His step didn't falter even though his jaws were clenched, and he barely even blinked until we made it all the way to them. The two soldiers in front of us stepped to the sides to make way, so in tune with Taland's very thoughts it was scary as hell. I looked at his profile, wondered what it was like in his head.

Fuck, he looked like shit.

"You okay?" I asked, even though he obviously wasn't.

"I'm fine," Taland said, just like I knew he would.

We made it to the other side and turned to look at the soldiers, all standing in a perfect line, their shoulders inches apart. Their eyes were closed and their chests still, their hands loose at their sides. I still hadn't gotten used to how real and *fake* they looked at the same time, and I didn't think I ever would.

Then they all opened their eyes at once, and a scream caught in my throat. I could have sworn all their attention was on me, just like I felt Taland's.

Four of them moved, left the line and started to pick up things from the forest floors—twigs and rocks and leaves that made no sense to me at first.

"What are they doing?"

"I need to create a ritual circle to help me focus the magic better, the same one Titus used," he said.

"Oh." I swallowed hard. "So, you just *thought* about it and they got to work?"

"Pretty much."

"That's..." I had no word, really. *Terrifying* and *fascinating* and *mind-blowing* and *dangerous* just didn't cut it.

"I know what it looks like," said Taland. "I suppose it is strange for you to not *see* me communicating with them, but I do. I talk and they hear—I just don't talk in words."

"Yeah, yeah, you talk in *thoughts*," I teased. "It's just telepathy—no biggy."

"I wish I could show you, sweetness," he said, raising goose bumps on my forearms.

"I think I'm fine." I really didn't want to know what it was like to have all those people inside my head, listening to my thoughts while I listened to theirs.

"Yes, you are. This is going to take a little while, I think," he said and led me to where those four soldiers were arranging leaves and sticks in a perfect circle between two trees.

"What exactly are you going to do here? Do you know?"

Taland flinched. "Not with a hundred percent certainty. It's just a handful of memories that I came across from when Titus did the binding ceremony with the soldiers. We never really learned Binding in school, but I've seen it a couple of times and what he did was very similar—with a few changes in shape. The memories of the soldiers are frail, incomplete, but Titus used the same spell to trap all of them and I think I can combine those memories they still have together to create the full picture of what I need to do to release them."

I nodded. "So, it's *Binding*."

"Yes, and no," said Taland. "It's soul-linking mixed with the curse. Greenfire and Whitefire magic combined, which is what concerns me the most. I haven't had this bracelet or all these colors long enough to know how to separate them, how to use one at a time."

"You can do it," I said, and it was easy to sound certain because I was. "If there's one person out there who can, it's you, Taland. You can separate the colors and you can do the spells. You can set them free and set *yourself* free as well."

The way he looked down at me for a moment...

"There's a chance I might not make it."

I squeezed his hand on instinct. "What...what do you mean?"

"We said *no more secrets* and I don't want to keep this from you, so there is a chance I might not make it, baby. Not a strong chance, but a chance."

If he'd cut off my head right now, I'd have been less shocked. "But...but *why*? How?" I didn't even know what kind of a question because my brain was suddenly refusing to work.

"I'm connected to them on a deeper level than even I understand. There's a very good chance that I'll be able to separate myself from them without any major changes to me, but I don't know for sure. Not right now." He turned to me, took my face in his hands. "Hey, look at me. It's going to be fine."

He was serious, too, but I didn't have it in me to laugh right now. "Then we're *not* going to do this."

"We talked about it," he whispered.

"Yes—*before* I knew that you were in any kind of danger!" I said—*shouted* the words out. "Taland, we are not going to risk your life for anything." That I even had to say this was absurd to me.

"It's the only way. I'll be careful. I'll—"

"*No,*" I cut him off. "No, no, no—just *no.*"

"I have to try," he insisted.

"You don't."

"I have to."

"You *really* don't!"

"I can't live like this, damn it!" he said, and this time he shouted, too. It was like he put his hand inside my chest and pulled my heart out.

Closing his eyes, he let go of me and turned around with his hands on his head.

"I can't...I can't live like this. I will not shut them out—I won't do it. And I can't live with the weight of them on my shoulders."

Goddess, it was like he was slicing me wide open with those words.

Tears in my eyes. I wrapped my arms around his waist from behind and hugged him, cheek against his shoulder blade. Fuck, I wanted to break something, make something disappear—preferably his pain. I wanted to take it somehow, pull it out of him, carry it in my own body so he didn't have to suffer another second.

All of this was because of me. Because he'd wanted to save me. Because he couldn't stand the idea of me being hurt, and now I was in *this* position. Now *I* had to stand back and watch him potentially *kill* himself trying to set free these soldiers. These strangers that he'd tied himself to —*for me.*

Taland spun around between my arms and hugged me to his chest, kissed the top of my head and promised me that we were going to be okay, that he really didn't think that he was going to die doing this. Maybe he'd be wounded, but it would not kill him. He'd recover, he said.

And after what felt like hours to me, I finally forced myself to come to terms with it.

This was Taland we were talking about. It was Taland, and if he said he couldn't live with this burden, then he really couldn't. If this was too much for him, then it really was too much—so much that it would have probably driven another man insane already. I had to suck it up and deal with it and stand by his side and make sure that he made it out alive no matter what.

He wasn't alone, damn it—he had *me* and that meant

something. That meant a great deal. I would not give up on him no matter what. I'd first give up on the whole damn world.

"I'll be right here," I said, both for his benefit and mine. "I'll have the bracelet. I'll use it. You will be fine." I knew spells—I knew a lot of spells. Fourth degree ones, so powerful they came *this* close to healing death itself as if it were a disease. That bracelet was my superpower.

It would be perfectly fine. We'd make it out of this just as we made it out of everything else.

"We will," Taland said, leaning back to look at my face, wipe the tears from my cheeks. No more of them were coming though. Old tears—and I wouldn't cry again until we were on the other side of this. "I trust you, baby."

"And I trust you."

He smiled, kissed my lips gently. "When we're done, we leave. We won't get more than twenty-four hours before they find out the soldiers are gone."

"Through the waterfall. We leave through the waterfall trail." There was a trail that we hadn't explored, but it led to the bigger waterfall pool down the mountain, and we'd take it from there.

"It's a plan," Taland said.

I kissed him with my everything, locked my arms around his neck and held him to me for a little while. A part of me thought this might be the last kiss we ever shared, but I drowned that thought with all my strength because it was a liar. This was not our last kiss—not even close. We both knew it and that's why we were smiling.

"We got this," I said.

"We got this," he said.

Then we let go and stepped back—and one of the

soldiers standing in line behind us broke formation and started to walk down the mountain as fast as he could without running.

CHAPTER 20

Rosabel La Rouge

At first, I thought Taland had told him to help the others who were still arranging those leaves and rocks and sticks into a three-foot wide, complicated circle to enhance the spell Taland needed to perform.

But then even he turned and looked at the soldier who was still rushing down the mountain, and he disappeared from our sight within the minute.

"Where's he going?"

"The wards are being tested," Taland said. "He's just going to get the IDD to back off, no worries."

I sighed deeply, thinking this was a good thing, that if they came to try to break through the ward now, they wouldn't for another few hours at least. Enough so that Taland could finish the spell and rest for a few hours, heal if he needed to, and then we could be on our way.

The plan made perfect sense in my head. We were

dressed and we had everything we needed—the bracelet. The rest we could figure out on the way.

When the soldiers were done preparing that circle with different shapes and Iridian words, they stood up and moved back. Taland gave me another kiss on the forehead before he entered it, stood in the very middle. He didn't once look down to make sure everything was positioned right, I imagined because he trusted the soldiers, too. Or maybe because he simply saw through them?

His lips stretched into a wide grin and he winked at me. For a moment, even with his eyes all white, it was like we'd gone back in time and we were just a boy and a girl going to school together, falling in love. So...*open*.

That's because Taland was relieved. He was *happy* to finally be doing this, to disconnect himself from these soldiers.

And I knew it was the right thing to do. We couldn't keep these men here, trapped in our time, tied to this world still when they no longer belonged here. They belonged with Iris. Their souls *deserved* to be free.

But that didn't mean that it hurt less.

So, when Taland kneeled on the ground and raised his hands toward the leaves and the stones that surrounded him, I turned my back to him for a moment, just to gather myself, to breathe while he chanted slowly. To remind myself of why he was doing this.

Not just for himself, but for these soldiers. These unfortunate men who'd been trapped here for so long, and now they stood here, motionless, forced to serve Taland, to obey every word he *thought*.

"You'll be free," I whispered, though I wasn't even sure if they could hear me. "You'll all be free soon."

Then Taland stopped chanting abruptly.

It could have very well been that he finished the spell—one to keep the magic secure and inside the circle, very standard stuff to start off any big spell with.

But when I turned, I found him looking down the mountain, and he was slowly standing up, too, arms lowered. It didn't look like he had any intention of continuing whatever spell he'd seen in the memories of the soldiers right now.

"Taland?"

I went closer because I could have sworn that he wasn't breathing at all. He wore a simple black shirt that was tight enough around his torso so I could see that his chest was still. He didn't turn to even look at me at first, and when I went closer, I saw nothing down the mountain. Heard nothing at all, just the animals of the forest.

"What is it, Taland? Is it the IDD?" Because that soldier had gone down there and he hadn't returned, but others weren't rushing after him like they would do if he needed help. They were all linked—the other soldiers would know.

"No," he said, shaking his head, finally looking at me. "It's my brothers."

My stomach fell all the way to my heels. "Your brothers?" Barely any voice came out of me. "Why? What...what do they want?"

They hadn't come to look for us, not even once. They had never come close, and we had talked about it, Taland and I. We figured they were laying low, that they were still tending to their wounds, regrouping, that they couldn't get close to us because of the number of soldiers that seemed to be permanently stationed around this mountain.

"To talk," Taland said. "They want to talk."

I looked at the trees again, expecting the face of Radock Tivoux to simply materialize among those leaves. A thousand questions, a thousand instincts came over me at once. Within the minute my mind was a chaotic mess again.

"Sweetness," Taland said, and I knew what he meant.

"Let them come," I said. "I think we should let them come up here."

"Are you sure?" Taland asked, and I wasn't. Not even close. I was half convinced that it was my fear talking, that my subconsciousness was convincing me because I wanted to postpone that spell as much as I could, even unknowingly.

No, I wasn't sure, but then again... "There must be a reason why they are coming here *now*."

"There is, I think," Taland said, closing his eyes for a moment. "Radock looks...desperate."

It shocked me all over again that he could *see* his brother from all the way up here, just because one of his soldiers could. *Fuck.*

"Let them come," I repeated, just because I knew that if we didn't see them, didn't talk to them, we'd regret it later.

Taland nodded. "They're on their way."

He stepped out of the circle and a long breath left me involuntarily, like my body was suddenly relieved even if I didn't want to admit it to myself. Taland took my hand in his and guided me to the side, closer to the soldiers.

"What do you think happened?" I whispered, trying to prepare myself for whatever they were coming to talk to us about.

"I'm not sure, but it doesn't look good," Taland said, white eyes squinting. "They'll be here soon. I'm sure they'll tell us."

I looked at him. "You sound suspicious."

He smiled, put his arm around my shoulders. "I am. It's

Radock we're talking about. He always has some sort of a hidden agenda."

"I'm not worried," I said, resting my head on his chest. "Not with these guys around."

"Good," he said, kissing my head. "There's absolutely nothing to worry about."

We really believed that, and neither of us even considered that we were about to be proven wrong very soon.

It was like I'd been picked up and thrown back into the past, to a time when it was normal to see people other than Taland, when I actually lived with Madeline and Poppy and went to work at the IDD—and that time I actually went searching for the Tivoux brothers, too, in hopes of finding Taland. That was...how long ago, *three weeks*?

That's all the time it had taken me to get used to a life alone with Taland.

Now that I was watching Radock and Seth and Kaid Tivoux walking side by side with Amelia and Zach Mergenbach as they came to us, guided by the soldier, it felt like I was in a dream. It felt like time had slowed to a crawl, and the closer they got, the farther away they seemed.

Until the soldier stepped to the side so we were all facing one another, and they were *right there.*

He didn't get back in line behind us, though. He stayed there with his hands at his sides, obviously at Taland's orders.

"I'll be damned," Radock whispered as he looked at him, then at Taland, and the other soldiers behind us.

"You actually brought back Titus's army. Not bad, Tal. Not bad," Zach said, nodding his head.

"Hey Rora, remember when you thought Taland was

normal?" Seth said, bringing a fist to his mouth as he laughed.

"Enough, guys," Aurelia said, her eyes on Taland. "Enough. We see you two are well. I'm sure you see that we are, too. Thanks to you."

"We are," I said, and my voice sounded strange to my own ears. "And we're glad you are, too." None of them looked wounded or weak in any way. They were all clean and dressed as well as always.

"Good," Radock said, and he didn't look away from Taland at all. "I don't know how much you can see with those eyes, brother, but I imagine you saw us through his." And he nodded his head slightly to the side, to where the soldier who'd brought them up here stood.

"I see enough," Taland finally said. "I don't see why you're here, though. The fight is over. I'm sure the Council can no longer get to you, so..." His voice trailed off, and I watched Radock intently, waiting on a reaction.

He smiled bitterly, looked down at the ground for a moment.

"Is that a way to welcome your own brother?"

I thought Taland might laugh, and in those moments, I regretted telling him everything about how I came to find him in Silver Spring. I regretted telling him the truth about meeting his brothers, but I never actually thought we'd be face-to-face with them again. That they'd come here to confront us like this.

That was naive of me, but I really believed that we were done with...well, *everything*.

Except Taland didn't laugh. He sounded very calm when he asked, "The same man who not only turned his back on me, but refused to help my girlfriend even after she told him she saved my life? The same man who ordered her killed, too?"

The words were like rocks falling in the pit of my stomach. I wanted to squeeze Taland's hand, beg him not to say anything, not to mention me, but that was just my fear talking. Besides, I hadn't lied to him about a single thing—Radock *had* ordered his brothers to kill me when I went to him for help. And Taland knew exactly what he was doing, so I stayed put.

"Things were different then," Radock said.

"Things are the same as always," Taland said. "You're no different than the people who used you and turned on you when you no longer served their purpose, Radock." His calm was to be envied. "I assume there's a reason why you're here?"

"Hold your horses, Taland," Zach said, raising his hands. "That's a mean thing to say, boy. Whatever your differences, you're still family."

"And more importantly, we're all in this together whether you like it or not," Aurelia said.

"Funny how *family* only means what you want it to mean when it's convenient," said Taland.

"The boy has an army of dead soldiers to command, so he's grown balls," Kaid said, hands fisted at his sides as he forced himself to smile.

"He's always had balls—it's the audacity that surprises me," said Seth.

And I could tell just by how Taland's grip around my hand tightened that he wasn't about to say anything nice next—but before I could tell all of them to shut up for second, Aurelia spoke.

"Simmer down, children," she said. "Let the adults speak here for a moment, will you?" She flashed me a grin.

"Rosabel, good to see you. We're all glad that we're all in one piece. We've come for a reason and we want to talk. Can we go somewhere to sit down and do just that? You know, like *adults?*"

I swallowed hard, looked at Taland, who only looked back at me. No expression on his face, and I knew that he would rather we talked here. He would rather his brothers and the Mergenbachs be on their way already because he was uncomfortable in his skin right now, but the fact that they'd come meant something, and I wanted to know the reason why they'd bothered.

"Of course," I ended up saying. "Follow us."

We turned around, Taland and I, and the soldiers behind us stepped aside to make way. Taland looked at me only for a split second but he said nothing, which was almost worse.

"I want to know why they came," I said in a whisper as we led them up to the house.

"Then we'll know," Taland said, perfectly calm still.

"Are the soldiers really necessary though?" He had four of them walking with the others. Though they kept their distance, they were perfectly alert of everyone's movement.

"I don't trust them near you," Taland said. "They're just a precaution." He brought my hand to his lips and kissed the back of it. "It's okay. We're safe."

As if I didn't know that. "It's not that. It's just...a feeling," I muttered. A bad feeling in my gut that had started the moment I saw the others coming up that mountain. Because of that reason Aurelia mentioned—the reason why they were here, *now* of all times.

"Let's hear what they have to say first," Taland said, as if he, too, had that same feeling gnawing in his gut, that premonition that whispered in his ear even before we made it to the porch of the safe house and decided to stop there to talk. There were no chairs, but the wooden top of the railings on both sides was as wide as benches, if any of them wanted to sit down for real.

"We're all ears," I said to Aurelia when we stopped in front of the doors, standing in a wide circle, while the four soldiers who'd followed us remained just outside, looking away. That didn't mean much, though—they could see through Taland's eyes just fine.

"So, you just get them to follow you around like puppies?" Seth asked as he watched them curiously.

"And how exactly do you do that? How do you give them orders?" Zachary asked.

"Are they really one hundred percent obedient to you?" Kaid.

"How are they walking around when they're obviously not breathing? Some creepy shit going on here, I swear..." Seth again.

"Boys, let's behave, shall we?" Aurelia said. "We've got more important issues to discuss."

"But I doubt that, really," said Radock. "What could be more important than the dead army you command with such ease, brother? You've *become* one of them yourself, it seems. The eyes give you away."

"If you're trying to pick a fight, Radock, you will not win this round, either," I said because he was fucking infuriating, and it wasn't fair to Taland at all. He saved us, all of us, when he brought back Titus's army. He *saved* us. He deserved more respect than this, even without them knowing what it was costing him to keep those soldiers alive.

Seth laughed. Zach, too, but he masked it with a cough. Aurelia grinned, step forward with her hands on her hips.

"We're not here to pick fights, actually. We're here to ask for help," she said.

"Help with what?" asked Taland. "You're perfectly capable of handling Selem, are you not?"

"It's very obvious that you haven't watched the news recently. Not that they show much of the real world, but still," Seth said.

"We haven't," I admitted, pretending my heart didn't just trip all over itself. "Why?"

"Because everything's gone to shit, Rosabel," Aurelia said. "The Council has turned on the people. They've been killing Iridians left and right, especially Mud, and imprisoning people based on *rumors*. There are no trials, no proof needed—it's a fucking slaughter out there."

No way, a voice in my head whispered, while the other said, *of course they did...*

"That's true, actually. While you've been up here, hiding away from the world, the Council has gotten busy. They're accusing people of being Selem, people who've never even heard about us before, just to have an excuse to kill them. Anything counts as a crime against the Council now—a simple expression of disappointment in their leadership suffices," said Radock, hands in the pockets of his black pants as he slowly began to pace forward and back.

My heart beat in rhythm with his footsteps. For a moment there, I couldn't see any of their faces at all, too focused on the chaos inside my head. Until Taland squeezed my hand because he must have felt my muscles clenching, my whole body turning rigid. Not with *shock* exactly—this was the Council we were talking about, and from them I expected anything.

"But...why?" I whispered, shaking my head. "Why would they...*why?*"

"Fear, mostly," Radock said. "They'll pick any excuse, but it's because of fear. Because they are no longer in complete control of the world, and they are no longer the most powerful people in the world, Rosabel—you two are." He pointed two fingers toward me and Taland. "I imagine that doesn't sit well with them."

"They feel weak because they can't get to you," Aurelia said. "And weak people are the most dangerous kind out there—especially those with authority over trained soldiers, such as the Council."

"They're in panic and trying to convince themselves that they're in control," said Zachary. "IDD soldiers are raiding houses, communities, schools even, based on very little intel."

"They're killing first, asking questions later." Seth was grinning ear to ear as he raised his hand toward me—a phone. He was offering me a phone.

I took it without really thinking about it, and found a video already playing on the screen, the sound off.

A video of IDD soldiers with machine guns in their hands, and wands and staffs and bones, too, walking into a neighborhood where more soldiers were already raiding the houses, kicking the residents out. Two of the houses were on fire, and men and women and children were out in the street, most wearing pajamas, looking around, confused. Afraid.

It was nighttime so I knew the video wasn't live, but I almost felt like I was standing right there, as terrified as them to see the soldiers walking in and out of houses, setting things on fire, dragging out the people who had most likely refused to come out of their homes on their own.

I was repulsed by every little detail—of how they beat a

man in front of his wife, who screamed and raised her wand at them, and then two other soldiers grabbed her and slammed her against the asphalt. Meanwhile her neighbors, two women holding two small dogs in their hands, watched and cried and didn't dare get even close to help them.

Yes, I was disgusted, but I also couldn't look away. I also couldn't stop taking in every detail of how, whoever was recording, moved deeper into the wide street to show how soldiers were dragging another man and woman outside of a one-story house, while a magically enhanced drone flew over it, and another two soldiers were chanting furiously at it, one waving his staff, the other holding onto his necklace made out of bone pieces. Fire exploded from both their hands, orange flames mixed with green and white at first, before they shot for the door and front windows of the house, and it exploded.

The man and woman screamed, and even though I couldn't hear the real sound, I could imagine it just fine in my head because I saw their faces. I saw how they tried to free themselves of the grips of the soldiers, until one of them waved his wand, and the Bluefire that erupted from it wrapped around their bodies and paralyzed them so that they couldn't even move anymore. They couldn't move— they could only watch their house going down in flames slowly—and then Taland grabbed the phone from my hand.

"That's enough," he said and threw it back at Seth.

Only when I looked up did I realize that my eyes were full of tears. Only when I opened my mouth did I realize that I couldn't produce enough voice to speak just yet.

"Tell me about it," Aurelia said with a sigh, and she wasn't smiling anymore. "I was the same the first time I saw something similar. They've...lost it. Completely lost it."

"That's...that's..." *barbaric* I wanted to say, but I couldn't spit the word out.

"They need to be stopped because they are not going to stop themselves," Radock said, still pacing around the porch, looking at the trees, mostly the four soldiers right outside. "Not until they've either killed or imprisoned every single person that they feel slightly threatened by."

"And we're not talking just about mages who can do fourth-degree spells—but third-degree, too. Even second in some cases. They have all the records, anyway. They've been gathering data for the past few decades, so they're having a fairly easy time finding everyone on their lists," Zachary said.

"Most Mud have fled their houses and are in hiding, as well as any Iridian who can do third-degree spells, who got away in time. Fourth-degree casters were the first ones to get hit so most of them are either dead or in the Tomb," Aurelia continued, and it was like they were repeatedly stabbing me in the same place at once.

"Simply put, they're destroying anyone who poses a threat to them, no matter how little," Radock said. "And again, they will not stop until they've figured out a way to destroy you and your soldiers, too, little brother. Then, their reign will be absolute."

"Exactly like David Hill wanted to do," Kaid said, and my stomach twisted violently. I let go of Taland's hand and went to sit on the railing. I just needed a moment to rest my shaking legs.

Taland was right behind me, and the others came closer to us, too.

"That's why we came here," Zachary, who'd sat not two

feet away from me, said. Taland stood behind me with both hands over my shoulders like he *really* thought someone might attack me any second. "That's why we had no choice but to ask for your help."

"Alone, we can't defeat them. Not even close with how paranoid they've become," Aurelia said.

"Shoot first, ask questions later," Seth repeated as he sat at the very end of the railing, resting his back against the pillar. "Remember that, Rora?"

I did. The Devil operated his entire neighborhood in Silver Spring by that philosophy, and I'd seen exactly what his community had looked like.

"But with your *trata*, Taland—" Zachary started.

"Don't call them that," Taland cut him off, his voice strained. His whole body had become so tense so suddenly. I could tell by how he squeezed my shoulders. "They're not *things*."

I remembered what I'd read in that book in Madeline's office about the Delaetus Army, how Titus had referred to the soldiers as his *trata*, which translated to *things*. Taland was right—these soldiers weren't that. On the contrary. If Zach could hear them and know their stories the way Taland did, he'd never dream of using that word to describe them.

"Okay," Zach said, raising his hands as if in surrender, a weird smile on his face. "Okay, I won't. But with your *soldiers* then, we can put an end to this madness once and for all."

"If not *things,* what are they? The way they follow you, the way they watch us, the way they do magic—they do it through *you*. They are not their own persons, they're yours." Radock came toward us as he spoke, analyzing the soldiers outside. "So, what are they, really? Because they are not men."

"They are," I said, a sudden feeling of *protectiveness* over those soldiers coming over me, something I definitely hadn't had before.

"They're men, Radock. All of them. They were tricked by Titus. He tied them to his soul with this curse, took away their free choice, their bodies, their *everything*. But *they are* men. More courageous men than most I've met," Taland said, and while he spoke, Radock raised his brow and smiled like he was pleasantly surprised.

I did not like that smile at all.

"Very well," he said, as if he'd wanted to hear exactly that. "It seems you know them, and they know you. It seems you've had enough time to get comfortable with them. Do you trust them?"

This time when Taland spoke, I heard the grin in his voice, too. "More than I trust you."

Radock's hand flew to his chest, over his heart. "You wound me," he mocked.

"You will be plenty wounded the next time you turn against me and mine. Those men will make sure of that," Taland said.

Radock laughed and it was heartfelt. "Little brother, you make me proud."

"And now I can finally sleep at night," Taland dead-panned, which made Radock flinch a little.

"Enough with the drama, boys," said Aurelia, rolling her eyes. "Taland, the Council has gone batshit crazy. They're on a killing spree and we can't stop them on our own. We need your soldiers to fight them. Kill them. Hopefully bring a new, better era upon the world for everyone, Iridian and human alike," she said in a single breath. "That basically wraps this whole thing up nicely." She winked at him. "So, say *yes* and let's just be on our way and kill some councilmen and councilwomen, and then we can all go on vacation or hide out in mountains all we like. How about that?"

Goddess help me, but that actually sounded like a fucking dream.

For a moment there, I was completely caught up in this fantasy of life without the Council, without the IDD coming for us, a life where the Mud weren't *Mud* and the Iris Roe didn't exist and the IDD actually worked the way it was supposed to, and the people knew exactly what happened in the world they lived in, and the Tomb was *not* controlled by the biggest criminal alive, but by the IDD.

For a moment there, I actually thought I might be *happy* living off this mountain, not in hiding or on the run. Just... living.

For a moment there, I imagined Taylor Madison and all other kids like her not having to go to human schools and keep away from magic. I imagined them being a part of *us* as they should be.

"Did you not hear me?" Taland's voice pulled me out of my head. "These are men who have been tricked into linking their soul to Titus. Not just them, but all the other soldiers who died during the War of Mages—they're all trapped here unwillingly." I reached up my hand to touch his over my shoulder, already knowing what he was going to say. "I will not make them fight another war. I'm going to set them free."

Silence for a good second. All eyes were on Taland.

Then, Kaid said, "I'm sorry but I think I heard you wrong. I could have sworn you said that you were going to *set them free*."

"I did," Taland said, and Kaid shook his head.

"In that case, I'm *really* sorry—but have you lost your fucking head completely?!"

"Are you *mad*, Taland?" said Seth, sitting upright now, curious again. "Are you fucking bonkers? Set *who* free— these super soldiers who could literally give you the entire world in the palm of your hands? Set *those guys* free?!"

"You can't be serious," Aurelia was saying, while Zach held his head in his hands and shook it, at a loss for words.

And Radock stepped closer to us, too. "What in the name of Iris is the matter with you, boy? You awakened Titus's army. You can command it—we saw. We all saw how they fight. We all see how well they obey you." His wide dark eyes were full of disbelief. "Do you have any idea what that means? Do you know that they are the reason we're all still alive? The Council hasn't even come after us for fear you'd send the soldiers after them. They've left us alone, Taland. They're *terrified* of your army."

"Those soldiers are the only chance we've got," Aurelia said. "We can't beat them—nobody can, Tal. *Nobody.*"

"The world will go to shit if you...*set them free,* which, by the way, *what the actual fuck?!*" This from Zachary.

"Who wants to set free super soldiers?"

"Why even bring them back if all you're gonna do is let them go?"

"Can you give them to me? Does that work?"

"They *can't* be set free—their purpose is to serve. That was always Titus's curse. He made them into slaves, and you can't just *unmake* them!"

They all spoke almost at the same time, and I understood exactly what they meant, how this looked to them from outside—*easy.* They saw Taland like this all-powerful mage who had super soldier slaves doing his bidding without him even having to speak an order out loud.

Maybe that's really what he was on the surface. Except this whole thing went much deeper than that.

"That's enough," said Taland when Zachary opened his mouth to speak again. "Enough. You don't need to understand anything, and you may think of me whatever you like, but I'm still going to set them free."

In the silence that followed, I heard what he didn't say to them, what we'd talked about all night. All those stories, the way it made him feel to carry their burden on his shoulders...

It was wrong, so fucking wrong that they were tricked and bonded and had to suffer like this for the past seven centuries. Cruel, evil—pick your favorite word.

But at the same time...

"We won't survive it," Aurelia said. "Without them, we won't survive this outrage of the Council, or their new regime. They have plans. They have *monstrous* plans on how to keep the people under control, and they're not playing around. This is serious, Taland." And she suddenly sounded terrified.

My heart grew heavier.

"Oh, he knows how serious this is. He knows the Council," Radock said, putting his hands in his pockets again. "But apparently these soldiers are more important than we are." He came closer and it made me so damn uncomfortable that I stood up just to keep him away from Taland. I didn't trust this man, either.

But then he said, "What about *her* then?" My stomach fell. "What about Rosabel? How are you going to keep her safe from them when come—and *they will* come. As surely as I am standing here, they will come."

"Step back, Radock," I said, despite my better judgment, despite the part of me that wanted *me* to step back and let them talk about it. But since he'd already put *me* in the conversation, I wasn't going to back down now.

"He's right," Zach said. "Without those soldiers to keep the Council off your back, they'll find you. Even if you hide, they'll find you eventually. You saw what it's like out there."

I looked back to find Taland had closed his eyes, jaws clenched, hands fisted.

Fuck, he needed to be away from everyone right now.

"We'll need a minute," I said and grabbed him by the wrist the next second, pulled him to the doors.

"We don't have a minute—we don't have any time at all!" Aurelia said, but I didn't stop.

"I know, Aurelia. We'll be right back."

Taland walked with me, let me drag him all the way to the door while the others complained, told us that the Council was moving, that they weren't giving anybody a second chance, not even a *first*. And I knew that, I knew that very well, but I also knew what they didn't—how much it cost Taland to keep up this curse, to be linked to those soldiers the way he was. His pain was my pain, and we were going to take a moment no matter what they thought or what the Council was doing. Taland deserved a fucking moment.

I locked the doors and led him all the way to the porch on the other side of the house, from where we could look at the trees and the bright blue morning sky, where only animals moved and birds sang. No soldiers and no Council and no Selem—nothing, just us.

Letting go of a long breath, I turned around and I wrapped my arms around his torso before the first tear slipped from my eyes.

It was going to be a long day.

CHAPTER 21

Rosabel La Rouge

We didn't let go of one another for a while. It was easier to talk like that, anyway. He kept me grounded and I did the same for him.

"Talk to me," Taland said.

As if on cue, angry tears burned my eyes. "They're fucking *sick*." Just as sick as David Hill, as my grandmother —as fucking Titus had been. Power-hungry assholes with no limits and no care for anyone but themselves.

"They are," he whispered, kissing the top of my head. "Don't lie to me, sweetness. Tell me what you think."

I held onto his shirt with all my strength and squeezed my eyes shut tightly. It hurt everywhere all of a sudden. I just wanted to run away and disappear.

I bit my tongue and pressed my lips together as my silent tears wet his shirt because I didn't want to *talk*, damn it. I knew what the consequences to both options were very well.

On the one hand, if Taland saved himself—which I wished he would do despite everything—he'd doom everyone else. And if he tried to save everyone else, *if* he even could with only thirty soldiers against the Council, he'd doom himself. There was no telling what it would do to him to keep those men linked to him like this. It had already drained him completely in less than two weeks.

"It's an impossible choice, Taland. What can I even say? It's an impossible choice," I finally said.

He pushed my hair away from my face and reminded me, "We've faced the impossible before."

"What do *you* think?" I asked.

"I think a lot of things, but the most important is, what the Council can do to the world if we don't stand in their way. And also what they can do to these soldiers if they get their hands on them somehow."

That made me stop breathing for a second.

"What do you mean?" I dared to asked, even though I was pretty sure I didn't even want to know.

"There are ways to take control of them," he said. "Only a Laetus could do it, but by now I have no doubt that they've charged Nicholas, have given him colors, have *prepared* him for the bracelet." Shivers ran down my back because I believed that, too. The Council had been ready to drain me and try to take my energy to give it to Nicholas before Taland came and stopped them.

"How? How could they possibly—you ruined everything Hill had with him on that mountain!"

"But who's to say that they haven't already found a copy of the original curse?"

Fuck, I was shaking. "Taland, that's—"

"It's okay, sweetness. I would have to allow it. Even if

they find the spells, I would still have to...*share*—and I am not going to do that."

I laughed bitterly and leaned back to look at him. "Let's be honest with ourselves here for a minute," I said.

"I am honest," he said.

"Good, good," I said, stepping back to lean against the edge of the table. "So, I need you to promise me that then."

"Of course, I wouldn't—" he started, taking my face in his hands, but I cut him off.

"Promise me that if we do decide to go down there and fight, you will *not* let any Council member take control of your soldiers for any reason, Taland. *Any* reason—including if they get their hands on me."

He didn't miss a beat. "That's not going to happen."

"I know it's not, but unless you can promise me that, I can't really talk to you about going at all. I just want to make sure we're on the same page, that's all."

Taland clenched his jaws so I heard it. "No."

I grabbed his wrists. "Promise me."

"No." He kissed me on the lips. "They won't get their hands on you. Nobody will touch you."

"Then promise me—it shouldn't be hard. Promise me." He didn't. He just continued to hold onto my face and touch my forehead with his. "Come on, promise me, *please*." Because I wasn't going to risk this—not this. If there was a chance that we gave the Council the only power that could stop them, I wasn't going to agree to it.

"They won't come close to you—I promise you that," he finally said.

"Taland, I—"

"I promise you *that*. There is no way that they will gain power over those soldiers because they will never come close to you. That is the best I can give you," he cut me off.

And I knew by the tone of his voice that he wouldn't budge. For now, it was going to have to do, but that didn't mean that we couldn't negotiate later on. I could get through to him, I thought.

But right now, the others were waiting on the porch, and we had a decision to make.

"Okay," I reluctantly said. "Okay, fine. I'll take it. Nobody's going to take those soldiers from you. The question is, do you want to fight?"

"Of course, I do," Taland said, lowering his head. "I want to fight. I can't just let them win. If things are as bad as they say they are, and the soldiers are no longer here, the Council is going to get to us eventually. They'll find us no matter where we run."

"But if we do fight, the soldiers..." I shook my head, squeezed my eyes shut. "They'll remain under the curse."

Taland put his fingers under my chin and raised my head. "It's temporary."

"I know that, but they're already becoming too much, Taland. Remember how I found you last night?" He'd been out there, carving their names on trees, and he had no idea he was even doing it. "There's a reason why we decided to try to release them right away."

"Sweetness, I don't think it's a choice anymore," Taland said, his voice soft, gentle. "We're not going to let them kill innocent people in a fit of rage. Look me in the eye and tell me you can live with yourself if we do nothing right now."

Goddess damn him. "I can if it means *you* get to be free, too."

Except it was a lie and he knew it. "Sure—for one day and two and three, but what about the fourth? What about the first week and month and year?" His sad smile said it all. "I know who you are, and you know who I am."

Yes, I knew. And I was well aware that neither of us was ever going to be happy if we walked away now.

Here I was, thinking I'd pull Taland aside and he'd convince me to stand back, give me all the reasons why it was a better idea to do nothing, when I knew that *he* would be the first to refuse.

"We're fools—that's what we are," I said, and I was crying now and laughing when he wrapped me in his arms again.

He laughed, too. "I think we're worse than that. We're fools *in love*."

That, we would be for as long as we lived.

～

Everything changed so suddenly again. We invited the others inside the safe house, into our living room, and Taland told them that we'd decided to fight. Seth wasted no time in grabbing our laptop and pulling up a news channel, where they were talking about the number of people that had been imprisoned without trial in the past three days.

Fifty-seven people—that's what the news said. Fifty-seven people were put behind bars for no reason and no trial or chance to prove their innocence, and Seth insisted that twice that many were already dead in the past week alone.

The Council wasn't planning to stop. Apparently the IDD had started a systematic *cleanse* of Baltimore first, and then they had plans to expand through the whole country. They were the Council—they called the shots here. The IDD was under their orders—Headquarters and all offices throughout the States.

"We have word that every CEO of every IDD base

around the country has been invited in for briefing in person. They've been assigned roles and numbers, have been ordered to see through their new program step by step," Radock said as he drank the wine Taland had offered him.

"Which basically is to wipe out third- and fourth-degree casters completely. Those who resist, die. Those who don't, go to jail for one charge or the other. They're bringing people in for parking tickets—any reason goes," Aurelia said.

"Is this information coming from Cassie?" I asked because the idea that she was still inside Headquarters when the Council had lost control like this freaked me out.

"It is," Zach said. "She's chosen to remain inside. Said that she could help us a lot more by feeding us whatever information she could, rather than be out here."

"She also said to tell you *hi*," Aurelia said.

I swallowed hard and drank from my bottle of water, urging myself not to start cussing—or worse, *cry* in anger. It was Cassie's choice. She knew what she was doing. She was a smart woman—one of the smartest people I knew.

"I'm assuming you have a plan," Taland said from where he stood behind the couch where Aurelia, Seth and I were sitting. It wasn't a big room, our living room, but it fit us just fine.

"We do. Go to the Council's chambers and kill them," said Zach, raising his wine to us, and Radock, who sat beside him, nodded.

"Exactly. There really isn't much more we *can* do. We could organize small attacks and push back soldiers when they come for certain areas we have people in, but that would just make them double their forces and come back twice as hard," he said.

"We have to uproot the Council from their position completely. We have to *kill* them all," said Zach. "That's the only way to stop them. The IDD soldiers and agents and every other employee they have is loyal to the Council. They are not going to abandon them because being in the IDD provides them and theirs safety from this cleanse."

I believed that with all my heart. Every person who worked for the IDD was loyal to a fault to it—and to the Council.

"So...that's it? We show up to their chambers and we kill them—that's it?" Because it sounded so...*simple,* but I also knew that when dealing with situations like this, nothing ever truly was.

Look what happened last time when we all went after David Hill.

"If you have a better idea, Agent La Rouge, we're all ears," Radock said, and I knew he called me that to try to get under my skin. I wasn't about to let him.

"Just La Rouge to you, Radock," I said, and his smile only grew. "And because I am a *former* IDD agent, I know what they're capable of. I know that if the Council is using even a quarter of their forces to protect themselves, it's going to take a lot just to get to them—assuming we make it to their chambers." Which also reminded me, "Do you even know where they're located?"

"We do. They're no longer keeping it a secret," Aurelia said. "But you're right—it's a damn fortress, that building. Full of soldiers and agents, not to mention *the Council* themselves."

"How many people do you still have?" Taland asked them, and Radock looked at Aurelia first, then Zach.

"About two hundred," Zach finally said. "They've hit

most of our communities. Have killed a lot of our people already."

"That's not going to cut it." Two hundred wasn't enough.

"Except it is," Kaid said, standing from where he sat on the armrest of the couch near Radock, his eyes on Taland. "With your army, we can get through easily. In West Virginia, we all saw what they are capable of."

I looked at Taland, too, the question in my eyes. Everything that happened in that valley from the moment I fell from the landing and until I passed out was a blur to me still. I'd been wounded, tired, so weak.

Taland said, "I think so, too. They can get past any defense they have. They can get to the Council members."

And I believed him, except... "They'll know we're coming. They'll be prepared."

"They will," Radock said. "I am actually counting on it, and I think they will want to fight themselves because they want the soldiers. They'll try to take Taland out quickly, and I don't think they'll trust others to do that." That actually made a lot of sense. "Your soldiers will fight them, while the rest of us keep everyone else off their backs."

The more he spoke, the more *I saw* the whole thing unfolding before my eyes. Maybe because I'd been in a lot of fights, or maybe because I'd been face-to-face with death so many times, but I felt like I could taste the blood on my tongue, feel the magic in the air, hear the screams in my mind.

Goddess, I *didn't want* to do this anymore. I never wanted to have to fight anybody ever again, but I knew I had to. All of us did. Like Taland said, there was no way I'd ever be able to live with myself if I sat back and watched now.

But if we were all lucky, *this* might be the last fight any of us ever needed to have.

For a while there, everyone was lost in their own thoughts, trying to imagine a scenario in which this worked in our favor. Incredibly hard to do, or maybe just for me. Because I knew what the Council was capable of. What the IDD was capable of.

"We'll have a system that David designed himself," Zachary eventually said. "I'm sure he never expected the day would come when we'd actually use it, but I believe it's a good system. We might have only two hundred people to fight with us, but if we know what we're doing, they'll be enough." Then he looked at me. "And if we have help from the inside, that would be even better. I'm sure Madeline Rogan is still in charge of the—"

"*No.*" I spoke so fast it was almost funny.

"He's right, though," Aurelia said. "She is in charge of the IDD army right now—there is nobody more qualified that the Council trusts. If we can get her to help us—"

"She'll serve us to them on a silver platter," I cut her off, too. Just the thought of actually working with Madeline or trusting her in any way made my skin crawl, made me want to start screaming at their faces until they came to their fucking senses. "You remember how you found me when you came to her mansion. She had already served *me* to the Council. They were about to kill me when you arrived. Right there in her office, on her couch, in front of her eyes."

They all flinched and lowered their heads, except for Radock. "What if we offer her something, though? She doesn't care about *you*, but I'd say she cares a great deal about herself."

"There's nothing you can offer her that she doesn't already have." Money, power, the Council's favor—and now she got to run the IDD and command its army, too, at least until they picked someone else to do it.

To her, that was *everything*.

"We still have Cassie," Kaid said. "She can still give us information."

"What little she has access to isn't going to be very helpful to us," Radock said, then looked up at me. "La Rouge here is a former agent, like she said, and she might know a thing or two about how they build their defenses."

"In such a way that you die if you get close," I said because I knew he was trying to mock me. "They'll have three layers of protective wards, if they're treating the Council chambers like the Headquarters, which they probably are. And they'll have three soldiers assigned per head of opponent, with another three lying in wait close by."

"Which is basically what they did in West Virginia," Aurelia said in wonder. "And that's fine, isn't it? We can put David's strategy to good use. We'll separate our forces into three, deal with the wards, and the soldiers, and then..." She looked up at Taland as her voice trailed off.

"I think Radock is right," Taland said. "The Council will be there themselves, and the soldiers will engage with them right away. If we're lucky, we won't have to make anyone else fight at all."

"You're certain they can defeat all the members," said Radock, and Taland nodded.

"Half of the soldiers, if not more, will be destroyed, but they can defeat them." The ease with which he spoke left no room for doubt.

Suddenly, Radock stood up, and everyone else followed. I did, too, and Taland was already beside me, taking my hand in his.

"That's all we really need to know," he told us. "Pack

your bags then, brother. La Rouge. We're going back to the real world."

Hold on, I wanted to say.

This is too fast, too sudden.

I was getting used to living here with Taland, watching movies and reading books and being at peace for once in my life.

Just hold on a minute!

The words remained inside me, though. I'd always known we were living on borrowed time when we came here. The fact that we were surrounded by the IDD, and that every day soldiers had to go down there to get them to back off was proof enough.

And even though I knew what was happening out there in the world, and I knew what Taland and I decided to do when we spoke in private earlier, it still came as a surprise to me. As a shock to have to leave. *Now.* Just like that.

But we did.

Taland put his arms around my shoulders, and I put mine around his waist. We took a moment just to breathe in, to prepare mentally, and the others waited outside to give us a little space.

We didn't really take much with—we didn't have a lot of things that belonged to us here. Not even the clothes we wore were really ours.

Fifteen minutes later, we walked out of the house together and we didn't look back.

CHAPTER 22

Rosabel La Rouge

Soldiers ahead, at our sides, at our back.

"So, they just *know* everything?" Aurelia asked as we went down the mountain, far away from the wide pathway at the front of the house, in a much denser part of the forest that covered this mountain like a green blanket.

"If any of us has seen it, they know it," Taland said. "The soldier who found you and brought you to us saw. The rest know where you came from."

"That is…" Aurelia shook her head, but she couldn't find the word she was looking for, so she never finished her sentence.

Apparently, we weren't going to walk away from this mountain through the main pathway because it was chock-full of IDD soldiers and wards. We were going to walk away through an uncharted pathway, where there were no soldiers and no weapons and no wards to slow us down.

"*Insane* is what it is," Seth said after a moment.

"It's okay, brother. Who knows—we might convince Tal to abandon those ridiculous ideas when this is over. I have faith," said Radock who was walking in front of us with Zach and Amelia, and he turned and looked at Taland in such a way that I wanted to tell him to keep his eyes in front of him.

My body must have gone rigid and Taland must have noticed because his arm was still around my shoulders. He pulled me closer and kissed my temple and said, "We're going to be just fine, sweetness. Nobody will see us."

"You can't be sure of that," I muttered, even though we both knew it wasn't the IDD who made me want to start running in the other direction right now.

"I can. Zach and Amelia created this ward themselves. They know what they're doing," Taland said. "Nobody's down there. I can *see* it."

He could *see* it—meaning one of the soldiers was already at the edge of the mountain, and Taland could literally see through his eyes.

Goddess, it was like I was only now realizing what that meant. How...*incredible* that really was.

"It's not that," I said with a sigh.

"And my brothers can think whatever they like." He kissed my hair. "That's not going to change a single thing."

I wanted to believe him, but...

"Me, too," Zachary continued, throwing us another look with a sneaky little grin. "It would be a shame to let all of this power go. This is next level stuff, Tal. It really is."

"Think it through is all we're saying," Aurelia said. "You could be invincible." She thought about it for a second. "You *are* invincible."

"Which makes me wonder, why in the fuck would you want to give that up?!" This from Kaid.

"Because he's not well in the head," said Seth. "This is sad, really. Fucking *sad*."

"Can't you just give it to us or something? If you don't want 'em, give 'em up. We'll adopt them," said Kaid again, and every inch of my skin rose in goose bumps.

The thought of those soldiers the way I knew them, with all the stories Taland shared, *belonging* to someone else to do with them as they pleased made me sick to my stomach.

No. Fuck, no—none of these people could have them.

Again, Taland pulled me closer to and whispered in my ear, "Ignore them, sweetness. None of it matters."

And he was right, of course.

But the others kept on talking and I couldn't help but be afraid that they'd somehow find out that Taland could *share* the soldiers with someone else if he chose to. I couldn't help but feel like they would be just as big a threat as the Council, and as ridiculous as that idea seemed on the surface, Radock was *absolutely* someone who'd use *me* to get Taland to do his bidding. He wouldn't even hesitate. There was no doubt in my mind about that part.

Which was why it was important to keep that information to ourselves.

When we made it to the bottom of that mountain, there really were no cars and no IDD, just the soldier that Taland had sent first, waiting for us. I looked at him and I tried to figure out which one of them he could be, what his name was, his story.

I couldn't, of course. The helmets didn't let anybody see their faces, even notice the color of their eyes from a distance.

"Our cars are just a couple minutes away," Kaid told us, nodding ahead at the large trees.

Before walking under the thick canopy of the forest, I looked up at the sky and I saw the little machine far away— so far it looked like an insect to the untrained eye. But I knew what it was. I'd seen those magically enhanced drones countless times, had gone on missions with them leading my way with the team. Maybe there were no soldiers on this side of the mountain to stop us, but the Council had eyes here as well.

The Council saw us, possibly live right this very second, and they knew we were coming. They would prepare and they would put up the fight of their lives. I had no doubt about it.

I just hoped for our sake that what was left of the Delaetus Army really made the difference we thought it would make.

~

It took us almost five hours to get back to Pittsburgh. The farther away from the safe house we traveled, the heavier my shoulders became.

The soldiers had to *run* behind us until we reached the nearest town from the mountain and found a big enough vehicle to fit all of them in. A bus would have been ideal, but all Radock managed to buy was an old van that barely fit twelve of them, and a large truck for carrying trees that we made work for the rest.

Taland assured me that they didn't feel discomfort and they didn't mind sitting so close together, that the wind didn't bother them, that they weren't uncomfortable in any way. Still, I couldn't help but feel guilty. I couldn't help but feel they were vulnerable out in the open like that, where anybody could see them, attack them, or call them in at the very least.

But the Council already knew where we were—they'd seen us through that drone. And we weren't trying to hide, Taland said. *They should know we're coming,* and they did. I had no doubt about that.

Even so I didn't stop fidgeting until we made it to that warehouse near The Diamond Club where Radock had ordered Kaid and Seth to kill me the night I came looking for them.

The bad memories settled on my shoulders, too, but the warehouse attached to the strip club hybrid had plenty of space to accommodate the soldiers. Ten remained outside, spread out to watch the perimeter. The others came in, took their places by the walls of the room we brought them in— I'm sure by Taland's orders. And once they did, they all closed their eyes in unison as if they'd clicked off completely. Like they'd *disconnected.*

This because it was easier on Taland's mind when they were asleep—less voices in his head, less information to process at any given time.

Meanwhile, Radock and the others continued to look at him, to be amazed, *fascinated* by the way he and the soldiers were connected.

Don't get me wrong—I was, too. It was amazing and fascinating and incredible, but they only saw half the story here. They only saw what Taland allowed them to see— which was the surface. The *benefit* of this curse, if there even was such a thing. They had no idea about the voices, the pleading, the stories that Taland carried in his head every second. They had no idea what the price to pay for such control over these men was.

And a part of me was certain that they *wouldn't* be paying this price at all if it was them. If any of them had had the power to awaken the Delaetus Army, they'd have had no trouble silencing the soldiers even when they were awake. They had what it took to wield such weapons—just like David Hill would have had. Like Titus did.

Not Taland, though. His heart was too pure. He could never live with the guilt of knowing he did nothing to *help* these men—and neither could I.

So, in the end, it didn't really matter what they thought, just like Taland said. It didn't matter if Radock hoped to change Taland's mind about releasing them, or if they thought he was a fool for wanting to in the first place. They couldn't stop us. When the time came, when the Council was no longer the Council, Taland could do the ritual and release them.

Then and only then would the two of us be really free as well.

For two days, we remained in the warehouse, slept in these rooms made of concrete walls and low ceilings that made me feel like I was suffocating any time I felt a little anxious. There were no doors to these rooms, and so we could hear the others sleeping in the ones near us in the basement as well. I barely got any sleep at all.

Taland was the same. Not just because of the rooms or the uncomfortable mattress, but because of the soldiers, too. Their voices that he was trying extra hard to keep at bay now that we were in the company of others. He didn't want them to know, he told me that first night when we went out for a walk to get some air behind the warehouse. He didn't want anybody to know the toll it took on him because he didn't trust Radock not to try to take advantage of it somehow.

The plan was to attack the Council in their chambers—which was on the other side of the city from Madeline's mansion, at the very edge—on Saturday, which was three days away. I thought we needed more time to get properly ready, to make sure we prepared as many wards as we could. To make sure that we'd gathered every single person who wanted to fight against them, to train them just a little bit longer on basic combat spells. It surprised me because the moment they put out the call, over three hundred responded—people who'd never been in Selem before, people who'd been of the Council through and through. I guess they didn't agree with how they were handling the public now that they felt threatened, that they feared their control had slipped. And it wasn't just in Maryland; the IDD had already started to go absolutely crazy in every other part of the country as well.

It was chaos, worse than anything I could have ever imagined, which was the story of my life. Reality had a way of finding more twisted and surprising ways to *be* than what any of us had the capacity to foresee.

Meanwhile, Taland insisted that we shouldn't wait at all, that the bulk of attacks on both the defense forces of the Council and the wards would be done by his soldiers. Radock and Aurelia didn't agree, though. They wanted to save the soldiers for the Council because they knew that they couldn't win against them.

We alone couldn't win against them, unfortunately. That I knew. Taland and I had beaten Hill only barely—together, using the bracelet and our Laetus magic, *after* he was already exhausted by having used those soul vessels to basically give flesh and skin to the soldiers, prepare them to *be alive*.

Imagine what *five* people with that kind of power could do, and then add countless soldiers and state of the art weapons and protection wards and shields and gadgets...

Yes, the soldiers of the Delaetus Army were going to have a lot on their hands. And we couldn't really control what happened when we got there, but what we could do was calculate our risks and give ourselves the best chance we could prepare for.

That evening, while the others planned and plotted and made a list of all wards and shields and spells to use when we first got to the chambers on Saturday, I decided to go to bed a bit earlier because I could hardly keep my eyes open. My head was killing me as well from lack of sleep the previous nights.

I had plenty of time for a nap, I thought, when I lay down and the two soldiers who came with me stopped just outside the doorway on other side to keep watch. I thought about the ocean, of calming, foamy waves and a bright blue sky with no cloud in sight. Of an empty beach with just me and Taland on it, nobody else.

It worked. I must have fallen asleep at some point because the next thing I knew was that I heard my name being called.

My eyes popped open right away, but my ears took a moment to adjust to the sounds around me, to understand what was actually happening. Someone was right outside the doorway, calling for me to wake up, waving his hands around to get my attention.

Seth.

I sat up, heart in my throat already.

"They won't let me through!" Seth was saying, pointing

at the guards. "Just tell them to let me through! I'm not going to fucking hurt you, for fuck's sake—I'm your master's *brother!*" he ended up shouting at the face of the soldier on the left.

I jumped off the bed and I went to Seth, completely disoriented still, pushing him back to give the soldiers a bit of space.

"What happened? What happened, Seth?!"

My words were slurred together, my voice thick, and I thought I knew exactly what he was going to say—*The Council is here; they're right outside the door!*

Except... "Come upstairs, *now*," was what Seth actually said, and cursing under his breath as he gave the soldiers another look of pure rage, he turned around and stared running down the narrow corridor that ended with the stairway.

"*Seth!*" I called because I needed to know why he'd come down here to wake me up like this, but he didn't stop. And I had no choice but to go back and put my boots on, then run behind him like crazy, while the two soldiers ran after me.

A million thoughts, each new one more terrifying than the last, rushed through my mind. I thought they'd found us—which wouldn't have been difficult to do considering we weren't trying to hide. The Council knew where we were all along, and the only reason they hadn't come to us was because they knew we would go to them and they wanted to fight us on their territory—which was smart of them.

But something must have changed because they were here. They must have come to terms with fighting in *our* territory now because possibly over a thousand soldiers were outside, waiting for us, and I couldn't get to the top of those fucking stairs fast enough!

Eventually, though, I did.

Eventually, I made it down the hallway and to the main room where we usually hung out to plan, and I found everyone there still, hunched over the large table where the map and all those plans and lists were. Taland heard me coming in, and he started walking toward me, his eyes—though white—alarmed. He reached out his hand for me and I nearly fell on my face because I always seemed to want to just *let go* when he was near me. But thank the goddess, I didn't.

"What happened? Seth woke me up—are they here?!" I asked breathlessly, but Taland shook his head.

"No, baby. They're not. But you need to see this." He kissed my forehead and led me to the table where there was a phone in the middle, right over the map where we'd drawn our potential plans of action.

The screen was on and it was showing something—a picture.

At first, I didn't realize what the hell it was, but the more I looked at it, and the more I leaned in to see...

The scream caught in my throat. This time, my legs did weaken, and if I hadn't been holding onto the edge of the table, I'd have fallen to the ground.

The picture on the screen was of Cassie, tied to a chair with her head to the side, motionless, bleeding, bruised.

Cassie, all alone in a dark room with a strong bright light falling on her body so we could see her face and know it was her.

"She was captured this morning," Aurelia said, her voice deep, dark, strained, like she, too, was trying to hold back tears.

"They sent us this ten minutes ago," said Radock.

"She sent us intel about the number of soldiers they

have lying in wait at their building. They must have caught her as she sent the message out," Taland told me.

White noise in my ears. "Is she..."

"She's alive," he said because I couldn't even say that word, couldn't focus long enough to keep my eyes from blinking to see if her chest was rising and falling.

Get a grip, Rora, my own mind called to me when I wanted to cry out in relief. *She's alive.* Cassie was alive, and I needed to be able to *think* about how to keep it that way.

"It's a trap," Zachary said.

"It's really not," said Kaid. "They know where we are. We know where *they* are. *Bait* is what this is."

"I agree," Taland said. "They want to lure us out, get us to go to them sooner. They don't want us to be more prepared."

"Then why not sent forces to attack us?" Aurelia asked.

"Because they know they can't win," said Radock. "Not their soldiers alone, at least. Not against ours."

Ours, he said, and it took me biting my tongue hard to keep from reminding him that these soldiers were not his by any means. They were Taland's, and Taland's only.

"And they won't be coming here themselves—too risky. They feel safer in their own home," said Kaid.

"So, the question remains, really—do we take the bait?" said Radock.

"I was of the mind to leave sooner, to stop them from killing more people, in the beginning," Zachary said, and his eyes were rimmed red, like he was holding back his own tears as he looked at the screen. At Cassie tied up like a fucking animal, bleeding. Unconscious.

Goddess help me, I will burn them alive...

"But now I'm not so sure," Zach continued. "Now, I'm

thinking they sent us this bait because they *don't want us* to be better prepared for a reason...right?"

My eyes closed. I couldn't keep looking at that screen for a second longer. My mind was full of images of Cassie's face, full of those laughs and the strange way she talked, the warmth in her gaze when she looked at me, the way she'd always been there for me, even when everybody else I knew turned their backs on me. Regret ate at my insides, too—for not forcing her to leave Headquarters, for allowing her to stay there with those people, for not being more afraid that she'd get caught. For not going there to get her out myself.

So many things...

The others were arguing—some of the mind to go *now* because the Council was already feeling threatened if they sent us that picture, some of the mind to wait and prepare better because they obviously didn't want us to—and if they didn't want us to do something, then that was exactly what we needed to do.

A part of me agreed with the latter. If they were trying to force us to go to them sooner, chances were that the Council was afraid of what we could do if we saw our original plan through. It made sense when I looked at it as an agent, it really did.

And then...

"Enough, all of you," Aurelia said, slamming her hands on the table. My eyes opened to find her looking at Taland who was by my side, and she said, "It's futile to argue about who wants what right now. We all know that Taland is the only one who can make the call here."

I swallowed hard, and though everyone was looking at Taland, I felt the heat of Radock's attention on *me*.

"Which means..." He smiled, showed me all his teeth, the fucker. "Rosabel will decide for all of us."

My heart skipped a long beat. Taland's hand closed around mine while I still gripped the edge of the table with all my strength.

Goddess, I wanted to slap that grin off Radock's face so badly, but the fucking table was between us, and it was a big table. I'd have to walk all the way to him to reach him, and my legs couldn't carry me just yet.

"What's it going to be, baby?" Taland asked, and Radock flinched—I saw it because my eyes were on his face still.

And he *hated* it—oh, how he hated that my opinion mattered to Taland more than his. He could try to mask it with his words and his smiles all he wanted, but he fucking hated that I was more important to Taland than him.

Suck it, asshole, I thought, and had we been in another situation, I'd have flipped him the bird, too.

"What do *you* think—do we really need to wait?" I said to Taland instead because I knew exactly what *I* wanted to do, but I couldn't carry everyone's lives on my shoulders. Not based on a *feeling*, at least.

And Taland said, "We don't." I looked up at him. "Three days is not going to make a difference. The soldiers will fight the same way." Once more, I envied his calm. The way he spoke—so perfectly sure of himself.

"They called," he continued, nodding his head toward the phone on the table still showing Cassie's picture. "It's only fair that we answer."

The corners of his lips were slightly curled. I so rarely saw him smiling since we got here that my stomach tied up in knots at the sight of his beautiful face.

"Then we will," I said, and there was no guilt weighing my chest down at all. If he thought we were ready, then we were. I believed it. Everyone else in the room believed it, too.

Radock clapped his hands.

Some cheered and some cursed under their breath while Taland and I held each other's eyes.

"Looks like it's already time to party!" Seth shouted.

It was no party, but it was time, all right. It was time to get rid of the Council that had ruled our world for centuries now. The same people whose job had been to *protect us*, who were now slaughtering their own, killing innocent people, taking *back* the power they were so terrified of losing. Taking back complete control.

It was no different from what Titus had tried to do at all, except the Council had found a way to make it look legal, too.

No more.

Taland pulled me to his chest, and I rested my head on his shoulder for a moment, just to gather strength, to breathe in deeply, to get the image of a bleeding, tied up Cassie out of my mind. It worked, but only halfway.

"Hey, look at me," Taland said after a moment, and I did. His white eyes had become so *normal* to me now, like he'd never had color in them to begin with.

"We're going to get her out."

"And we're going to take *them* out as well. Once and for all." I strangely sounded much more confident than I felt.

Taland grinned. "I love it when you talk dirty to me, baby," he whispered against my lips, and it was impossible not to smile.

"I'll talk dirty to you all day when this is over." When Cassie—no, *the whole world* was safe from the likes of the people who made the fucking Council.

"It's a promise."

Taland kissed me—right there in front of all of them.

Some told us to get a room and others called for us to keep going, that they loved to watch (Seth and Aurelia), but we didn't care. We kissed for a moment and we breathed each other in, and when we let go, we were both *fuller*.

Then we got to work, and I didn't allow myself to consider even once that we would not make it out of this alive.

CHAPTER 23

Rosabel La Rouge

Three hours to Baltimore.

"I want to sit with them," I said to Taland when we put on our warded leathers and prepared to ride to the city together with a small army of people, and a thirty-man army of cursed Laetus.

Talk about *unbelievable.*

"Of course," said Taland, just when I expected him to want to argue about it, to tell me that I was better off in a car with him and some of the others. After all, it had been a hassle to figure out transportation from Pittsburgh to Baltimore for all the people who'd joined our cause. Most had their own cars, but plenty didn't. Aurelia and Zach had made deals with a transportation company and a rental, and from what I understood, it had cost them a shitload just to get everything in place so we could leave at the crack of dawn.

Surreal. We were leaving for Baltimore—to fight. The

Council, the IDD—*to fight*. We were all going to a battle we weren't sure we would win. In fact, most didn't think they'd ever make it back. You could feel it in the air, see it in their eyes, the way all of them wanted to say something to someone, *anyone,* but then chose not to at the last second. Chose to hope because wasn't that all that we had right now? *Hope* and the desire to change the world we lived in, the time that was ours. Hope for a better life for those who came next.

Taland and I would ride in this old school bus with eighteen soldiers. They were already inside, but I stayed by the doors and waited for him while he went to clear things with Radock and the others.

While I waited, I watched the people walking and running to and from the cars and vans and all buses that had blocked the road in front of the warehouse completely. The sun had already turned the sky grey, but it was dotted with darker clouds. Angry clouds, like the goddess was angry that this day had come.

Truth be told, at that point, I wasn't really a believer. If I allowed myself to be, I feared I'd lose my grit and will to fucking *destroy* the Council and everyone who worked for them, not just for what they had done to Cassie, and to me, and to Taland, but for what they'd done to everyone. How they'd twisted the world, what they'd made it into for us, for Taylor and everyone like her.

No, I wasn't going to have mercy, not today. I couldn't afford to, and that was fine by me.

"Scared?"

I looked toward the truck behind us where the rest of the soldiers were waiting to be transported, to find Aurelia holding onto the side mirror, one foot on the stair of the truck cabin. She wore navy blue leathers that looked almost black from here, and her hair was done on a thick braid that went down her back, and her halo shone brightly over her head—her protection spell activated. Their father had created special ones just for her and Zach with his blood when they were just children. Just like Taland's mom had made her sons those charms.

It made me wonder what more I'd missed, not only when I lost my parents, but when I was left with a grand-mother the likes of Madeline, too.

"Can't you see my knees shaking?" I deadpanned, and Aurelia threw her head back, laughing. She looked so petite holding onto that mirror like that, her body leaning back, and she almost looked like she was going to fall any second. She was stronger than most people I knew, though. She'd survived the Devil—and probably a lot more fights than I knew about, and I actually respected her. Zachary, too.

"I'm shaking, too—with laughter. It's going to be a good day today, kid," she said with a wink.

I shook my head. "You're barely ten years older than me," I reminded her, just because I didn't really want to dwell on the fact that today was *not* going to be a good day at all.

Even if we *won*, how many people would lose their lives?

"Twelve, actually, but who's counting?" Aurelia said with a grin that didn't quite reach her eyes. "You okay?"

The question took me off guard. I looked around at the people rushing to get to their transportation vehicle while Kaid and Radock and Zach screamed orders from some-where close by. It was like I'd been thrown back in time to preparations before a mission at Headquarters, to be honest, and...

"I am," I said, surprised. "I'm okay." It wasn't a lie at all.

I'd done this before—and for the same people I was fighting against now. Except back then I hadn't known *why* I was doing it, even if I thought I did. Back then I'd been running from everything, from *change,* and now I was running toward it.

I was okay.

"Good," Aurelia said.

Even though she was far enough away that I couldn't really see all the shades of blue in her eyes, I saw enough to know that she wanted to say something else. In the last second, though, she changed her mind—or maybe I was just seeing things.

"Let's kick some ass, shall we?" she said and basically threw herself inside the passenger seat of the truck, a big grin on her face as she waved at me through the windshield.

I waved back, laughing at myself. She was someone I'd want to hang out with in the future, if we survived this thing.

"I do love the sight of that."

I turned to the other side, to Taland slowly coming to me, a small smile on his face, his white eyes focused on me. He wore black leathers, almost identical to mine, and he'd cut his hair shorter again. I already missed it longer, but he could grow it within weeks—just as long as we survived.

Funny how everything had taken a pause, how everything had moved to *when this was over.*

And what if we never saw the other side?

"The sight of what?" I asked, breathless by the time he was in front of me.

"This." He tapped his finger to my lips. "The sight of you smiling."

299

There I went, smiling all the way that very second. He was magic.

"Smiling as if we aren't going into battle," I muttered, resting my forehead on his chest.

"I think that was more *smiling as if we were*," Taland said, kissing the top of my head.

"Why would I be going to battle smiling?" I asked, wrapping my arms around his waist.

"Because you know we're going to win." He said it so simply—like it was an undeniable truth.

I looked up at his wide white eyes. "What did they say about us riding in the bus with the soldiers?"

"I don't know—I didn't wait around to hear it," Taland said. "Do me a favor, sweetness?" He pushed my hair behind my back, smoothed it behind my ears.

"Anything," I said.

"Stop worrying."

Laughter burst out of me. "Anything except that."

He leaned down, brought his lips to mine. "Stop thinking about losing."

Well, damn... "I can try."

A siren sounded somewhere ahead near the beginning of the road, and most of the engines came to life. It was already time to go.

"I'll take it," Taland said and kissed me. "You realize that you will be safe no matter what."

"It's not *me* I'm worried about." *Him* first, and then everyone else later. *Me* I could handle.

"Remember what you promised me, baby."

"Promise me something, too, then," I said when he opened the passenger door of the old bus for me to get in—and it was already awfully familiar, this feeling, this situation. Exactly like before we went to that valley looking for Hill.

"Anything," he said with a grin.

"Don't die." That was still the most important thing of all.

"Deal."

So many cars on the road, trucks and busses and SUVs. We didn't move as fast as I'd have liked, but we were moving. Taland drove in silence, and he seemed perfectly at ease any time I looked at him. It would be a while until Baltimore, but nothing was going to stand in our way, at least. No— the people we would be fighting were waiting for us at the end of this journey that could very well be our last.

The human police and military were not getting involved in this—a deal they made with the Council, apparently, though I was pretty sure they didn't have a choice. Still, I was thankful for it. The last thing we needed was their blood on our hands, too.

Eventually, I slipped between the front seats and moved to the back. I leaned against the window right behind the passenger seat, and I stayed there for a while, watching the soldiers. They didn't exactly look uncomfortable, though they barely fit the seats with those armors and those huge swords I had yet to see drawn out. I tried to figure out who was who, if theirs was a story Taland had told me, if I knew how they'd come to be here—always trying. The idea of being trapped like this had never even occurred to me, and I couldn't begin to imagine what it was like to be them. Just like with a lot of things lately, this, too, made me wonder what more happened in the world that was so absurd I could never even imagine it before I saw it happening.

Shivers washed down my back and my eyes were full of tears, which I only realized when I blinked and they moved down my cheeks.

"I'm sorry," I said to the soldiers, but they probably didn't hear me because of the old bus's noise, and I barely let out any voice. I knew it meant nothing to them, that they were being forced to be here once more, just when they thought they were going to be set free. A *sorry* wasn't going to make a difference.

"Are they...angry?" I asked Taland when I went back to the passenger seat.

"No. They are calm. Preparing. They enjoy fighting, I think," Taland said.

I was glad for it. It was better than to force them to fight, I figured, but what the hell did I know?

I didn't dare look back at them again all the way to Baltimore.

~

I'd forgotten.

The sight of soldiers and guards dressed in the IDD uniforms, carrying guns and anchors. The smell of the magic of the wards about them in the air. The sound of shouts and orders, of footfalls while men and women rushed to stand in formation, preparing for a fight. The weight of weapons on me—how I'd forgotten. The tightness of a holster around my torso, the weight of guns and knives strapped all over my body. The rush of my blood, the echo in my ears, the pounding of my heart—I'd forgotten in such a short time.

It wouldn't be long, though. I'd been taught by the best IDD trainers for six months and regardless of how I felt when I first got to any mission site, when the fighting began, I would be calm. My instincts would take over and they would be in charge of my body. That's how I'd always survived.

Even so, right now, I felt like I might suffocate on thin air.

Everything had become so *real* in the past minute. We'd arrived at the Council's chambers, a building I had seen before, I thought, but I was sure it had looked different then, and I'd heard it was the private property of a very rich guy, or something like that. It was a house as big as Madeline's mansion, with a grey facade, lighter in some places, darker in others. It had a much more gothic feel, though, with gargoyle statues on every corner, snakes carved around the window frames, and a dark red rooftop that looked like the whole building had been just slightly dipped in blood. Looking at it now, I realized they must have spelled the place because there was no way that I'd have seen this house and not stopped to analyze it before. No way wouldn't I have known it in detail—it was absolutely breathtaking in a very *dark* kind of way.

Or at least it used to be—before there were lines and lines of soldiers standing in front of its wide, glossy doors. Doors that were open.

"They're here," Taland said, and every inch of my body was covered in goose bumps as I rose on my tiptoes to see better. I still couldn't see them, though, but when I tried to move forward, toward the lines of people coming together at the front of the road, Taland stopped me.

We, the truck behind us and only a few other cars had come so close to the building, had stopped right on the sidewalk, while the rest of the people who'd come to fight here had left their vehicles a little farther away, basically in the middle of the city. By now, I had no doubt that any civilian who lived nearby had been evacuated, or at least they'd have run away themselves when they saw what was about to happen here.

"I can't see them," I whispered because the crowd of people that had gathered around us, and the IDD soldiers that were standing in the front yard of that house that was the Council's chambers made it impossible to see the doors.

"It's going to start raining soon," someone said from behind us—Aurelia, walking toward us with Zach. They'd left their truck right behind our bus, and the crowd was *pouring* all around us to get closer to the house.

She was right—the sky was grey, the clouds angry, and I still couldn't shake the feeling that they were angry *at us*. All of us for ending up here because of our greed for power.

But before Taland could say anything, the crowd in front of us parted. A moment later, Radock came through with Kaid behind him. Seth was nowhere to be seen.

"They've been waiting," Radock said, his black leathers melting on his frame, and he looked so different without a suit. So much younger with a clean-shaven face and chopped hair. His eyes were brighter, too. More alert.

He was ready to fight, I realized. All of them were.

"Good," Taland said. "It won't make a difference."

"What about Cassie? Can we see her?" I asked.

"Already tried to do a foresight and a search spell. I got nothing—the place is too well guarded," Aurelia said. "She's in there, though. We'll find her as soon as we kill these people."

"Taland, we will need you safe at all times," Radock said. "You will not engage in the fight personally."

"Noted," Taland said. "There are *more* people."

More?

"The word has spread," said Radock, looking around the crowd. "I think we're close to five hundred right now, but more could be on their way."

"People have grown tired of cowering back," Zachary said with a proud grin. "More will definitely join when they see us here."

"We won't wait, though," Kaid said. "I don't think we could if we wanted to. They will attack. They're ready."

"So are we," said Aurelia, and she, too, sounded confident.

Meanwhile, I couldn't keep my hands from shaking. Maybe because I'd already fought with these people— on *their* side? Maybe because I could guess how many lives would be lost here today?

"They want a word with us. We will go to them. Me and Zach and Aurelia," Radock said to Taland. "And your soldiers."

As soon as he said the words, all the soldiers who'd been sitting in the bus, and the ones in the truck Zach parked behind us suddenly moved in unison and came outside, stopping all around us, pushing the crowd farther back.

The people looked. The people whispered. The people pulled out their phones and started recording.

"Lead the way," Taland said to Radock, completely unbothered.

I thought we were going to go with. I thought that, when Radock, grinning like all his dreams had suddenly come true, turned around and went through the crowd again, we were going to follow.

Kaid did. Aurelia and Zachary did. Fifteen Laetus soldiers who forced the crowd back as they moved did.

But we didn't.

"Taland?" I said in question, and I even took a step forward to tell him to keep moving, but with my hand in his, he stopped me.

"No, sweetness. We only watch."

He must have lost his damned mind. "I want to hear what they are saying!" If the Council wanted to speak to Radock and the others, fucking hell, I wanted to hear it!

But Taland said, "Then you will."

"What are you—"

I stopped speaking when Taland pulled me toward the front of the bus, then began to *climb* to the roof of it, urging me to follow. I could hardly believe it, but the need to see, to know where the Council was, where everybody was stationed, didn't let me argue. If I tried to run to them now, I wouldn't make it—and I also didn't want to be away from Taland. So, I followed, climbed on the hood of the bus, grabbed Taland's waiting hand and he pulled me to stand with him on the rooftop.

Then, I saw.

My breath caught in my throat.

At first, I thought maybe I was imagining things, or I was seeing wrong, but I wasn't. *All these people…* and not just the soldiers in front of the chambers, and others standing by behind the monstrous house we could barely see the sides of. Not just them—but *our* side as well.

Radock hadn't been kidding. More had joined us, and even more were coming—I could just see the endless lines of cars parked in the streets and sidewalks behind us as more and more civilians came toward the crowd, some with weapons in their hands, some with only their anchors. All of them ready to fight.

Right there, in the middle of the city.

Buildings were much farther away than I'd realized.

This place had definitely been spelled with illusions before, because there was an open space, possibly over a mile, in front of the chambers, with a fountain in the middle that was barely noticeable now in the sea of bodies. Thank goddess, the houses, the shops, everything was far enough away that I could hope the damage wouldn't be too severe by the end of this.

Meanwhile, what looked like an open field behind that house was brimming with more soldiers, I had no doubt about it. We saw a few of those who were standing to the sides with machine guns in their hands, watching, but there would be more. A lot more.

"How many—" I started, my voice breathless, but Taland answered before I could finish the question.

"Three hundred in the front. I don't have eyes on the back yet," he said, those white eyes of his scanning the area like he was a damn robot instead of a man.

I stepped closer to him, took his hand in both of mine, and he squeezed my fingers. "Breathe, sweetness. We will be okay."

"I can't *breathe*," I said. "Taland, all these people. They don't compare to the IDD. Those are *trained* soldiers against unarmed civilians." The death toll was going to reach numbers higher than I was prepared for.

But Taland said, "Look." And he turned to look behind us again, toward the city.

There, four of his soldiers were pushing civilians back, separating the majority of those who were coming closer from the group that had already settled in front of the chambers.

And that was a good thing, but it wasn't enough.

"Do you want to hear?"

I whipped my head to the other side again, to the

307

house, to find that Radock and the others had already stopped in the narrow space between two groups of a hundred and fifty IDD soldiers, standing in ten perfect rows on either side of the front yard.

The Laetus that Taland had sent with them were at their front and back, keeping them safe, and the Council members had come all the way outside, too. They stood in a triangle with Helen Paine at the head, shoulders back and chins raised.

The blood in my veins turned cold.

"Yes," I whispered, and then Taland's voice transformed completely.

"*We're glad you could join us. We've been waiting for you for days now.*"

For a moment, I was confused, and I almost asked him what he was saying, but he continued.

"*It's our pleasure. We had some logistics issues to figure out, but here we are.*" Before the last word left Taland's lips, I saw Radock waving his hands to the sides, and realized *he* had said that.

And the first to speak had been Helen Paine.

Taland was repeating everything they were saying because he could hear it through the ears of the fifteen soldiers who were down there with the others.

"*And you've brought friends,*" said Helen, and Taland repeated the words for me. We were too far for me to read her lips from here, but I could have sworn that she was smiling.

"*They insisted on coming to meet you, since you ran away last time,*" said Radock, and if I'd been there, I'd have been itching to slap him on the back of his head.

Because right now we didn't want the Council angry. We didn't want them to be more pissed off than they already were. A fight was inevitable, but what if we could make it end very quickly?

Wishful thinking, though. All the Council members were here. At the sight of Nicholas standing behind Helen, my stomach turned.

Had they somehow made him Laetus, too? Had they charged him with another source of energy? Could he use the bracelet now like we could?

I *really* didn't want to find out.

"*You're far too kind to bring them to us,*" said Taland—but the words were Helen's. She brought her hand to her chest, too. White leathers covered her from head to toe, and it was obvious that she was here to fight. "*Exactly where they belong.*"

Taland didn't even take in a breath before he continued, "*I believe we agree on that. This is where they belong. Where* we *belong. In charge of this country you've so thoroughly screwed over—starting with us.*"

This from Zachary, I thought, because the others had turned their heads toward him. Their backs were to me, so I couldn't see their faces.

"*I'm afraid you've got your priorities twisted. We were, are and always will be in charge of this country and its people,*" Taland said while Helen spoke, and maybe the people heard her, too, because I could have sworn that the whispers and the voices of the crowd around the bus, waiting for the fight to break out, turned louder.

"*You are nothing but leeches feeding off the people you should serve.*" Definitely Aurelia, and she even took a step closer. My heart skipped a beat. Zach immediately put his hand over her shoulder, but she continued. "*We fought together, and we—*"

"*And you won—congratulations!*" Helen actually clapped

her hands. Goddess, how I hated that woman. "*We never said we'd be allies once the fight was over. We were well within our rights to order your execution—you've committed more crimes than I care to remember. You are nothing but ordinary criminals.*"

I squeezed Taland's hand so tightly it was a miracle he didn't move away. He just continued to repeat every word they were saying for me, and he even tried to imitate the tone of their voices.

"*Yet we still won against you, too,*" someone said— possibly Radock. "*That must have bruised your ego a little bit, and I'd have enjoyed the thought had I not had bigger issues to deal with right now. But things are as they are, I'm afraid. We fought together. You betrayed us in the end, which didn't come as a surprise to any of us, really. Today, your betrayal to this country finally comes to an end.*"

If Radock sounded half as sure as Taland did right now, I didn't see how Helen and the others wouldn't believe him.

Then she raised her head. "*Enough with the chitchat— you are all delusional, I'm afraid. Hand over the bracelet and what is left of the Delaetus Army, and we will let you live.*" Every drop of blood in my veins turned to stone. "*There does not need to be a battle here today, Tivoux. These people don't need to die. Call your brother down here, and let us set things in order once and for all.*"

Taland looked at me then, and I found he was smiling. "Hear that?" He told me. "They just want the bracelet and the soldiers—that's all."

I shook my head, envious once more of his easy nature. "I don't suppose they'll like it when you tell them *no.*"

"Let's see—my brother and Aurelia are still laughing." He nodded his head forward, and indeed Radock and Aurelia had their heads thrown back. *Laughing,* while Helen and the other members watched with their hands folded in front of them.

"You certainly have the right to ask, Paine." This must have come from Radock.

"I am not asking," said Taland, and this he said in almost a hiss.

"However, the answer is no," Radock continued right away, as if she hadn't even spoken. It was so strange to be looking at them from this distance while Taland repeated everything they said to me in real time, and while the people grew louder and louder. Taland must have heard it, too, because the fifteen soldiers he'd stationed around the bus began to slowly push them farther back.

"We will not be giving you anything anymore. You've taken enough," Taland continued—and whether it was Radock or Aurelia or Zach who spoke didn't really matter. *"Now, it's our turn, and if you don't surrender, we will not stop until we've taken over."*

I expected to see Helen laughing now, but she didn't. Instead, she took a single step forward, her eyes on Radock —must have been him who spoke.

"Do you have any idea who you're dealing with, you pests?"

Pests, she said, just like David Hill. Goddess, she was no better than him. In fact, she just might be worse.

"We will destroy you, then take our bracelet and our soldiers," Taland continued, and my heart was thundering in my chest at the idea of the likes of *her* commanding the soldiers of the Delaetus Army. The world would come to an end for real.

"This is your last warning. Back away—or die."

Taland and I looked at each other. I reached out a hand for his cheek and tried to smile, but I couldn't bring myself to do it. Despite everything, despite how much he'd suffered, my goddess, I was so glad that *he'd* brought the army back. That *he'd* been the one to use Hill's spells, that they were tied to him now—nobody else.

Because if Taland hadn't done what he did, the Council would have done it themselves. There was no doubt in my mind about it, and they wouldn't have cared about the injustice done to these soldiers. They wouldn't have hesitated to silence their voices—would never even *consider* setting them free. They'd have used them as their weapons to take over the world completely, exactly like David Hill had tried to do, and Titus before him. By now all of us would have been dead.

So, yes, despite his pain, I was glad these soldiers were Taland's now. And if I'd had any kind of hope left that we could leave here without a fight today, it was gone now. Disappeared completely.

"May Iris stand with those who deserve this victory," Taland said, and I had no idea whose words they were, but I agreed wholeheartedly.

Then, it began.

CHAPTER 24

Rosabel La Rouge

Guns fired first. My instincts were already taking over and I turned, ready to jump off the roof of that bus and into the fight, but Taland was still holding my hand. He refused to let me go.

And my mind ran away from me when I began to *see* the fight going on around us, when I felt the colorful magic in the air—and not just from the soldiers, no. Taland was chanting, too, and the magic wrapped around us before it disappeared, locking us in a ward while the people fought.

The IDD soldiers, the Laetus—and the people.

Screams filled my ears, but I was too shocked still to join in. Too consumed by the sight of all that magic, all the guns that were firing, but not for long. Bullets were only effective when there were no wards to keep them back, and by the time everyone lost control of their wards, they would all be too immersed in fighting with magic to think of weapons.

The civilians, that is.

The IDD soldiers? They were trained to use both, just like I had been. Which was why I knew that it wasn't going to be a fair fight from the very beginning, but...

Colors.

So many colors were in the air, and they were coming from the hands of Taland's soldiers. They were not engaging in the fight but all thirty of them had their hands to the sky. None were chanting, yet colors were bursting out of their palms and the magic was falling like sparkly fairy dust onto the crowd.

"Protection," Taland whispered, before I realized that his hands were raised, and he was so focused on what was happening around us that his eyes looked different. I couldn't put my finger on it, but it was like he was trying to see everything at the same time—and he was succeeding.

"They don't need to fight," he continued, and I watched in awe as the IDD soldiers dropped their weapons and turned to their magic.

With their wands and bones and staffs they chanted furiously, but their spells couldn't get through to the civilians at all. All those people around us screaming and shouting spells, throwing knives and guns—not bullets—at the IDD soldiers, and they were perfectly fine. None of them were being hit because twenty-one of Taland's soldiers had spread their own colorful magic around them —or was it *his*?—and they weren't fighting, either. Most of them had gathered to create a line between the IDD soldiers and the civilians screaming their guts out at them. They'd created a line of bodies, and the strangest thing— the IDD soldiers were *not* attacking them.

Not a single gun was aimed at Taland's soldiers. Not a single spell fell on them, either, and right now I had no idea whether that was intentional or not, but the Council members were still there, still in front of those doors, watching. The people screamed like mad, and they tried to get Taland's soldiers to let them through to the IDD because they'd gathered courage now. They'd gathered courage because they still hadn't been truly threatened.

"Taland," I whispered, and I wasn't calm yet, not even close. "Taland, I'm going in."

"No," he said.

"Yes, Taland. I need to find Cassie. She—"

Suddenly he was in front of me, his eyes on my face. "It's not safe," he told me, and had it been anybody else, I'd have probably been terrified.

But this was Taland, no matter how his eyes looked right now, and so I took his face in my hands, too. I rose on my tiptoes and whispered against his lips, "*She could die.*"

"She won't," he said, his voice thick.

"You don't know that. I know you're scared, but I'll be fine. I'll—" *Be back in a minute,* I wanted to say, but he didn't let me.

"If you die, all will be lost."

The words died on my tongue.

"I can't...I can't just stand here and watch, damn it!" I understood what he was saying because I felt the exact same way, but I had to do *something*.

He said, "Trust me, sweetness," and all my complaints faded away. "*Trust me.*"

"I do." I trusted him more than I trusted myself. More than I trusted anyone in the world.

Taland nodded, didn't smile. He didn't kiss me, either, but turned to face the crowd again, the soldiers...

Meanwhile Radock and the others were still behind the line of Laetus soldiers who were facing the Council, and he was most definitely smiling as he looked up at us. We were maybe twenty feet away atop the bus, and the sea of bodies between us would make it impossible for him to get to us quickly, so he stayed put, but I saw his smile. I saw how he was *proud* of Taland, how he was greedy. It was so clearly obvious it made my stomach twist and turn. Made my instinct scream against him.

Then Taland spoke.

"We will only fight against the Council."

Every single person out there held their breath, myself included. Not because I heard the soft voice of Taland standing beside me, but because I also heard those same words leaving the mouths of the soldiers who stood before the Council, and their voices were anything but soft. Anything but normal. They were...robotic at best. Monstrous.

Fucking hell, they *spoke.*

Again, I found myself gripping his arm, not afraid of the Council or the battle or anything, no—just terrified of the fact that the soldiers were right there, standing tall, not hiding, and the IDD was *not* attacking them yet.

"Taland, what are you doing?" I whispered, and every person around looked up at us, at *him.*

"Ending this once and for all," Taland told me. "They're here. They came here personally, and nobody should have to die for them. But if they're cowards and won't face my soldiers..." His voice trailed off and he took a deep breath, and said, *"We will only fight against the Council."*

Again, the words amplified when leaving the lips of the Laetus soldiers, in that strange voice, so powerful.

But now, the crowd went crazy.

Suddenly, they started to cheer. Suddenly, they started to call Taland's name and raise their fists in the air, and

Radock and Zachary were laughing where they stood, and Aurelia was looking at me. Just as terrified as I was.

Every instinct in my body came alive. To push them down again was torture.

"We will only fight the Council!" said the soldiers together with Taland one more time, and then the crowd continued—*fight, fight, fight, fight!*—in unison, like they were all being controlled by the same mind, too.

I held my breath, fisted my hands, looked at Helen Paine as she stood in the shadows of the building, watching...

Goddess, the whole thing was surreal, a scene from a movie or a book—not real life. All those people—and more were coming. So many cars behind us—like riots. Like a true fucking battle. Eleven Laetus soldiers were around our bus, and the rest were there, waiting...

Helen stepped forward and waved her hand around, and a sword appeared between her fingers.

The crowd stopped screaming all at once.

"Very well," her magically enhanced voice echoed. "We shall fight."

~

We were all waiting for it, yet it still took us by surprise when she moved. When all of them moved. Everything went to shit so quickly, yet it would take us all a while to actually believe in what our eyes were telling us.

I let go of Taland and went to the edge of the bus's rooftop and watched, with my heart in my throat and my breath held, as Helen and Flora and George ran forward with swords in their hands and met three Laetus soldiers halfway. They'd drawn their owns words, too, and they were indeed bigger than those of the Council.

The sound of metal hitting metal took over the air. The first raindrop fell on my cheek as if the sky had begun to cry.

People moved away from the front of that house—including the IDD soldiers. They made room for the Council members and the three soldiers—no, *two*. The one in the middle was on his knees while Helen touched the top of his helmet with her hand covered in white flames and ran her sword across his neck.

Taland sucked in a deep breath. I turned to him, terrified, to find his eyes were rimmed red and he was holding onto his own neck, lips parted while he drew in air in short gasps. By the time I was beside him, and I looked out at the fight again, the body of the soldier had turned to a skeleton right there on the concrete in front of Helen's feet, while she, gripping her sword with both hands now, waited for the other two who were aiming for her.

"Goddess, help them," I whispered, my hands over my chest to keep my heart from exploding out of me, and I watched how the other Council members joined the fight, and how the IDD soldiers kept moving farther and farther back to give them more space.

Nobody wanted to die here today. Not the IDD and not the people who'd had enough of the Council's twisted ways. Nobody wanted to die, and so it was no surprise to me that they were all standing back, moving, *hoping* that they didn't have to engage.

Who could really blame them? After all, what we were witnessing here today was something beyond our wildest imaginations. The way the Council members fought, and the way the soldiers who'd been dead for seven centuries fought—none of us could compare.

They moved like they had lightning in their veins. They called for magic like they were the gods of it. They endured so much more than they should, and whether it was wards or their own persons, I had no idea, but they weren't immune to one another forever.

Though details were lost to me, probably blocked by my own brain to protect my sanity, I still saw how they hit the ground when they did—Ferid first, holding his neck with both hands, before a solider grabbed him and *tore him* apart by the shoulders like he was made out of paper.

Three more soldiers turned to skeletons, their flesh and skin and blood becoming dust on the concrete while the others fought around them, and another three from the ones who'd been standing guard around the bus joined them as well.

Then Natasha with her fiery red hair hit the ground on her knees, and a soldier tried to kick her on the side of her face, which would have undoubtedly decapitated her, but at the last moment Flora with a golden sword in her hand cut off the soldier's leg completely. He fell, and she failed to see the other behind him, who had already raised his hand toward Natasha's face. His magic, bright and colorful, consumed her, made her skull explode in the next minute. Her blood and brains decorated the ground while Flora screamed, and swung her sword harder, and chanted even more furiously as her Redfire charged at the soldiers again and again.

Then she killed the one whose leg she'd cut off, driving her sword right through his mouth, if I could see correctly, while at the same time both George and Nicholas attacked a soldier who was one his knees, one with his magic, the other with his katana.

The soldier fell to the ground—and Taland's leg gave up. He hit the rooftop of the bus on one knee, as if he was calling for my attention.

Goddess, he looked *awful*. His every muscle was strained, eyes wide open like they were about to pop out of his skull, skin slick with sweat and so pale, every vein in his forehead and his neck protruding while his hands shook and he tried to straighten his fingers but couldn't. They seemed to be stuck light that, curved like hooks, paralyzed.

I grabbed him and I pulled him to his feet, carried half his weight as well as I could. I called out his name, and I tried to get him to look at me, to focus on me, but he didn't.

Because if he did, if he lost track of his soldiers, they were all going to die at the hands of the Council.

The crowd screamed. I turned just in time to see Flora hit the ground on her side, while two soldiers pulled her apart—one had her by a leg, the other by her head. They tore her apart and Helen screamed as she cut off the head of yet another soldier, and every muscle in Taland's body clenched.

He could feel it.

Every time his soldiers' physical bodies were destroyed, he felt it.

"We're close," I told him, though I didn't know if he could hear me over the screams of the people. They were trying to break through now, to get in the fight.

And they were right. *Now* was the time.

"Taland, I'm going to join the fight. Keep going—it's almost over, okay?"

His hand wrapped around my arm, and I thought he was going to tell me to stay put again, that he had it. And I knew he did, I knew that, but...

"You don't have to do all of it on your own. It's almost over," I whispered, and he was still looking ahead at the fight, keeping control of the soldiers. But Taland wasn't planning to stop me again.

"Take the bracelet," he said through gritted teeth, and he pulled my arm up again, but only to bring my hand over his wrist. Over the bracelet.

I didn't argue—he knew exactly what he was doing. I just took the bracelet and put it on.

It had never occurred to me that anything in the world could replace my father's ring as my anchor, but this did. This bracelet had become mine—maybe because it was *his* as well, so completely.

I kissed Taland's cheek. "I'll be right back." And that was a promise I intended to keep.

I didn't reach for guns or knives. I just jumped off the edge of the bus, finally feeling a little bit of relief. My heartbeat had gone steady and my head clear. And when I ran forward, three of the soldiers who had been standing guard around the bus were already clearing the way through the crowd for me. All I had to do was run.

Of course, they stayed right behind me as I did, and we weren't far from where the Council was fighting—and *losing*—but it still took me a good few minutes to get there because of the crowd.

Radock's face was in front of me.

"What are—"

"*Move!*" I shouted a couple of feet before I got to him, and began to chant my spell at the same second.

Radock heard. Looking like he swallowed something wrong, he moved, and the two remaining soldiers from that line they'd created to separate the crowd from the fight stepped to the sides, too, to let me through.

One.

One last soldier stood in front of the remaining Council members, and they all attacked him at the same time. I knew he wouldn't make it—he was wounded, and even if they didn't feel pain, they could still be worn down by cuts and blood loss just the same. So, he tried to raise his hands and release his magic, but he couldn't do it before Helen's sword went through his chest and the left side of his torso as if it were butter.

The soldier fell—*that's okay.* My spell was already at its end and my hand raised, the skin of my palm heated in such a familiar, yet strange way.

The look on the faces of George, Helen and Nicholas when they saw me standing there was priceless—you could tell they hadn't seen me coming. I was tempted to smile as the last word of my spell left my lips.

Helen raised her sword at me as she screamed, *"Attack!"*

Too late.

Colorful magic burst out of my hand so fast, so powerful, it threw my arm back and nearly tore it off my shoulder. An energy blast almost the same size and intensity as the one I'd used to break the screen of the Regah chamber hit the Council members hard. Their wards had weakened from all that fighting, and *they* were tired, too. Wounded. Bleeding.

There was no way they could stop the impact.

The ground shook and groaned—not just from my magic or the angry clouds pouring rain on us, but from the shouts and screams of the people behind me, as well as the IDD soldiers who were trying to attack, I thought.

Their spells fell on the surface of the ward Taland's soldiers had wrapped around the people, and *they* tried to push through, too. They couldn't, not yet—but it was over. All the remaining Council members were on the ground.

Iridian words came out of my lips like daggers. I didn't need to think or look at my surroundings or wonder if I had enough juice in me for one more fourth-degree spell while they were down to seal their fates for good—I did. Three soldiers walked with me, and as I chanted, Helen raised her head, her nose bleeding—and her hand.

Her Whitefire magic shot for me lightning fast, and I'll admit I didn't see it coming. For a second there, I thought I wasn't going to be able to move away in time—and I was right.

Except the soldier who'd been beside me did, and his back was suddenly right in front of my face. His body absorbed Helen's magic and he didn't make a single sound.

Then he fell to his knees and the flesh on his bones began to melt away into nothing—and Helen screamed once more. No words this time—just a scream because she knew.

I looked back—at Taland standing alone on top of that bus, hands fisted at his sides, shoulder rigid.

I love you, I thought, then turned to Helen who was trying to reach her sword where it had fallen, while Nicholas's eyes were closed—though he breathed—and George was staring at the sky but couldn't move.

The Council. *This* was what was left of the Council.

"You...you..." Helen was trying to speak, and I slammed my boot onto her wrist hard just as she touched the edge of her sword with her fingertips. Again, she screamed in frustration.

"Do me a favor, baby," I said, racing to catch my breath because that spell really did take a toll on me. "Drain them for me, will you? I really want to keep them alive."

I didn't need an answer, of course. Taland could hear me just fine through his soldiers that were by my sides, and even though *I* didn't know enough to separate the colors of my magic yet, his soldiers did.

The look of pure terror in Helen's face when my words

made sense to her was something I'd take to the grave. George closed his eyes in surrender. She opened her mouth to scream again, but the Whitefire magic that *poured* onto her body from the soldiers' hands didn't give her the chance.

Drained. She would be drained, unable to access her magic at all. She would be *chained,* too—in the Tomb, together with other criminals like herself. And we would be there to make sure she remembered how she screwed the whole world over, and how powerless she'd become because of it.

The deafening screams of the crowd behind me filled my ears. Helen was no longer conscious, but she was breathing. Her chest rose and fell steadily, and I turned around to see what was happening.

Nothing.

The crowd was jumping up and down with their fists raised in the air. The IDD soldiers remained right there where they were, guns and anchors in hand, looking like they had no clue what the hell to do.

And I wondered for a brief moment why they hadn't even tried to stop the soldiers. Why they hadn't protected the Council or why they hadn't attacked when Helen ordered them to.

I wondered, but the thought escaped me instantly when I saw Taland, on one knee on top of that bus, and Radock and Zachary and Aurelia looking at him. Talking.

There was no way I could hear them over the screams, and I was surrounded by body pieces and skeletons wearing armor, so I couldn't get to them as fast as I'd have liked but...

I read two words on Radock's lips.

Stop him.

Zach and Aurelia and Kaid who'd been somewhere in the crowd were already moving, pushing the people aside —toward Taland.

My heart fell all the way to my heels. Radock turned, and when he saw me standing there with my eyes on him, he flinched.

Fucking prick, I thought. "Get me to Taland, now!" I said.

I didn't know if Taland would hear me and order his soldiers to take me to him, or if the soldiers by my sides could understand and obey me themselves, but they moved. When I started running, thinking they'd just clear the way for me again, one of them grabbed me by the arm, and *threw* me.

He threw me right on the back of the first.

The scream was stuck in my throat. I moved on pure instinct when I wrapped my arms around his neck and my legs around his hips, hanging onto him like a fucking monkey as the soldier ran.

So much magic.

My eyes were watering and my nose was almost completely blocked and my body screamed in protest— Goddess, these bodies contained so much magic. Taland hadn't been kidding when he said they *ran* on it—they really did.

Gritting my teeth, I held onto the soldier with all my strength anyway, and—

Radock was in front of us, hands forward, screaming, "*Stop!*"

The soldier did. He stopped so fast, so suddenly, I swear it felt like I slammed onto a brick wall with my chest, even though I was literally hanging on his back.

"Get out of my way," I said through gritted teeth.

"It's over," the asshole said. "It's over, okay? The soldiers will not attack. The Council is gone—it's over."

"*Move, Radock!*" I shouted at the top of my voice because the crowd was now moving farther away on their own, and I could see how his brothers and the Mergenbachs were trying to fight the soldiers standing around the bus to get to Taland.

I could see Taland, who couldn't even stand on his own feet anymore.

"It's *insane* to give them up!" Radock screamed. "It's insane! We will only knock him out, talk to him when he wakes up. He'll be safe! He'll be—"

I raised my hand at him and began to whisper a spell—fuck if I cared who he was right now. I wasn't going to let any of them near Taland.

Fuck them. Fuck *him*—he didn't get to decide what Taland did with *his* soldiers.

Colorful flames came alive in the palm of my hand.

Radock cursed out loud in frustration and finally moved out of my way.

I stopped chanting at the same second, pulling my magic back to save energy. "Run!" I shouted at the soldier, and he did.

My eyes were locked on Taland's.

I'm coming.

CHAPTER 25

Taland Tivoux

The screams had become louder than ever before. The rain had stopped pouring. My body was not my own. I wanted to stand, was desperate to move, yet I couldn't. The weight kept crushing me under, pushing on my shoulders, weakening my legs.

But she was coming.

I watched her as if from another world. This was what I hated most since I'd called those soldiers back to life—that only a part of me seemed to really *be here* in this world, and the other part was somewhere far away. Maybe in another time.

The voices screamed louder as the soldier ran to bring her to me—they didn't like me to think of them in names. This one carrying her was Benion Otes, father of twins whose mother had died in childbirth. He pulled them out of her himself at the crack of dawn in their cabin near the mountains, and he had to kill her with the same knife he cut the cords just to end her suffering.

I saw his story, carried his pain over and over again, felt every struggle and every ounce of desperation, but most importantly, I heard his voice, too. His pleading. *All* of their pleadings to set them free.

And I was going to. By the goddess, I was going to release these men from this curse if it was the last thing I did.

But first, Rosabel.

She hung onto the neck of the soldier still. Eleven of them were left standing, the rest lost to the fight with the Council members. Had I been stronger, they'd have killed them sooner, but it didn't really matter, anyway. Just because their bodies died and the soul vessels David Hill used on them disappeared, their souls were still tethered to the curse. To *me*. The way they screamed my name and *pulled* at the very essence of my being had driven me over the brink of insanity that first day, I was sure of it. It was just Rosabel who somehow held me together for a little longer.

Then she was in front of me.

The way she moved was quite fascinating. The way she jumped off the soldier's back and climbed on the rooftop of the bus kept me grounded, focused on her rather than the voices. That's how she saved me every second of every minute and she didn't even know it, didn't understand it, not fully.

"We have to do it *now!*"

I read the words on her lips as she put her hands on my face, and her touch gave me energy, too. I was already feeling *more* of my body.

"We can still leave," I said, though I wasn't so sure. I'd

seen this coming, but I hadn't really anticipated that I'd lose so many soldiers and so much of my energy in this fight. I'd been sure I could get us out of here afterward because Radock had always been a greedy man. He would do everything in his power to try to stop me from giving up the soldiers. I wouldn't put it past him to keep me sedated if only he could, until he either got through to me or he got me to share the bonding with him. Neither of those things were acceptable, though, but now I found myself barely standing, and *the voices-the voices-the voices* were so hard to handle. All of them. One hundred and twenty soldiers. One hundred and twenty souls pulling mine under.

"We *can't* leave, Taland."

Rosabel.

"Focus on me. We will do the ritual right now. There are still eleven soldiers left. They'll keep everyone away. We do it right now, right here. We let them all go."

That sounded like a dream.

That sounded like *a solution*—to everything because... well, the Council was gone. I had no doubt Radock and the Mergenbachs would be taking over. The IDD soldiers hadn't even broken formation, and they wouldn't, not now. Not when they had nobody to lead them anymore. Not when they didn't want to fucking die for no reason and no reward.

I blinked these strange eyes that were able to see so much more than a man was meant to see. Energies and colors so vivid, surrounding people, hanging in the air—the very souls of the soldiers that hung on mine.

My brothers were fighting the soldiers, trying to get to me. They were trying hard.

And Rosabel was no longer touching me—she was on

her knees in the middle of the bus's rooftop, and she was drawing.

A knife in her hand. She'd cut her fingertips and she was drawing a ritual circle on the pale-yellow paint with her blood. She was drawing it exactly like the soldiers had made it for me in the forest.

I stood up, tried to silence the voices, just for a moment. Just until I got to her.

It worked.

"Baby, what are you doing?" I asked, though I knew.

She looked at me and she was *bright*. Not just her aura, but her brightness slipped through her eyes, too. I saw her light. It was the most beautiful light of all.

"I'm drawing the circle. They're not going to knock you out, not before we're done here," she said, and her determination had always fascinated me, but now it did so more than ever. We were surrounded on all sides, but she couldn't care less about the screaming and the shouting of the crowds, about the IDD soldiers—or my brothers who were trying to get to me.

A command sent to my soldiers, those who remained—which was really merely a thought. All I did was think about them pulling up a new ward around us, locking us in, and it was done.

Colorful magic exploded around us, rose up in the air into a dome. My brothers were pushed back by the strength of it—they couldn't even fight the soldiers anymore, couldn't get close.

At least for a little while. Because that ward came *from me,* and regardless of the fact that the curse amplified my power, I was spent almost completely. The fighting, the trying to keep up with both the voices and my own self, it had exhausted me so thoroughly.

No more.

Rosabel was right. The time to do it was *now*. I watched as she continued to draw the shapes with her blood, and she'd remembered almost all the details. I reminded her of the rest, and she had the circle ready for me within minutes.

Then she stood up and put the bracelet around my wrist.

Whatever it was about us, whatever had happened on the Drainage in the Iris Roe, it had connected us. I never lost power over my soldiers when *she* had the bracelet. It was like we were one and the same when it came to magic.

"Go!" she said, pushing me back into the circle. "Go ahead, Taland. Do it. Set them free."

Tears in her beautiful eyes.

I reached for her cheek. "Don't cry, sweetness. We made it." Because even if we didn't, and even if I felt like I was about to tear myself wide open, I hated to see her hurting. Worried.

I hated it more than anything else.

"We'll make it once we're done here." She held my hand with hers, turned her head and kissed my palm, and just like every other kiss she'd ever given me, it imprinted on my skin. Made me alive.

I smiled. "Then let's get done here fast."

The memories of the soldiers were inside my mind forever and I lived them as if they were mine, as if I was *them*, as if I'd been with them right under their skins at every moment these memories were created. I knew how each one of the hundred and twenty ordinary men had turned into weapons, had linked themselves to one soul without fully comprehending what they were doing. Regret gnawed at all of them. Not a single soul wished to have done what they did, to have agreed to work with Titus, who'd promised them so much. Who'd promised not only to take all their problems away, to ensure their loved ones lived healthy and wealthy lives, but he'd promised them immortality, too.

Now, it was time I undid that curse he'd sold to them as a gift.

I'd thought this through for days without realizing it, and then for only hours deliberately, so I knew what to do, at least. I finally saw all the pieces of the spell with which Titus had ensnared the souls of these men, had turned them into what they were today. I collected pieces of it in their minds, their memories. I remembered the words they'd heard exactly as he'd said them.

Now all I had to do was reverse it.

I winked at Rosabel to tell her that I was okay, even if I wasn't, not really. I didn't know what would happen to me here and now, if I would survive it, if I even had the power to see all of it through. After all, there were a hundred and twenty souls here, inside me, that didn't belong in this time or place.

"Don't die," she told me, but she smiled. She shone even brighter when she smiled.

"Wouldn't dream of it," I said, and for once I really prayed that I wouldn't. Because it was over. The Council was gone. There was nobody out there who was coming for us anymore. We could be free for real, she and I.

If everything went right, we *would* be.

So, I began.

My brothers called my name. They screamed it at the top of their lungs. The crowds did, too, except they *cheered* it.

The moment I began to whisper the words of that curse

in reverse, the souls felt it, *knew* what I was going to do. They let go of me, stopped pulling me down, stopped screaming at me to help them, save them, set them free. Stopped pushing all their pain and their misfortune to the center of my mind.

Titus had silenced them, had shut them off completely, had *ordered* them to never let a single thought or word escape into his mind.

Now, I was going to set them free once and for all.

The curse wasn't long. That man had been a monster, true, but he'd put together a curse of this magnitude with just over a hundred words, which was unheard of. Fucking genius—if only he'd used it for something *good* instead of this.

As it was, I chanted the words and I released every ounce of magic I had in me into the circle while I looked at Rosabel, at the fire in her eyes, the brightness of her own soul. Her pureness. By now I was sure that the goddess had made her for me, just as she'd made me for her. She completed me in ways I never knew I needed to be completed.

I smiled at her as well as I could so she'd be at ease.

But when the pain began, I wasn't able to keep it up for long.

It came slowly at first, from everywhere, every line of blood Rosabel had drawn, every soul connected to me, every word of the curse that Titus created.

Then, with the last word, it came all at once and crushed me under.

Gritting my teeth, I held back from making a sound when the pain tore me wide open, sliced me right across the chest. My legs gave and I fell to my knees, hands fisted tightly as I forced myself to stand still, to take every ounce of pain I was going to have to take, to get this over with once and for all.

Taland, look at me, baby. Keep your eyes on me.

Rosabel's face was in front of me, just there, almost close enough to touch if I had the energy to raise my hand. She was there, kneeling with me, always with me, taking care of me—even when I didn't know it. Even when I thought she betrayed me.

Then the souls began to break the bond to me, to set themselves free.

I felt the first tearing off me like a page off my book. Painful, bloody, *loud*.

He screamed, the soldier, one who'd died in the War of Mages seven hundred years ago.

Then came the others.

The pain was unlike anything I'd ever felt before. I forced my eyes down for a moment, just to look at my body, to see that my skin wasn't being peeled off me—*how is my skin not being peeled off me?* I could have sworn that it was.

Rosabel called my name. I tried to hold onto her, tried to focus on her, to endure the pain, but it was impossible.

A muffled scream left me when my skin tore, too, for the first time.

Blood exploded. My clothes were in pieces. Rosabel screamed louder.

But the souls didn't stop.

Something's wrong.

Titus didn't feel an ounce of pain when bonding these men to himself. *I* didn't feel any kind of pain or discomfort while I chanted the necromancy spell from that mountain the day they ordered Rosabel killed. Reversing a curse should be the same as creating it, yet now, something was wrong, I was sure of it.

I just couldn't figure out *what* until the twentieth soldier tore himself from me.

I was dying.

And *they* were being unraveled.

No time to regret or to panic or to think. There was only time to feel the pain of them as they separated from me, *not* free in the least, no. They were being undone instead.

Whatever our souls are made of, theirs were being *unmade* because Titus was no fool. The only way out of his traitorous deal was complete annihilation, it seemed, and the worst part was that I could do nothing to stop it now.

I'd chanted the spell, had given it my magic. Now as they came out of me, they tore me apart, too—not just my soul, but my body as well.

Pieces of me died with them.

Then there was Rosabel.

"Look at me!"

I did. Her hands were on my face and she was right in front of me. She'd entered the circle of the ritual. Her wide eyes were full of horror, no fire left in them, only darkness. She spoke, moved those beautiful lips, tried to hold me in place while my body moved to the sides as it ripped apart again and again, while the soldiers screamed, wailed, begged me to make it stop. Begged me to save them—yet again.

I thought I did, though. *We* thought we were setting them free.

All I'd done was doom them for the rest of eternity. All that pain and suffering and magic—gone as if it had never existed. All of them would be just *gone*.

"Let me through," Rosabel was saying, over and over again. And only when her words made sense did I force every ounce of my attention on her. "Let me through—let me have them. Please, Taland, give them to me!"

Never, I thought. The idea of *her* feeling this pain in my stead made me want to tear the world apart just as those souls, that curse was tearing me. I no longer had the energy to look down at my body, to move at all, but I felt it just fine how much of me it had already consumed.

Wrong, wrong, wrong. We'd done it all wrong. I'd made mistake after mistake after mistake, and the most fatal one was to trust that a man like Titus hadn't tied up *all* loose ends before he created this curse.

"Please, Taland, please!" Rosabel shouted, and I was dying. I was leaving her.

Something in me stirred.

"Look at me, baby."

Again, I did.

"*Trust me.*"

These words left her lips in a whisper.

These words I heard all the way in what was left of my soul.

"I know what I'm doing," she said, bringing her lips closer until they touched mine. "You asked me to trust you and I did. Now I'm asking you—*please!*"

Every instinct in my body was rioting. Every shallow breath I took already belonged to her anyway. Even the screams in my head, the speed with which the curse undid those souls in the same order that it had bound them, slowed down.

I heard nothing, saw nothing but her. Everything else just...stopped.

"*Trust me.*"

How could I not?

CHAPTER 26

Rosabel La Rouge

Taland was dying right in front of my eyes. He was being torn apart completely by the very souls that he was setting free. He was being torn apart *literally*. His clothes were near gone, and there was almost no inch of skin on him left without a cut, without blood.

Taland was dying, and if I couldn't stop it, I was going down with him.

The world around us no longer mattered. I'd made him this circle with my own blood, damn it, and I wasn't going to let him die in it all alone. The soldiers and the crowd and the IDD—none of it mattered except for this: I would try to stop whatever was doing this to Taland, and if I couldn't, I'd already accepted my fate. There really was no better way to go, anyway.

I begged him to let me through, to *share* the soldiers to me, so that maybe I could carry at least half the load that setting them free was putting on him.

Taland finally agreed.

I felt the switch as if it flipped somewhere in my own mind, and the world around me turned dark.

Suddenly, there was no bus underneath me, no lines drawn in my blood. There was no Taland in front of me, either. It was just me—and everything I had just *seen* happening to him with my own eyes felt like it had happened to *me*.

I couldn't even begin to explain it if I tried, but it's like for a moment, we eclipsed each other, Taland and I. In my mind, we were in perfect alignment, perfectly connected, truly *one*. We didn't exist as individuals at all for as long as the darkness kept me under, and I was completely disoriented until...

The pain began.

I'd seen those tears on Taland's body, had heard his screams, had felt the horror in his every breath. Yet now, it was *me* who'd been torn apart, and *me* who'd screamed, and *me* who'd been horrified with every breath —not him.

Just me and those souls, so many of them tied to my very core, and they were now tearing that core apart little by little, like tearing pieces of the fabric of my soul.

Almost a hundred of them, and the more I tried to hold in that scream, to hold back the pain, the faster that number declined. Ninety, eighty six, eighty-two, seventy-nine...

The scream came out of me and I gave it every ounce of energy I had left. Because I realized that these souls weren't being set free at all.

They were *disappearing*.

Their lights shone in the darkness I'd been thrust in, and I saw them only in the distance—until they were no more. Until they simply turned off, ceased to exist. *Gone* for good.

Goddess, this was wrong.

And I had no idea how to stop it.

Soon, the lights came to me, grew bigger and brighter and warmer against my skin that was being torn apart exactly like Taland's had been. I thought I knew what I was doing, thought I would carry the weight of their release together with him so we could both see the light at the end of the tunnel, but this was no tunnel at all. The only light came from the tricked souls of those soldiers, who were now being released from their linking with Taland—*no*.

They were being released from their bond to *me*.

I got to watch them as they flickered off and died like they had never breathed the air of this world at all.

Lights all around me—and the soldiers were screaming. Goddess, I heard their voices in my head and I couldn't stop screaming myself, hoping to make them stop.

So heavy. So all consuming. I'd give up my life just for a second of silence.

How I'd taken being alone in my head for granted all my life. How I wished I could go back to when I only heard my own voice...

Now, I heard them all, begging, pleading, their lights *sticking* to my skin—*stop, please stop, don't let us go!* they screamed in one language or the other, but I understood all of it. Of course, I did—our souls were linked together.

So much light died in front of my eyes, and I couldn't stop it, didn't know how. No thoughts in my head except for them, their pain, the way they dimmed, the way they turned off, never to be seen again—and the way they all took a part of me with them.

Now *I* was dying, it seemed, and the more I screamed,

the heavier the souls, and the *bigger* those sources of light became. Until they morphed into humanoid figures, and grabbed me by the hands and feet, and pulled me down as they begged—*please, please, please, please!*

Over and over they begged.

A mistake. All of it, a mistake. I couldn't stop tearing, and the lights around me wouldn't stop going off. It had been a mistake to start this ritual because this wasn't going to set them free at all.

But there had to be a way, right? Wasn't that what always happened—wasn't there *always* another way?

"Remember the quest for a body that had come to its death by natural causes?" I asked Taland—or Taland asked me, but it was also my own voice.

So strange. None of it really made any sense, but that didn't mean that all of it wasn't *real* to me. The dark and the souls dragging me under and my fight to keep afloat as if I was in water and only my head was above the surface.

"Remember those beautiful moss-green eyes and the impossible task of getting an animal the size of a vulcera to bond to a person without accessible magic?" I asked or Taland asked—it really didn't matter.

"Remember how she lay on that ice? How impossible the challenge given to us seemed?"

And finally, *"Remember how it became perfectly possible then?"*

There was always another way. The Iris Roe had taught me that, even if it had scarred me for life, had almost killed me on multiple occasions.

There was always another way.

"Stop!"

I screamed it at the top of my lungs. I called with my everything—and again, half my voice could have been Taland's and half my thoughts could have belonged to him, but we were one. We'd *become* one through magic, and now, with these tears in our bodies and our souls in pieces, disappeared with long-dead soldiers into this never-ending abyss, we were one physically, too.

The souls stopped pulling. The lights stopped flickering, dying. So few of them left—only sixty. *Half* of what they once were. Only half.

But they stopped. They heard me. They listened.

I urged them to come forward, to slip under my skin, to see into my mind the way I saw in theirs. To see all I'd gone through, all that I'd ever thought. Everything from the very beginning.

I was completely bare in front of them.

There is always another way, and I promise you I will find it. I promise you with my life that I will set you free if we stop this spell right now, break free of it together.

I wasn't sure if they believed me, or if they even heard the thoughts in my head in the state they were in, screaming and begging and pulling at my limbs. I wasn't sure if they saw what I was trying to show them, if they knew what it all meant. The vulcera and the ice statue of the roc and the dead crow on the rooftop and the legs of Madame Weaver with tips as sharp as blades. I wasn't sure if what I promised could even be done, but I bet my life on it —quite literally. Because without them I couldn't make this stop.

And I didn't wait for an answer. I gave every ounce of me, all my energy and every bit of magic in my veins to the bracelet and aimed at the curse that had pulled them and unraveled them so mercilessly, had simply turned off their lights. I aimed to destroy it just as thoroughly as it had destroyed those souls, as thoroughly as it had torn through Taland and through me.

I didn't know if the soldiers joined me, if they helped.

But when I gave it all away, I stopped hearing their voices in my head, and I stopped seeing their lights in the darkness.

Light—the kind that comes from the sky. Not overly bright, but it was there and I could see it, though barely. I could see it and I chased it with my everything because I knew that if I couldn't get to it, everything would be lost. I knew that if I couldn't get to it, I would never see Taland again.

Nothing ever motivated me the way Taland did. Nothing could ever make me want to get out of my own skin so badly. And I launched at that light with my entire strength, which grew the more aware of myself I was, the more I awoke from that never-ending darkness. The more I realized that nothing was pulling me down anymore and nobody was screaming in my head.

My eyes opened.

The light over me had seemed brighter than it actually was. The sun continued to hide behind thick, grey clouds that no longer even wept—a visual representation of the earth's anger at what had happened. What *we'd* done. Us—all of us.

The fear was strong, forever present in my very bones because of what my life had looked like since I could remember myself. Always fear. Always running.

But right now, I just needed to sit up and look.

Since sitting up was out of the question, I tried to move my head, at least, to see where I was, where Taland was. I began to hear noises, but they seemed to be coming from every far away. The more I blinked the clearer the image of the sky in front of me, the smell of blood and magic in my nostrils. The smell of something *burning*.

My heart was in my throat. I managed to turn my head to the side just slightly, desperate to see where Taland was.

I saw.

He lay next to me, on his side, eyes closed, hair all over the place, blood all over him. His skin was torn everywhere, big and small cuts, surrounded by fresh and dried blood. A scream built up in me because my heart simply couldn't handle the sight of him like that, but...his chest.

It *moved*.

Taland was alive.

The sky could have been mine. The earth and all the seas—but it still wouldn't compare to what I felt in those moments.

Until something else moved, shook me to my core.

We must have still been lying on the rooftop of that bus because it moved, and it sounded like someone was climbing it.

Get up! my mind shouted at me.

I couldn't.

All I could do was look up at the sky and thank the goddess that Taland was still breathing—right until they came, from all sides at once, and looked down at me.

The soldiers. What remained of the Delaetus Army. Men whose souls were tethered to my own, wearing helmets and armors and white in their eyes.

I expected a lot of things to happen in that moment. For them to kill me, stab me, burn me, call to me in that awful, robotic voice, throw me to the ground—or pick me up and put me on my feet.

I waited, but all they did was look down at me, eyes unblinking, bodies perfectly still.

Do something! I wanted to say, but of course, I couldn't. At least Taland would be okay, wouldn't he? These soldiers were his...*weren't they*? They wouldn't hurt him.

Safety, said another voice in my head—and I could have sworn it belonged to someone else. But it must have been me, my own self trying to think of a safe place, of somewhere to take Taland to, somewhere where *nobody* could hurt him. Not the IDD, not Radock, not the soldiers.

I had no such place in mind, though. Taland was always the one who knew the places and had the plans to keep me safe. All I had was my room at the mansion that was never really my home.

The darkness claimed me again.

CHAPTER 27

Rosabel La Rouge

I knew that ceiling well. Perfectly white, perfectly *perfect* in every line and every corner. There was no other like it, I was sure, and it was the ceiling of my bedroom at Madeline Rogan's mansion, exactly as I saw it every morning when I woke up, and every night before my eyes closed to sleep.

I was in the mansion, and this time, when I tried to move, I could.

This time, when I made to sit up, I did.

The ringing in my ears intensified. Block dots in my vision but the faster I blinked the more they faded, until I could actually see light coming through the windows.

It was my bedroom, all right. And the sun was shining outside, the sky was blue, and I was in my bed, naked, and... *not alone.*

Every inch of my body froze in place again when I realized that the figures against the walls on all four corners of my room weren't furniture—they were soldiers.

Soldiers of the Delaetus Army with their eyes closed and their hands loose at their sides. Eyes that opened the second I considered screaming until my lungs burned.

They were alive. Four of them were alive, and they were somehow in my room and *I* was somehow in my room and—

I screamed. Taland was in bed with me.

It took me a good moment to gather myself, to stop shaking, stop crying, clear my eyes of the tears and finally reach out a hand to touch his skin. Warm. He lay on his back, eyes closed, a lot of dried blood on his body—but no wounds. Not a single wound or scar or mark was anywhere on him, and he was most definitely breathing. He was breathing steadily and when I put my hand over his chest, his heart beat just as it should against my palm, and I about died of relief all over again.

What the hell had happened? How had we ended up here? Was I dreaming? How—

"Not a dream. We brought you to safety, Mistress."

The way I jumped out of my bed would have been funny to anybody watching.

I jumped and moved back and I eventually hit the wall, I thought, because I didn't fall when I should have. I didn't fall to the floor so I could close my eyes and urge myself to wake up.

"What...what...what..." The words wouldn't come. Someone had to answer me because someone just did—in my head, and I needed to make sense of this before I started screaming again, this time to never stop.

We brought you to safety, Mistress.

Those same words—except nobody *said* them. Not out loud. They just...popped into my head, at the center of my mind, in that voice—that same voice I'd heard before. That same voice that I was sure I'd heard for a long time now, every single day.

But I hadn't, not really.

I shook my head as my mouth opened and closed a million times, and I looked at the soldiers, all four of them around me. *They* were speaking to me. *They* were speaking right into my mind. They were here, right here, in my chest, under my skin, inside my skull.

They were—

Another scream ripped out of me when my view shifted, when something dragged me through a tunnel, and then I was looking at me.

Yes, I was looking at me from all four corners of my room. I was seeing myself, naked and covered in blood just like Taland, and my eyes...

Goddess, my eyes were white.

My legs gave up on me and I hit the floor on all fours, and the views disappeared. It was just the floor in front of me now and this urge to throw up, except I couldn't because I had nothing in my stomach.

Footfalls.

Don't!

They stopped.

Don't come near me. Get back!

They did.

Meanwhile my heart all but beat out of my chest.

I somehow managed to fall back and sit on the hard-wood floor, press my back against the wall, wrap my arms around my knees, pull them to my chest. I was shaking, though I was too shocked to cry.

I was shaking because I remembered, because I knew exactly what the hell was going on.

A promise. I'd made a promise.

An arrangement, said the voice in my head—a single voice that belonged to them. To all of them.

My eyes closed and it was so difficult to let go of this breath. So difficult to allow my muscles to relax. So difficult to allow myself to *feel.*

All of them. Sixty-one souls, their light as bright as it had been in that darkness. Eleven of them alive. Around me. Four in my room, another seven outside in the hallway. Just behind that door.

And they were connected to me. They were my *limbs.* My thoughts.

My...*responsibility.*

"*An arrangement,*" I whispered because it was too scary to *think* the words and know that they heard them. Too scary still to talk to them without making a single sound.

An arrangement. You promised to find a way to set us free without condemning us to destruction, in exchange for our service until the day that you do, said the voice. *Our* silent *service.*

Silent, he said—or was it they? Same difference, I thought. But he was right, it was silent in my head. It hadn't been, not when I was in that dark. It had been so, so loud...all those screams and those pleadings, all the cries and the stories and the images...

It was silent now in my head.

For as long as it took the sun to set behind the horizon, I just sat there and looked at nothing and I tried to process what had happened.

Taland. The fight. The Council. The look in Helen Paine's eyes. The rage in Radock's. The blood on Taland. His screams—*my screams.*

The way those lights had faded from existence, swallowed by that dark forever.

Fifty-nine souls lost as if they'd never existed. I mourned them, goddess help me, as if they'd always been mine. I mourned them and I felt the void their destruction had left in me as clearly as I felt the cold wall I leaned on. It was a trap indeed, that curse, in every sense of the word. There was no way out of it, unless you ceased to exist. Both the master and the soldiers.

"I made you a promise," I said to the room. "I will keep it. I will set you free as you deserve, or I will die trying." My voice shook, but I thought the words, too, and so I knew they all heard them. I knew they would all know that I meant them with my whole being.

These men had not only endured the unbearable, but they'd come back and had helped us defeat the Council, without any of us meeting our end. Not a single civilian or soldier. No deaths but theirs. *None.*

The cruelty of a man had brought them here, but I had faith that there was a way around it. I had faith that I would find it, and I had no doubt that Taland would help.

So, I stood up. The wall held me, offered its support like an old friend. My legs shook until I made it to my bed, to the red satin robe that I always kept there. I put it on, not because I was embarrassed or shy. These men had seen my soul, had seen me naked in the full sense of the word.

"Who healed us?" I asked, thinking they'd tell me it was them.

Madeline Rogan, the Mistress's grandmother, they said instead.

And that certainly surprised me. "She's here?"

Yes, Mistress. Waiting. She healed you, then we brought you to your safety, as requested.

Except I didn't request shit. This room was the only

349

place I really knew, but that's what they'd seen. The image of it—that's what they'd seen in my mind.

"Can you not call me that?" I said, because that name made me feel like I wasn't...*me.* "And what about Taland?"

Two of them who stood on the other side of the room stepped forward. *Shall we awaken him?*

"Goddess, no," I breathed, raised up my hand on instinct. "No, I—"

The bracelet was around my wrist. Cold and heavy and fitting me exactly right.

I lowered it again, brought it to my chest. "Let him rest," I whispered. "Stay with him while I clean myself up."

Yes, Mistress, the voices said, and I, pretending that I knew what I was doing, that I was strong enough to handle all of this, went for the bathroom door that was right next to where the soldier was standing by the wall.

I looked at him, and his name was Lind, and I thought, *Don't call me that, Lind,* this time only in my mind.

He said nothing.

I didn't dare look in the mirror or anywhere near it in the bathroom. I'd already seen more than enough through eyes that weren't mine. The water of the shower fell on my head and it was like a touch caressing my skin as it washed away the blood and dirt. I kept my eyes on my feet, on the pale pink tiles while the water went down the drain. But by the end, that same water that comforted me became too heavy on my shoulders, each drop a reminder of all those memories in my head that weren't mine.

It was over. Everything was already over. The memory of the look on Helen Paine's eyes said so. The pain that had sliced through Taland's body and mine said so, yet I still couldn't convince myself of it. It was going to take a while.

In the closet, I avoided the mirror again, eyes on my feet

until I got dressed in my own clothes that felt as foreign to me now as every other thing I'd ever put on that didn't belong to me. But when I went back into the room, nothing had changed. The soldiers were still there and Taland was still sleeping, and I don't know why there were tears in my eyes, warm and stinging.

Those, too, I ignored when I grabbed towels and a small bucket from the bathroom, filled it with water, and went to sit at the corner of the bed to clean his face, at least. I don't know how long I did it, but eventually my hands stopped shaking every time I wiped the blood off his cheeks and forehead, and cleaned his neck and his chest. Eventually those tears I was pretending didn't exist stopped falling, and the more I focused on his steady breathing, the more grounded I felt.

Then I wondered where Madeline was and what she thought of this whole thing, if she was going to—

Outside, Mistress.

The voices that popped into my head brought all my other thoughts to a halt, and that wasn't all. Suddenly I was being dragged down that tunnel again, violently. I stopped breathing and suddenly I saw a lot more than what was in front of me.

I saw the hallway outside my bedroom through the eyes of a soldier who must have been standing right in front of my doors, and I saw Madeline with two of her guards near the wall across from him, waiting.

Stop! I shouted in my head, and then I was back to seeing from my own eyes, and Taland's clean face was there again while I breathed like I'd been racing.

Goddess, how was I ever going to live like this? How was I ever going to get used to this? Taland had made it look so easy. I'd never once heard a word of complaint.

"Wake up," I whispered, touching his cheek gently, and I wished he would open his eyes for me, but he didn't.

He needed rest. The thought of how he'd been torn apart, clothes and skin and flesh right in front of my eyes, terrified me. He was going to need a lot of rest.

So, I put the towels and the bucket away and I pressed my hand in the middle of his chest and I called for a healing spell, even though he looked okay. I called for a simple one, second degree, to search and mend minor damages, just in case Madeline had missed something. Highly unlikely, but I needed to feel like I'd done *something*.

Colorful magic rushed down my arm, slipped out of my skin and into his, heating his chest for a moment.

A deep breath later, Taland fell in a steady rhythm again. His eyes remained closed.

I stood up and went to the door, feeling like there was no ground beneath my feet.

"Sta—" I stopped myself.

I thought, *Stay with him.*

Yes, Mistress, the voices responded, and I no longer wasted another thought to tell them not to call me that. I just grabbed the handle and pulled the door open.

The hallway was much brighter than my room, where I'd only had the nightstand lamps on. Ricardus, the guard whose eyes I'd seen through just now, stepped to the side, and my breath caught in my throat to find Madeline right there, exactly like I'd seen her. Red suit without a wrinkle in sight, silver hair perfectly done, red staining her lips, and those golden round earrings I didn't think I'd even recognize her without...

She was here.

"Rosabel," she said, and her voice echoed in the high

ceiling—or maybe it was just me. I forced air down my lungs without ever giving the slightest expression, but the way she was looking at me suggested she wouldn't have noticed even if I'd have flinched. Her focus was on my eyes, which I understood. I'd seen myself, too, through the soldiers in my room, and I knew what they looked like. *White,* completely white. Just like Taland's had become. The reason *why* was there, scratching the surface of my brain, trying to get my attention, but I was barely coping with all these new memories and views and thoughts and senses being dumped into my brain at the same time so I was constantly blocking everything I could block on instinct.

"You healed us," I said, and my voice sounded even worse than earlier.

"Of course," Madeline said.

Of course, like healing me was a very normal thing, like she'd done it all the time, all my life.

"Let's talk, shall we?" she then said, and every inch of my skin crawled.

My first instinct was to say *no,* to tell her to leave so I could go sit with Taland until he woke up, make sure he was safe, but...

I *could.* I could make sure he was safe through these soldiers, and I really, so desperately needed to know what had happened, how the fight had ended, if Selem had really taken over—I *needed* to know.

"In my office. You can eat there, too. Come, Rosabel."

Eat.

Could it be that my limbs were still shaking the way they were because I needed food?

Possibly. *Probably.*

I looked back at the room again, at the bed, hoping

maybe Taland had opened his eyes, but he was still sound asleep, his face now clean. He looked...peaceful.

I would leave most of the soldiers with him. The ones in the room, and another five outside, I thought. And I was going to think the words clearly, too, except the moment I stepped outside, two of the soldiers on each end of the line they'd made in front of my doors moved with me, while the five remained. Ricardus took his place in front of the handles again, a mountain of a man that I knew nobody could possibly get through if they tried.

I didn't need to think the words at all—I just needed to think like I normally did for them to understand, apparently. And judging by the look of pure shock on her face, Madeline was much more surprised by the fact than me.

"Lead the way," I said, and I noticed how her guards looked at the soldiers behind me. I noticed the one on her right, the same guy who'd smuggled me into the Iris Roe, had pushed me around to his heart's desire.

I'd been mad at him then. I felt nothing now.

Together all six of us made our way to Madeline's office through the empty hallways, and I found myself praying it would be over soon.

CHAPTER 28

Rosabel La Rouge

Taland, Taland, Taland.

When they opened the office doors for me and let me through, I briefly considered running back just to see if he was awake—and then I was shoved down that fucking tunnel again, and Madeline's office was not the only thing I could see, but my bedroom, too. Through the eyes of the guard—Lind—who stood by the bathroom door, I saw the bed and I saw Taland, sleeping, exactly as I'd left him minutes ago.

Then I was *spit back* into my own body—that's exactly what it felt like. Spit back out of that tunnel, and the office in front of me spun, and it was a miracle I didn't lose my balance as I walked ahead.

Still, I was completely disoriented, and so I made a big mistake.

I looked to the left of the office knowing full well that that's where Madeline's oval mirror was mounted on the wall. The reflection shocked me all over again, paralyzed me in place. I saw my face and my wet hair and my pale skin and my white eyes, and they held me captive for a good second. No air went down my throat as I looked at myself, at what I had become. My heart pounded and my hands shook—

"Rosabel."

Madeline's voice rang in my ears, pulling me out of my trance. Breaking whatever spell the sight of myself had put on me. I turned to find her waving her hand at the armchairs—the same ones where we'd sat when she brought me here from the Blue House. When Taland called her to come save me from his brothers.

Goddess, that felt like ages ago.

The new armchair—because I'd made the old one dirty by sitting on it, she'd said—looked even less comfortable than the old one had been. I didn't want to sit in it—I would rather stand when speaking to her.

She looked so different to me now—like a *little child* as she waited for me to respond. She looked...harmless, and for the life of me, I couldn't figure out why I'd ever been afraid of her. Terrified. In need of her love and affection—and most importantly, approval.

She was just a woman, wasn't she? She couldn't hurt me, couldn't even come close. Not anymore.

"I'm fine right here," I said, turning my back to the mirror slowly because I needed to be present, not lose my shit, and I needed to get this over with sooner rather than later. It wasn't just her—this place was full of bad memories. Not just because of when I came back from the Iris Roe, but the last time I was here as well. I could still hear the sound of her pouring her whiskey as she held me down on that couch on the other side of the room and ordered me to tell her everything.

"Very well. You need food. Fiona will be here any moment," Madeline said, and sat in her precious armchair, with that cup in front of her, her tea still steaming, the golden design on it, the oversize saucer just teasing those bad memories I had of the last time I saw them.

"What happened at the chambers?" I asked, and my voice sounded steadier already. I could focus on her. I could focus on the past rather than the present. I could...*put off* having to deal with myself right now, just for a moment longer. Just until it became a little easier.

"You won," Madeline said, and that smile on her face...

"Explain," I said, and half my mind was on Taland, but now my curiosity was the size of a monster, too.

"What's to explain? Your boyfriend killed most of the Council with the"—her cold amber eyes fell behind me, on the soldiers that refused to move a single inch, and her smile turned up a notch— "Delaetus Army itself. Helen, George, and Nicholas survived. They're locked up, Helen and George completely drained, and Nicholas—well. He already was." She leaned in, grabbed her cup. "You won, Rosabel. With *my* help, of course."

There was a knock on the door behind us, and suddenly I felt like I should start running. The soldiers moved on their own, or perhaps pushed by my own thoughts, to the sides of it immediately, and when it opened and Fiona walked in, she stopped dead in her tracks, almost dropping the tray full of food in her hands.

Stand down! I thought and almost screamed out loud, and the soldiers stepped back again, right behind me.

Fiona, the elf who'd served my grandmother her entire

life, and who'd always been nice to me, looked at me with a brand-new light. With pure, raw *fear*.

"We'll take it, Fiona. Thank you."

One of Madeline's guards was already there, taking the tray from her hands.

Fiona couldn't look away from me at all.

Hi, Fi, I wanted to say, and wave, and smile, do anything at all to get that look off her face. *I know how it looks, but it's me. It's just me!*

Except she didn't wait around for me to gather myself. She moved back and the guard closed the door before he took the tray to the table without a glance my way.

I kept staring at that door for a good moment after, and the image of Fiona's terrified face remained with me for years to come.

"Sit, Rosabel. Eat. A healing spell is only as good as the energy your body has to spare for it," said Madeline, her voice so lightweight. So...carefree. The kind of voice she'd never before used when I was around.

I sat down because I needed my strength. I sat down because I needed to be doing *something*.

"Speak," I told Madeline, and it seemed I couldn't bring myself to say more than a word or two at a time right now.

Madeline drank her tea and continued to smile as she looked at me. The shock had passed, and she was most definitely not afraid of my white eyes. If anything, I'd say she was *admiring* them. Admiring *me*.

"Well, the young Tivoux challenged the Council to a fight—I'm sure you remember that part. And they accepted because they were arrogant enough to think they would win and take over these..."

Once more her voice trailed off, her eyes moving to the soldiers behind me lightning fast.

"*Men,*" she concluded. "They were wrong, so they lost. The elder Tivoux and the Mergenbachs burned down the chambers afterward, imprisoned Helen, George, and Nicholas. The soldiers took them to Headquarters, secured them in the jail cells. It's still pretty chaotic—"

"Wait, wait, hold on a moment," I said, and my head was already buzzing, and fuck, I felt so...light. The room was starting to spin, too, so I had no choice but to reach for a piece of bread on the tray that Fiona had brought me. I didn't check under the silver dome still, afraid the smell of whatever was on that plate would make me want to throw up. I hated the taste of bile.

"When did they burn the chambers?" Because as far as I could remember, that building had still been there when I passed out.

"Right after you were brought home."

This isn't my home, I thought, but didn't say.

"By your soldiers, you were brought home. They can drive—did you know that? They drove that bus across the city and to the mansion." She seemed fascinated by the fact.

"And the civilians?" I asked, then bit into the piece of bread, and taste exploded on my tongue.

Fuck, I was hungry. So hungry my stomach was screaming at me now as I chewed.

"All well. Nobody died," Madeline said as she sipped her tea.

"Soldiers?"

"Back in their homes, I suppose." She shrugged. "Right after they locked up Helen and the others. I released them until further notice."

I released them, she said. I swallowed the bread. "You really were in charge of them."

"Of course," said Madeline. "There's nobody else who

has the power or the knowledge to command an army except for me. Only IDD directors are trained in that area, and since you took Hill out, it was a no-brainer. I was in charge and I foresaw the whole thing from Headquarters." The way she looked at me, her unblinking eyes wide...I held my breath. And she said, "I chose not to engage in the fight. Would have been useless, anyway, don't you think? And the soldiers knew it, too."

I shook my head again and again as that specific memory reared its ugly head—of Helen Paine shouting to *attack,* yet none of the soldiers standing in formation had moved. None had even shot their guns or called for spells.

"That was *you,*" I breathed, and I don't know why I hated that so much.

"It was," Madeline said. "Like I said—there was no point in killing soldiers when the results were obvious the moment Flora was torn apart. They were incredibly valuable to Selem afterward, anyway. They helped in clearing the civilians, arranged transportation for them and the surviving Council members to Headquarters. They handed over Agent Martins, and let them into the building, too."

My heart fell all the way to my heels. *Cassie.* The reason why we'd gone to the Council so soon in the first place. She'd been captured and beaten half to death, tied to a chair, and they'd sent us her picture.

"Is she okay?" I asked in a breathless whisper, so damn guilty that I hadn't thought to ask about her first. Cassie had been my friend, my only true friend.

"She is. Healing in the infirmary, last I heard," Madeline said.

"Which was when?" How long had I even been out?

"About three hours ago." My heart slowed down the beating instantly and I took another bite absentmindedly—

just the relief giving me a false sense of relaxation for a moment.

"And when did the fighting end?"

"Just last night," Madeline said. "You..." she put her cup down, shook her head at me once. "You've exceeded my expectations, Rosabel. You've truly outdone yourself. I have never in my life been more proud."

That's what she said—those exact words. Those words that I thought I'd die to hear my whole life, and I waited now, breath held and hands fisted. I waited to feel... *something*.

Maybe a sense of accomplishment?

I felt absolutely nothing.

So, I ignored the words easily and instead said, "Radock and the Mergenbachs have taken over Head-quarters?"

"They have," Madeline said, not surprised in the least by my change of subject. "They've declared *democracy*, believe it or not. They're planning elections for the new Council—*elections*," she repeated and even laughed a little. "The people are going to choose the new leaders now. They want balance." She shrugged. "I suppose we could try. I don't think we ever have before."

"And the IDD?"

She looked up at me, those old, curious eyes. *Greedy* eyes.

"Well, they know as well as everyone that the IDD is very much needed. Without it, none of us could ever dream of order on any level."

I nodded. "As an independent institution." Something the Council would collaborate with, but not control.

Madeline arched a silver brow. *"Independent,"* she repeated.

"Yes," I said. "And *you* will stay far away from it from now on."

I braced myself. This was Madeline Rogan, and power was her oxygen. There was no doubt in my mind that she'd betrayed the Council the moment she saw that they were not going to win. And she did it just so she could make claims after. She gave command of the IDD soldiers to Selem because she wanted something out of it—possibly wanted to run the IDD again. She thought she was more than capable—and I agreed. Physically, old age had yet to leave a mark on her.

But she would never, *ever* take that position again. No matter what she did or how she planned to go about it, she was *not* going to be in charge of the IDD, and now I was going to feel her wrath, so I prepared myself. Prepared to push back against her arguments, threaten her if I needed to.

Except...

Madeline raised her hands in surrender, crossed a leg over the other, and smiled. "Done."

Every thought in my head died a quick death. I blinked and I waited for her to start laughing or tell me that I was being silly or something—*anything* but her silence.

"Done," I repeated when she refused to say anything else.

"Done. I am retired, am I not? I am not fit to be in charge of the IDD anymore. I will stay far away from it."

She spoke the words and I heard them, saw her lips moving, too, yet I still couldn't believe them.

"What I *can* do, though, is bring the richest Iridian families of the world on board with this new...*regime,* if you will. They are powerful people, and they can cause a lot of trouble for you if they so please. I can help you bring them over to your side."

Impossible.

No fucking way in hell—no way.

"I don't...I don't understand," I said truthfully after a good minute because I was more shocked now than I had been in any other situation so far.

"What's not to understand?" Madeline asked—cheerful, so fucking cheerful I wanted to run from her. Her smile scared me more than her sneer.

"Power," I choked. "You...you've always wanted power."

"True," she said, folding her hands over her thigh. "I always have. For me. For our family. For our blood—and we have it." Her eyes scrolled down my body slowly, and for the first time in my life, she wasn't disgusted by me. She was *in awe.* "Power falls on you—more of it than *I* ever had, more than I imagined. Our bloodline will continue to rule the world whichever form it takes. I have faith in that," Madeline said. "I have faith in *you.*"

My eyes closed and I wanted Taland so much that I was dragged into the tunnel once more, and I saw him lying there, sleeping, through the eyes of all four soldiers who were watching him in my bedroom.

Fuck, I was *never* going to get used to that.

Drawing in a sharp breath, I looked at Madeline again, focused on her face. Her eyes. Her smile.

She was a monster—I knew that my whole life. It's just now that I *confirmed* it that hurt especially deeply. I hated that I was related to her, but I will not lie and say I wasn't *relieved* that she wouldn't make me fight her. I would have —don't get me wrong. I would have fought her tooth and nail.

But, fucking hell, I was exhausted, and I just didn't want to.

"So long as *you* take over the IDD, of course," Madeline added a heartbeat later, and this time I smiled.

And I stood up. "Maybe."

She stood with me, her smile suddenly vanished. "Not *maybe,* Rosabel. You *will* take over the IDD. You've earned it." She came around the table, and I knew she wasn't going to attack me or anything—of course not. Not *now,* at least.

But even so, I had this strange thought, this strange desire—to see fear in her eyes.

The soldiers moved. They moved so fast they could have materialized on either side of her, and the way she moved back...

Tongue between my teeth, I called for every ounce of my willpower to stop from smiling. Her guards were behind her, but they didn't engage. They looked just as scared as Madeline, in fact, and she turned three shades paler right in front of my eyes while she looked up at the soldiers, one then the other, then back at me.

"They're very protective of me," I said—this I couldn't keep inside. And I was going to reach for the tray on the table, except the soldier on the left—his name was Iohannes—leaned down and grabbed it before I could move.

Damn, they were good. So fucking good it terrified me.

Meanwhile Madeline took a step back, shook her head. "We can talk later if you need more rest," she finally said in half a voice.

"No, Grandmother. I will be leaving soon."

"Surely you can stay. This is your home. Where are you—"

"*Not* my home," I said, exactly like I thought it when I first came into this office. The same office where so much of my life had changed through the years.

Today, it changed again—and for the last time.

"Rosabel," she said, and she had the audacity to sound *sad*.

"I'll be taking this with. Taland might want to eat before we leave." I pointed at Iohannes, as if I really thought she would even look at the tray in his hands—she didn't. She just stared at the soldier, at what little of his eyes she could see through the helmet, and she turned paler still.

One of the highlights of my life.

"Think about it," Madeline said when I turned around to leave. "Just...just think about it. The IDD is power. With it you can—"

"I already have more than enough power—just like you said." I pulled the door open, walked outside and the soldiers followed me. "And if I do decide to work with Selem, you'll be sure to hear about it."

She called after me, Madeline, as if she really believed she had any right. She told me to reconsider, that she would teach me how to be a *good director,* that she would show me everything I needed to know about the IDD.

On my way back to my bedroom, I smiled, but not because I was happy. I smiled because I'd come to a point in my life where *none* of what I ever considered to be worthy was anymore.

It occurred to me to go knock on Poppy's door and see her—she was probably awake—but I couldn't. I was too exhausted, too impatient to talk to Taland.

Too much of a coward to see the look in her eyes when she saw mine.

So, I went back to my bedroom and I sat on the bed, and I ate some food while I watched Taland breathing.

I tried not to think at all about anything—until he finally woke up.

CHAPTER 29

Rosabel La Rouge

I didn't want to freak him out. I saw him moving his fingers first, then raising his hand to his face slowly, eyes closed. Because of mine, I didn't want to freak him out, and so I thought about getting up and moving away from the bed, to give him some time to adjust to the sight of me.

Goddess, for a moment I wished *none* of it had happened. I wished I could just go back to the old me. I wished that I *had* gone back to the old me and I just didn't know it yet because I was still too cowardly to look in the mirror.

Yes, moving away from him seemed like a good idea at first, except I remembered when I was in his shoes—unconscious—and when he was in mine—bonded to the Delaetus Army. I remembered how he, too, had stayed away from me when I woke up at the safe house. He'd figured I would need some space, but I hadn't. Goddess, no, I hadn't needed space from him. Not ever in my life.

So, I forced myself to sit still on the edge of the bed and wait for him to open his eyes. My breath was held and my heartbeat erratic, and then I saw the colors on him, the pink on his cheeks and all the shades of brown and black in his eyes.

All of them, just like before.

Then those eyes fell on me.

Taland was *shocked* to say the least, as shocked as I had been when I first saw him in that safe house. He sat up slowly, watching me like a hawk, taking in every little detail of my face, and finally settling on my eyes again.

Tears slid down my cheeks and I hardly even noticed. I waited and waited, stood still until he reached out his hand for my face, touched a tear with his fingertip.

Smiled.

"It worked."

He sounded like him. He looked like him. He smiled like him.

My arms were around his neck and I was on top of him the next second, shaking as I cried and laughed at the same time, probably made it close to impossible for him to breathe. And Taland held me to his chest, too, squeezed me until my ribs hurt, but who cared? We were laughing and we were crying and we were alive together.

I don't know a thing closer to impossible than this.

We took our time, probably wrestled each other on the bed for a few minutes. He was naked and mostly covered in blood still, but neither of us minded. He could take a shower later. Right now, we needed to just laugh together and keep touching and hugging until reality no longer felt like a dream.

So, we did.

. . .

"How loud?" Taland asked, looking at the soldiers stationed in each corner of the room, especially at Lind who was near the bathroom door through which we'd just come out of. Taland had showered while I'd watched, had washed all the blood and dirt off his skin, and now he was wrapped up in towels and walking around the room, slowly but surely. He wasn't even close to losing his balance, though he was weak. He still needed to eat, and I'd saved him plenty of food on that tray.

"Not at all," I said, watching him closely still, part of me replaying how that curse had cut at his skin. I kept expecting him to fall on the floor again, bleeding, even though I knew he wouldn't.

Taland turned to me, surprised. "They're not pleading?"

"No," I said, shaking my head, unable to keep that small smile off my face. "Will you sit with me and eat? I'll tell you everything."

He reached for my hand, and when I took it, he brought it to his lips and kissed my knuckles. "Lead the way, sweetness."

We sat on the bed and I put the tray between us just like he'd done the last time we'd been in my room. Before this shitshow began.

He ate slowly while I told him what I knew how to tell him. About how he'd allowed me to carry the curse, how it had felt like we were one and the same wherever that dark place the curse had taken me to was.

How I'd heard the souls of the soldiers, had seen their lights, how I'd spoken to them. How they'd dragged me down, then let me go.

"I thought it would release them," Taland said, his eyes darkening just like they used to before. I'd missed the way he looked with colors in his eyes, but I missed it now, too, how he'd looked without.

And that gave me a sense of calm. Made me not want to shy away when he looked at me. Because maybe he didn't mind my eyes exactly like I hadn't minded his. Maybe he, too, thought white eyes could be beautiful.

"So did I. I thought releasing them was what was killing you."

He swallowed a piece of meat, looking down at his lap. "There is no way out. No way out of the curse. Releasing them means destroying them permanently. *Undoing* them."

"It does," I said. "I felt it."

He looked at me. "How many are left?"

"Sixty-one," I reluctantly said. "The rest..."

The rest were already gone. We didn't know exactly what happened beyond death, but we did know that our souls moved on, that they existed—whether in a different place or realm, or in a different shape—didn't matter. Our souls existed, and that had always been my greatest consolation because I could handle life knowing that my parents were still somewhere. That I would still be *somewhere* when I died. It made life worth living. It made waking up in the morning make sense. It made *trying* make sense.

But to think that I would be completely destroyed after this was over...*why bother*?

"Fifty-nine soldiers," said Taland, shaking his head. "I should have known better."

"We all should have known better—starting with the Council. Don't you dare blame yourself. You were trying to set them free." Knowing him, that's the first thing he'd feel, and guilt just might be the most dangerous feeling in the world. A silent killer. Merciless.

He smiled bitterly. "And instead ended up giving them to *you*."

"You did. We survived, Taland. And now we figure out how to set them free for real," I said, reaching out for his hand. He took mine on his lap and inspected my fingers.

"What if we can't?"

"There are ways. It's magic—there are always other ways." This I believed in with my whole heart. "We won't rest until we find one that works."

"Had anybody else said that to me, I wouldn't have believed them—but you?" He pulled me by the arm and I leaned over the tray on the bed to kiss him. "My stubborn little criminal. You, I believe."

I grinned. "Smart guy."

"Just lucky." He kissed me again.

"So, now what?" I asked when I sat back again and urged him to keep eating.

"Now, we go to Headquarters to see my brothers, I guess. Understand what they are up to. See what their plans are. Tell them ours."

I arched a brow. "We have plans?"

"We do. To figure out ways to release these soldiers once and for all. To make sure the world will always remember their sacrifices. And we're going to help them build this new world, too. It's only fair, don't you think?"

Shivers rushed down my back. That definitely sounded like something I'd want to do.

"With great power comes great responsibility," I whispered, looking at the soldiers standing by the walls, their eyes closed at my request.

"True," Taland said.

But... "What if I fuck it up?" Because these soldiers were

people. It wasn't just my life on the line, or Taland's—it was their souls.

"Sweetness, there's a reason why they chose to submit to you willingly. A reason why they're not screaming in your head right now," Taland said. "They see beyond the physical, deep inside of us, too, and they chose to trust you."

It all sounded amazing, and I thought I might even believe it one day, but right now...

"Can you just tell me that you'll be there to stop me whenever I want to fuck it up?"

Taland laughed. I probably said it a thousand times, and I'm going to say it a thousand more—I absolutely adored his laugh. It was perfect, genuine, and it made me smile and feel like I was on top of the world no matter the circumstances. Apparently, it even worked if I tied my soul to dead men and swore to work for the rest of my life to set them free. It worked even when my eyes turned completely white, too.

"Every second of every day. I'll be right there with you forever," he said and pushed the tray back on the bed so he could drag himself closer to me, pick me up and sit me on his lap.

"Through summer breezes," I whispered, wrapping my arms around his neck, touching my lips to his.

"Through fucking hurricanes," he promised.

And then we kissed.

CHAPTER 30

Rosabel La Rouge

Breathe, Rora. Breathe.

The soldier sitting across from me drew in air, and I was pretty sure the other three in the SUV behind us did the same.

I noticed that when I was talking to myself, when I was reminding myself things this past day—like to breathe or take a minute to relax—they did it, too. I never told *them* to do anything, but they did. They actually breathed, expanded their lungs, even though they didn't really need oxygen. And sometimes they closed their eyes and lowered their heads when I did, as if they needed to be mirroring me every chance they got.

It was...strange, to say the least. To have these men, eleven here, physically, and another fifty in my head, with me at all times. It had been over forty-eight hours since they'd become *mine*, since I'd made the deal with them, and a full day of me being *awake* to actually acknowledge it, and it still felt like I would never get used to it.

Taland, who was sitting beside me in the back of Madeline's fancy SUV, squeezed my hand as if to remind me that he was there, and I appreciated it. It helped more than anything else.

We'd spent the night at the mansion because he'd been too weak still to even move properly, and I had been much more exhausted than I'd first thought. We decided to take a nap before leaving, but when we woke up it was already five a.m. Fiona brought us breakfast in the room, and the soldiers stayed right where they were, and I even got to hug Poppy while we walked out. She was definitely freaked out by my eyes, by the soldiers following me around, and she was relieved when I said I couldn't stay right now, but that I'd call her and make plans to meet with her soon. I didn't blame her, though. She just needed a bit of time to come to terms with this, get used to the idea of this new me—and so did I.

Then we could just relax and talk, I hoped. Maybe go out to dinner—*not* in the mansion. Watch a movie. Just...be in each other's company.

I'd like that very much, I thought.

And now we were on our way to Headquarters to meet with Taland's brothers and the Mergenbachs, and I really wasn't looking forward to it. Especially since that talk with Madeline had left its imprints all over my mind, and I hadn't stopped thinking about it at all.

All in due time, though. I didn't want to get ahead of myself. It's why I was telling myself to breathe, and why the soldier sitting across from me had. His name was Fergus. He was Irish and he had bright red hair you couldn't really see under that helmet. But I remembered how it used to look in the surface of the lake near his house where he went for a swim every morning to wake up properly. That, paired with his deep blue eyes, could turn heads any day.

Any of the *old* days, that is.

"Is it strange?" I asked him, though I didn't really mean to. But I had to know—was it as strange for him to be here, in an SUV—something that he couldn't even dream about in the time he was alive?

It is, Mistress, Fergus answered in my mind, though it still sounded like all of them were talking at the same time.

And? Do you want to, like...explore more? I asked without speaking this time.

We have explored, he said, and just now I started to notice the accent that they all seem to have—the same accent.

What about those? Can you take them off? I asked next, looking down at the bracelet around his wrist.

We can't remove our armor, said Fergus.

Are they...anchors? I wondered, squinting my eyes at the bracelet. Nothing much to see on it, though. Same color, same metal, just the band thinner than mine, and closed together.

No. Our anchor is you, Mistress. And we are yours.

Before I could ask him to explain, Taland said, "I hate to interrupt whatever conversation you're having, baby, but we're here."

"Oh!" I said, surprised to find the Headquarters building in front of us and the SUV slowed down. "I'm sorry. It's not a secret—it just comes naturally to speak to them *internally* when they do."

Taland chuckled. "I know. It really does. Don't feel bad about it. I don't mind."

Of course, he didn't.

Unfortunately, there was no way that we could just keep driving this SUV on our own and go somewhere, hide from the world right now, so when Taland got out and held his hand out for me, I took it. Let him guide me outside. Fergus came out, too. So did the other three soldiers who'd driven behind us.

"What the..." My voice trailed off when I looked at the street to find that the other seven I had specifically told to *stand back* at the mansion until I sent someone from Headquarters to pick them up were *running* together in pairs, coming right behind us.

"I don't think they like to be apart from you," Taland said.

"That's *insane!*" They'd run all the way here? "*Fuck!*" Now I felt bad...

"You couldn't have stopped them if you'd tried," Taland said. "Come on. Let's get going."

He took his hand in mine again and led us to the main doors of the building, where none other than Ashley Cameron waited for us with a huge smile on her face.

There were barely any guards around the front yard of the cross-shaped building. Very unusual, but things had changed. It was best to keep that in mind. Nothing was the same anymore—and neither was I. So when Ashley led us inside while her hands shook and her cheeks almost melted off her face, I didn't mind. When every person I knew in the building, and new ones I'd never seen before, stopped what they were doing and moved back toward the walls and watched me with their eyes wide and mouths open, I didn't mind. I reminded myself that this need to hide my eyes, to look at the floor so nobody saw them, would pass. I'd get used to it. And maybe, if I could figure out *why* they had turned white, when I had the time and the will to go through the memory of every soldier to better understand the man that Titus was—maybe I could undo it. Maybe I could get my own eyes back.

Until then...

Cameron led us straight to the elevator which only took you up to the director's office. Taland's brothers must have made it their own now. She said nothing when she stepped aside to let us into the car, but even though the space was big, it still didn't fit all of the guards. Six remained outside—the same ones who'd run all the way here, and I'd been too distracted by my fear and panic to notice.

Stay here, boys. Keep watch, I thought.

Yes, Mistress, they said and turned their backs to the elevator, formed a line in front of it before the doors had slid closed.

Cameron had already backed away with an alarmed look on her face, but she'd be just fine.

"You're nervous," Taland said, kissing my hand as we climbed up to the top floor. "Don't be."

"I just want to get this over with," I said. "I want to know what to expect. And I want to go see Cassie."

"And we will. Soon." He turned, grabbed my chin and pulled me closer, kissed my lips. "Everything will soon fall into place."

It was like he gave me the world, put it right in the palms of my hands.

The doors of the elevator slid open. The office of the IDD director was in front of us, with all three Tivoux brothers and the Mergenbachs and a woman I hadn't seen before but Taland had told me about—Violet Asher, Blue-fire, one of the elder members of Selem. She was well over sixty, and it was easy enough to recognize her based on the description he'd given me when we were in the safe house on the mountain: *long wavy hair that touches her hips and wraps around her shoulders like a silver blanket, not like normal hair does.* He'd been absolutely right—it looked like a piece of fabric instead.

They were all close to the screens that were mounted on either side of the room right off the entrance, and the long tables in front of them.

When they saw us, they all stopped. They all came forward and they were all smiling.

"Your shift starts at eight—or didn't you get the memo?" Radock said, tapping the watch on his wrist.

"Give them a break, won't you?" Aurelia said, nudging him playfully on the shoulder. "Welcome, Tal, Rora. We've been waiting for you." And they clapped.

They actually clapped, and none of them looked even remotely disturbed by the white of my eyes or the sight of the soldiers behind me.

Of course, they didn't—they'd been ready to knock Taland out just to get him to keep them around, and they'd succeeded in a way. The soldiers were still here, even though I wish they were free instead.

But I kept that in mind as we walked deeper into the room to the main table opposite the elevator doors where the Director probably sat. The walls around it were completely made of glass and they showed the city surrounding Headquarters like they were 4K images instead of the real world.

The others came closer, shook our hands and patted our shoulders, all smiles and good moods and sparkles in their eyes.

It didn't exactly surprise me, and it didn't surprise Taland, either, but he said, "So, we're just going to pretend that you didn't want to knock me out and keep me sedated for...how long, exactly? Until you figured out how to take the soldiers from me?"

He said it all with a cheerful voice and a smile on his face, but what did surprise me was that none of the others even flinched.

"Pretend? Absolutely not!" said Radock.

"We wouldn't have kept you *sedated*, kid," Zachary said with a wide grin. "Not *all* the time."

"It's nothing personal, brother," said Kaid. "All we wanted was the soldiers on our side. After all, it's thanks to them that we all made it. They died for us. It's the least we could do to try to keep them alive."

Taland and I looked at one another. These people had absolutely no idea what they were talking about or what the soldiers even were. I couldn't blame them, though. Taland hadn't had a clue when he first brought them back, and I didn't, either, when I asked him to share them with me. It's not something anybody else could hear since everything happened *inside* our heads.

And we wanted to keep it that way. I could tell just by the look in his eyes and the small nod he gave me—the less the people knew about the Delaetus Army, the better. We could handle this on our own.

I nodded back.

"But all's well now," Aurelia said. "Rosabel has them—that's perfectly fine by us. You're on our side...*right?*"

I am on the people's side, I thought, and I said, "Yes, I..." My voice trailed off and I took in a deep breath, held her eyes. "Actually, I'm just on the people's side."

Her smile turned up a notch. "Then we're all in the right place here."

I nodded. "Cassie?" My heart skipped a beat at the mentioning of her name, even though Madeline had already told me. I just didn't let myself believe anything she said—old habit.

"Awake. Healing. I'll take you to see her as soon as we're done here," Aurelia said, and the next breath I took came so much easier. *Goddess, thank you,* I prayed.

"That's a deal." I had no doubt that Cassie wouldn't mind my eyes, either. And even if she freaked out, I still planned to give her the hug of her life.

"Like I said, there will be no pretending, little brother. We did what we thought was right. Your soldiers saved us all. Whether they're yours or Rosabel's—I really don't care. They died so that we didn't have to. That I will not forget," Radock said then.

Do you hear that? I asked in my mind, and the ease with which I thought that took me by surprise because it came so naturally. So quickly.

We hear, Mistress, the soldiers said, and I don't know why that made me feel better. Why it was important that they knew what they'd done for us, how much their help had changed the world we lived in.

It had changed *everything.*

"Fair enough," Taland said. "I appreciate the honesty."

"Now sit down—all of you. We're facing a completely new era and we have a lot to talk about," Radock said, waving for me and Taland to get behind the large table, to turn our backs to that beautiful view of the city while the others were dragging and rolling chairs from all parts of the room to come together.

The soldiers followed behind me, pushing Radock back as they went. Not on purpose, but they demanded space and they were pretty big fellas. Not that I felt bad, to be honest.

One of them—Lind again—was already pulling the chair back for me to sit as I went around the table.

Thank you, Lind, I thought, and sat down, feeling all their eyes on me, but strangely it didn't affect me as much as I thought it would.

Like Taland said, we were here now, the people who had stood up and fought, the same ones who'd taken down the old system, and were on the cusp of creating a new one. I actually didn't mind being here at all now that I sat with them and they were all talking at the same time, his brothers asking Taland questions, before they turned to me.

In fact, it felt...*right.* Like I was meant to end up right here all along.

It felt like I had a voice now, and though I'd never thought about it before, that mattered. It was exactly what Madeline had talked about when she lectured me on power —having a voice and making a difference in decisions that would affect the people. Our people and the humans. The entire world.

I *wanted* to be here. After everything, I *wanted* to change the things that I spent so long fighting against. All of us here sitting at this table did.

"Shall we begin with the most obvious?" said Radock, folding the sleeves of his shirt up to his elbows, a silver pen in his hand and a pad in front of him.

I didn't know what the most obvious was, but I smiled together with the rest of them, and nodded. Taland and I looked at each other for a moment, and he seemed just as calm as me. He felt that being here, now was the right thing, too. Where we were meant to be all along.

Together, we began.

. . .

A week later

It took a thought to get them to leave me alone for a minute, but even then, half of them had their eyes on me at all times. They didn't care about people seeing them or about freaking others out—they spread around the neighborhood like nobody else in the world even existed. So long as some of them could see me, the others were cool enough to stay in the car with Taland.

I'd assigned two to him personally, to be with him at any given time, despite his complaints. He didn't need babysitters, he told me, just like I told him back when the soldiers obeyed to *his* thoughts.

And I agreed. They were seven-centuries-old soldiers, not babysitters.

It's not like he could do anything about it, though, which I loved to remind him of. Just like I couldn't do anything about when we were in that safe house and he had them following me around every second we weren't in the house.

It was still funny to see the look on his face any time he came out of the bathroom, though. I lived for it. It had been a week since we found out we weren't going to die, after all, and I had over a thousand pictures on my new phone of him coming out of the bathroom and realizing that two soldiers were on either side of the door, waiting for him.

Priceless.

We lived in a penthouse now—only because of the soldiers. I'd have preferred a small apartment, to be honest, but small apartments wouldn't fit eleven soldiers in and still leave space for us to live, so a penthouse it was. Only temporary until we found a house that we both loved. Right now, we needed to be close to Headquarters, so living in the city was a must.

After all, we were the new Directors of the IDD.

There was no telling how much work there was to begin with, let alone to also *change* the entire system at the same time as mending the damage the Council had left behind, *and* making sure that criminals didn't take over completely while we were busy looking away.

That, too, was temporary—or at least we were promised it would be. In that meeting with the Tivouxes and Mergenbachs, we'd decided to stay and work for this *new era,* as Radock liked to call it, simply because we'd fought too hard and gone through too much not to make sure that the world ended up a better place for real at the end of it.

At first, when Radock asked us to take over the IDD, I hadn't been all that sure about taking on *more* responsibility. We could help with other things, I thought, until Taland turned to me and said three words: *the Iris Roe.*

That game that had been my doom and my salvation. My blessing and my curse. That game that was the reason so many lives were lost regularly—and *legally.*

After that, it had been a no-brainer. I'd accepted my position alongside him and our first act as the newest directors of the IDD had been this: *no more Iris Roe.* The game would be permanently shut down, the playground reconstructed—and it was just the tip of the iceberg. So much in the City of Games that needed to change, but the Iris Roe, at least, would *never* happen again.

Taylor Maddison would *not* be happy about that, I figured, but that's only until she saw what I brought for her in my pocket.

It was dark, past ten p.m. when I finally made it down

the street from the human neighborhood, to the trailer where she still lived with her family. They hadn't been captured or killed by the Council in those weeks of blinded rage, and for that, I was so thankful. So many had lost their lives—we were still putting the names on record. Far too many—but the lights were on in the trailer, and Taylor Maddison was alive.

She always knew before when I came to visit, but right now as I looked behind the trailer where I'd caught her coloring once, there was nobody there. I looked back at the road, at the black SUVs Taland and I traveled in—again, because of the soldiers who insisted on staying with me all the damn time—and I knew he was watching me. I'd wanted to do this alone first, and he could meet Taylor later.

He really wanted to, and I loved him more for it.

A moment passed and Taylor still didn't come outside, but I was dying to see the treehouse that carpenter had promised me he'd build for her, and I knew she would find me eventually. She always did.

So, I slowly moved to the back of the trailer, past the clothes that had been hung out to dry, and into the small forest where I spent so much time with her before. Where I got the peace and quiet—and *will* to keep going when it felt like there was no way out of the maze that was my life.

I went deeper, slowly, eyes wide, and for a moment, as I tried to see everything, I accidentally sort of *switched* to what Taland called *all-eyes-mode,* and I was suddenly looking through the eyes of the two soldiers who'd went all around the houses, and I knew for a fact that they were in the forest with me.

They were—and Edric, one of the soldiers, had eyes on the little light that was coming from the tree.

From Taylor's tree.

It didn't scare me anymore, to be dragged down that tunnel. Not saying I was used to it, just that it didn't freak me out as it did in the beginning.

Still, I preferred to be looking through my own eyes only, so any time I slipped, I quickly came back. A smile on my face as I rushed to get to the treehouse.

Two minutes later, it was right there in front of me, better than I could have possibly imagined—and light was indeed coming from inside.

Tears in my eyes. It was a big tree house, big enough to fit Taylor comfortably. I thought about calling her name, but then figured I should make sure she was alone first by walking around the tree to search for the shadows up there.

Except...

A head popped out of the window of the tree house.

"Who's there?" Taylor Maddison called, and my heart all but burst right out of my chest.

Our eyes locked.

I remembered mine were white now. She was a kid and she could be scared of me.

Sun glasses, Rora. Sun glasses!

Except this was Taylor, and she wanted to win the Iris Roe when she grew up and she'd broken into the IDD Headquarters once just to see me—of course, she wasn't going to be afraid of some eyes without color.

That's why she was smiling.

Instinctively, I raised my hand and waved. "Hi."

She said nothing, only disappeared for a moment, then reappeared on the other side of the tree, climbing down a ladder I couldn't see very well from here—and to be honest, I couldn't move for a good moment.

Long enough for her to run and jump in my arms and hug me with all her strength.

Yeah, she didn't care about how I looked, and if she could hear the soldiers nearby, hiding in the dark, she couldn't care less about that, either.

Her big eyes sparkled, and she said, *"Come see my tree-house!"* without giving me a moment to even look at her, to see that she was okay.

"Will I even fit in there?" I said, laughing, as she dragged me to the other side of the tree, to the ladder.

"Yes, yes, you will. Come on!"

I didn't think I'd ever seen her so cheerful, so...*carefree,* exactly as a kid should be. That alone made me want to do everything in my power to keep it that way—but first, the treehouse.

She had a gas lamp there, an old one she got at the dollar store, she said, because using an electric light didn't *fit with the vibe.* She had a couple of cushions and a lot of coloring books, a lot of colors and blankets, too. A tablet was playing music on a low volume, and she was *glowing* as she told me about the day the guy I'd hired came here looking for her, asking to see the tree where she wanted the treehouse. She said she immediately knew that it was me, and she couldn't wait for me to get back so she could show me.

Like *she knew* for a fact that I would.

Fuck, I loved this kid, and I didn't even realize how much until my heart about burst at seeing her so damn happy. With a treehouse—just a treehouse. A space for her to just...*be.*

"Tell me everything," she then said, sitting cross-legged on a cushion, the lamp between us. The guy had really outdone himself—it really was big enough for both of us to sit comfortably.

"How much have you seen already?" I wondered.

"All the videos that are online," she said, and I flinched. Yes, a lot of people had recorded the battle, recorded Taland and me on top of that bus, the fight of the soldiers with the Council, though those we'd taken down already by sending out a magically enhanced virus to destroy them completely in any device across the world. Nobody needed to see all that blood being spilled in that way.

But the rest remained.

"Okay, so...a very bad guy was trying to bring back an ancient army from—" I started, but...

"David Hill, the IDD director and the Delaetus Army. Yes, yes, I know. And?"

I burst out laughing—how could I not? Of course, she knew everything. They'd given it in the news on human channels, and most importantly, social media.

So, I wrapped things up for her as well as I could without telling her the especially ugly parts, and she listened intently, hanging onto my every word until I finished speaking.

"No more Iris Roe," she finally whispered, and her shoulders slowly hunched, and her eyes slowly lowered to the light between us.

"No more Iris Roe," I confirmed with a nod.

"I suppose it's for the best," she said, and I smiled—she was making herself say that, but I could see the tears pooling in her eyes. She was devastated about it because the Iris Roe to her represented a chance at magic.

She fucking loved magic.

I held back a smile as I reached for the inside pocket of my jacket and pulled out an envelope. It was thick, and her name was embossed on one side in beautiful golden cursive letters.

"This is for you," I said and handed it to her.

She tried—oh, how she tried to smile, but she only managed to look like she was in pain when she took the envelope and read her name on the back of it, and...

She stopped. Looked at me again.

"What's this?"

"Open it," I urged her, so impatient I probably looked ridiculous.

But Taylor opened the envelope slowly, her hands slightly shaking, until she pulled out the thick piece of paper I'd put in there myself after I signed it.

I watched her eyes, unblinking, as she read every single word written on it, then started from the beginning.

Shook her head.

"I don't...I-I..." Again, she looked at me as if she was waiting for me to tell her that it was a joke.

"Go ahead, read it for me," I said instead, and it took her a moment to breathe and to stop stuttering. To read those words out loud.

"*Dear Miss Maddison,*" she started. "*We would like to invite you to attend the Iridian School of Chromatic Magics this coming fall as its student. Your presence would honor us, should you choose to accept. We l-l-look forward t-t-to meeting you and to learn about our world t-t-together. Signed, Martin Emanuel Pascal, Headmaster, and Rosabel La Rouge, Co-director of IDD.*"

Taylor barely choked the words out, then closed her eyes and gathered her knees to her chest and cried in perfect silence. Her little body shook as she held on tightly to that letter, and she just cried.

I pushed the lamp aside and went closer, hugged her to

my side and let her have her time. I pretended I wasn't crying, though my cheeks were just as wet as hers.

"What do you say, huh? Do you accept?" I asked when she calmed down and stopped shaking and leaned her head on my shoulder.

"But...but I'm Mud," she said in that small voice, and I leaned back, raised her head to me.

"Laetus," I told her. "There is no such thing as *Mud*."

"I don't have any magic," she whispered, and this time I laughed.

"But you do! You just can't access it right now, and that's okay. Because when you finish your studies and when you learn everything you need to know, you will receive all the energy you need to unlock it. It's in you, Taylor. And it's waiting."

"Like...like when I made light?" She looked down at the palm of her hand, fascinated, eyes red and cheeks wet.

"Exactly like that," I promised her. "Exactly like that."

Together, we sat at the edge of the tree house where a part of the wall pulled to the side like a door. Taylor had requested it from the carpenter, she said, so she could sit and watch the moon again like we used to. We barely fit together, but we made it work.

Eventually, we both calmed down, and no more tears came out of us, and our hearts slowed down the beating, too.

Eventually, I found her smiling like she was right there in the sky with the half-moon she was staring at.

"They say you're the youngest director the IDD has ever had," she said after a while.

"I am," I said. "Just turned twenty-one three days ago, actually." I still signed my contract with the IDD when I was twenty, though. Technically.

"Happy birthday, Rora," Taylor said, and my smile was so big it hurt.

"Thank you, Taylor."

"Is it real, though? That letter? Is it..." Her voice trailed off, her eyes wide with fear suddenly.

"Of course, it is. The Headmaster, Mr. Pascal, wrote and sent me the invitation himself." All I'd had to do was make a call.

"So, will all Mud be going to school with the Iridians now?"

I touched her face, pushed her hair behind her ear. "Laetus *are* Iridian," I told her. "And, yes, you will all be going to school together from now on."

She blinked and blinked and blinked...

"Is this a dream, Rora?"

There went my tears, stinging my eyes again.

"No, Taylor. It's not a dream," I said. "It's just the real world becoming right again."

I often thought about that question Taylor had once asked me, about what it meant to be Iridian. Back then I hadn't had a clue how to answer, but now I did. Being Iridian is being just like every conscious being out there, no matter the species. We're all the same, and we're all one thing—lost souls waiting to be loved so we can find our way home.

That's how I felt now—*home,* not in a penthouse, but in my skin. Thanks to Taland and to Taylor, too.

There was still so much to do, so many things to figure out. Not just about how this new system would work and how much of the old would remain, but with the soldiers, too. With the curse. With all this power that I had now and what I could do with it.

I never asked to be here, and I never imagined that this was where I'd end up, but I was not going to back down now. Together, we would make it, Taland and I. We would see the world as we wished it was when we were only kids because there are ways. There are always other ways. I have faith in that.

And most importantly, I have faith in myself.

I've tiptoed through most of my life. Now I am going to slam my feet down with all my strength to let everybody know that I am here.

—THE END

*Thank you for reading **Iridian**!*
This is the final book in this series and I hope you enjoyed the story.

If you did, will you take a moment to leave a review on Amazon? Reviews are an incredible help to authors, and just a few words should do it (or a simple rating). I'd appreciate it very much.

To be notified about future releases, you can follow me on Amazon, social media, or visit www.dnhoxa.com.

For more books, turn the page!

Sincerely,
Dori Hoxa

MORE BY D.N. HOXA: FALL OF THE SEVEN ISLES SERIES

Mama Si's Paradise (Fall of the Seven Isles #1)

The girls in Mama Si's Paradise live like royalty. Real-life princesses. Dolls, she calls them, and what they do is entertain her very beautiful, very wealthy guests.

They hide the true face of the Paradise so well...

Good ole me went in there to apply for a housekeeping position after I caught my boyfriend cheating, and he kicked me out. Nobody in town was hiring, so I thought, what the hell. Even though I knew what that place was, I went.

Then Mama Si saw me.

She took one look at me, told me that the vacancy was no longer available, but that she had a better offer to make me—to become one of her dolls.

I accepted because she promised me freedom. She promised me power. She promised me magic.

She lied.

My whole world turns upside down for me within days. I end up bitten by a dragon and stuck in an isle where the sun never shines. Stuck in the Evernight Court, as the bride-to-be of one of the five Evernight brothers who rule the Seven Isles—what is left of the world of magic on Earth.

They're powerful vampires, hungry for new blood, desperate for an heir, each more breathtakingly beautiful than the last—and all of them trying to make me theirs.

I pretend to play along while I search for an escape from their Isle and hope to make it back home in one piece.

Except the Evernight brothers are not easily fooled. Secrets hang in the air, and there's a storm lurking in the distance that nobody seems to know about. The more time I spend in their midst, the more I am convinced that I will never find my way back, that I will have no choice but to accept my fate in the Isle.

And the first question is, **which one of the brothers will make me their bride?**

THE HOLY BLOODLINES SERIES

The Elysean Trials (The Holy Bloodlines, Book 1)

Elyseans are so wise...

Elyseans are so beautiful....

*Elyseans are **divine**...*

<ins>Elyseans are power hungry assholes with a god complex.</ins>

Yes **gasp** I said it. Sue me and bring out your pitchforks.

Unfortunately for me, the deadly Elysean Trials are right around the corner. Despite my unpopular opinion on them and anything Olympian-gods related, when they unleash their strange blue birds to select mortals around the country as candidates, one of them chooses me.

Naturally, I politely tell them to *shove it*, but that's the thing about Elyseans: they're not used to taking *no* for an answer. So together with my legal guardian, they force me to go to their trials just two days shy of my eighteenth birthday—and for what?

A chance to attend the Academy of Divine Light and Beauty. A chance to become Elysean... What a joke.

They can keep their Academy and their magic, but I will finish their trials because I have no other choice. I will survive these monsters disguised as gods because my freedom has never been closer.

My own kind can't stand me, but that's nothing new. The Elyseans despise me—especially Shade, a descendant of Hades, who commands darkness with a wave of his hand and is sinfully beautiful, even when he's reminding me of how perfectly powerless against them I am.

But the more I get to know him, the harder it gets to ignore who he really is, and the more *impossible* it gets not to give in to my attraction for him.

And the deeper into the trails I go, the more I learn, and the more I realize that Elyseans are not the perfect god-like people the world paints them to be.

Worst of all, my past might not be quite like I remember, either...

THE REIGN OF DRAGONS SERIES

King of Air (The Reign of Dragons #1)

Being stuck in a time loop sucks, especially when I die on the same day, at the hands of the same man, over and over again.

But in Life Number Seven, I'm determined to change my fate.

To do that, I have to run away from my father, the dragon king of all shifters, and the most paranoid man I know. He and his men are near impossible to fool, but I switch places with my lady's maid and manage to make it all the way into the woods—right before I get knocked out cold.

When I wake up, I find myself a prisoner, and my captor is the son of my father's worst enemy. Just my luck.

Lucien Di Laurier is a cocky bastard who thinks I'm an object to be owned. It doesn't help that he's dangerously sexy, and can literally control the air in my lungs with a wave of his hand. He wants to get his revenge on my father for killing his, and that's why he's after the dragoness...never realizing that I'm right there, in his home. Thinking I'm just the maid, he vows to *break* me until I tell him everything he wants to know.

But things don't go as planned for either of us. Secrets have a way of coming to light, and his just just might be worse than mine. And when we both finally learn the truth about one another, will we be able to stand together against the sickness that has plagued the world and created this time loop?

Or will I have to go back home, and wait to die for the seventh time?

THE HIDDEN REALM SERIES

Savage Ax (The Hidden Realm, Book 1)

I heard the stories about Savage Ax. They're whispered among vampires everywhere in the Hidden Realm.

He's dangerous, merciless, a predator even among monsters...but nobody told me that he was dangerously sexy, too.

Now, on top of having to go searching for a vampire out there in the human world infested with sorcerers, I have to do it with *him* by my side.

Handling Savage Ax didn't seem like a big deal—despite his looks, our covens are sworn enemies. Despite his reputation, I have the green light to get rid of him if needed. And it's all fun and games, empty threats and dirty words at first...

But there's a spark of madness in his eyes that draws me in. Something about the way he takes what he wants, even from me, and gives no explanation in return. Something about the rough touch of his hand that melts all the ice I've spent years layering around me.

The farther away from home we go, the easier it gets to forget who he is. Who I am. Where we are.

And that's exactly where my real troubles will begin...

Savage Ax is the first book in The Hidden Realm series, written in 2 POVs, packed with magic, mayhem, and explicit romantic scenes intended for mature audiences.

PIXIE PINK SERIES

Werewolves Like Pink Too (Pixie Pink, Book 1)

What's worse than a pink pixie living all alone in the Big City, eight thousand miles away from home?

A pink pixie who's stuck behind a desk all day, taking calls and managing monster-fighting crews without ever seeing the light of day herself. *That's* what.

For two years, I worked my ass off to prove myself to my boss, and prayed for a chance to do the work I left my family behind for.

And I'm finally about to catch my break. I've got an undercover mission with my name on it, and it's everything I've been dreaming of since I got here.

Until I find out that Dominic Dane will be my partner. That self absorbed, narcissistic werewolf who humiliated me in front of all my coworkers on day one, and loves to pretend that I don't even exist.

It's bad enough that he tried to kick me out of my mission. It's even worse that he's sinfully hot and fries braincells with a single look of those gorgeous green eyes.

Now, on top of having to kick ass on my first mission, I have to pretend to be his *girlfriend* for three days, and keep my ridiculous attraction to him under control, too. So much for catching a break.

Lucky for me, I've got a secret weapon that's going to help me handle Dominic Dane, and it's God's best gift to mankind: chocolate. Armed with as many bars as my purse can fit, and with my wits about me, I'm going to survive the gorgeous wolf-ass one way or the other—and *win*.

Also by D.N. Hoxa

The New York Shade Series (Completed)

Magic Thief

Stolen Magic

Immoral Magic

Alpha Magic

The New Orleans Shade Series (Completed)

Pain Seeker

Death Spell

Twisted Fate

Battle of Light

The Dark Shade Series (Completed)

Shadow Born

Broken Magic

Dark Shade

Smoke & Ashes Series (Completed)

Firestorm

Ghost City

Witchy Business

Wings of Fire

The Marked Series (Completed)

Blood and Fire

Deadly Secrets

Death Marked

Winter Wayne Series (Completed)

Bone Witch

Bone Coven

Bone Magic

Bone Spell

Bone Prison

Bone Fairy

Scarlet Jones Series (Completed)

Storm Witch

Storm Power

Storm Legacy

Storm Secrets

Storm Vengeance

Storm Dragon

Victoria Brigham Series (Completed)

Wolf Witch

Wolf Uncovered

Wolf Unleashed

Wolf's Rise

Starlight Series (Completed)

Assassin

Villain

Sinner

Savior

Morta Fox Series (Completed)

Heartbeat

Reclaimed

Unchanged

Made in United States
Troutdale, OR
01/29/2025

28491851R00257